Torn

Books by Karen Turner:

All That & Everything

Broughton Hall series:
Torn
Inviolate
Stormbird
Counterpoint

Torn

Karen Turner

Published in 2023 by Karen Turner

www.karenturner.com.au

First published 2013 by Palmer Higgs Pty Ltd
Reprinted 2014, 2021

TORN

Designed and typeset by Look Up Media
Original design and typeset by Palmer Higgs Pty Ltd

Cover image by bigstock.com

ISBN: 978-0-6450002-1-4 (pbk)
       978-1-922219-84-8 (ebk–ePub)

A catalogue record for this book is available from the National Library of Australia

For Stuart
Elephant shoe

PROLOGUE

The old woman woke from a disturbed sleep. Her candle had reduced to a stub plunging much of the room into darkness. Her legs moved stiffly as she shimmied over the edge of the bed and her toes groped for her slippers. A bony hand supported the small of her back as she shuffled across the threadbare rug on the floor. Fumbling, age-crippled fingers lit another candle from the dying one, and she watched as yellow wax dripped onto a tin plate, before sticking the new candle upright in it.

The additional candle threw a wider arc of light around the room and her solid wooden dresser, mirror, and writing-desk, fashioned in a heavy bygone style, emerged from the thick shadows. Other than her bed, these were the only furnishings.

She stood like an arthritic question mark, muttering to herself while tying the belt of her robe. The local villagers did not think odd Meg's habit of talking to herself. They had known this woman all her life – known her family and her history. Some more ancient ones remembered her mother. Yet Meg herself considered such conversations terribly odd and, in a curious irony, this was often what she muttered about. But not this night.

Her long grey hair, streaked with the straw colour of her youth, was escaping its plait and she blew it impatiently from her face as she drew up a chair and eased stiffly onto it – for she could no longer sit elegantly – and bunny-hopped closer to her writing-desk.

With a clean sheet of vellum, straight from its box, before her, she dipped her pen into its inkpot and did not hesitate; for months of deliberation had led to this sudden lucid knowledge of what she must do. She did not know why she felt such compulsion, nor did she care. But the responsibility was hers and it would be done this night.

On the top right-hand corner of the page she wrote the date – 14 March 1871 and her hand, steady now, seemed guided by its own will.

You have found the diary, as I knew you would. Are you a relative? I know not. But I have spoken with you in my dreams and I have seen you sometimes in my waking hours. You walk these halls, your lovely auburn hair swinging with your step. I know not if you are aware of me, for somewhere deep inside I know that you do not exist in my time. And for this reason I entrust this to you.

Allow me to introduce myself …

The old woman wrote without pause for a quarter of an hour. When finally she laid down her pen she did not read over the words, but spent several moments massaging her crooked fingers and contemplating a tin box on the dresser.

With the page held between thumb and forefinger, she flapped it dry before folding it carefully in half, and half again, then leaning her meagre weight on the desk, she pushed herself up and shuffled over to the dresser. She opened the tin.

The diary stared up at her. Its scuffed red–leather binding was aged but had survived quite well; its yellowed pages were intact.

She held it with hands that had resumed their tremors and slipped the single folded page under its cover.

Back at her desk, she extracted a square of oiled canvas from the drawer and wrapped the diary with great reverence before replacing it in its tin, then with a gusty sigh of finality, closed the lid. Meg tucked the tin beneath her arm and took up her candle.

The elderly house groaned in the darkness as it settled for the night and Meg muttered about old ladies with creaking joints as she navigated the grand staircase with experienced steps.

At the bottom she turned right and tottered up the hall; left, down four steps; left again, four more steps, and into the kitchen. She gave no thought to the lavish meals prepared for important guests in this room a century and more ago. Nor did she recall the times when, as a small child, she had hidden beneath the cook's table, waiting to pilfer a chunk of biscuit dough. She shambled through the room grabbing a serving spoon from its hook as she went.

The door to the kitchen garden was as stiff on its hinges as Meg, and its grinding protest sounded foreign in the quiet of the night.

She had always disliked the kitchen garden because of the grubs that crawled there, but tonight she was compelled to consign her burden to where it would remain safe.

Shadows seemed to detach from the walls and corners of the old house with a life of their own, following, watching … always watching …

Meg shivered.

She jerkily eased herself to her knees on the cold, hard ground. The winter's snow had only recently melted and the earth remained frozen – her task would not be easy.

There was no breeze to extinguish her candle, and the full moon shone like a disk of ice between scudding clouds – a witch's moon, someone from her past had called it, but she could not remember who, and had not the time to think about it now.

She grasped the serving spoon with two hands and found a

relatively soft spot beneath a clump of long-dead thyme and began her work, first scratching away the weeds and debris, flicking at a snail or two, and when she had cleared a space, she set about digging.

She dug and scraped, heedless of the brittle dampness hanging in the air, and oblivious to the night creatures rustling and calling to their mates in the overgrown garden. Nor did she hear the laboured rasping of her own breath as she worked for what seemed like hours by the screaming of her back, until the tin sat comfortably in a grave about 10 inches deep.

Before filling in the hole she sat back on her heels. Running her finger over the lid of the tin, she felt her initials stamped there – *MMW*.

"Margaret Maria Washburn." Her voice was a thin thread of vapour that lingered before her face. "Were it your life, would you have lived it differently?"

The night seemed to fall silent and Meg cocked her head as though listening. The shadows gave no reply.

The filling of the hole was easier than the digging. The old woman finished her dirty work, then rubbed and massaged her stiff joints into movement before heaving herself to her feet.

Spoon in one hand, candle in the other, and without a backward glance, she shuffled slowly through the kitchen door. The sound of it closing echoed resoundingly after her.

CHAPTER 1

1808

"Miss Alex!"

The shout startled me and my eyes snapped open. Janet, the maid I shared with my sister, was rushing across the lawn towards me.

Breathing heavily and with her chestnut curls escaping her cap, she leaned over me. "I thought I'd find you here – lying in the grass with that dog. Look at the state of your dress!"

"Who cares about my dress?" I drawled grumpily, shading my eyes as I squinted up at her. "I was dozing – you scared six months out of me."

"Sorry, miss." She did not look apologetic in the least. "Sir Simon sent me to fetch you urgently."

I sighed resignedly. "What does he want?"

"A pair of coaches arrived."

"So? Why does he need me? Who are they?"

She shook her head. "Don't recognise the colours, miss, but they look important."

I nudged the dog with the toe of my boot. "C'mon, Jemima. Up you get."

Janet briskly led the way up the lawn to where a path met the terraced walkways of the gardens behind our house. Broughton Hall had belonged to my family since the second Charles. It was grey with age and lichen, with large mullioned windows like all-seeing benevolent eyes watching over the park, gardens and bordering forest.

As we rounded the side of the house, my eyes slid towards the drive and porch to where two shiny wine-red coaches, each with four well-matched grey horses, and bearing an unfamiliar gold crest, stood rocking gently. Their occupants had not yet emerged and my siblings waited at the foot of the porch steps. I ranked between them in age and was the proverbial thorn between two roses, for Simon and Anne were extraordinarily attractive.

A young wine-liveried footman opened the door of the lead coach and unfolded the steps.

Jemima fussed around the horses' hooves causing them to move restively. I clutched her collar tightly and watched a rotund, fair-haired gentleman appear from within the coach.

"Gently now, m'dear," he said as he offered his hand to a second person behind him.

As the woman stepped down Anne gave a small gasp and I consciously closed my mouth.

"Remember yourselves," Simon hissed, for our manners were momentarily forgotten at the unexpected sight of our mother. Pausing before us, she straightened and regarded us haughtily, her early yet obvious pregnancy displayed defiantly.

Simon was the first to recover. "Welcome home, Mother," he stepped up to kiss her cheek. "We had no idea you –"

"Oh Mother! You're home!" Anne cried and her excitement caused Jemima to leap and almost jerk me off my feet. The horses stirred, clanking their harness, and unsettling the coaches.

"Alexandra, control that dog!" Mother commanded. The chastisement stung and I tightened my grip on Jemima's collar.

Mother did not respond to my siblings' greetings. She appeared tired, her eyes shadowed and the blue of her travelling gown lent her face a sallow tinge.

Our housekeeper appeared beside me. "Lady Broughton, you look weary, may I —"

Mother raised a silencing hand and proceeded towards the porch leaving Mrs Grainger to silently draw up her bosom.

The young footman waited beside the coach. His appraising eyes swept over us, pausing, if only for a moment, on Anne. He had a pleasing face and appeared no more than 18 or 19 years old, and I made a mental note to suggest Simon should keep an eye on our pretty sister.

Finally, Mother's maid and companion emerged from the coach and I wondered, as I always did, why Mother kept her around. Eleanor, a waspish creature, was tall and rail-thin with a face that looked as though she perpetually sucked a lemon. Her hair was exactly the same as every other time I'd seen her — bright orange-red and clawed back in a tight chignon.

She was utterly faithful to Mother and I reminded myself to be careful as her eyes rested on me. To avoid her gaze, I studied the big, rather jolly-looking blond fellow now offering Mother his arm as she ascended the stairs. As if I had voiced my curiosity, she paused on the porch and faced the gathering of her children.

"This is Gerrard Washburn, Earl of Thorncliffe. He will live here." Turning, she presented her straight back to us and entered the house.

I was too stunned to remember my manners, but Anne sank into a practised curtsy as though King George stood before her.

Lord Thorncliffe hesitated and his hand toyed with his ear lobe. Offering a quick, apologetic smile and nod to the three of us, he then addressed his young footman. "Very well, Jeffrey. Have the coaches unloaded."

I looked at Simon and he shrugged. "Annie?" he said.

Turning to our sister, I saw with dismay that she had already sidled over to where Jeffrey was directing others wearing the wine livery in the unloading of the coaches. Easily distracted though, he made Anne a courtly bow with a somewhat jaunty lift of one eyebrow.

I quickly grasped my sister's shoulders. "Come, Annie, it's almost time for dinner," and shoved her towards the porch.

"We'll have to watch that one," Simon said, pointing with his chin in Jeffrey's direction as Anne disappeared into the house.

"She won't discourage him," I said. "And she won't be able to resist the flattery either."

"No, she won't." My brother made a rueful expression, then bent towards my ear. "Council assembly … bring Anne … my office in an hour."

As we climbed the porch steps Janet was waiting by the door. She glanced doubtfully at my boots. "Mrs Grainger's had the maids beating the rugs. She'll skin you alive if –"

"Pooh to Mrs Grainger! I'm going upstairs. I'll be in my room. Come, Jemima."

Holding my skirt in one hand, I pushed open one of the two enormous oak doors at the front of our house and stepped into the cool entry hall. It smelled of old wood and beeswax and had a great staircase directly before me and rooms either side; the parlour on the right and a morning room on the left.

True to form, Mrs Grainger stood guard, one large, square hand resting on the newel. With a face that threatened thunder, she held the power to strike fear into disobedient children with a single glance. She regularly examined our boots and clothing before grudgingly allowing us entry into our own house. Not even Simon, for all his looks and charm, could escape her inspections, and while he and I were forced to endure her recriminations about wallowing in stable-muck like commoners, Anne's proud perfection extracted merely a grunt.

Mrs Grainger's dignity had taken a blow with Mother's disregard but she seemed to have recovered well enough, for now she watched disdainfully as my dog and I headed for the grand staircase and slid past her, effectively avoiding her scowl.

&

An hour later, I gave the briefest of knocks before Anne and I entered Simon's office. It was an entirely masculine domain with dark wood-panelled walls and unfussy furniture, unchanged since our Papa's death some five years ago.

The room was chilly. Being rarely used – Simon generally did his estate paperwork in the library – no-one had thought to light a fire and since the windows overlooked the eastern boundary of our property it did not enjoy the afternoon sun.

Simon was seated behind Papa's heavy old desk. I took a seat opposite and Anne did likewise, sitting primly upright and flawlessly turned out, as though we were expecting exalted visitors.

My brother was more practical than my sister. Simon wore an old linen shirt beneath a green woollen waistcoat and a pair of dun-coloured trousers, attire perfect for a country gentleman – though he would look as well in rags for he was tall and in good proportion for his 17 years. His merry nut-brown eyes and beautiful smile reduced sturdy milkmaids and broad-shouldered washerwomen to giggly, brainless twits before him. It baffled me as it stoked my pride in him, the older brother who nurtured my penchant for mischief and adventure.

"I have had the opportunity to speak with Mother," he began. "There's … unexpected news." He looked at me significantly, "Her post at court has been terminated."

"Oh dear," Anne murmured.

"Yes." Simon continued, and his voice seemed deeper, "She didn't say a lot, but I am given to understand her return to Broughton Hall is permanent … and it seems," here he paused and gave a slight grimace, "Mother's return is on the King's orders and that man, her escort, is to be … well, they're to be married."

Instantly, Anne burst into a flood of tears while I stared at him in stunned silence. Now, I was not an unfeeling girl. Certainly I had felt Papa's death in some manner all those years ago. But I had never thought Mother might remarry, though she was young enough, perhaps no more than her late thirties. So, I received this news with a strange kind of allegiance towards Papa.

Anne continued her sobbing and Simon reached for the bell-pull, rang for a maid, and we watched dispassionately as our younger sister leaned heavily on Janet and was led away.

"She would not do it without an audience," Simon commented drily as Janet closed the door.

I murmured something distractedly; I was wondering what Mother's return might mean for Simon. Since Papa's death, Simon had run our estate well and efficiently, despite his youth. He wouldn't officially take over his inheritance until his majority, yet I wondered, would Mother's return, with a new husband, change all this?

"Sime?" I waited for him to look at me. "This is so strange … I mean, what do you think it means … for you and everything?" My expansive gesture included the house, land, tenants, everything Simon was currently responsible for.

"We'll see. Collings has practically run this place for years and shall continue to, I expect. But it's not something you need to worry about. I think Mother's first duty would be to marry you and Anne off to some ageing farmers who need good women to knead their bread and bear their children."

I stared at him in alarm but he quickly smiled, "Stop snapping those brown eyes, Zan! I'm not serious." Then sobering, "Mother is in a bit of a mood. Being sent home has aggrieved her."

I nodded, knowing as he did, that to be expelled from court was no small matter. Yet my 14 years of life-experience was too limited to imagine what could have caused such dishonour, and I said as much.

He considered for a moment before answering. "We may never know, but one thing is certain – we will see some changes around here."

∾

We sat stiffly correct at supper that evening, not daring to speak. Mother directed Simon to the head of the table while she sat opposite. Lord Thorncliffe, ruddy and damp-browed, took the seat to her right. Maud, Cook's new girl, served a vegetable broth followed by stuffed goose and roasted vegetables. The steaming, fragrant bowls and platters were arranged before us, then Maud discreetly withdrew.

Cook's offerings remained largely untouched as Simon, Anne and I merely picked at our food, such was the brittle tension in the room. Only Lord Thorncliffe seemed to have an appetite, addressing his plate with gusto and quaffing enough wine to fill three farmers.

When Mother spoke, it was almost with relief that we placed our cutlery politely on our plates and turned to her.

"You have eyes – you know that I am with child." Her stony gaze rested on each of us in turn. "The child is due in five months – early in the new year. As I'm certain Simon has advised you, Lord Thorncliffe and I shall be married."

We nodded in unison and I shot furtive glances at my siblings. Simon was staring at Mother, his lips clamped firmly together. Anne's eyes were glassy with unshed tears, her fingers pressed to her mouth.

Meanwhile, Lord Thorncliffe studied the intense ruby-colour of his wine, his mouth unconsciously turned down.

Mother, having paused to allow us time to digest this news, now continued. "The wedding will take place next month. It shall be private – the three of you and Lord Thorncliffe's children. They will travel from my lord's estates in the south. Afterwards, they will live here with us."

Mother served herself from the teapot and the only sound in the room was the heavy pouring of the steaming liquid into fine china.

Finally, Anne broke the silence. "Mother, if you please," she said, tentatively. "How many, and how old, are Lord Thorncliffe's children?"

"Patrick is almost seventeen, of age with Simon, and …" Mother turned questioningly to Lord Thorncliffe but he remained diverted by his wine. "Gerrard?"

He started slightly. "Er … sorry, m'dear?"

"How old is your daughter, Gerrard?"

"Oh, Maeve," he gave a short laugh, more like a bark, and tugged at his earlobe. "Well, er … let me see now … she was born in ninety-six so she'd be … er … twelve."

Mother looked around the table at each of us. "Anything else?"

We were silent as we filed from the room. And later, alone in my bed, I knew instinctively that the only life I'd ever known, was gone forever.

I was born Alexandra Rose Broughton on 22 May 1794, one of three children to Lady Miriam Broughton and Sir Dudley Broughton. We were not an important family, but my mother brought money to her marriage.

My Papa had been a naval officer and, in this class-conscious time, a baronet with estates and tenants. He had a respectable lineage but not a farthing in his cash-tin. Mother, daughter of a successful merchant, married him for the potential she saw in his title: he married her for her wealth. He presented her to the King, where from gratitude of her husband's fidelity to the crown, she was offered a posting in Queen Charlotte's court. Papa promptly returned to sea, making only infrequent visits to England which resulted in Simon, myself, and Anne – in that order – and we grew up as orphans in the reign of mad King George III.

Prudent investing of Mother's money had made us prosperous. Our house and estates – Simon's inheritance – were well maintained and brought steady income: our tenants were happy and healthy.

Yet these were difficult times for England under the reign of a King whose declining sanity resulted in public *faux pas* at best. In this age of debauchery, despotism and unrest, he was known to be utterly faithful, even boring, though his eldest son, George IV, was the opposite. Prinnie to his chums, was extravagant, impulsive and known to have a fondness for the ladies. It was to this group that Mother gravitated.

Meanwhile, across the Channel, the French had executed their King and much of their aristocracy and at the turn of the century Napoleon Bonaparte had proclaimed himself Emperor of France. By 1803, England was again under French attack – by Napoleon's Continental System, intended to cause considerable damage to Britain's trade.

But I was only a child and content to be so. My brother, sister and I ensconced in our country home in Yorkshire, were blissfully unaware of the future gaping before us and how European events would shape our lives.

And this night, after Mother's unexpected return, I drifted on the cusp of sleep, and was vaguely aware of *the lady* gliding silently through my room. I cannot recall when it was that I first saw her. It seemed that she had always been there, floating without a sound from room to room with a strange, purposeful expression. I never thought of her as a ghost, for weren't ghosts expected to frighten you? And she was pretty, if somewhat oddly clothed …

And while I lay there, stirring restlessly, the winds of change swirled and cried about our house.

CHAPTER 2

The following morning, I rose at my customarily early hour to wash and dress. Janet assisted with the numerous buttons up the back of my gown but made no attempt to dress my hair – for it, like Medusa's, had a life of its own and persistently escaped pins and ribbons to riot in coiling tendrils about my face. Anne, conversely, demanded her hair be coiffed every morning as though a visit from Queen Charlotte herself was expected.

Following Janet into my sister's room I found Anne before her mirror – 13 years and already the coquette! "Good morning, sister," she greeted me brightly. I watched her preening – preferring to squint into the mirror than wear spectacles – as Janet brushed her glorious mane and twisted it into a shining plaited rope that hung down her back.

My sister was a rich brunette with dazzling hazel eyes and a rose complexion. Her leaning towards plumpness would doubtless see her become a voluptuous beauty, though Simon and I, faithful to sibling tradition, teased her endlessly with chants of, "Butterball! Butterball!" Anne, seemingly the quietest of us, exacted her revenge last week by filling my riding boot with custard – a reprisal I discovered by squelching my stockinged foot into it.

"You seem to have recovered well," I said, thinking that Simon's cynicism about Anne was warranted.

Her face fell dramatically, "Oh Alex, I'm trying so hard to be brave."

"I see. In any case, it will be lessons as normal this morning so I trust your bravery holds out."

She wrinkled her pert nose. "Lessons … pooh! Who needs lessons? Soon, Mother will obtain a position for me at court. I shan't need lessons then." Her musical voice and sibilant lisp were not affectations but she was already aware of their power. The stable lads, target practice for her as yet imperfect skills, tumbled over each other like puppies for a mere second of her attention.

"It appears there's no court position for Mother let alone you and besides, you know if you don't attend lessons Master Baxter will report it to her."

"Mother won't be home long and when she returns to London, she'll doubtless take me with her. You'll be sorry you poked fun at me."

"Ooh you're a right one, young Miss," Janet said, angling a wink in my direction and tying off the plait with a silk ribbon, the same lilac shade as Anne's dress. "Come get a wriggle-on. If you stare into that glass any longer you'll wear it out."

Simon was already seated at the breakfast table as Anne and I entered. Cook was laying out a basket of freshly-baked bread and a bowl of honey. The spherical woman greeted us with a broad-faced grin.

"Where's Beth?" I asked, setting my napkin over my lap.

"Abed, Miss Alex, with the 'ead cold. There's fruit compote for any wantin' it."

"Thank you, Cook," Anne said feebly, "but I haven't much appetite today."

Simon looked at her. "Unwell, Annie?"

I snorted scornfully, "She was well enough two minutes ago. Stop the theatrics Anne." I turned to Cook, "Compote would be lovely, thank you."

Anne made a face at me and poured herself a cup of tea. Undeterred, I dripped honey on a hunk of bread and applied myself with great enthusiasm, taking perverse pleasure in forgetting my table manners before Cook. She was constantly reminding me of my birth station and my mother's expectation of a good husband for me. "Yer name will count for naught if yer cannot eat like a lady," she warned as she returned with a steaming bowl of stewed fruits. "What gentleman will want yer for his wife if yer shovel food into yer gob like a smithy shovelling coal?"

Simon leaned over and commented *sotto voce*, "Or Agnes shovelling swill." I erupted with mirth at Simon's reference to our scullery maid, whose father was a local pig-farmer.

Cook shook her head and made a tutting sound. "Sir Simon, I'd expect better from yer. As lord an' master, yer needs to learn respect for those beneath yer."

"As lord and master, Mistress Cook, you needs must learn respect for me," he responded in mock pomposity.

Immediately the large woman dropped to her knees, her pinny twisting in her hands, "Oh kind sir, pray have mercy upon a lowly matron such as I!" Then, hauling herself upright, she glared ruddy-faced around the table. "Get on with them meals yer disagreeable lot before I take the broomstick to yer!" We broke into laughter as Cook haughtily returned to the kitchen.

Lessons were conducted in the library where sharp-faced Master Baxter reigned. My papa had been more liberal than his contemporaries and had instructed Master Baxter to expose Anne and me to the same subjects as Simon. Consequently, our lessons included history, Latin, English literature, music and mathematics. I was good at history and literature, but I excelled with figures which, though amusing, was useless since I was destined to make a good marriage, breed children to further my future husband's line, and fall in love – probably in that order. I should have no use for mathematics.

Twice weekly, music and dance were included in our curriculum. The day following Mother's return Master Baxter, repairing to the parlour, stationed himself at the piano and barked his instructions. Compared with Simon and Anne's grace, my dancing was barely adequate despite my love of music.

"No, no, no!" Master Baxter cried. Leaping to his spindly legs and standing before me, he demonstrated. "Like this, young leddy, one … and two, one … and two – try it … other foot first – no other foot!"

Behind me, Anne sniggered but I ignored her and tried again. Master Baxter exaggerated a sigh. "Stop!" he commanded. "Young leddy, do you derive pleasure from this?"

"No, I –"

He leaned his vulpine snout towards me and his beady eyes narrowed. "It escapes me why a girl-child – gifted in the masculine study of numbers – should be so inept in the pursuit of social arts."

Immediately incensed, I opened my mouth to release an angry retort.

"Master Baxter," said Simon, effectively slicing my reply. "If you would be so kind as to resume your seat at the piano, I shall step my sister through the dance."

Simon turned to me, "Zan, try –"

"No!" I responded angrily. "I've no desire to learn the stupid dance anyway."

The front door slammed behind me as I escaped into the late-afternoon sunshine. The trees in the park cast thin shadows across the lawn and neatly raked gravel drive, and the dying scents of summer hung in the air as I stomped to the ancient oak tree adjacent to our house. With my skirt hoisted unseemingly high, I found my foothold and scrambled into the branches, then shimmied on to a sturdy bough to relax with my back against the trunk. This was my favourite hiding place. I loved to perch here, unseen by anyone below, breathing the verdant foliage and surveying our beautiful, terraced gardens, orchard and long, curved drive.

At length, Simon emerged from the house with Jemima at his heels. I watched as he leaned on the porch balustrade and scanned the gardens and park. His eyes eventually rested on my Great Oak. Grinning good-naturedly, he straightened and descended the stairs, strolling unhurriedly towards me.

"Do you plan to stay there all night, you grouch? Shall I have your supper sent up?"

"You could join me – if you dare climb this high."

From climbing trees, to seeing who could spit the furthest, my cheerfully irreverent brother had led me into all manner of hoydenish activities. Ordinarily he'd find my challenge irresistible, but his response surprised me. "Not now. I agreed to ride over to the Goodmans' place with Collings this afternoon to have a look at their roof. It's in need of repair before winter."

He turned and I watched his receding back in dismay. Until now our lives had melded into one wondrous round, and Simon and I had been inseparable.

This life was all I knew and Broughton Hall the only home. The winters here were icy – the stone of our house seemed to absorb the cold and no fire roared enough to dispel it. But if the winters were bitter, the summers were long, glorious days when Simon and I ran wild through fields of swaying yellow grass, wildflowers and disgruntled bees, with Jemima galloping alongside.

Anne found our outdoor pursuits dirty and undignified. I was aware that in a corner of her heart she resented the closeness between Simon and me, but in my childishly-selfish way, I gave it little thought.

Annually over summer, our escapades were interrupted by the arrival of our Mother, always with a contingent of friends from court – coachloads of them. During this time we were painfully reminded of our manners and behaviour.

Our quiet country estate was transformed by glamorous ladies in the most sumptuous silks and satins, gliding sensuously about, laughing with affectation and tinkling with jewels. The gentlemen fawned over them and competed for their attention in high-collared shirts, elegant coats and long leather boots, with glinting, rakish swords hanging at their hips.

Anne would sigh dreamily over the extravagant clothes and glittering jewels. "I simply cannot wait until I may wear such beautiful clothes. I shall have a ring on every finger and all the gentlemen will vie for my attention – just like Mother."

One hot night, I lay restlessly on my bed as the sounds of clinking crystal, music, and laughter drifted up from the gardens below. Unable to sleep, I slipped unnoticed, outside by the servants' stairs.

The grotto was a secluded corner of our garden, walled by a tall hedge on three sides and stone on the fourth. It had been designed by the builder of Broughton Hall – a wealthy merchant who had owned several ships that plied their trade between Bristol and the Indies. According to local narrative, he'd never lost a ship to either pirate or element and, crediting God as the source of his luck, built and dedicated the little corner garden – complete with statue of Our Lady, a trickling fountain, and stone benches – to grateful contemplation of his good fortune.

We Broughtons were not a religious family, but maintained the grotto for its tranquillity. Seeking solitude, I was drawn there on that night, but as I approached, I thought I heard vague whispers and sighs. Innocently curious, I pushed aside a curtain of foliage and silently slipped inside. I paused in surprise.

The light of a single lantern revealed my mother, leaning against an ivy-covered wall, one slender leg on the bench, her skirt lifted to expose her stockings and garters. A man was leaning over her, his face buried in her bosom, his hand working between her thighs.

I could only see his back, but recognised the shiny grey coat he wore for I'd seen this young man, not more than Simon's age, only that afternoon toasting my mother and her cronies with champagne beneath the Great Oak.

Neither was aware of my presence, or that I hurried away, sweat dampening my young forehead, confused and inexplicably frightened by what I'd seen. I told no one of my experience, but the image was burned forever on my memory.

While our summer visitors were here, our house bulged with people and Cook always brought in two or three village girls to assist in the kitchen.

One of these girls was discovered in a pantry with a gentleman visitor. Young as I was, I did not understand the ensuing trouble. The lass was dispatched in disgrace to her family while Cook groaned and became even more harried.

Finally, after what felt like six months but was in reality only one, they all departed in a frenetic storm of dust, perfume, servants and horses to their own estates before returning to London's winter round of parties and balls.

My mother lingered, passing the heat of summer in the relative relief of the country. But as August arrived she was gone and the trees in the park began turning gold and red, and our tenants prepared to bring in their wheat harvest.

Before the dust had settled behind her, Simon and I had donned old clothes and joined the farmers in the fields, sharing their back-breaking toil, their rations and their cheerful freedom, all the while delighting in the scandalised outrage of our sister, for such work ought to be beneath us.

Cutting and bailing was hard graft but culminated in a great celebration, revelry in which my brother and I participated to the full.

❧

But all this was about to change. Mother was home under mysterious circumstances with a new husband, and my brother, my friend and partner in crime, was already growing away from me.

CHAPTER 3

Summer was well gone and the trees in the park were red and gold, their leaves beginning to fall. The last of the fruit in our orchard was ready and I had agreed to help Simon gather the plums. Dashing quickly to my room, I changed into my favourite attire – a cast-off pair of Simon's breeches. They were comfortable and practical, affording freedom of movement; I'd wear them all the time if I could, since I regularly tripped on the hem of my dress and earned Anne's contempt.

I was in a hurry lest Simon began picking fruit without me. Jemima and I bounded down the staircase and on my way along the hall I caught a glimpse of someone in the parlour. Ever watchful for Mrs Grainger, I slowed to a decorous walk and cautiously peeked into the room. Rather than our fearsome housekeeper, I was surprised to find a well-dressed girl about my own age.

"Hello," I said.

Startled, she whirled around and returned my greeting with a quick curtsy and genuine smile. I decided it would be foolish to curtsy in breeches so bobbed my head in response.

She was wearing a lemon-silk dress with white-lace edging, which did nothing to hide her chubby figure. A white bonnet hung carelessly from one hand and white gloves were scrunched in the other. She cocked her head as she looked at me and, rather than coquettish, the glance was quite charming and entirely artless.

"Hello," she replied. Her smile made her eyes shine and she had an unfashionable spattering of freckles on her nose.

"I'm Miss Alex Broughton. Is your mother visiting with mine?"

She nodded and her glossy, auburn curls bobbed about her face. "We've only just arrived. Is that your dog? I do love dogs – I'd love to have one of my own. May I pat it? Does it bite?"

"This is Jemima," I said. "She's a girl, and you may certainly pat her."

Instantly my acquaintance dropped her gloves and hat on a table and crouched before Jem, whose tongue and tail responded enthusiastically.

Remembering Simon in the orchard, I shuffled restlessly and craned my neck to see through the window though I knew the view didn't extend that far.

"How long will your mother be?" I asked. The girl straightened and Jemima sat between us looking from one to the other, baring her teeth in a wide grin.

"Oh, she'll be ages – she can talk forever when she gets started. I was looking for a book or something to read while I waited. I hope you don't mind."

"No, but … who are you?"

An apricot flush washed the skin beneath her freckles. "Saints alive! You must think me entirely rude! Miss Julia Chapman."

She extended her hand and we held each other's fingers as our mothers would do. Her hands were lightly tanned, as were mine, and her eyes were like chestnuts. I liked her instantly.

"I'm supposed to be helping my brother in the orchard. You can come if you like." She smiled faintly and then to my own surprise, I added, "Do you climb trees?"

Her reaction told me all I needed to know. Her eyes glinted

mischievously and her mouth twitched. She said, "Only if you don't tell Mama."

I rejoined with an air of solidarity, "If you don't tell mine. My brother's waiting. We're picking plums."

She winked slyly and gathered her gloves and bonnet. "Then let us get started."

By the time we reached the orchard Simon had a wooden crate ready. Julia, unlike other girls who met my brother, did not go all daft when I introduced them, and I liked her even more for that. After a quick no nonsense exchange of greetings, we set to work. I scrambled into the aged limbs of the largest tree – a talent I was secretly proud of – and Julia easily clambered up beside me, further winning my approval. She began immediately picking the ripened fruit and placing them in her upturned bonnet.

Simon climbed into the tree beside ours and tied the ends of a net round a narrower branch to form a sling.

The three of us talked between the trees, laughing and swapping stories and before long I felt as though I'd known Julia for years. At times we stopped to eat a fat, ripe plum, and the blood-red juice trickled over our chins and hands.

The Chapmans were from Harrogate. I'd heard of them before – successful business people, though untitled. Hardly my mother's social equal, however she and Mrs Chapman spent a good two hours together while their daughters scrambled through a number of trees, laughing and chattering like sparrows before we realised that time had escaped us.

Except for the plum-coloured stains inside her bonnet – at which she shrugged, stating happily, "No-one will see," – and a couple of dusty marks on the skirt of her dress, Julia looked as though she'd spent the entire time in the parlour.

The three of us were waiting innocently on the porch as Mrs Chapman and Mother emerged.

"Oh there you are," Julia's mother said. "We were wondering

where you'd taken yourself." Mrs Chapman was taller than Mother, and carried herself with a soft and comfortable grace. Her russet hair and smiling mouth were engaging, and the scattered freckles across her nose were features I'd already noted in her daughter.

"Miss Broughton and Sir Simon were showing me their lovely gardens, Mama," my accomplice said ingenuously.

"How lovely." Julia's mother responded though her eyes skimmed critically over my masculine clothing.

Later, as their coach trundled down our drive, Mother's experienced eye regarded me with an entirely justified suspicion.

~

I was sitting in the library window. Open in my lap was a book about Ancient Rome and I flipped its pages absently. My attention was focused directly below where I could see the front porch and the steps leading to the drive. The gravel created a divide between the two halves of our garden.

To my right was an expanse of lawn interrupted by the Great Oak and the wide grassless patch beneath its limbs. On the left was more lawn, a rose garden, and terraced walkways. Six stone steps led to further garden beds; an additional four steps led to the orchard. An ancient stone wall separated the orchard from property owned by our neighbour, Eliard Jackson. Jackson owned the grumpiest black bull alive; such was his scowling demeanour that I was certain the creature was costive and trespassers did so at their own risk.

One of the stable-lads was busily raking the gravel – Mother insisted this was done each morning, and the dry, scrape-scrape sound filtered up to me. The drive curved to the left and disappeared into the thick, green foliage of the birch trees that sheltered our property from the public lane some quarter mile from where I sat. It also served to effectively screen Collings' cottage from the main house.

Lord Thorncliffe's children were expected today and I bore the knowledge with thorny resentment toward the changes Mother's return had wrought.

My mind drifted to the breakfast room that morning. I had been sulkily moving my food around my plate, peeved that my idyllic existence was being so drastically altered. Lord Thorncliffe attempted to catch my eye and offer a conciliatory smile hoping I'd return his approach, but I would not. I was sullen, sour and not pleased with the fact that I was being subjected to a stepfather, stepsiblings, and a newborn brother or sister, in so short a time.

"I am so looking forward to having a new brother and sister, Father," Anne gushed sycophantically and I rolled my eyes at my plate. "Simon and Alex are exceedingly poor company." Her mutinous expression challenged me and I glared at her in response.

"Perhaps, Gerrard, this is as good a time as any to …" Mother prompted with a pointed nod of her head in Simon's direction and I groaned inwardly; not another surprise.

Lord Thorncliffe stammered and reached for his ear and before he could respond, Mother had leapt in, "Simon, Lord Thorncliffe's son will be staying here only until the university year resumes. It is intended that he continue his law studies at Oxford. Perhaps you should go with him – your future would benefit and I think you've probably outgrown Master Baxter."

I watched my brother curiously. He had been riding the estate early this morning with Collings and held a genuine care for his land and tenants. The latter, perhaps enticed by the young master's good looks and considerate nature, were quite taken with him and he wore his adult responsibilities well.

Over the years he had casually mentioned following a path into medicine, with no real expectation of the opportunity arising. Given the choice, would he opt to stay here, or would he grasp the chance to go to university? I for one, would be devastated should he leave, and clasped my hands together tightly beneath the linen tablecloth in a silent plea that he would decline the offer.

He was slow to respond, but finally he addressed Lord Thorncliffe. "I think I would like that, Sir. The property is managed well under Collings. It will still be here when I return."

"Good, good." Lord Thorncliffe smiled. "Er … We must consider your subjects, of course, and I shall prepare all the paperwork. You should be able to depart for Oxford with Patrick."

And just like that, the turning upside down of my life was complete. Anne began babbling excitedly about her scholarly brother, while Lord Thorncliffe and Simon discussed the subjects necessary for medicine. Mother reclined in her chair, a look of quiet satisfaction on her face, and when I asked to be excused she nodded in reply.

That had been this morning, and now, as Simon joined me in the library, we sat briefly in companionable silence before he spoke. "You know, I've always wanted to be a physician."

"You hadn't mentioned it for some time. I thought you had changed your mind."

"I'd put the idea aside — resigned to remain here, though of course we couldn't have foreseen the current turn of events, could we?"

"So you're happy then?"

"Yes I am," he said, firmly. "And Mother seems pleased."

"Why wouldn't she be? Sending their sons to Oxford is what people like Lord Thorncliffe do. Mother has ever aspired to be more than the wife of a mere baronet."

"And now she's about to become a countess." Simon finished.

"And you're prepared to leave this — your home, your inheritance?"

"Collings has been helping me become more involved with the tenants lately and I rather enjoy it — they seem to like me too."

I snorted indelicately. "The tenants' wives and daughters like you. The men respect you because they've watched you grow up and know you're not a brute."

"But I wasn't expecting an opportunity like this, Zan. An opportunity to study medicine …"

"So you'll leave your lands in the hands of a stranger," I stated, unfairly.

"Collings is no stranger – he knows the place better –"

"Not Collings," I said with significance and he frowned.

"Lord Thorncliffe? He wouldn't be involved. Collings will remain in charge and besides, this place is my inheritance – no-one can change that."

"I suppose not," I mumbled.

"Why are you upset? Do you think I'll be so absorbed in anatomy and biology that I'll not have time to marry you off?"

I thumped his arm playfully. "Don't be a rat, Simon. I'm in no hurry to bear the brats of some cranky old man so don't make any plans."

"And that's for me as well," said Anne coming into the room.

"Well now Annie, dear little vixen, the sooner you are foisted on some old fart the better for everyone."

Simon and I laughed but Anne dropped an elegant curtsy and rose, skirts lifted perfectly as she stepped up to an imaginary dance partner and held out her hand, "Your majesty, I would be honoured to share this dance with you."

We laughed again but Anne thrust her chin out. "You may laugh now, but there are big things in store for me, I can feel it." She hugged herself rapturously. "I shall go to court, and ladies will envy me and gentlemen will fall in love with me. And you, dear brother and sister, you'll be bowing to me."

Simon and I looked archly at one another and my brother said, "If you say so, Annie."

"I do, so you'd best be nice to me now, for I won't forget it if you're not."

"Really?" I asked. "So what are these big things that are in store for you, or can you not share them yet?"

"Oh, you'll see," she lisped coyly.

Simon nudged me, "Thinks she's going to ensnare Prinnie and be a king's favourite."

Anne looked smug. "Don't laugh – Jemima get your wet nose off my skirt – you never know what could happen."

I nodded then. "That's true, because I'll wager you didn't know you were going to fall on your backside in front of Jeffrey yesterday."

"Oh, be quiet about that!" Anne snapped.

"What's this?" Simon's face lit up, mischievously.

"Leave it be, Alex," my sister warned.

Ignoring her, I said, "Yesterday morning – remember it had rained? Anne and I were walking out past the stables, and Jeffrey was polishing Lord Thorncliffe's coach."

"Alex, please don't. It was embarrassing enough then, don't have me relive it."

"I'm sorry, Annie. Simon, you won't believe this – she lifted her skirt to step over a puddle, and just as she did," I could barely get the words out for laughing, "she said, 'good morning Jeffrey', and at the very moment he looked up, she put her foot into a huge horse turd. She slipped in it – oh, it was so funny!"

By this stage Simon was doubled over with laughter and I was breathlessly gripping my ribs. "She landed, plop, on her arse, right in a great pile of horse-pooh. Jeffrey ran over to see if she was alright, but even he was laughing so hard … she had to sit there in the muck until Jeffrey stopped laughing enough to help her."

Anne was looking fit to kill. "Well," she snarled, "I hope you've enjoyed yourselves at my expense," and with queenly dignity, swept from the room.

Simon and I exchanged glances and broke into renewed laughter. When finally we sobered, Simon said, "Our sister's going to be a handful. I pity the poor fellow who marries her."

"Oh, you're such a hypocrite," I said accusingly. "You play the gallant with every maid who glances your way. Now that our sister is proving to be a female version of yourself, you have a different view."

"Perhaps now, but the day I marry it shall be for life. All I'm saying is that Anne is our mother all over again. Haven't you wondered why she's the only one of us Mother has ever seemed remotely interested in? It will be all about money and position where our Annie is concerned."

I pondered his words momentarily. "I hope I marry for love. Promise you'll not contract me for money or position."

"It probably won't be up to me. I expect it will be Mother's decision."

This gave me little hope, but what else was there? What else for any well-bred girl my age? A year, perhaps two, before the obligatory London season where I would be presented at court and shown off at an exhausting and pretentious round of balls and parties until a mutually beneficial arrangement could be made with an outwardly suitable stranger. Every girl wanted to marry for love. Plain little Laura Hindley – daughter of one of Mother's Leeds friends – confided last week while her mother visited mine, that she'd already met her love.

Laura had refused to divulge the identity of her suitor which then prompted a parade of eligible bachelors through my mind. With no result, either for Laura or myself, I decided it was not worth the effort for I had more pressing things to consider – a new brother and sister, Simon going away, Mother with child … only Jemima was constant, my beloved companion. Everything else seemed to be changing and the growing pains were sharp as my childhood began to slip away.

"Look," Simon interrupted my thoughts. He was pointing toward the drive. "They're here."

CHAPTER 4

Simon and I, followed by Jemima, clattered down the stairs and arrived, breathless and expectant, on the porch. Lord Thorncliffe was there, eager and ruddy-faced at the foot of the steps, Mother beside him and Anne beside her.

The crested, wine-coloured coach had already rolled to a stop and Lord Thorncliffe's children were stepping down as I grasped a handful of my skirt and stood between Simon and Anne.

The two blond siblings, dressed in expensive travelling costumes and bearing the weariness of travel on their faces, turned to their father. Lord Thorncliffe embraced them fervently, his great bear-like arms pulling them both to his chest. I watched sullenly as he proudly introduced his son, Patrick, and daughter, Maeve. "Their mother, my late wife, was Irish," he stated, unnecessarily.

Patrick was, as my mother had said, Simon's age. Though not as tall, his physique evidenced a more active lifestyle than my brother's and the remnants of a summer tan spoke of long outdoor hours. Unsmiling, he pushed shaggy honey-blond hair from his eyes and appraised each of us in turn.

He looked fatigued and his expression was distant, yet the structure of his face was such that I thought, if only he smiled he could be attractive − not like Simon, no-one could be attractive like Simon − but Patrick had a well-proportioned face, a straight nose and full lips and, while his thoughts were unreadable, his eyes were the most startling green, glittering with intellect and a touch of irony.

Maeve was short, about Anne's height, though slimmer than my sister. In contrast with her brother, her quick gaze darted excitedly to each of us with hopeful friendliness. Maeve was a very pretty girl, and her bottle-green-velvet travelling gown and matching hat, tied with gold-velvet ribbons, suited her fair colour. She had the bearing of an elegant lady coupled with the flighty little gestures of a sparrow. She studied each of us with an impish smile twitching her lips and I reluctantly conceded that I could come to like her.

With no regard for decorum, she ran to Mother and hugged her enthusiastically. Unaware of that lady's surprised expression and heedless of the lack of response, she threw herself in turn at Anne, me and finally Simon. She caught us up in a whirlwind of energy, leaving us quite taken aback.

Completely oblivious to her impact, Maeve clapped her hands and executed a series of little jumps. "Oh, it is so perfectly *marvy* to have a new family," she gushed. "Two sisters and a − oh, goodness! *Missy!*" In a flurry, she turned back to the coach and indecorously showed us the creased seat of her gown while she dragged out a wooden crate from which emitted faint mewing sounds.

It was all too much for Jemima. The dog reacted before I could and bounded forward, leaping at the crate in Maeve's arms.

"Jemima! *No!*" I cried, but too late as my dog threw the slight girl off balance. Even as I lunged in a vain attempt to grab Jemima's collar, Maeve stumbled and dropped the crate.

"*Missy!*"

We watched in horror as the wooden box splintered open and a thoroughly-affronted white cat launched a spitting, clawing attack on the dog.

Chaos erupted. Simon grasped Jemima's collar and hauled her away but the cat attacked again. The dog squirmed in a panicked frenzy and a bright bead of blood appeared on her snout.

"Jemima!" I shouted again.

"Someone hold the cat!" cried Anne.

"Steady lads, *whoa* …" the coach driver attempted futilely to calm the horses. He leaned back in his seat, pulling the reins taut but the coach rocked back and forth as the horses danced in fright and Jemima barked furiously.

A stable boy attempted to grasp the horses' halters but ducked immediately to the side, narrowly avoiding the startled, side-stepping animals.

Simon continued to hold Jemima, and Maeve was clutching the squirming cat to her chest, but the infuriated feline lashed out to rake her face. Maeve's cry of pain changed to one of alarm as, in a tumble of white fluff, the animal leapt free, streaked across the lawn and disappeared among the trees in the park.

Jemima squirmed frantically, desperate to give chase. Had I been holding her rather than Simon she'd have surely broken free; as it was, she began a high-pitched yelping.

"Boy," Gerrard addressed the stable lad, "go fetch some help – find that cat."

The lad nodded and dashed away.

Maeve began to cry and her father folded her against his broad chest.

Suddenly Mother was at my shoulder. "Alexandra, I have warned you about that dog in the past. Bring the stableman now. I shall see he knocks it on the head. It is more trouble than it is worth."

"But Mother," I pleaded. "She's only being a dog. Please, I'll keep her tied up, I –"

Mother held up her hand. "We've had this discussion before Alexandra, and I'm in no mood to continue it now. Anne, run along, fetch the stableman."

Anne stood rooted to the spot, her eyes wide with dread, "Mother …" she began softly.

"Go Anne, I've had well enough – go now."

Still Anne hesitated. "Mother, please don't ask this of me …" she said, her lisp more pronounced than normal.

Maeve stood in the circle of her father's arms. She glanced at me apologetically, then turned to Mother, "My lady … please …"

Mother ignored her. "*Now!*" She demanded, in a voice that made the horses toss their heads in fright again. "That dog has to go, Alexandra, you've been warned time and again … useless cur … get rid of it," she turned to Anne. "Go! I'll not repeat myself again."

"Mother, no!" I wailed, while Anne continued to stare at Mother. This could not be happening. My eyes darted frantically from face to face, and came to rest on Simon. He'd been looking at Patrick and now he turned to me.

"Simon … please …" I begged and tears ran unchecked down my cheeks.

He shook his head. "Zan –"

"*Please …*" I cried again.

At that moment, Patrick spoke up – his first words since arriving.

"Give me the dog. I'll take it to the stableman." Mother eyed him curiously for a moment before nodding curtly and pointing to the side of the house towards the stables.

"*No!*" I screamed and lunged towards Jemima but Simon was already dragging her in Patrick's direction.

"Mother no … *please … please!*" I was screaming now and Jemima, confused and suddenly aware that she was in great trouble, cowered on the ground. Leaning over, Patrick easily scooped the frozen dog into his arms and walked away.

"*No …!*"

Simon tried to pull me into his arms but I fought him.

"Alexandra! Go into the house!" Mother commanded but I paid no heed. "*Alexandra!*"

I stopped and turned to her. "Why are you doing this? Why would you kill my dog?"

"I said, go into the house now, and I'll not say it again."

"Do as she says," Simon said firmly.

"How can you do this? You of all people … Simon?"

"Oh for goodness sake, Alexandra, do as instructed for once in your life." Mother looked weary, but she was not going to back down. I looked at Anne's stricken face, at Gerrard wiping Maeve's tears with his handkerchief, and knew nobody would take my part.

I let myself go limp in Simon's arms, long enough for him to relax his hold – this was my cue. With an explosive burst, I broke into a run but, hampered by my skirt, I'd only gone a few yards when a strong hand grasped my arm, all but jerking me off my feet.

"Simon! Let go …!" I struggled desperately, screaming and slapping at him. "What's wrong with you …?" I sobbed, "Let go … *let … me … go!*"

"Alex, stop it!" he shouted into my face, "It's too late …"

I beat at his chest with my free hand but he gripped my chin, forcing the direction of my head. That's when I heard the crunch of gravel and saw Patrick's return, his face set like stone.

"See?" Simon said, gently. "It's over."

I cried until my head ached and my eyes were so swollen I could barely open them. I held the pillow to my face and screamed until my throat hurt, but still the pain throbbed and constricted my chest. How could this have happened? How could Mother have ordered such a monstrous thing? I thought my heart would break apart from grief and anger.

And Patrick! How dared he? He no sooner arrived and … I could not even shape the words in my mind.

"*Oh Jemima …*" I cried and turned to my pillow again.

Was it quick? *Oh God!* Please let it have been quickly done.

How I hated Patrick. I'd known him less than ten minutes and I hated him with every drop of blood, every bone in my body. Was he trying to win favours with my mother? Surely if he'd not interfered I could have reasoned with her. And as for Simon … We'd always defended one another, but when I'd needed his support … nothing! The sooner the two went to university the better. And as for the others … they could all go to the moon in a basket!

Some time later there was a tentative knock at my door. "Miss Alex, I've brought your supper." It was Janet. I didn't answer. "Miss Alex?" The door opened slightly, there was a pause, then it closed quietly and I was alone again – with Jemima's cold, empty basket beside my bed.

~

Appropriately, it rained that night. I remained in my room, having no desire to see or speak to anyone. By morning, my head was pounding mercilessly, and when Janet brought a breakfast tray, I turned away.

"Cook made it especially," she said, smiling cautiously. "Fruit-bread, still hot from the oven. Oh Miss Alex … I'm so sorry."

I stared vacantly at the drapery around my bed and, though the bread smelled good, I could not stomach it. Janet rinsed a cloth in cool water and bathed my face. I didn't speak; I had no words. I hated everyone. I particularly hated Patrick.

Finally, to my relief, Janet left me in peace and I continued to stare at my wall – I may even have slept, for I started slightly at another knock at my door.

"May I come in? It's Pat." His voice was soft and hesitant but instantly my blood began to boil and hot tears of rage welled in my eyes.

"You get the *hell* away from me!" I swore at the door.

Defiantly, it opened and his tousled blond head appeared. "*Get out!*" I screamed, but he slipped inside: infuriatingly, in the face of my anger, he was calm. I took up a glass from my side table and hurled it with everything I had. Sadly, it missed its target and smashed against the door.

"Whew," he whistled, running a hand through his hair and staring at the wreckage. Then, as though nothing untoward had happened, he approached my bed. "I need to tell you something." The soft timbre of his voice did nothing to dispel my anger.

"I've no desire to hear it." To my intense shame, I began to cry again and clutched the pillow to my face.

"I rather fancy you do, Alex, for your dog did not die. She's alive and well, and has just eaten her fill of roasted pheasant – pilfered from the kitchen."

I stopped breathing, my body trembling fitfully. "Liar! You are … the most … hateful … creature," I sobbed. "Are you … proud of yourself? I raised … Jemima from a … newborn pup … kept her alive when she would have died … and … now you come here …" I couldn't continue.

He watched me for some seconds until I began to grow calmer. "Will you listen?" I didn't respond and he went on, "I took the dog to the stables because I could see no other way – your sister is too young and would only have repeated your mother's orders to the stableman. I merely asked the fellow to take care of the dog until your mother finds herself more … amenable."

His extraordinary, green gaze studied my face.

I took a deep breath and dared phrase the question. "Jemima is alive?"

He nodded, "Want to see for yourself?"

"She's alive?"

"Yes."

"You made me think all this time … that she was … I broke my heart last night."

"I apologise for that but I feared you'd brain me with something heavy had I visited earlier."

The hope that sprang within me was such that I overlooked his poor excuse. "Come, let's see your mutt." He offered his hand but I ignored it.

"How are we to hide this from my mother?" I asked suddenly. "She will find out eventually, and will probably throttle Jemima with her own bare hands ... and the two of us for good measure. *Oh!* She's going to hate you," I added, for the first time allowing my heart to lighten.

He looked at me for a long moment, before saying quite soberly, "She already hates me. Well, your flea-bitten beastie awaits."

❧

Jemima was indeed alive and exceedingly pleased to see me. I hugged her and she squirmed, yelping joyously and licking my face. Patrick leaned impassively against the wall of the straw-filled stall and I glared at him periodically to make certain he knew I was still angry for having caused me to endure an entire night of wretchedness.

"If you're interested," he said in a quiet drawl, "Maeve's feisty feline was located behind a fallen tree in the park."

I fondled Jemima's floppy ear. "I'm glad," I said with sincerity, adding grudgingly, "I suppose I should thank you."

He shrugged and executed a somewhat mocking bow before taking his leave.

❧

I made an appearance at supper that evening and Maeve, with an angry-looking scratch on her cheek, smiled shyly when I took my place beside her. "I am so sorry, Alexandra ... your poor dog. Had I known, I'd never have collected Missy at that moment."

"It's alright, Maeve — really," I said truthfully, and patted her hand for emphasis.

"Then we may be friends as well as sisters?"

I faltered, surprised, for in the hubbub of their arrival, I'd forgotten that Maeve and Patrick would become our stepsister and stepbrother. Until now it hadn't been real, but I took a deep breath and responded evenly. "Yes, Maeve."

"*Marvy!*" Her silver-blond curls bobbed happily.

Glancing in Patrick's direction, I noted a vague smile on his face. He furtively tapped a sly finger against his nose, then applied himself to his meal, while Simon raised a single eyebrow at me – a trick he usually employed to make the village girls blush – and I realised then that he too, had been party to the ruse. He must have fathomed immediately what Pat was doing when Jemima was taken to the stables, which is why he'd insisted, *trust me.*

And then, the greatest surprise of all; Lord Thorncliffe caught my eye with his wide grin. They were all in on it – oh, to have a devious male mind!

Now watching this man who was set to become my stepfather, I felt the first stirring of solidarity with him – something that I'd never felt with either of my parents. A slow smile, despite my best efforts, crept across my face and I quickly stuffed a chunk of bread into my mouth to hide it.

CHAPTER 5

Patrick and Maeve joined our lessons. The corner of the library where Master Baxter reigned with grim-faced authority was rearranged to fit two extra places, and the classes I'd previously attended with an attitude of bored resignation, suddenly erupted with unseemly mirth.

Patrick, from the first, showed neither respect for, nor fear of, our teacher, and, though he demonstrated some marked aptitude for such subjects as languages, literature and history, he clearly found little of interest in other subjects. Nor did Master Baxter's rigid manner inspire him to anything further than a cheerful persecution of the harried tutor with a wit far sharper than the older man could deflect.

If Master Baxter had deigned to smile, just once, it would have been so much the better for him; but his lack of humour and straight-backed disapproval made him an irresistible target for Patrick's incisive impudence. Frequently distracted, Anne and I evoked many a "pay attention young leddies" from the unhappy man.

But if her brother drove him to distraction, Maeve compensated with her polite participation at lessons, and her capable, if somewhat dreamy, attention to learning.

Music classes were another matter and Master Baxter, along with the rest of us, could not help but be charmed, for the abilities of the newcomers set them apart.

Pat owned a beautiful Stradivarius and was possessed of a passion for music that was equalled only by his skill, while his sister whirled and skipped through even the most complex of dances with the lithe grace of any forest sprite.

Many an afternoon passed with Master Baxter at the piano, accompanied by Patrick on the violin – playing with dark passion, sensitivity, or wild abandon, as called on by the classical composers. And Maeve danced, her sinuous movements capturing our starchy teacher in silent awe.

After lessons, Anne and Maeve took themselves to the drawing room or to the gardens, while Pat simply disappeared, often not even returning for supper. I saw him once lying in the long grass at the edge of the park staring at the sky. Another time I heard the plaintive strains of his violin as he sat against a tree and played soulfully to an audience of wild ducks.

While Maeve was open and candid, her brother's reserve pricked me with curiosity. I caught myself watching him, and wondering what he was thinking, and I was aware that he watched me also: I was gratified to note his surprised admiration when I demonstrated my understanding of Pythagoras' theorem.

They say that still waters run deep, and I knew this to be true when one evening he discussed with his father a building project he had in mind for their Devon estate. He drew a diagram, suggested the materials, and argued which tradesmen should be employed.

His father leaned forward to examine his son's work. "You've done your ground work, that's clear. Very impressive."

"So, what do you think?" Patrick prompted, his eyes shining passionately.

"Talk to the builders. It's your decision."

"I'll draft a letter tomorrow to that fellow we know in London."

As he rose to leave, Patrick bent to gather his papers and Mother looked pointedly at his tousled hair and hanging shirt-tails, and sighed loudly. "Have you no care for your appearance?"

Patrick appeared to give her question due consideration before responding flatly, "No."

She stared, aghast, as he left the room. "Your son, Gerrard, is a future earl. He ought to dress and behave as appropriate."

"He's quite aware of his lineage, Mim."

"Nevertheless, you must speak with him."

Lord Thorncliffe tugged his ear lobe and nodded absently.

I was not the only one fascinated by our new brother, for Simon joined Patrick's orbit and began to enjoy his company where he'd once enjoyed mine. Despite my own attraction to him, I felt the first steely jab of resentment. In my childishly naive way, I considered Patrick an intruder and hoped to deter him with frowns and smart remarks.

And as my irritation grew, so my behaviour deteriorated. One morning I virtually shoved him aside in order to take my seat beside Simon for our lessons. Patrick merely regarded me with an expression of bored contempt.

The brother and sister were quite opposite – where Maeve was bubbly and excitable, Patrick was distant, with a quiet dignity. They were the last of a historic, well-bred lineage, and Maeve, with her easy smile and delicate manners, did her noble ancestry proud. Patrick, on the other hand, was brooding and irreverent, denying any claim to aristocratic roots by his dishevelled attire.

Soon enough, Anne, too cunning by half for one so young, also took to studying him. One afternoon, he lounged casually in a chair by the parlour window reading a book. My sister's gaze was focused intently, her eyes sagaciously appraising, and it was one of those moments when you know something intuitively; and I knew then that, already at her tender age, she was weighing up his social and financial worth.

I studied him myself and found a paradox; a young lord shunning the pretensions in which his kind voraciously indulged. I saw intellect and humour lurking in his eyes and, though he was gifted with a quick mind, he remained a private thinker who kept his opinions to himself. My sister saw none of these things.

So Anne sat, with one glossy curl twirled about her finger and a cheeky pout at the ready, waiting for him to glance her way. Engrossed as he was in his book, he must have felt the tingle of being observed and looked up. The smile this 13-year-old coquette offered was designed to entice him as surely as it did the lads in the stables. But he merely lifted a mocking brow and returned to his reading.

Blushing with the sting of rejection, Anne dropped her pose and stalked from the room.

∾

Mother's marriage to Lord Thorncliffe was, as planned, a very quiet affair presided over by Wolstone's vicar. The five of us, and Eleanor and Jeffrey, joined the bride and groom.

Mother wore a lovely, velvet gown in deep blue with white lace trimming the high-waisted bodice, effectively concealing her pregnancy

Lord Thorncliffe wore buff trousers that hugged his paunch and tapered neatly to his polished, Hessian boots. His blue coat was the colour of Mother's gown. It buttoned tightly over his belly and white lace frothed at his cuffs.

The ceremony complete, the earl and his new countess' health was drunk and Cook, Janet and Mrs Grainger were invited to join the toast.

In the weeks following, the days shortened and the last of the autumn leaves drifted across the terraces.

Winter brought grey and rainy days with lead-bellied clouds and promises of early snow that forced us all indoors, though rarely in one room. One afternoon, we five Broughton-Washburn siblings were engaged in various activities in the parlour. Anne and Maeve were reading poetry to each other while Pat and Simon played chess by the window. I was writing a letter to Julia.

Eleanor slunk into the room and regarded us down her sloping nose. "Miss Broughton," she announced, her eyes on Anne, "the Countess requests your assistance with a piece of needlework she believes you are particularly able with. You will attend her rooms immediately."

Anne shrugged, "If she feels I can do a better job."

"She clearly stated that it must be you – not your sister." The woman jerked her pointy beak in my direction. "It is well known *her* work with the needle leaves much to be desired."

Anne grimaced apologetically at me and passed the poetry book to Maeve.

"Well *that* was an important piece of information," Patrick drawled. Pausing, Eleanor eyed the young man speculatively. He had risen from his chair and was leaning casually against its back.

"I did not address you," she remarked caustically.

Patrick shrugged. "In any case, a quick word, if you would be so kind." Her painted eyebrows rose in bored inquiry. "It never ceases to amaze me, just how – I'm not sure how to say it – how a delicate flower such as yourself, Miss Eleanor, has never ensnared a husband? I'm completely bemused." He approached her, hands out in supplication.

Clearly confused and uncertain as to the direction of his thoughts, Eleanor hesitated, curiosity outweighing suspicion.

"Do you deliberately withhold your favours? Do you enjoy frustrating the gallants with your elusive charms, your almost ..." he searched the ceiling for the right word, "*surreal* beauty?"

He sighed melodramatically and I felt the first flicker of unease as I saw an unidentified expression cross his face. I would recognise that look in years to come, but for now we were all transfixed as he drew close enough to touch Eleanor's cheek in a strangely intimate gesture.

"What man could resist the stir in his loins, his quickened heartbeat?" A flicker of wariness flashed across Eleanor's pinched face but she was trapped in the moment. His hand dropped to tenderly stroke her neck. "Perhaps in the stringy folds of her throat he could find such strength."

Eleanor's face registered concern, and the room grew tense as we all sensed something terrible was about to happen. Eleanor went to speak but Pat placed one finger lovingly against her lips. "Nay, mistress, I wouldst have thou silent, for it could possibly be the spite that drips from these thin little lips, or the acid from this forked tongue."

Turning quickly he announced to his audience, "Oh no – 'tis none of these fine attributes. The reason the lovely Miss Eleanor will die a virgin spinster is …" suspended for an interminable moment we waited as he paused significantly, "this bloody-ugly wig!" And with a flourish he grabbed Eleanor's chignon and wrenched it from her head.

None of us had ever suspected that it wasn't Eleanor's real hair. The woman screeched in horror and I have the image of her mortified face forever burned on my memory.

For what felt like minutes she stood screaming and screaming, her hands vainly attempting to hide the stubble on her pink-grey scalp before she stumbled from the room.

Patrick, the wig held aloft like a trophy, swept the floor with it in a most courtly bow before booting the door shut.

"Disgusting thing", he muttered regarding the limp clump of hair distastefully, then with a mock shiver, tossed it into the air where it hooked on the ceiling candelabra, swinging jauntily. "Disagreeable, bitter and twisted old crone," he continued and, returning to the chessboard, moved his knight, and declared calmly, "Check."

Maeve recovered more quickly than the rest of us, having no doubt experienced her brother's unpredictable cruelty before. As for Simon, Anne and me, we'd never witnessed such malice and, though I had no love for Eleanor, I could not help but feel sorry for her.

"I'd best attend Mother," Anne said in a subdued voice.

I doubt Eleanor reported Pat's stunt to Mother, in fact it was never spoken of again, but as the rest of us continued to endure Eleanor's disdain, she stayed well away from Patrick.

CHAPTER 6

As had ever been our habit, Simon and I, with Jemima in tow, passed our study-free afternoons roaming the park, but winter's rapid descent forced us to remain indoors playing cards, music, or, in Simon's case, reading the papers from London.

He was fascinated with the progress of the Peninsular War, often reading aloud and questioning the decisions of the leaders. I didn't pretend to understand military strategy, but was intrigued by Simon's interest that resulted in much tutting and sighing over his adjudged ineptitude of the two commanders, Sir Hew Dalrymple and Sir Harry Burrard.

In August that year, the French, led by Junot, had been trapped by the English in Portugal and cut off from their supplies. Soundly beaten, they called for an armistice that the English accepted, resulting in the Convention of Cintra being signed.

Though victorious, the events that followed did nothing for English military pride, for Dalrymple forced the English to transport the French, with all their arms and supplies, back to France in English ships.

Simon veritably exploded as he read this latest. "So much for a military coup! What was the Government thinking of putting those two old farts in charge? That young fellow – what's his name, Moore – he'd have made a better fist of it for certain, or that Wellesley chap."

I nodded judiciously with absolutely no idea who these fine gentlemen were, though I did note some weeks later, that Dalrymple and Burrard had been recalled to Britain where their resignations were accepted and they were replaced by Sir John Moore. Simon smiled, satisfied, as though the appointment had been made on his express advice.

But my brother was changing; the increasingly rare moments when I had him to myself were no longer spent cheerfully exchanging village gossip, or dissecting British military strategy, for his interests expanded to encompass our new brother and his ostensibly impressive history. Patrick has been to court, you know; Patrick has been to Ireland. Patrick, Patrick, Patrick!

I made my displeasure known by sulking and offering only monosyllabic responses to which Simon seemed oblivious. He invited Patrick to join us in our afternoon pursuits and, more often than not, the invitation was accepted. I was feeling cheated of my special time with Simon, and observed their growing camaraderie resentfully. With the cumulative wisdom of my 14 years, I endeavoured to make the newcomer so uncomfortable he would remove himself. Yet, having witnessed Eleanor's humiliation at Patrick's hand, I operated warily.

I decided to ignore Patrick as if he didn't exist, and it did seem, for a time, that I was succeeding – until I chanced to see Pat and Simon exchange a contemptuous roll of their eyes. Disappointed, I realised they were in accord and that I risked alienating Simon altogether.

To further confound me, as I grew to know Patrick better, I discovered that I rather enjoyed his presence during our lessons. Stubbornly I renewed my efforts, making full use of my talent for sarcasm, but even then my campaign wilted when he turned to Simon and said, "Am I expected to believe this puerile little nonentity is related to you and Anne?"

Good for the soul, was how Janet described him. Perhaps he had charmed her as he charmed everyone – my sister, our servants, and even Mrs Grainger called him, the young lord. He definitely had his attractions with his dishevelled, careless manner and witty repartee, but he was an interloper, and it riled me no end that no-one else could see it. Simon's behaviour was a betrayal of our partnership, but he merely shrugged off my displeasure and accompanied Patrick into the park to shoot arrows at targets on trees.

Meanwhile, Maeve was bewitching and likeable, a fact that only served to increase my moodiness. She and Anne had become immediate companions and passed their time before a cheerful fire; reading, talking or sewing together, with Missy curled on the settee between them.

Alone to contemplate my position, I became even more disagreeable. So much so, that Patrick cornered me late one afternoon in the parlour. I was watching from the window as Collings made an inspection of the rose garden.

"I know what you mean by all these infantile displays," he said, startling me.

"I –"

"Don't bother. Any denial insults us both." His normally pleasant looks were transformed by his scorn and I prayed he would go away but he made no move to leave.

Very well, I thought, rising slowly. I faced him and blurted out, "We didn't ask you here to disrupt our lives."

He moved explosively, his hand shooting out to grip my chin and force me to stare into his hard, emerald eyes.

"Now, you listen to me," he snarled, and I whimpered stupidly in surprise. "I couldn't give a tinker's cuss what you think, but I'm here and so's my sister and you'd better get used to it. I'm not interested in your petulance, nor is Simon, thank God! Even your scheming sister's less unpleasant, so stop behaving like a spoiled little bitch!"

He flung away from me, slamming the door on his way out, leaving me in the gathering dusk, trembling and stunned and with a renewed wariness of his cruel capabilities.

∾

It was early December and Patrick celebrated his seventeenth birthday. Lord Thorncliffe surprised his son by arranging for Pat's horse to be brought up from their estates. Equus was as beautiful a creature as I'd ever seen; a black mare, strong and tall with a fine, intelligent head. Now my stepbrother enjoyed a new freedom; galloping through the woods, hurdling fences and charging through the park – fearlessly and dangerously. Simon attempted to join him on the laughably inadequate Oliver, who grudgingly responded to Simon's urging, and took every opportunity to loiter in the lush grass at the edge of the forest.

Other times, with their saddle-bags bulging, the two boys disappeared for entire days. In my more grown up moments I knew my resentment was churlish and unreasonable, but watching their easy camaraderie as they laughed at some shared joke only built on my towering sense of betrayal.

Simon's tolerance ran out one clear, frosty morning. We were enjoying unseasonably pleasant days for December and I stood on the neatly-raked gravel drive while he waited before me, hand extended, "Come on, Zan," he said, smiling beguilingly, "we're going to follow the stream and eat lunch. The snow will be here soon and then we'll not be able to go out."

I could have saved myself, but like a lemming, I ran obstinately to my own destruction. "No!"

"C'mon, we'll have fun – just like we used to."

"It can't be like it used to," I snapped, angling a significant glare over his shoulder to where Patrick lingered. My stepbrother's face was inscrutable, but he was studying me closely, his eyes like cold jewels.

"Leave her, Sime." He turned and stalked away.

"You go to hell!" I shouted at his back and saw Simon's brow pucker.

"Zan …" he began sadly, then shook his head and turned to follow Patrick.

Dropping to the ground, I scraped a handful of gravel and threw it with all my passion at Simon's retreating back. I've always been a good shot and this was no exception. The stones hit their target but my brother's steps did not falter.

❧

And so, as Christmas approached, I drifted about, reading or wandering through the woods with Jemima. Simon was despondent and sought occasions to talk with me that usually ended unhappily because he couldn't understand how I felt.

"If you would only get to know him, you'd like him – he's fun, Zan." We were sitting over the chessboard in the library as rain beat steadily against the windows.

"I don't like him," I said, replacing his bishop with one of my knights.

"Hmm, you're getting good at this," he muttered thoughtfully. "Why don't you give him a chance?"

I glanced up. "He called me a spoiled little bitch – I'm not like that, Sime."

"Aren't you?" He studied the chessboard. "What do *you* call your behaviour, then?" I lowered my eyes as tears pricked their backs. His voice was gentler when he spoke again. "We had fun when we were two. What fun if we were three?"

"I don't like him," I repeated for it was all I could say.

He sighed and pushed back his chair, indicating our game was over. "Have it your way, but you're the one losing out."

The weather turned and suddenly overnight it brought snow and bitter winds. Prevented from riding, Pat began spending his time in the stables grooming Equus, or simply lying in the hay with a book. Daily I collected Jemima and hurried away so I could avoid him, but one morning I stood at the stable door staring bleakly outside. The snow lay thick on the ground and heavy in the trees, rendering impenetrable our usual paths through the woods. "You'll not want to walk out today," Patrick said. I started slightly for I'd not expected him to speak to me. He reclined in the hay in Equus' stall. She was standing comfortably, head hanging low in a light doze. Jemima traitorously ambled to him and I silently berated her. Obligingly he fondled her ears and peered over at me.

There was no malice or antagonism in his face and I felt a twinge of shame as he studied my sullen expression. I looked outside again to hide my confusion. The snow swirled on an icy breeze and turned the forecourt to muddy slush where the lads had walked back and forth during their morning chores. The trees in the park were grey and skeletal, and leaden clouds hung in the sky.

Patrick's eyes continued to linger on me. I gave an involuntary shiver and obstinately called Jemima to the entrance where the wide stable door was hooked to the outside wall to keep it from banging. Immediately a sharp gust of glacial wind blasted me in the face.

"Don't go out there just to be stubborn," he said, coming up behind me. He unhooked the door and pulled it to, latching it shut against the blustery weather.

Through the window I could see the storm moving in and the clouds boiling above the naked trees.

"Have you forgiven me my verbal attack the other day?" The bluntness of his question caused me to pause. Uncertain how to respond, I made an ostensible contemplation of the weather.

"If I've taken Simon away from you, I assure you it wasn't deliberate," he continued gently while I remained staring wordlessly outside. "Simon and I will be leaving for Oxford soon. Shouldn't you be enjoying your time with him? You're upsetting him, you know."

"I never wanted to hurt him," I murmured. "But no-one cares how I feel. No-one understands."

He took my shoulders and turned me to face him, his head cocked to one side. "That's not true. I do know. I understand that everything you've ever known is upside down."

His calm empathy caused my hackles to rise. "Oh you're so experienced, such a man of the world," I shrugged off his hands but he merely stared blandly at me and, in the face of his composure, I suddenly saw how childish I was.

"Do you realise," I continued, doggedly, "that in less than one year, I shall have added three new siblings? Your father installed as my papa? How can you know how I feel? I don't even know myself," I finished in a whisper.

"You're young yet," he said, not unkindly, "your inexperience is telling on you. In time you'll come to realise —"

"You pompous swine!" I snapped.

He shrugged and rested his arms on the window-ledge to watch the storm gathering over Jackson's field. Jackson's celebrated bull was nowhere to be seen, probably tucked up in a warm barn somewhere.

"Yes, I suppose that would have sounded pompous," he conceded. "But you can't —"

"Don't tell me what I can and can't do," I snarled, confident that my 14 years made me quite fearsome.

His brows rose beneath his hair. "This has been difficult for Maeve and me too —"

"Oh, I'm sure it has been — you just march into our home and take over our lives and —"

"Haven't you ridden that hobby-horse to death?" Now his face darkened and he shoved away and returned to Equus' stall. When he spoke, his voice was barely audible, "Yes, very fine for me, all nicely mapped out." His mouth twisted bitterly. "Since Father was often away, I was learning the running of our estates under the guidance of our steward. Then, he summoned me to London; in his misguided way he thought I would enjoy it there. Oh, I learnt a lot at court, but not the way my father intended for it was expected that I would spend my youth in meaningless, privileged pursuits, marry a suitable maid, then apply myself to the business of producing a string of heirs – hearty Washburn stock. My thoughts on the matter were … are … irrelevant." He shook his head angrily. "I shall never conform to expectations. I left court, returned to Waterville, and wrote to Father explaining that I'd remain there until the Oxford year resumed."

Up to this point he'd been contemplating his hands, but now he seemed to arrive at a decision. "Coming here was not part of my plan, nor was it my intention to disrupt your life. Maeve and I were not consulted, we were instructed. Further, I know full well your mother's reasons for marrying my father. She cares only for wealth and position, and expects that if she bears a son, it will further cement her social standing."

I stared at him with growing contrition. He mimicked my petulance, "*You don't know what it's like for me. The privileged world we live in makes no concessions for our individual desires.*"

I turned away, as with dawning self-realisation I saw myself as he must – childish, ignorant and selfish. I trawled my brain for something to say but nothing came, and finally, I capitulated and my arms dropped to my sides. He could be hateful and his words cruel, but he was right. I had conducted myself appallingly. I had been self-absorbed and foolish – everything he said.

My nose was running with the dampness in the air and I swiped at it with my sleeve as I gathered my thoughts. In the tail of my eye,

I saw he had returned to his book and after several long minutes, I drew in my breath and said quietly, "I have behaved dreadfully."

Without lifting his eyes he replied, "Yes. You're also unworldly, quick to unreasoning anger, and childish in the extreme – a feisty kitten who thinks she's a lion."

Realising immediately that he was trying me, I carefully modulated my voice. "Are you terribly miserable here?"

He didn't respond initially. He finished his page before closing the book and laying it beside him. "I wouldn't say miserable. Perhaps … unsettled is more apt. Maeve adjusts better than I. She accepts things more readily. Acceptance, like patience, is a virtue and I am not virtuous."

This last was delivered with a smile that softened his features and caused me to look away in embarrassment for I was beginning to feel repentant of my recent behaviour. "Virtue is never left to stand alone. He who has it will have neighbours," I recited softly.

"Ah," he said with surprised approval, "the feisty kitten quotes Confucius."

A small spark of solidarity with this complex boy flickered within me and, with some circumspection, I moved to sit beside him in the sweet-smelling hay, vaguely aware that we'd laid the first shaky foundations of a bridge across a chasm; a flimsy bridge nonetheless, and easily rocked by words of anger.

And since he seemed to be in a rather expansive mood, I said, "You were born to inherit a great title and vast wealth. Does this not make you happy?"

He smiled wryly. "It would be silly to say I wasn't happy with that. Maeve and I will never know poverty. Our rank will gain us entry and privilege. But there are more worthy things I'd like to spend my life doing."

"You sound like Simon, though he's by no means in your position. Simon is very grateful of the opportunity to go to Oxford. Is this what you want too?"

"No." He locked his hands behind his head. "There's a whole world out there; sights to see … places to go. And while England's at war, here am I, safely ensconced in this plot in the middle of nowhere."

I bristled at his description of my home but decided not to test our tentative ceasefire. "You'd like to travel then?"

"Yes, but not for travel's sake. I'd like to go to the Iberian Peninsula and actually do something worthwhile."

"You mean the war! How would killing and being killed be doing something worthwhile?"

He shrugged. "Napoleon's a little upstart – everyone knows it, and we all complain, but what do we do about it?" I watched him as he pondered his own words. "Yes, that's what I would most like to do."

"Maeve would be devastated, and your father wouldn't be happy."

"I'm old enough to buy an officer's commission – Father wouldn't stand in my way."

"Funny," I snorted, "my mother might. She's ever been focused on Simon making a good match – by that she means wealthy – his family responsibility and all. She will probably be the same with you."

"She already has plans for me. Another reason to go abroad."

I grimaced in commiseration. "Mother carries your father's child, doesn't she?"

"Without doubt." He shot a wary glance at me before continuing. "Our parents have been engaged in a liaison for some time. So, the problem – which worked well for your mother – was that the King, mad though he may be, is a very prudish man. He ordered their marriage as punishment, and for the benefit of the child. Their banishment from court demonstrates the King's disapproval; convenient for your mother since she is now a countess and wealthy beyond her wildest fantasies."

I was quiet while I took this in. Finally, I said, "Are you worried for your inheritance?"

"No – the bulk of that comes from my maternal grandfather – it's secure, along with Maeve's portion. I disliked your mother since I first met her at court. She's a schemer, a fortune hunter."

"I can't deny that!"

"Have you read King Lear? No? Well, you should. You'd recognise her among the characters."

We fell silent and the only sound was the wind howling outside and as I watched him, his eyes softened and he seemed to be looking into the distance. "Some day you must visit Waterville Place," he said pensively. "I think you'd be fascinated with its history – although it's quite unusual, it is very beautiful. My grandfather, aided considerably by his fertile imagination, re-designed it after he bought it."

"There is every chance we – the family, I mean – shall visit."

"In any case," he said, with an abrupt change of subject, "what do you think of your family now? I mean, after our talk. Shall we be friends?"

I drew up my knees and wrapped my arms about them. "I think we may be friends."

"You're not sure?" he said, teasingly.

"My hobby-horse has been put out to pasture. We can call a truce," I announced magnanimously.

The crooked half-smile he gave transformed his face, and I liked it. His lips were full and expressive and curved down at one corner. "Truce," he agreed, and we shook on it like farmers. "Equus likes you," he commented matter-of-factly, as the horse leaned towards me and snorted into my hair.

I laughed spontaneously; her steamy herbaceous breath tickled my neck, and I was rewarded with another lopsided smile.

Rain had begun clattering on the shingle roof creating a warm and cosy atmosphere within the stall. I stretched with unladylike ease in the straw and Jemima snored lightly at my feet. Patrick lounged casually beside me, his book forgotten.

"So, what happened to your mother?" I asked.

He blew out his breath. "She died."

"I supposed that much. Was it —?"

"A long time ago. In childbirth … the baby was lost too."

"Did you know her?"

"I was about seven at the time, so I knew her only as much as a seven-year-old can."

"I don't mean to be nosy …"

He smiled again and his eyes held a glint of irony. "Yes you do, but I don't mind."

"So your father raised you?"

He nodded. "In a fashion. Like I said, he was away a lot — at court. Maeve and I spent time in Ireland with my mother's family — we have cousins there."

"So what's court like?"

"See, you are nosy."

"Perhaps I'm getting to know my new brother," I rejoined quickly.

"Ask Maeve what sort of brother I am."

"I've already seen a few sides to you," I said arching my brow significantly and thinking of the Eleanor incident. "Did you like it at court? How old were you when you went there?"

"I was fourteen. I only stayed for two years. Father secured me a posting in the Queen's stables." He considered his horse for a few moments. "Equus's mother was one of the Queen's horses — Father purchased her for me when she was only a few months old. When I returned to Waterville I took Equus with me."

"And now you're here."

"And now I'm here."

"But what about court — is the King mad as they say? And the ladies — are they as beautiful?"

He laughed lightly. "Yes to the first and no to the second. The King does not involve himself in court society. All the interesting events are held by the Prince of Wales – now *that* fellow knows how to enjoy himself."

"So he'll make a good king some day?"

"Doubt it. Parliament is pushing to have him made regent but I think he's too irresponsible … too interested in throwing parties to be reliable. Let's not forget we're still at war – Napoleon is determined to control Europe and hold Britain to ransom. Parliament and the Queen are trying to keep the Prince under control and they can't manage that now – imagine if he were Regent! It will be worse when he's King."

"But –" I was interrupted as Equus shifted her stance and a low rumble crept from beneath her tail. "Oh Equus!" I exclaimed, laughing freely for the first time in months.

Pat held up his hand. "Wait for it."

"What?"

"Horse fart," and just as he said it, the stench of fermenting vegetation filled the stall, leaving us gasping and giggling. We covered our faces as best we could, scrambled to our feet and ran to the stable door, pushing it open to breathe the newly-cleansed air. I turned to Patrick, and his face was made attractive with laughter. "Hungry, brother?" I asked impulsively. "I believe Cook has baked orange biscuits and if you distract her, I shall steal a handful for us to share."

He grinned, with no hint of mockery for once. "Very well, L'il Sis, let us see what we can purloin from the kitchens." He shoved the door closed behind us, and we ran, leaping puddles and mud on our way.

❧

Christmas descended quickly and Mother's condition progressed so that she made only brief appearances outside her rooms.

The festive season had previously been celebrated quietly by Simon, Anne and me, with only a brief exchange of gifts. We had always purchased gifts for the staff, and Simon had instructed Collings to distribute coins and food to the tenants.

This year, Simon decided to extend the tradition to include a Boxing Day party on the snow-blanketed lawn. He arranged for braziers to be set up at strategic points for warmth and had instructed Cook to plan a sumptuous feast. Maeve and Patrick launched themselves into the festive spirit with a contagious fervour that helplessly infected their Broughton siblings.

Pat, Lord Thorncliffe and Simon went into the forest and cut a fir which they dragged through the snow amid much stumbling and shouts of laughter. Maeve and Anne visited Wolstone Market and returned with a treasure-trove of coloured beads and baubles. The parlour sparkled brightly and the clean, sharp tang of pine permeated the rugs and furnishings and crept in to the hall to greet those entering the house. Some weeks earlier, Anne had charmed the stableman's son, who had a talent for wood-carving, to produce a collection of miniature figures. These, she and Maeve had painted in red, green and blue, and now they hung in the tree from gold threads.

Even Mother seemed relaxed. She observed our gaiety from her couch, smiling like a benevolent queen.

Christmas Eve arrived and the household staff were invited to join us around the tree. Maeve and Anne danced to Simon's piano and Patrick's violin. There was much laughter and carolling and Cook was dispatched to the cellar for a third bottle of her special plum wine. My only sadness was that Jemima remained alone in the stables. Though I visited her daily, she'd been raised indoors, was part of the family, and I hated the thought of her being outside.

Emily brought in a plate laden with marchpane holly leaves, and another with mincemeat tarts that were swollen with fruit and spices, and we ate, sang and swapped stories before a roaring fire. Some time later, I relaxed in my chair watching the glittering, cheerful scene, a forgotten smile on my face, and aware that I had enjoyed this evening more than any in recent memory.

Suddenly Mother clapped her hands and we turned as one. "I don't believe I can continue to look upon these mysterious parcels a moment longer," she declared, indicating with a flourish the brightly wrapped gifts beneath the tree. "Maeve, Anne, will you ladies do the honours?"

Maeve squealed with delight and threw herself with inelegant eagerness to the floor beside the tree.

Anne, more dignified, joined her in handling each boxed package carefully, reading the tags and announcing the recipient's name.

"Simon!"

"Mother!"

"Ooh! Another for Simon and it smells so sweet it must be from a girl," said Maeve, giggling.

"Probably Katie, the farrier's daughter," suggested Anne.

"Or her mother," I added with a wink in my brother's direction.

Simon scowled with mock annoyance and read the label, "It's from you, Naughty Puss." Maeve glowed beneath the affectionate nickname, bestowed after the Missy incident on her arrival.

"Father, this is from Mother."

"To Cook from the Countess."

"To Alex from Simon."

And so it went on.

Much later, we each had a pile of gifts before us. I had received a lovely bottle of scent from Simon, a red leather-bound journal from Patrick, various trinkets from Anne and Maeve, and an assortment of books from Mother and Gerrard.

Cook made a pot of thick, aromatic chocolate. I sipped my drink and reflected that Mother had been in uncommon good humour, regaling us with funny tales of the King's misdemeanours and public displays of madness, though her descriptions of the parties held by the Prince had Anne's eyes bulging.

"There are rumours," Mother said conspiratorially, "that Prinnie's favourite is with child again."

"No!" Gerrard was genuinely surprised. "Again you say? To his mistress? High time that wife – what's her name – gave him another."

"Caroline," Mother supplied. "They have lived apart for … let me think, well, since Princess Charlotte was born. She has that boy, of course – claims she adopted him, but *everyone* knows the child is her own bastard. The Prince *must* get a son with his wife, but cannot stand the sight of her.

"If it is true that the mistress is in … er … a delicate condition, then her star will most definitely be on the rise."

"Indeed, though if she's with child, she'll need to be on her guard." Mother then described the outrageous lengths some of the court ladies would go to in order to attract Prinnie's attention and their conspiracies behind closed doors to bring one another into disrepute. One had to be constantly on one's guard against scandal. From the pleasure Mother derived in the re-telling, I judged she was among the agitators.

Suddenly the door opened. Until that moment I hadn't realised that Patrick had slipped away. When he came into the room my hand flew to my mouth and I stifled a gasp of shock. The gathering fell silent while I, unable to breathe, stared fearfully at Mother. Patrick was leading Jemima into the room.

Mother nodded toward me with a small smile. "Alexandra, this is my Christmas gift to you," she said, magnanimously. "Those disrespectful boys there," she waved imperiously at Patrick and Simon, "confessed their crime and I have decided to forgive you all this conspiracy, and return that wretched hound to your care."

Jemima sat, uncharacteristically obedient, at Patrick's side, though I sensed her excitement and desire to run to me.

"Mother, thank you," I said softly.

"Hmm," she said, grudgingly. "It is on condition."

"Anything …"

"Your brothers have endeavoured to drill some manners into it – see that you keep up the training."

"Yes, Mother – thank you."

"Don't thank me, thank them. I was furious when Simon told me my orders had been undermined. As head of this house, he must learn the consequences of his actions."

"Well … thank you in any case," I said, reverently. "And the two of you also," I added to Simon and Patrick and it dawned on me that Patrick's daily visits to the stables were not for Equus' benefit alone.

"Needn't thank Patrick," Mother grumbled, "If he were alone in pleading your case, I'd have had them both, human and dog alike, knocked on the head."

Pat grinned – almost as handsome as Simon when he wasn't guarding his expression – and passed the leash to me. "The mutt has received a reprieve, and is hereby returned to you."

So Yuletide came and went and it was the most joyous I'd known. Mother's unusual affability no doubt contributed to the congenial atmosphere about the house. And a week later, when the parlour clock struck midnight on New Year's Eve, hugs and good wishes were exchanged between Broughtons, Washburns and their combined staff.

CHAPTER 7

January crept slowly by. Heavy snowfalls transformed the park into a glittering white landscape and made it impossible to venture outdoors. Master Baxter was spending the festive season at Kendall with his family and had not yet returned, and so, free from lessons, I spent much of my time reading those books that were more to my liking than my tutor's. I wept over Shakespeare's star-crossed lovers, knew irony in the tragedy of Oedipus the King, and marvelled at Donne's image-laden words.

Poetry was all the rage at court and I felt quite the modern woman one snowy afternoon with a companionable fire, Jemima at my feet, and lost in Shelley's poetic visions of the moon. I closed my little book, and quoted from memory,

> *Art thou pale for weariness*
> *Of climbing heaven and gazing on the earth,*
> *Wandering companionless*

I thought I was alone until Patrick completed the last lines for me.

> *Among the stars that have a different birth,*
> *And ever changing, like a joyless eye*
> *That finds no object worth its constancy?*

He was leaning against the door frame but now he came forward. Pleased to see him, I made space beside me.

"Do you understand it?" he asked.

With our recent hostilities still so near the surface, my hackles rose immediately. "Of course," I snapped. "I'm not a fool, you know."

"I never suggested you were, Miss Prickle, but generally the empty-heads who profess to enjoy these works, do so because it's fashionable. They've not the slightest idea what our most expressive Master Shelley was on about."

"Well, I'm not one of those empty-heads," I said firmly, and rising with much dignity, stalked out, Jemima trotting behind. Congratulating myself on my cleverness, it was only as I shut my bedroom door that I realised how silly I'd been. Patrick had clearly sought a conversation and in trying to act grown up I'd proved myself the opposite.

Master Baxter returned and lessons resumed. Simon and Patrick began preparing for their journey to Oxford and, even though they'd be commencing midway through the term, Simon was as excited as a boiling pot. Patrick, conversely, seemed rather apathetic, and I recalled his bitter words about life being planned for him. Still penitent over my childish behaviour, I resolved to redeem myself before his departure and awaited a likely opportunity – that presented itself sooner than I'd expected.

I was passing Patrick's door one afternoon when I heard the jaunty sounds of his violin. Now, music had ever been one of my great loves, and I had knocked at his door without a second thought.

The playing within ceased abruptly. "Yes?"

I opened the door. He was seated cross-legged on the rug before a cosy fire, the violin positioned beneath his chin.

"I heard you playing. May I come in?"

As usual his expression gave nothing away but he bade me enter with a jerk of his head. Holding the instrument by its neck, he rested its body on his knee watching as I shut the door.

"It's beautiful," I nodded towards it and sat before him on the rug.

"It is a Strad," he said simply.

"I know."

"How?"

I looked up sharply but his face showed only interest.

"The signature on it. I saw it at Christmas when you laid it on the settee."

"Well, there you go …" he said, "and you'd be right for it bears the moniker of Senor Antonio Stradivari himself. But all that means is that the instruments are crafted to his design. Many are misled: the signature does not prove authenticity."

I must have looked perplexed for he added, adopting a perfect imitation of Master Baxter, "But I heppen to know, young leddy, that this particular specimen is genuine."

"Oh? How so?" I rejoined.

"Well, young leddy, since Gerrard Washburn's father, the then Earl of Thorncliffe, personally brought it back from Stradivari's shop in Cremona – he toured Italy and France in his youth, you see. But without the benefit of such information," he leaned forward, dropping the charade, his voice low," you need only touch and hear it to know its pedigree. Here …" he passed the instrument and I held it with respect.

"Feel the wood … its texture … it's like silk. And this …" he plucked a string. "Feel it? It's alive."

I did feel it. Almost afraid, I reverently returned the instrument to him as he continued. "But to play it, to hear its voice, is to truly demonstrate one's respect – one's passion," he whispered.

"Well then," I addressed the violin, "Sing for me, Senor Stradivari."

Pat made much of cracking his knuckles and flexing his fingers, took up his bow and positioning the instrument below his chin, began to play.

With eyes closed and face set dreamily, he played a haunting, mournful tune I didn't recognise but which prompted me also to close my eyes and lose myself in the glorious chords.

For several minutes I listened, spellbound, as the notes lulled and swayed me, swelling, filling the room. I breathed them in, as they lifted me on a crest of sound and held me suspended on resonant threads, building dynamically to a violent crescendo that burst through to the other side, retreating in a final, plaintive minor chord.

My throat constricted with the beauty of it.

Motionless for a long moment, I sat with eyes closed, breathing as one in a trance. When finally I opened my eyes, I met his green gaze. "That is how you know a genuine Stradivarius," he said huskily, letting the instrument rest on his thigh.

His eyes, smoky and deep, continued to hold mine with an intensity of emotion that tightened my chest. The urge to touch him was a physical thing yet I remained motionless, afraid to break the spell.

Suddenly the door burst open and Maeve, Missy in her arms, and Anne barrelled into the room. "Oh Pat that was *marvy*," his sister gushed, oblivious to the weight of feeling between her brother and me.

"We heard from the hall," Anne added. "May we join in?"

"Play that Congreve – oh what's the name of it? My favourite one." Maeve plumped to the rug beside her brother, settling Missy on her lap.

Anne carefully arranged her skirt about her and added, "Yes a Congreve, and we shall sing along."

A warm wave of well-being washed over me. Patrick's eyes had continued to hold mine, and now we smiled as one conspirator to another. Without comment, he raised the Strad and launched into his sister's favourite tune and she began to sing in a thin pure tone. Upon recognition, Anne and I joined in.

> *False though she be to me and love,*
> *I'll ne'er pursue revenge;*
> *For still the charmer I approve,*
> *Though I deplore her change.*

> *In hours of bliss we oft have met:*
> *They could not always last;*
> *And though the present I regret,*
> *I'm grateful for the past.*

We made our way through many more songs before the afternoon was over and, each time Patrick's glance met with mine, the thrill of something shared ran through me.

Mother joined us for supper, and large though she was now, she seemed in good spirits.

Retiring to the parlour afterwards, she and Eleanor stitched baby clothes. Eleanor's habitually disapproving face beneath the flaming red wig did not inhibit the merriment of the evening as a giggling Maeve told us how Tom, the baker's son, had inadvertently baked his mother's entire store of apples saved for the winter.

"She wanted to dry them, you see – out in the sun – sun-bake them. He thought she said to bake them."

Simon and I laughed heartily for we were well acquainted with the unfortunate Tom's lack of sense. While Mother's mouth twitched slightly, Eleanor's expression never changed. "When Mother Croft came home from the market," Maeve continued, "she found every single one of them shrivelled and brown like those shrunken heads you see in books about natives in the africas … oh, poor Tom."

"Poor Tom indeed," Lord Thorncliffe remarked from behind a newspaper. He turned to his son and Simon, "Seems there's still much trouble on the continent."

"Oh Gerrard, why ruin a pleasant evening with talk of war." Mother grumbled.

"Good grief, woman! Our troops have been there since July last year!"

"If it were *that* important, Isabella Camelleri would have mentioned it in her letter. She reports that things are wonderful in Italy at the moment."

"Well it *is* affecting us … damned difficult getting a good brandy these days." Lord Thorncliffe swirled the rich liquor in his glass. "In any case, it's strangling Britain's economy."

"Isabella Camelleri?" Simon interrupted. "Didn't she visit some years back?"

Mother nodded absently and failed to notice as Simon jabbed his elbow slyly into Patrick's ribs. That individual, roused from reading over his father's shoulder, turned to Simon.

"Isabella Camelleri has two of the most *charming* daughters a fellow could meet.

"Is that a fact?" Patrick responded, with interest.

Simon began extolling the virtues of the two young ladies, descriptions that were aided in some large measure by imagination, for many years had passed since their last visit.

Lord Thorncliffe watched the boys' exchange indulgently for a moment before returning to his paper. "It says here – wait-on, I've lost the spot, 'Napoleon himself, led two-hundred thousand men into Spain', there – Spain. Nowhere near your friend in Italy." He continued. " 'The thirty-thousand British soldiers, led by Sir John Moore, fought their way through Burgos, Sahagun, Benavente and Cacobelos. Finally, after valiantly defending La Coruna, Moore was killed, resulting in an evacuation of the British troops. Napoleon has passed control to Nicholas Soult, and has returned to France.' "

"That tyrant must be stopped or Europe will not know a moment's peace," Simon stated with conviction.

"And when he's done with Europe, he'll march on Britain," Patrick added. "You know, Sime, they're always after soldiers — they've commissions available."

I swallowed hard, awaiting Simon's response, but it was a moment before he spoke, "Yes, but I'll wager they'll want doctors too. If I could gain some medical training first, it would go well."

As one, Maeve and Anne cried, "You can't go to war!"

"You could be hurt," Maeve reasoned.

"Or killed," Anne added dramatically.

Mother spoke without raising her eyes from her needlework, "You each have responsibilities at home — it's out of the question."

"They accept junior officers," Patrick continued.

Mother sighed and put aside her work. "Gerrard, say something!"

"They're right, they do accept junior officers."

"That's not what I meant!"

"Madam!" Patrick said suddenly, his eyes blazing vividly, "You may bully your son, but you may not bully me. What I choose for my future is no concern of yours."

Having not heard anyone speak so to Mother; Simon, Anne and I stared in open-mouthed amazement.

With great dignity, she raised her chin and said, "Be assured you have my unconditional blessing to go and get yourself killed. But you'll not take my son with you. Eleanor, gather my needles and things, I shall retire now."

☙

Two nights later, I was awakened in the small hours by the sounds of a banging door and the pounding of urgent feet along the hall. Jemima leapt from her basket and I poked my head into the corridor in time to accost a pair of scurrying housemaids carrying hot water and linen. Eleanor, poker-straight and empty-handed led the way.

"Judith!" I whispered hoarsely to one of the maids. "Is it Mother's time?"

"Yes ... oh dear," she said, flustered and glancing nervously at the frowning Eleanor. "Why do babies always make you feel so unprepared, even though you know they're coming?"

"Has someone been sent to fetch the midwife?"

"Get a move on," snapped Eleanor, glaring at me. "This is no place for you – go back to bed."

"Yes, Albert ..." the maid threw over her shoulder as she disappeared down the darkened hall.

"So, to bed I returned, but not to sleep. By the glow of a single candle I awaited news, but it wasn't until the sun was above the horizon and I'd broken my fast that Lord Thorncliffe, far too excited for a man supposedly giving his name to another's child, announced that Margaret Maria Washburn had arrived at 8.07 am that morning, 17 February 1809.

With her pretty, little face and fine, blond hair, she bore no small resemblance to Maeve, if slightly pinker – a fact that was noted by all but mentioned by none. Recalling our conversation in the stables four months earlier, my eyes met Pat's knowingly over the crib.

Meg was an unsettled baby who cried a lot and Mother quickly engaged a wet-nurse. In her early thirties, round and cheerful, Clara was full to the brim with the latest village gossip. She was alone in the world, having lost her own child five months earlier and her husband a year ago in a farming accident. She moved in to the nursery and took up her position in our household with calm efficiency.

When Clara was not busy feeding Meg or taking care of other baby associated tasks, I visited. Unlike Mother, Clara was fond of Jemima and didn't mind the dog being in the room with us, and before long my afternoon routine included visiting Clara and Meg. Many hours were spent in cheerful conversation over tea and biscuits and, though there were some years between us, I enjoyed her company and we soon developed an unlikely friendship.

But the days remained short and cold, and the snow deep. It piled against our house in sodden mounds and weighed heavily on the naked branches of the trees in the orchard. The Great Oak looked forlorn; its only companions in winter were a family of squirrels. The pines in the park and forest glittered with a million icicles where their needles had frozen, while the other trees sagged like weary old men.

I was feeling stifled. Generally the melt would have started by now but the long winter was continuing to make a desert of our garden, restricting my outdoor excursions to brief strolls along the terraces. From frustration, I suggested Simon accompany me on a walk through the forest. Feeling the strain himself, he agreed and invited Patrick to join us.

The residual traces of resentment over Pat's friendship with Simon lingered, but their departure to Oxford was imminent so I stoutly contained my annoyance and forced a smile.

The mist swirled and floated between the trees, lending an enchanted feel to the forest as we crunched through the snow. Simon chattered excitedly about the upcoming trip to Oxford, though Patrick remained quiet and kept his thoughts to himself.

They strode out, their long legs carrying them with ease, while I, hampered by my voluminous winter skirts, struggled behind.

As the snow began to fall again, they moved in and out of view between trees and over logs, and when they rounded an enormous oak, Jemima bounded after them and they were lost from sight.

I navigated the giant tree – tugging irritably when my skirt snagged – and their voices grew faint, and then were gone.

I stared about me with irritation. Their tracks should have been visible and easy to follow, but they disappeared round the base of a tree so broad a man on horseback might have hidden behind it. And with the snow falling as it was …

I studied the ground and found only my own tracks. "Blast," I swore out loud. The grey and white landscape gave nothing away. The skeletal trees, with their limbs protruding from the mist like gnarled fingers, were making me feel slightly jumpy.

"*Simon!*" My voice fell dull and flat, blanketed by the snow. "*Jemima!*"

Nothing.

"Damn and blast!" The snow was quickly obliterating any remaining foot-prints and the enshrouding mist didn't help – white on white. I circled the tree once more, increasingly frustrated.

"*Simon!*"

I listened hard. Nothing.

They had been heading towards the river. I shot a glance behind me and paused. Was I mistaken or was that a flash of blue from Simon's coat disappearing behind a tree? They were circling, staying out of my sight. Damn them!

Deciding to catch them at their own game, I feigned confusion and called out again, then continued round another large tree and down a slope and, sneaking a glance over my shoulder, I saw them – Patrick with Jemima in his arms, and Simon, darting from tree to tree. They had doubled-back and were following – good – they thought they'd fooled me.

"*Simon! Patrick!*"

I was nearing the river. It was full and fast and gave me an idea. Bunching my heavy velvet skirts I increased my pace.

"*Simon!*"

I skirted a large pine and, relying on the obscuring mists, ducked out of sight. Now I ran as quickly as I could down an embankment toward the river. I arrived on the lip of a four-foot drop into the swiftly-flowing water. A number of fallen logs rested on the bank and one, conveniently, was partly hidden by undergrowth right by the edge. It was this that I ducked behind, flattening myself and tucking my skirt around me so that nothing showed. Scanning my surroundings, my eyes lit on a broken branch – big enough to splash, small enough for me to toss. I pulled it towards me, threw several handfuls of snow to cover my tracks, and then waited.

"*Simon! Patrick!*"

They were closer, I could hear them. I held my breath …

Suddenly the still air was shattered by the most piercing, the most frightened scream I could wrench from my lungs. I followed it by tossing the log and was rewarded with a satisfying splash as it hit the water.

The sound of their approach halted momentarily, followed by Simon's alarmed shout, "*Alex!*" They were running towards the river, making no attempt at stealth now. I pressed myself smaller behind the log in preparation.

"*Alex!*" they shouted in unison and there was worry in their voices.

Simon arrived first, I could hear his heavy breathing. I was tempted to spy on them but prudently kept my head down.

"She couldn't have fallen in, surely," Patrick gasped, arriving seconds later.

"She's not here," Simon's voice had an edge of panic in it. "She must have fallen … I can't see anything … this blasted fog."

"We'd see her down there if she'd fallen in," Patrick reasoned, though there was doubt behind his words.

"Zan can't swim, she's probably sank straight down or been carried away."

"But we'd be able to see her – what are you doing? You can't go in – you'll freeze!"

"You don't expect me to just stand here!"

All the while they were discussing my disappearance, I was gathering two good-sized snowballs. Cautiously now, I peered over the edge of my log. They were standing with their backs to me. Patrick had released Jemima and was watching Simon peel off his coat and gloves and edge closer to the bank.

"*Alex!*" Simon called again and I ducked behind my log.

"She's not there, Sime. I'd wager my allowance on it."

"Well, where is she then?" Simon rounded on him, and I had to act quickly before he plunged into the icy waters.

"Right here!" I leapt from behind my log and released the snowballs, my aim true, striking them each on the back.

As one, they whirled round. The relief on Simon's face quickly turned to anger. "Zan, that's not funny, we –"

"You bloody cow!" Patrick raged, his face flushed with anger. He lunged towards me and I shrieked, just managing to side-step him. I lifted my skirt and took off as fast as I could – which wasn't very fast for I'd only taken a few strides when Patrick caught the back of my coat and I stumbled. Simon fell into us and the three of us tumbled to the ground. Jemima danced about excitedly while I squirmed, flinging myself from side to side, attempting to break free, but Pat grasped my hands and held me firmly in place.

"You like snow?" Simon asked, his eyes glinting. He was laughing now as his anger subsided. "Try this …"

He shoved a handful in my mouth. I spluttered as it melted and gritted between my teeth. Kicking and fighting, the forest rang with my shrieks and Jem's barking. Simon scooped another handful of snow.

"Hold her steady!" He fumbled with the buttons at the neck of my coat.

"No!" I screeched and increased my thrashing. "Don't you dare Simon – Ahh!" A cold, wet, handful of snow was thrust unbecomingly down the front of my gown, followed quickly by another, and another.

Its iciness melted rapidly against the warmth of my skin and I could feel the dampness seeping through my clothes.

Finally, Pat released my hands. He threw his head back and laughed with such genuine pleasure that it stirred something within me. I'd not known he was capable of so joyous a sound. It echoed through the mist and infectiously tugged at the corners of my own mouth.

I scrambled to my feet, breathless and wet, and tried to glare down at the pair of them but found myself grinning instead. To cover it, I irritably kicked out and caused a spray of snow to shower Simon, but he gripped a wad of sodden velvet and dragged me to the ground.

At last we lay catching our breaths as the mist parted to reveal grey clouds scudding across the sky.

"All we need now is for it to start raining," said Simon.

"Would it matter?" I responded. "I'm soaked anyway."

"You could be wetter," Pat sniggered menacingly.

"Don't you dare. If I come down with my death it'll be your fault."

Simon jumped to his feet. "Well, I for one am getting very cold now." He grasped my hand and dragged me up. "C'mon, let's get back. I think we all need to thaw out."

∾

The weather took a turn for the better several days before my brothers' scheduled departure and Simon suggested a ride to Wharferidge. My own horse, Juno, was being treated for a cut to his foreleg that forced Simon and me to ride pillion on Oliver.

The melting snow turned the lane into an icy, brown slush and Equus was cautious, placing her feet carefully on the uneven surface. Oliver, a less gently-bred horse and more familiar with northern winters, clopped along casually and confidently. Though never sleek, he was scruffier than normal in his shaggy, winter coat. I straddled his broad back inelegantly and hugged Simon's waist against the sway of Oliver's round rump.

The countryside rolled by; tufts of grass and ancient rocks emerging from the snow. Black-faced sheep congregating around bales of hay watched our progress with mild interest. The lane followed the river, and several ducks gathered on the bank fluffing their feathers in the brisk air.

Simon began to sing *Greensleeves* and I attempted a light harmony half a step above his tenor. The effect was quite pretty, and Patrick listened in silence with his eyes half-closed.

As an inn appeared ahead, he interrupted our chorus. "Mulled wine, anyone?"

The thought of the wine, warmed and spiced, was instantly attractive and I nodded enthusiastically. I could almost smell the cloves and nutmeg, and suddenly my stomach growled hungrily.

"Splendid idea," Simon agreed happily as we drew even with the inn. Its damp stone walls glistened in the sun and a plume of wood-scented smoke curled unhurriedly from the chimney. Simon slid lazily from Oliver's back then assisted me, and a pair of grubby boys ran forward to take the horses.

Patrick gallantly swung open the door. The room was warm with the mingled smells of roasting meat and tobacco smoke. Patrons sat in groups of two or three, talking, eating, drinking and puffing on short-stemmed clay pipes, beneath the indifferent gaze of a serving-wench. Now she glanced up wearily, and I saw with no surprise a new interest cross her face, and enjoyed the rush of pride as her eyes sifted admiringly over Simon's tall frame, before passing unseeingly over me, to assess Patrick's casual grace.

I sat on a high-backed wooden bench before a scarred trestle-table and Patrick unceremoniously shoved me further along to take up the space beside me.

"Recognise her, Zan?" Simon nodded toward the bar where the comely young woman was furtively tugging her bodice lower.

I shook my head. "Should I?"

"That's Molly Starling, Jack's daughter. Remember they used to sell vegetables at the kitchen door? She was a child then."

Molly was approaching and, at close range, I recognised the abundant black hair escaping in thick tendrils from her servant's cap, and the broad nose common among her family. "'Ullo, Sir Simon," she said pleasantly, and her gleaming black eyes slid slyly in Pat's direction. "Wha' can ah be gettin' yers?"

Simon ordered three mugs of mulled wine and a plate of bread and cheese, and was rewarded with an inviting smile. I snorted but it went unnoticed as Molly turned to address Patrick. "An' this'd be M'lord Thorncliffe if ah guess araight. They's bar-wenches at 'Orse n 'Ounds been a-talkin' 'bout ahs like emeralds – no mistakin 'em they says." She nodded approvingly. "They says other things 'bout yer too," she added mysteriously.

Patrick's composure was unwavering. Lounging comfortably on the bench beside me, he returned her bold stare. "Do they indeed? How intriguing."

"Yer calls me if there's summat yer want," she went on, and the proposal in her voice was unmistakeable.

Pat regarded her appraisingly, "I just might do that," he drawled, and his mouth moved into one of his slow smiles. I watched, with growing annoyance, my companions following the swing of the girl's hips as she sashayed towards the kitchen.

"You two are –" I began but they both laughed.

"Settle down, Zan. Your hackles are showing."

"But she's so … so … *overt* and you're –"

"Don't worry Li'l Sis," said Patrick placatingly. "Harmless sport but I do believe our brother here may be tempted."

"Give over," Simon said, with a smirk.

Patrick laughed. "Ah, don't be so coy. Molly there casts a shadow over the quality of companionship you enjoyed the other evening."

"In my own defence, perhaps my perceptions were distorted by the bottom of the ale jug."

"Never a truer word have you spoken – ah, here's our delightful maid now."

I was slightly appeased by the sight of the food, for even though the inn was crowded, we had waited only minutes. The laces of

Molly's bodice had mysteriously unravelled to expose large fleshy mounds that threatened to spill free as she leaned further than necessary across the trestle. I heard Patrick's appreciative intake of air and I glowered at the girl without effect.

Molly took her time arranging the plates and mugs before us, and when finally she straightened, her eyes settled on Pat in blatant invitation. "I'll be o'er at t' coun'er M'lord, if yer needs owt."

Patrick responded pleasantly. "Thank you, Mistress Starling."

The girl's face broke into a broad grin and giving a blatant wink, she returned to where a waiting customer was served considerably less cordially.

"I'd say from that little … er … exhibition," Simon said with amusement, "she has set her cap firmly in your direction, *your Lordship*."

Patrick sipped his wine, "So it would appear. Perhaps I'll enquire as to what time she finishes her work." He glanced in my direction and offered a mock grimace in response to my glare, "Or perhaps not."

"You are rude and lewd," I said.

He shrugged. "And we receive prompt service – no harm. In any case, I'm more discerning than Sime. It's not my behaviour you should be concerned with."

"Bah!" Simon said playfully. "She could be just the type our young Thorncliffe here is looking for – marriageable age, child-bearing hips …"

"Ample and willing, more to the point," I grumbled and sipped my wine. It was deliciously warm and fragrant, and smoothed my frown somewhat.

"Undoubtedly the best attributes," Patrick agreed. "But you, my dear Li'l Sis, have been mercilessly exposed to the more boorish qualities in your brothers' characters, for which Simon profusely apologises."

I gave a bark of laughter. "*Simon* apologises?"

He leaned back and draped a casual arm across the back of our seat, letting his hand lightly brush my thickly coated shoulder. "*I* shall apologise for nothing."

My eyes widened and he grinned wickedly. "Apologies are expressions of regret – a concept that implies a person embraces more than a passing regard for the consequences of their actions. *I* have no such vice. I shall love where I will and give my heart to no-one. I shall enjoy to the full my essentially selfish life and sleep well at night – sated with good food, excellent wine, and affectionate wenches – like our Molly over there."

I stared incredulously at him but he merely took a long pull from his mug, his eyes sparkling merrily over the rim. Across the table Simon was watching with a curious look on his face. As I met his gaze, he cocked a quizzical eyebrow.

Something in the mood of our banter had changed. "Surely you're not so shallow," I said quietly, inexplicably disturbed, my eyes drifting to where Molly leaned on the bar watching steadily.

"He's teasing you, Zan," Simon said, soberly.

Patrick suddenly laughed – a reckless sound – and in brotherly fashion, pulled me against him in a brief hug. "Arguable, but 'tis no concern of yours Li'l Sis, so drink up and eat your lunch."

I stood on the porch steps beside Gerrard in the brisk, dawn air. Mother, in queenly fashion, had bidden Simon farewell the previous evening from her bed. Patrick had neither visited nor been expected to.

Maeve stood with her forehead pressed into her brother's chest. "Come now silly, you're wetting the front of my coat. It's not forever."

"But it's so far away," she sniffed.

He gently unwound her tentacles from his waist and she ran to her father who put an arm about her slim shoulders.

I clenched my jaw as a myriad of emotions worked within me. If only I could go with them, be educated, and live the experience of that wonderful university town. For the first time in my life I was aware of my deficit of choice, and I envied them their freedom, their male birthright.

More than this, rising up and threatening to overwhelm me was grief, for Simon was going away, and the thought distressed me more than I'd anticipated.

He held me tightly against his scratchy, woollen coat, and I knew that despite his excitement, he also was moved. I stood on tiptoes and whispered, "We've not been parted before."

He nodded solemnly, "I know," then took my face between his hands and kissed my forehead. "And it might be a while before I'm back – more than a year I should think. Pat wants to spend next Christmas at Devon."

I drew a long shaky breath. Anne was weeping noisily behind us and he turned to her now.

"S … Simon, you will write w … won't you?" she sobbed.

"Of course I won't write! I'll be far too busy cavorting and drinking – oh, and studying, of course." He hugged her quickly, and held his arm out to Maeve. "Come, Naughty Puss, and kiss me goodbye."

A flash of movement caught my eye. Patrick had swung into Equus' saddle and I hadn't said my farewell. I knew a stab of regret that I'd wasted so many weeks nurturing foolish resentment, rather than exploring the potential of his friendship.

He was smiling at me – that engaging smile I'd seen more frequently in recent times – and I drew closer.

"*Adieu*, Li'l Sis."

I nodded dumbly, confused and unhappy. It seemed so inadequate and I wanted something more, something undefined and unfamiliar. I wished he'd embraced me as Simon had, but instead, he held my gaze, his face closed, eyes searching. Suddenly he stripped off one leather glove, kissed his first two fingers and, leaning from his saddle, pressed them firmly to my lips.

It was an impulsive and strangely intimate gesture that left my emotions in disarray.

He too, seemed uncommonly uneasy and he immediately looked away, saved, as Simon on Oliver moved up beside him.

I retreated to where Anne stood with Maeve and her father as our brothers wheeled their horses' heads toward the gate and with a final jaunty wave, they loosened their reins and were shortly gone from our sight.

&

The household quickly settled into a new, rather feminine routine. Mother recovered well and was soon out of bed but continued to linger in her rooms for a further week.

Anne, Maeve and I attended our comparatively subdued studies each day, noting with amusement the return of Master Baxter's supercilious confidence.

Spring had arrived and each day new life was evident in the gardens. Buds burst into glorious bloom and nestlings in the shrubbery were learning to fly. In the forest, young fawns explored their new surroundings on gangly legs.

Jemima and I visited Clara and Meg each afternoon after my lessons. Sometimes Clara and I shared village gossip and stories. Other times we sat quietly, Clara sewing while I attempted to. I thought longingly of my brothers but, as the weeks passed, no letter arrived from Oxford.

Lord Thorncliffe was frequently absent attending to business affairs in Leeds. His irregular visits to Broughton Hall often accompanied a delivery of a new book for me and consequently, I was introduced to a range of exciting writers like Walter Raleigh and Lady Anne Lindsay. The story of *Auld Robin Gray* haunted me once I'd deciphered Lady Lindsay's Scots accented writing.

Meanwhile Mother noted my growing friendship with Clara and remarked that it was inappropriate for someone of my station. She suggested I invite my cousin, her sister's daughter, Charlotte, to stay, or perhaps Julia.

But I enjoyed my afternoons with Clara and my baby sister, and knowing Mother as I did, I knew that concerns that did not pertain to her social activities were of a fleeting nature and would soon be forgotten.

Having no prior experience with babies, I'd initially been wary of Meg, but as the months passed and spring became summer, the baby girl grew and I became comfortable handling her. I decided I would rather enjoy becoming a mother one day.

Mother's time seemed to be entirely occupied by the social events afforded by her status as a countess. So many invitations, so many women who'd previously considered themselves her equal, now curtsied deferentially before her – and she revelled in it.

She threw herself enthusiastically into society and the lion-head knocker on Broughton Hall's doors had never worked so hard. Throughout that summer, Mother attended an endless round of garden parties and balls, charity events and dinners. The prestige her presence lent each occasion ensured her diary was constantly full.

The county had a reasonably well-established society and the glittering events attracted others who travelled from nearby Lancashire and Humberside. Some even came from further afield, progressing from one country estate to the next, where they ate, drank and whittled their days away in idle, pointless pursuits.

One day Mother, attracted to a life of wealthy indolence in Leeds and York, disappeared down the drive in a cloud of summered dust. It was to be nearly a year before she'd return.

Gerrard now remained at Broughton Hall, and the household settled into a slumberous mood, and remained so as I, with the approving nod of my stepfather, joined our tenant farmers in the annual autumnal haymaking that heralded the approaching winter.

CHAPTER 8

It was June 1810, almost a year since we'd last seen Mother, when a pair of wine-coloured coaches lumbered up the drive and she alighted, fanning herself with a lace handkerchief and exclaiming over the heat.

A week later, Isabella Camelleri, with daughters, Catarina and Grace, their servants, and numerous trunks and boxes, descended on us. Lord Thorncliffe made good his escape to Leeds and left a household of women behind him.

Painted and perfumed, Isabella carried herself ramrod straight and managed to look down her prominent, aquiline nose at everyone – despite her diminutive height.

At 17 years old, Grace was, as her name suggested, quiet and serene. She was not especially pretty, but was crowned by the most glorious cascade of thick, chestnut hair.

Catarina, by contrast, at 19 years, was consciously beautiful with all the attendant confidence. Coolly sophisticated, she was a sumptuous example of everything modern and glamorous and, not surprisingly, Anne gravitated toward her. Catarina treated Anne as one would a pesky child; smiling indulgently from time to time, but for the most part ignoring her.

Maeve regarded Catarina warily, whispering to me one morning, "What sort of lady dresses round the house like that? Perhaps she thinks the King himself will arrive on our doorstep."

The Camelleris had been in London for the winter season where Isabella's cousin had presented them at court. Now, they intended to pass the summer with Mother at Broughton Hall before returning to London for another winter.

Anne's eyes shone at the prospect and she immediately embarked on a campaign to convince Mother that she should also go to London for her long awaited coming-out and to be presented at court.

"No!" was Mother's quick and simple response.

"But everyone I know is coming out this season. And you did yours at my age."

"It was different for me."

"Why? I could become one of the Queen's ladies." She leaned conspiratorially toward Maeve, "The Prince of Wales will notice me and I will become very rich."

Maeve made a noise of appreciation but Mother was not amused. "Alternatively, you could remain right where you are, marry Patrick, and become even richer."

Undeterred, Anne made Catarina her unknowing mentor, copying everything; from her manner of dress to the coquettish way she tilted her head, when a man — any man, servant, visitor or otherwise — was present. She evidently thought Mother would change her mind.

July progressed, bringing hot and cloudless days. Each evening, the seven of us made a pleasant feminine gathering in the cooling shade beneath the Great Oak. Over 50 summers, this magnificent tree had spread its boughs over those reclining beneath it, and in that time it had housed countless families of birds and squirrels.

Mother, Isabella and Catarina were talking quietly and sipping lemonade. I leaned back in my chair to stare into the arching foliage overhead, letting my gaze soften so the green of the leaves melded into one. Grace and Maeve were sewing and Anne was dozing.

Suddenly, Maeve's head jerked. "Visitors!" she announced, and then I heard it too – the unmistakable sound of horses' hooves. Maeve and Anne both leapt to their feet and ran to greet our unexpected guests as two horsemen appeared around the bend in the drive.

Mother tutted and shook her head. "Maeve and her brother have both suffered terribly from lack of discipline. It worries me not at all, except that Maeve wields such influence over Anne."

Isabella nodded but her gaze shifted beyond Mother as the two girls returned, triumphantly towing one each – Simon and Patrick.

"Oh dear," Mother murmured, "speak of the devil and he doth appear."

"Look who we have. Home at last – isn't it *marvy*?"

In the year and more they'd been away my brothers had changed considerably. Simon's hair was longer and he was tall and well-muscled and, if possible, his masculine beauty was even more arresting. His eyes scanned our little group and came to rest, predictably, on Catarina.

Patrick too was taller, leaner, but broader in the shoulders. His hair was sun-bleached to the colour of straw, shorter at the sides but long and tousled on top.

"Oh, how tanned your arms are," Maeve cried to her brother. Pat's loose cotton shirt was open at the neck and rolled up at the sleeves, and showed a goodly amount of brown skin.

He put his arm about his sister and squeezed her to him. "Indeed. And feel this … we've both been in the rowing squad and have muscles enough to crush naughty girls."

She squeaked with delight.

Dragging himself from Catarina's spell, Simon came to where I sat and pulled me into a tight hug. "Muh!" he placed a smacking kiss on my forehead. "Miss me?"

"Not much," but a betraying grin spread across my face.

"Excellent! I didn't miss you either."

Mother interrupted impatiently. "Yes, yes; now, Isabella, may I present my son, Sir Simon Broughton, whom I believe you met many years ago, and my stepson, Lord Patrick Washburn. Boys, this is Senora Isabella Camelleri, and her daughters, Senorina Catarina and Senorina Grace."

As the introductions were made, I noted that while Patrick paid no particular attention to any of our guests, Simon's eyes were continually drawn to the lovely Catarina.

Maeve and Anne elbowed one another and sniggered.

Wondering if Patrick had forgotten our budding friendship, I glanced his way and found his appraising eyes on me. Perhaps he was thinking I'd changed too, and the heat flooded my face. Before I could look away, he sent me a mischievous wink that caused my heart to skip. Turning then to Mother's guests, he and Simon bowed politely and excused themselves.

∾

I dressed with uncommon care that evening and arrived in the parlour just as Emily announced that supper was being served. Simon led Catarina into the dining room and, taking his place at the head of the table, wasted no time in engaging the Italian girl in conversation.

Though he'd always been completely comfortable in female company, there was a new sophistication in his manner that hinted his Oxford education included more than mere academia.

Patrick sat beside the tranquil Grace. He finished a glass of wine and was pouring another while appearing genuinely interested in her quiet conversation, and even as the plates were cleared and a large bowl of summer fruits and a second of fresh cream were brought in, she continued to entertain him.

Maeve and Anne piled their plates with slices of pear and plum, a sprinkling of grapes and berries, and a dollop of cream, before excusing themselves to go outside into the balmy summer night air.

It was customary at this stage for the ladies to leave the table but Mother and Isabella were engrossed in their conversation and seemed to be disregarding convention. Suddenly Grace laughed – a vivid sound that was at odds with her calm exterior. She artlessly raised a small hand to brush aside a stray hair, while her other hand toyed absently with her dessert spoon. Her complexion was petal-smooth and, unlike her sister and mother, she made no use of crèmes or powders. She wore an azure-satin gown that flattered her small bosom and my initial impression that she was plain was belied by her refinement and quiet elegance. She glowed beneath the warmth of Patrick's attention, a fact he had clearly not failed to notice, and a sly serpent of jealousy writhed in my stomach.

But then, he caught my eye and threw me his most disarming smile and all was right with the world.

Mother and Isabella departed to visit with some of Mother's friends in Leeds, and as though coordinated, Gerrard returned the following day.

"Hmph, sorry to've missed them," he said, with a cough.

Summer was at her apex now and days of breathless heat dragged by, but when evening arrived on a current of cool air, we gathered beneath the Great Oak to enjoy wine and pleasant conversation.

Later, as the sky darkened, Patrick and Simon rode down the lane towards Wolstone, generally not returning until dawn. They were frequently absent from breakfast, sleeping off the previous night's carousal, making their first appearance of the day at the dinner table, with faces haggard and shadowed with dissipation.

When I overheard them discussing Molly Starling or other village girls, old resentments bubbled within me, but I suppressed my jealousies with a new maturity for I understood that my resentment only served to chip away the foundations of our tranquil amity, and the fact that the weather was co-operative meant that I enjoyed many long afternoons in their company.

Days were spent soothing our hot feet in the river, or strolling through the forest, benefiting from its earthy coolness.

Sometimes Cook packed a basket with bread, cold meat, pickled onions, cheese and lemonade, and the three of us – always with Jemima – spread a rug beneath the trees where we ate and – in my case – read while they dozed away the remains of their nightly indulgence.

One such afternoon, I sat against a tree, a book of sonnets open on my lap. Simon was sprawled in the grass, one arm flung over his eyes, a dandelion stem between his teeth. The still warmth of the afternoon weighted my limbs and I breathed deeply of the summer-scented air. I looked to where Patrick reclined on one elbow, head tilted back to watch a bird in a tree. Its wings were held wide to gain some relief from the temperature.

As I watched, Pat's hair fell away from his face and his expression was, for once, unguarded. I studied the strong line of his jaw, the clear observant eyes, slightly-parted lips, and was spellbound. Captured thus, unaware of being observed, he was … beautiful. My breath caught in my throat and as he turned and met my gaze, I flushed hotly.

But his lips curved into a sleepy half-smile and my heart lurched. Returning hurriedly to my book, I was unable to read: this enchanted summer, my awakening womanhood had my emotions in turmoil.

For Simon made me so inordinately proud of the man he was becoming. He had kindness, wit and striking looks. He was tolerance itself, with a joie de vivre that was contagious. But beyond that, he was *good*.

And there was Patrick. Reserved and watchful, intellectual and humorous, he was gifted in so many ways, yet rarely offered glimpses into his soul. In the two years since I'd met him, he'd shown himself capable of extraordinary kindness, while possessed of a cruel ability to target weakness – a potent contradiction.

We made a trio, as though Patrick had allowed us entry into his world. And when his lips moved in that lazy smile, my chest tightened and my stomach twisted in a way that owed nothing to sibling fondness. My head advised caution, but my 16 year old heart was ripe and ready and I was powerless to heed the warning.

These two captivated me in different ways. Simon, who'd previously exploited his looks to wheedle an extra biscuit from Cook, or bargain with a market woman, carried a new confidence born of maturity and experience. No longer a boy, he was a man fully conscious of his allure and made powerful by his face and charm.

Patrick, on the other hand, was often aloof and reserved. He was an enigma, with a certain remoteness that I recognised, even in my innocence, was strangely compelling and, coupled with my growing awareness of his maleness, would have been quite dangerous had he not been so inaccessible. I was drawn to him, enticed to teeter on the edge of peril, and toy with my attraction. I knew his little gestures – like a fingertip kiss pressed to my lips, or a casual arm draped over my shoulders – were mere flippancies, part of his *laissez-faire* character that held little meaning for him.

Yet I struggled, that summer, against my reaction to his magnetism. I ignored the fact that he regularly drank to excess and sported with the village girls, focusing rather on the Patrick who recited poems while lying in the grass, who played violin in the dark, who challenged me in exercises of verbal thrust and parry; the one who was at once entertaining and frustrating.

Meanwhile, he seemed to have one weakness – Maeve. His best smiles were reserved for the sister to whom he was endlessly kind and affectionate. Clearly, she occupied an elite corner of his heart. But I sensed that he was beginning to treat me in a similar manner.

Stifling my fancies, I knew it was a combination of brotherly intimacy and affected gallantry – an exclusive offering, a privilege not extended to Anne.

Simon had always treated Anne kindly but he had no illusions about our pretentious and ambitious younger sibling, and it appeared Patrick hadn't either. He rarely spoke with her and seemed entirely impervious to her dedicated attempts to beguile him.

My realisation that he regarded me only as a younger sister did nothing to deter me, for I was intrigued by him and aware that I was playing a game I could not win. Nevertheless, I made my way to the stables each day, just before dinner, when he visited Equus. Having just risen after sleeping late, he was generally happy to be drawn into conversation and, though he typically gave little of himself away, he was an attentive listener. I made him laugh by describing Meg's latest antics and relating household anecdotes, and our friendship grew steadily.

One morning, I was in the rose garden with Meg when I turned without warning and gasped as my nose bumped his shoulder.

He gave a wry grin, "My apologies."

"No … I didn't realise you were there. I'm just surprised to see you about so early. It must want at least an hour until your usual rising time."

He caught the teasing note in my voice. "I returned early last night. Sime stayed out but I've had enough for a while."

"Growing too old for the wine, women and song are we?"

He ran a hand through his unruly hair, tousling it further, and laughed lightly. "I shall be nineteen soon and a man must know his limitations. What are you doing?"

"Showing Meg the roses."

He crouched to the little girl's level. "And what do you think of the pretty flowers then, Meggy?"

"Dat! Dat!" she responded waving her arms. He looked up questioningly.

"She's saying, *Pat, Pat*," I translated.

"Oh, I see." He curled an arm round her and rose, as she joyfully wrapped her arms about his neck. "I have an idea," he said to her. "Let us see if there are any ripe apples to pick. Then, we shall ask Cook to stew them with rhubarb and make us a treat."

"Sounds like a good idea to me," I said. "What do you think, Meg?"

"Dat, Dat!" she responded, and began a happy discussion in her own childish language.

"Good, that's settled." He nudged Jemima gently with his toe. "On your feet, doggle!"

Our visit to the orchard paid dividends and later that afternoon, Pat and I sat with Clara and Meg in the nursery, each of us enjoying a bowl of stewed apple and rhubarb, topped generously with sugared cream.

My friendship with Patrick was blossoming. I knew moments of immense happiness in his company, yet I was too young or too afraid to name the feelings awakening within me. Though Grace and Catarina were young, they were sophisticated in a way that I, country rabbit that I was, could not match and my painful awareness of my lack of social refinement grew.

At the supper table – those rare evenings when Simon and Patrick remained at home – Grace's eyes concentrated on Patrick as he spoke. She was animated and gay and not immune to his charm. She herself had an appealing manner that made me wonder if Patrick found her attractive in return. I pursed my lips contemplatively.

"We're going out to the park. Will you come?" Maeve interrupted my thoughts and I looked up in surprise. She added quickly, "Please say you will – it'll be lovely. Anne has asked Pat to bring his violin so we can have music beneath the moon."

"That sounds nice," I said, smiling.

"*Marvy!*"

We made a merry party of ten since we'd collected Janet,

Emily and Jeffrey on our way through the house. Maeve and Anne scattered a collection of rugs on the lawn and we lay beneath a vast indigo-velvet sky.

Simon produced a bottle of Irish mead from which he pulled the cork with his teeth. He drank enthusiastically straight from its neck before passing it to me.

I'd had mead before but not like this. I put it to my lips and took a larger swig than I'd intended. The fiery liquid burned its way down my throat and, once again, I demonstrated my lack of experience. Once my coughing fit subsided, no thanks to Janet's exuberant back-thumping, I relaxed on the rug and enjoyed the sweet honey aftertaste.

When Patrick took up his violin our revelry started in earnest. Janet kept time with a tambourine – a gift from a peddler who'd once fancied her – while the rest of us lent our voices. The evening air fairly rang with the sounds of our merrymaking and the bottle was drained and quickly replaced by another.

Giddy with mead and laughter, we jigged and bounded among the trees, stumbling into one another, whirling and shrieking for pure joy. I know that on this night we were truly enchanted, and was not surprised to spy *the lady* watching from a distance.

Her lovely auburn hair hung loose about her shoulders and she was wearing a voluminous white gown that rippled in a soft breeze and … and then she was gone.

Later, exhausted and more than tipsy, I contemplated the diamond-studded night sky. I was hoping to see a falling star so I could make a wish but my eyelids grew heavy and I let them close.

I awoke as Maeve – staggering, laughing and breathless – flopped on to the rug beside me, followed by an equally unsteady Janet.

"Oh Alex," Maeve gasped, "we must include Janet in our dance lessons – she's sorely in need of training."

"Strange, Miss Maeve," Janet slurred happily, "But I'm the one with the bruised toes."

"Oh tish, I dance like a fairy."

"Fairy what?" Patrick joined us on the rug. "Elephant?"

Maeve continued, unperturbed by our laughter, "Light on my feet, nimble and graceful – that's me."

Patrick leaned conspiratorially toward Janet and me, reaffirming, "Elephant."

"I shall ignore you all." His sister stretched sinuously and yawned.

An uncommonly disarrayed Grace crawled onto the rug beside us. She ducked her shoulder beneath Pat's arm and he shifted to draw her into a casual embrace against his side. She had a bottle in her hand and he took it and drank from it.

She was giggling tipsily, and when bent his head to whisper into her ear, I turned away.

"What a simply *marvy* night," Maeve's voice was thick with wine and she was drifting into sleep. "You know Alex, we really ought … spend every … night … beneath the stars … and …"

"Is that not so Alessandra?" Grace asked suddenly.

"Er … I'm sorry?"

"Your brother believes that the warmth of my country would be more to his taste than the cold of England. I tell him that while your English winter is severe, the summer is lovely."

"In that case," I said slowly, "the best result would be to divide one's year between the two countries – winter in Italy and summer in England."

"*Brava!* What better solution than this! *È molto bene, si?*"

"Perhaps," Patrick replied with a suggestive lift of one brow. "Do you think I'd do well in your country, Senorina Camelleri?"

She chuckled delightedly and snuggled further beneath his arm, "I think you would break many hearts, *Senor.*" She nodded in my direction, "the first being your sister's were you to stray such a great distance from her."

Patrick laughed dismissively. "That's doubtful. Alex'd be only too happy to see the back of me."

"Do not be so certain. All the little girls give their hearts to the big brother. Always, they are the first love." She smiled indulgently at me and I stiffened with annoyance that she would speak as though I were Meg's age.

"I'm not so *little*," I snapped but when Grace merely smiled my hackles rose and I added with a sharp edge to my voice, "And don't treat me like a child."

She looked contrite. "Forgive me, Alessandra. I did not mean to tease … it is that you are … *come si dice* … so fond of your brother and you are right – you are not so little. *Infatti*, I think –"

"Well, you're right," I cut her off sharply and said with deliberate emphasis, "I missed Patrick and Simon *both* while they were away."

To my eternal relief, she shut up and we fell silent momentarily allowing the chirrups and hoots from the nearby forest to take over.

"So," Patrick drank from the bottle again, then, his expression unreadable, turned to me, "you would discourage me from moving to Italy?" His eyes glinted wickedly in the dark and a vague smile twitched the corners of his mouth signalling danger.

Against my better judgment, I responded to his bantering tone. "I find that now you are returned, I did not miss you so much as I expected I would, so if you've a mind to go to Italy, I should be happy to help you pack."

I smiled sweetly and Grace laughed.

But Patrick was assessing me narrowly and seemed about to say something, yet despite his evident drunkenness, he grew solemn and appeared to reconsider. Dropping his arm from Grace's shoulders, he said, "Told you so. I'm afraid my little sister is not as enamoured of me as you presume, *Senorina*."

"It is perhaps that you tease her too much, *si*?"

"*Si!*" I agreed firmly.

His changeable, unpredictable mood shifted and he grinned mischievously. "Tease her too much? I've not yet started." He picked up a discarded cork from one of the bottles and tossed it at me.

I gasped in surprise. "You'll pay for that Master Washburn!"

"Are you threatening my person, Miss Broughton?" I knew he could easily better me in a war of words, but this game had suddenly turned irresistible.

"Far be it from me to threaten your person, My Lord, for I suspect you would derive an unhealthy pleasure in the planning and execution of your reprisal."

He lifted an eyebrow in response and reached for the wine bottle again. "Oh, indeed I would," he whispered intensely, drank, then wiped the back of his hand across his mouth, his eyes fixed on my face.

I drew an unsteady breath and glanced quickly at Grace. Her expression was one of vindicated satisfaction. She said softly, "*Allora, vedi ho ragione.*"

"*Forse ma, chi sa?*" Patrick responded. Replacing the bottle on the rug, he continued to watch me. "And you, dear Miss Broughton, may well derive a rather *healthy* pleasure *from* my reprisal."

I hadn't known he spoke Italian, but now was not the time to explore such discoveries, for I realised with an odd feeling of panic that we had slipped into a different game altogether, one at which, in spite of his inebriation, he was far more adept than I.

The confusion must have shown on my face for his tone changed once more and he laughed. "Apologies, Li'l Sis, I am teasing you abominably. I'm well aware that you are not a child, and in my ill-mannered way, tested my boundaries inappropriately."

This speech was delivered with only a hint of irony though he had arranged his face into a perfectly respectable expression.

His gaze held mine just a moment longer, but the game had lost its appeal and seeking diversion, I broke the spell. "Where's Maeve?" I asked.

"She retired to bed, Miss Alex," Emily replied. "Perhaps Miss Anne went with her, she also is gone."

"Miss Anne was talking with Jeffrey, last I saw," Janet said.

Patrick made a snorting sound and I looked at him curiously. He'd been strangely short with Anne lately but I couldn't imagine why. Naturally, his expression gave nothing away.

"There's no sign of Jeffrey either," Simon said, strolling over with Catarina on his arm and I wondered briefly where they'd been.

"Perhaps he escorted them to the house," I suggested.

"Miss Anne's wrap is still here." Janet held a silky shawl.

Simon and I exchanged a weighty look and, as the others began to gather rugs and the numerous empty bottles, Simon whispered, "You go that way – I'll start over there. If you find her, return here – and make sure she doesn't make a scene."

The forest was alive with the calls of assorted night creatures and, listening intently, I heard a rustling nearby and paused. But an owl launched itself from a branch and disappeared into the night and, though quite tipsy, I plunged deeper into the woods – I had no fears, for Simon and I had wandered through this forest all our lives.

Suddenly I heard it. The sounds sprung directly from my distant past: the unmistakable, disembodied sighs and murmurings of lovers. Before I could gather my thoughts, I came upon my 15 year old sister, backed against a tree, her bodice unbuttoned and exposing her young breasts like any common trollop, and pawing at her, his mouth on her throat, was Jeffrey.

I sobered in a rush.

"*Anne!*" My outraged cry bounced sharply off the trees. She reacted calmly, though Jeffrey leapt like a scalded cat and immediately vanished among the shadows.

"What on *earth* are you doing? And with a servant!"

Remorselessly, she took her time adjusting her clothing. "Oh be still, Alex."

"And carrying on like … like some peasant slut!" I stood before her, my hands on my hips.

"Oh, don't be so prudish!" She brushed off her gown and

tucked her hair into place. "Everyone's doing it but you, Alex – oh, and Maeve – and I mean *everyone*. Simon was in the scullery with that new kitchen wench last week – the one from Harrogate – saw them myself."

"I don't care about Simon. We're talking about you!"

"You'd care had you seen them. I reckon her titties were giving that table a fair polish!"

Disgusted, I grabbed her arm and spun her round. "Come on."

She resisted and yanked free. "You're jealous because you're already turning into a dried-up, frigid old maid. Your tits will shrivel into raisins and … *ouch*!"

The sound of my hand on her self-satisfied face hung in the air and we both froze in surprise.

First to recover, Anne wailed, "You hit me!"

"Where've you been?" Simon appeared, stepping over a log.

"Oh God, not you as well," she said with a resigned sigh." I might've known – where there was one, there'd be the other."

"I found her with Jeffrey … dress pulled down … he was all over her."

"Thank you, Alex," said Anne, "I was doing no worse than you, brother dear."

"It's very much worse. For starters, I can't get with child and foist some bastard brat on the family."

"He only wanted to kiss me."

"You think he'd stop at that?"

"Hmph!" She twitched her skirt at him and made to walk away but he grabbed her arm.

"How do you hope to find a suitable husband if you've done the rounds of the tower?"

"That's my business so both of you can take your long noses out of it."

With that, she jerked out of his grip and stalked off towards the house.

Simon turned to me, shrugging. "We'd better rejoin the others. What are you looking like that for?"

I grimaced. "She told me about you and that maid – Jane Carter, was it?"

He shrugged again. "So?"

"Sime, you can't do something like that and then preach the opposite."

"It's different for men."

"You're not a man yet."

"Tell that to Jane Carter."

"Simon!" I thumped his arm and he laughed.

"Don't take things so seriously, Zan," He draped his arm across my shoulders. "C'mon, silly, the others will wonder what's been going on."

The next morning Simon spoke privately with Lord Thorncliffe and Jeffrey was promptly dispatched to watch over Lord Thorncliffe's London address. The fact that homeless people were breaking into, and living in houses left vacant over the summer months, proved convenient, and nothing more was said of the incident in the woods. In fact, Anne gave no indication that she'd even noticed Jeffrey's departure.

Meanwhile, I gave considerable thought to the changed tone of the banter between Patrick and me and so, evidently, had he, for as our paths crossed in the hall he stalled me with a light hand on my arm.

"Alex, I must apologise for my behaviour last evening."

Something in me was dismayed by this but I said nothing as he went on, "In my own defence, I can only say that I had perhaps imbibed rather more wine than was suitable, and was tempted to tease you as … as I shouldn't have."

"I … I didn't know you spoke Italian," I said lamely.

He smiled. "I don't very well. My violin teacher was Italian." Then, gesturing dismissively, "Alex, there are sides of me that are not pleasant … it is not my intention to expose you to them – without provocation, of course," he added with a glimmer of humour, but I was unhappy that he evidently thought me young and in need of shelter from drunken innuendo.

"Having attracted your less pleasant side in the past, I'm fully aware of it. I thought we were friends, though." I added sarcastically, "I didn't mean to provoke you."

"You didn't. And I remembered for a moment that you are not truly my blood sister." With that, he was gone and I was left to ponder the meaning of his words.

∾

The weather was turning blustery and hot winds whipped dust about. It was not conducive to outdoor activity, so Clara and I remained indoors to indulge our common interest in poetry. I visited the nursery daily, taking Masters Shelley, Keats and Wordsworth with me. They were all the rage during this time, though I definitely preferred the works of William Shakespeare, despite feeling a little old-fashioned for doing so.

One particular day, armed with a compilation of Shakespeare's sonnets, I could hear Meg chattering in her childish language as I approached the nursery, and then I witnessed something I am never to forget.

Meg was in bed, supposedly taking her afternoon nap, and leaning over her was *the lady*, shimmering incandescently, and smiling down at the angelic girl. The child seemed transfixed by the vision and was waving her little hands about, attempting to touch her visitor.

At that moment my presence became known and *the lady* simply evaporated before my eyes. A magical moment, and for some long seconds after, I remained awestruck.

The spell broke as Clara bustled into the room with a plate of oat cakes, fresh from Cook's oven.

∾

Later that day, Patrick joined us. He came in quietly, aware that he had intruded on an intensely feminine domain. He didn't speak but sat cross-legged on the rug and set about re-stringing his violin.

I watched his graceful hands work lovingly and deftly, winding and tightening, stretching the strings, plucking to tune by ear and, if he glanced up and caught my eye, he smiled and returned to his work.

During those last humid days of summer, he joined us regularly and a new routine was established. I looked forward to his visits and, as he became more at ease in this womanly gathering, he related funny stories or recited rhymes he'd made up. He was a relaxed and pleasant companion – quite the opposite from the detached cynic he often appeared.

By the time August ended, afternoons with Patrick took on greater significance as his return to Oxford drew imminent. As the weather offered a few considerably milder days, we returned to spending our afternoons in the grass at the edge of the forest.

Full fathom five thy father lies;
Of his bones are coral made:
Those are pearls that were his eyes:
Nothing of him that doth fade,
But doth suffer a sea-change
Into something rich and strange.
Sea-nymphs hourly ring his knell:
Hark! Now I hear them – Ding-dong bell.

Clara was reading Shakespeare from my book. Bees were humming busily in a knot of lavender in a garden bed beside the drive, and a gentle breeze stroked the lush grass. I was lying flat on my back, eyes closed, enjoying the sun's warmth on my bare arms – my heart was quiet and my mind at peace.

"That's a little mournful, Clara. Pray, find something more cheerful, woman!" Pat berated in mock displeasure. "Master Wobbledagger wrote many lighter pieces. Read one of those."

"Hmm, let me see." Clara searched through the book.

I rolled on to my side in the grass watching Patrick playing with Meg. His hair fell into his eyes as he flopped on his back and lifted the giggling child in the air above him. His shirt sleeves were rolled up above the elbow and, with his tanned skin, he looked more like a farmer than the son of an earl. Then he spoke slowly, considering his words,

Soft as cotton in bales on high
The clouds scud 'cross the summer'd sky
Whilst day grows old on stealthy feet
Maketh bales of gold like harvest wheat

"What's that?" Clara flicked through the book.

"Something you won't find in there," he replied.

"It's not Shakespeare?"

He rolled over, placed Meg in the grass between us, and winked mischievously at Clara. "That, my dearest woman, was a Patrick Washburn original."

He picked a purple larkspur – they grew wild along the edge of the park at this time of year. Meg chuckled happily and snatched at the flower that her brother dangled before her.

Catching my eye, he smiled lazily. Something was growing between us; something familiar yet unknown – a feeling, a solidarity, something more honest than double-edged repartee. Leaning forward, he tucked the fragrant flower behind my ear, then, jumping explosively to his feet, he scooped Meg into his arms and held her high in the air. Jemima danced about excitedly, barking and eager to join the game.

"Shh, Jem," Patrick balanced Meg on the dog's back and the child shouted with delight, looking as though she were riding a hairy pony.

"What in heaven's name is going on here?"

In our excitement, we hadn't seen Mother's approach. Now she stood glaring imperiously at us, and Clara and I scrambled to our feet. "Clara, you are employed here supposedly for your sense of responsibility. Please return that child to the nursery immediately."

"Yes, my lady," Clara bobbed deferentially and took Meg from Pat's arms.

"You know, Clara did nothing wrong, and Meg was enjoying herself," Patrick said reasonably.

Mother's eyes widened with horror. "You question me before a servant?"

"Question you?" He snorted rudely. "Where to begin?" Clara turned and hurriedly waddled up the lawn toward the house. Meanwhile I stared transfixed as Mother flushed unbecomingly.

Her voice rose in anger. "Go to the house and wait in your room until I tell your father of your behaviour."

Pat stood his ground. Adopting Mother's imperious pose, he stood a full head taller and responded, "No."

The air crackled with tension as they faced one another. Mother's complexion was glowing with anger, while Patrick's stony face revealed no expression. "Sooner you are gone from here the better, you … you are the most audacious … disrespectful …"

Patrick held her eyes steadily and replied, "And you, Madam, are the most repellent – and you know why." Mother's hand clutched her breast and I was worried that she was about to swoon but as she opened her mouth to respond, Patrick bowed with supreme arrogance and returned to his seated position on the grass.

I remained open-mouthed in shock. Mother herself seemed

unusually confused. Her hands trembled, and her bosom rose and fell erratically.

Finally she turned to me and took a deep breath. "Alexandra, I sought you out because I wish to speak with you. I came myself because the afternoon is so lovely." She fanned her hot face with a fluttering hand and glared at Patrick but he had stretched out on his back with his eyes closed. The rudeness of his attitude was not lost on her but she ignored him. "I was mistaken. Come and see me in the drawing room at teatime." She turned and walked briskly up the lawn.

I watched her straight back as she marched away. "Wonder what she wants."

He moved to a sitting position. "Who knows – she loves her little intrigues, could be anything. Let's go back to the house."

As we strolled slowly in Mother's wake I turned to him, "You shouldn't antagonise her, you know. It is quite unpleasant."

He rounded on me angrily. "Don't take her part! You've no idea what's going on here."

"I'm not taking her part, but if there's something going on I have a right to know."

"If you had a right to know – you *would* know. Stay out of it!"

These were the first heated words he'd said to me in a long while and they stung. "I'm only … I thought –"

"When it affects you, then you'll have a right to think!"

"If you don't think it affects me, you're even more pig-headed than you appear. When you upset Mother, she takes it out on the rest of us – come, Jemima."

Full of righteous bravado, I stormed off ahead of him, but decided to fire a parting salvo. Turning, I waved an admonishing finger, "And you shouldn't be so self-satisfied, it's not always about you!" And then I tripped over my hem and fell flat on my face.

To fuel my intense humiliation, he doubled-up with hilarity – laughing so much he held his stomach and was unable to assist me – that only added to my anger. Finally, he wiped his streaming eyes and hauled me to my feet and when he tried to brush the grass from my skirt, I slapped his hands away.

"Don't touch me!" I shouted.

"I'm sorry … but Alex … that was … a wonderful performance. You can be so clumsy … one day you're really going to hurt yourself."

"Keep it up, Patrick Washburn, if you fancy a split lip."

That started him afresh.

"Oh do shut up!" I growled in exasperation, and fled home, my dignity in tatters.

Mother was enthroned on her winged chair with Lord Thorncliffe at her shoulder when she delivered the news. My knees threatened to give way and I felt sick in my stomach. I must have swayed for Lord Thorncliffe put out a hand to steady me.

"Here, Lass," he dragged over a chair. There was sympathy in his eyes but Mother's expression was inflexible – the decision was final.

"But … I don't understand."

"Oh heavens, Alexandra, what is there to understand? Lord Elginbury approached me several summers ago. Nothing was ever formally agreed, but recently our communications resumed, and yesterday a mutually favourable arrangement was achieved. You ought to consider yourself fortunate – it's an enviable position, a perfect match that will benefit both families."

"He has seen me?"

"Yes. The boy visited with his parents several years ago and attended the solstice ball. He thought you … suitable enough, even if you were in the garden wearing a pair of Simon's breeches when he arrived."

I cast my mind back to the last summer when my mother's court friends had visited but no-one stood out, particularly not a boy.

My blood began to boil and Lord Thorncliffe felt my shoulder stiffen beneath his hand. "Settle down, girl," he said gently.

Glaring, I jerked away. "My future is planned without consultation and you tell me to *settle down*!"

"Alexandra, that is quite enough!" Mother was on her feet, her mouth drawn to a thin line and her hard, blue eyes glittered dangerously. "This is not for discussion. Lord Elginbury would prefer you to be nearer twenty. Yet since he's unwell, it may be earlier. Either way, there'll be time aplenty to become accustomed to the idea."

"I won't marry him – you've not even asked me what I think."

"And what exactly *did* you think?" Mother demanded. "That you would be supported into your dotage? Don't be ridiculous! You are sixteen – girls your age dream of such a match, you should be grateful. Regardless, this is your brother's house. He will marry and have children and there will be no place for you here."

Under the truth of her words my shoulders slumped and the tears that had been threatening finally came.

"There, Lass," Lord Thorncliffe fished in his pocket and extracted a crisp, white handkerchief with a burgundy *GW* embroidered on one corner. "It is a fortuitous match," he said kindly. "Lord Hamish is the Sixth Viscount Elginbury, your betrothed – also Hamish – will be the seventh."

"She has ever been a difficult child. In any case it is done." Mother regally crossed the floor, and left the room without another word.

"You'll be well, Lass."

"B … but Mother … she doesn't care wha … what I would … would like."

"Of course she does, but she's thinking of the family too. Just imagine – to be settled … a household of your own and a baby. I hear Lord Hamish has a castle."

"*Oh no … A baby!*" I moaned. I was quite certain I didn't want to do *that* with some stranger. I began to cry with renewed fervour.

"Oh dear," Lord Thorncliffe muttered, fingering his ear lobe.

∾

It was a short time before supper when I knocked on Patrick's door. Doubtless he would share my outrage; I hoped he would approach his father in my support. At the very least, given his animosity towards Mother, he would be an ally.

He was seated in the casement watching Maeve and Anne on the lawn below hitting a ball between them with tennis rackets.

He made no comment at the sight of my tear-stained face, and when I gave him my news he returned to the scene below.

"Haven't you anything to say?" I cried.

"What would you have me say? I'm not surprised – why are you surprised? Besides, isn't this what all girls hope for?"

I stared at him in bewilderment. "I … I don't want to marry this … stranger. I thought … I *hoped* you might help me."

"Why would you think that? If I recall correctly, not two hours ago you were wagging a finger at me."

"You could speak to your father … I don't want to be married! Pat, I don't know what to do …" My voice ended on a mournful wail that even to my own ears sounded pathetic.

"How can I speak for you? As if anything I said would change matters."

"Couldn't you try? Please …?"

I gazed at him hopefully but he frowned in reply. "Look, you may be happy if you give this Lord Whatsit a chance."

"Hmph! I don't even know him."

"Come on, it's supper time. We'd best go downstairs." He rose and took my elbow, but I irritably pulled away.

"*Bastard!*" I muttered but he widened his eyes at me.

"Oh dear, such unladylike language."

He left his room and I thumped grumpily along behind him, all but bumping into him when he paused abruptly at the dining-room door. My head was aching dully from emotion, and my eyes were brimming again. Regarding me intently, he watched the emotions rising in my face, though his own was impenetrable.

With unexpected gentleness he brushed a stray hair from my cheek. "You're so young yet," he said, softly. "Be brave – betrothals are broken every day. Who knows what the future holds."

His sudden intimacy caught me by surprise, but there was no time to react. "Now," he wiped a tear away with his thumb, "happy face," and propelled me into the dining-room.

My brothers were returning to Oxford. They rode out a week later and we all, including Mother and Isabella, gathered on the porch to bid them farewell in the still, early-autumn morning. Simon came over to where I leaned against the balustrade.

Bending his head, he whispered, "Keep your eye on Anne, and look after yourself." He hugged me tightly before turning to our sister.

Mother and her friend needn't have bothered making an appearance for they huddled together on the porch, chattering like sparrows.

Patrick was laughing and trying to unwind Maeve's arms from his neck. With an effort, he extricated himself and turned to me. I was hugging my cloak tightly to ward off a stiff breeze.

"Alex," his leather-clad hands took mine. "You know I couldn't help you. When contracts are being settled ... others' opinions count for nought. Anything I might have added would not have helped."

"It is done now anyway," I said unhappily. "It is signed." I waved my hand dismissively. "But ... I have enjoyed your company this summer. I shall miss you." An uncomfortable flush crept up my neck.

"And I you. When you lower your quills you can be rather

agreeable." He added one of his wicked grins and kissed both my cheeks, then pulled me into a hug against his chest. He smelled of some spicy cologne, and I breathed it in, revelling in the strength of his arms about me. He released me abruptly and descended the porch steps, two at a time.

Simon had kissed Anne and Maeve and now sat on Oliver's broad back while Equus snorted and pawed the ground impatiently and nudged at Grace. She waited beside the elegant horse, her eager face was turned toward Patrick, and as he approached, he mouthed something that made the Italian girl snicker and colour hotly. Then, in full view of the gathering, he stood before her and raised her chin with his gloved finger. Her head fell back languidly, her eyelids fluttered down and he lowered his face to hers.

Patrick kissed Grace's mouth solidly, lingeringly, their lips moving together, and his hand plunged into her glorious mane to cup her head. Her arms coiled around his neck and they clung together, locked in a timeless lover's embrace.

My stomach lurched sickeningly. Not for a moment, after all the pleasant, companionable hours we'd spent together, had I suspected, and now I felt deeply betrayed.

Mother and Isabella had fallen silent with surprise, and Maeve whooped and squealed indelicately. Simon was grinning but Anne looked fit to commit murder. Her knuckles were clenched white and her eyes shot daggers at Grace.

Finally breaking apart, Grace smiled and flushed even deeper, pressing her cool hands to her cheeks. Patrick flicked a lascivious tongue over his lips causing renewed shrieks from his sister and, with a roguish wink to Grace, he swung easily into Equus' saddle, doffed his hat and joined Simon as they rode away.

That evening after supper, Mother and Isabella sipped Muscat from small gold-edged glasses, by the window. With heads bent together, they talked and laughed in whispers and I wondered how they could have so much to discuss.

Eleanor, of course, sat like a mannequin; seeing everything, saying nothing.

Maeve and Grace were sewing while Catarina and I quietly read. Catarina's book was in Italian and I could not even make out its title. My own book, *A Travelling Girl*, was the diary of a young woman working as a chamber maid to earn passage to New South Wales. There, she planned to be reunited with her father, who'd been transported for theft. I was fascinated by descriptions of that strange, distant land, populated by dark-skinned natives and exotic animals that kept their young in pockets in their fur.

A sudden squeal from the sofa raised my head. Maeve had caused Grace to glow pink with embarrassment.

"Grace and Patrick, Grace and Patrick!" she chanted. "Do you think he will ask for your hand?"

"We have not spoken of this," Grace pointed out uncomfortably.

"Perhaps he'll write a love letter, or a poem; Patrick writes wonderful poetry."

"He won't – don't bother getting your hopes up," Anne snapped with hostility. "He never writes – except to Maeve, that is."

"Simon said he will write to me," interjected Catarina confidently.

I snorted. "Simon says that to every girl. I wouldn't take it personally." All four heads swivelled in my direction and for perhaps the first time in our lives, Anne's eyes met mine in solidarity. Irritably, I snapped my book shut and gathered my things. "Bother it all, I'm to bed."

∾

Our Italian guests took their leave a couple of days later – rumbling out as they'd rumbled in, their coaches heavily laden with an excess of over-stuffed trunks. Travelling first to London, they planned to enjoy the season before sailing home around the coast of Spain and on to Italy.

Anne was strangely silent on the topic of joining them in London. I couldn't believe that she'd abandoned her campaign but something had definitely changed. In any case, the night before their departure, Isabella suggested that Anne, Maeve and I, spend the summer with the Camelleris at their villa near Sienna.

The dust had barely settled in their wake when Anne turned to Mother. "We will be allowed to go to Italy next summer, won't we Mother?"

"I thought you were going to London to be the favourite of the Prince of Wales?"

Anne laughed breezily, "Oh he'll still be there when I return."

"So you're really going to be the Prince's mistress, are you?" asked Maeve mockingly.

Anne wiggled her eyebrows in answer and her sister laughed. "Or I could marry Patrick. I'd be far better for him that poor quiet Grace. And he's to be the earl after your father – rich too."

Maeve narrowed her eyes speculatively as Anne continued, "Hmm. Wife to a future earl or mistress to a future king? Perhaps both."

Maeve grinned slyly then, "The Prince may not fancy you."

"Very funny, Maeve," Anne responded dismissively, but then noticed the teasing look on Maeve's face and said, "Oh, very well, Patrick would be a fine catch, but I shall explore my options." She playfully slapped Maeve's arm, "an earl may do well enough if I cannot snare a duke or a prince."

Mother cleared her throat delicately. "Alright girls, that's enough. You're getting on my nerves with this conversation. If you don't look out I shall marry the pair of you off to the next aged vagrants to pass our gate."

Unaccustomed to humour from Mother, we gaped at each other before exploding into laughter.

Later though, Mother watched Anne with interest and I knew instinctively she was planning the latest of her schemes.

CHAPTER 9

Mother poured a cup of tea for herself and took a sip. I stood patiently before her as she returned the cup to its saucer and looked up at me.

"Your betrothed is to pay a visit," she announced in her direct manner. "He will arrive tomorrow and will stay only for two days on his way through to London."

She paused for my response but when I remained silent, she continued. "You will behave yourself … comport yourself in a manner appropriate for a young lady. You will show due respect to Hamish throughout his visit."

She took up her knife and spread butter on a slice of bread. I think she expected I would return to the lesson she had summoned me from but instead I said, "Anything else?"

Frowning at my sarcasm, she glanced contemptuously at Jemima who stood beside me, swinging her tail amiably. "He does not like dogs."

∾

He arrived before dinner on a glossy bay gelding accompanied by a groom riding a second horse. Looking for all the world like a young dandy, he stood on our gravelled drive brushing the travel dust from his fine coat.

Lord Thorncliffe descended the porch stairs and proper greetings were exchanged before my husband-to-be was shown into the house.

Standing in the library window, I watched through a gap in the drapery. After he disappeared from view I flopped into a large over-stuffed chair, delaying the inevitable. The library door burst open.

"Alex! I've been looking all over – he's here!" Anne ran over and grabbed my hand. "He seems awfully nice … he's waiting for you. Come *on*."

I entered the drawing room, a wad of skirt clutched in my damp hand, and beheld a dark-haired and not-unpleasant-looking young man standing by the mantle. His expensively tailored coat seemed better suited to Whitehall than here in the country and, as he turned toward me, I was struck by the lack of warmth in his hard, black eyes.

"Thank you Anne, you may leave now," Mother said.

"Ah, Alex," Lord Thorncliffe stepped forward with a false smile painted on his face and made the introductions.

In his early twenties, Hamish was only slightly taller than me. His pale complexion seemed rather womanly to me and his expression of practiced boredom would not have been out of place in a fashionable London drawing-room. But he took my hand and brushed his boyish moustache over my fingertips with inflated courtliness. His hands were smooth and white, the nails clipped and manicured and, even in his youth, he carried a soft paunch, far removed from the hard, athletic physiques of my brothers.

I sensed caginess in him, and wondered if he also was uncertain about our betrothal. But he greeted me with dutiful politeness and said, "Pleased to meet you," in a pleasant Scots burr.

"Good, good," Lord Thorncliffe clapped him on the back. "Care for a wee dram – as they say in your parts, eh lad?"

"Aye, thank you My Lord," Hamish replied.

Mother and I were served plum wine, while Lord Thorncliffe poured two glasses of an amber liquid from a crystal decanter. Offering a glass to Hamish, he raised his own and toasted our families.

The conversation was painfully stilted but I made no effort to improve the tension. I replied to Hamish's questions with, "Yes, My Lord" or "No, My Lord", and no silent admonition from Mother would unbend my attitude.

Hamish, for his part, appeared equally unimpressed with me. How our parents could possibly consider this a good match was beyond me. Resolving to break the betrothal one way or another, I drained my wine and offered my glass to Lord Thorncliffe. Dutifully, he refilled it and I quaffed the second in one gulp, enjoying the fire in my throat and the dark flavour of aged summer fruit. The potent liquid went directly to my head and, regarding this entirely unsuitable young man through a tipsy haze, I began to snigger stupidly.

All three heads turned as one and of course Mother looked disapproving. I rearranged my face and presented my glass for another refill.

∾

"Would it be so very terrible to marry him?" Anne asked. We were watching from the parlour window as Hamish and his groom rode away.

The two days of his visit had passed reasonably quickly though Mother had engineered several opportunities for the two of us to be left unconventionally alone. His inane conversation and clear disinterest in me made the thought of marrying him even less attractive.

"I think he's perfectly beastly," Maeve commented from the settee. She hadn't even deigned to come to the window, and now she wrinkled her elfin nose distastefully, adding with a mock brogue, "Aye, and he simpers like a wee girlie."

Anne whirled about indignantly. "He does not. You're only jealous that he's not marrying you!"

Maeve snorted in response and pulled Missy on to her lap.

I turned away from the window. "If you like him so much, Annie, you have my blessing to steal my betrothed."

"Oh, would that I could," she cooed. "He has spent time at court with Prinnie – no wonder he's so charming."

"He talks only about himself and is far too vain and arrogant for me. But in any case, what of *your* plans for the Prince?" I asked, sarcastically.

"Mere whimsy. Oh, Alex, you don't know how lucky you are." She plopped on to the rug, her rose-satin skirt billowing around her, and sighed wistfully. "Hamish's family owns a castle. Oh, how I wish it were me marrying him."

"So do I," I said truthfully.

"He makes Simon and Patrick look like oafish farmers."

"He makes Simon and Patrick look like real men," Maeve interjected dryly.

Anne made a rude face. "Of course he's not like other men – he has something … oh, I don't know … he's different – you can tell straight off."

"And isn't that the first true word you've said on the subject," Maeve said. Holding Missy to her bosom and heedless of the white cat fur on her blue gown, she said, "You have my sympathy, Alex."

❧

Autumn turned to winter, and Christmas was only a month away. I missed my brothers terribly and tried not to wonder whether they corresponded with Grace and Catarina.

Much of my time was spent with Meg and Clara – reading, talking, engaged in nothing particularly constructive. It was during these tedious grey days that it occurred to me that this would be the pattern of my life, without a husband: an endless passage of time marked only by the changing seasons. Unpleasant as that thought was, I preferred the life of a spinster to life as wife of Lord Whatsit – as Patrick called him.

Nevertheless, in an effort to break the daily routine, I decided to visit Wolstone markets. I wanted to buy some suitable fabric to make Meg some clothes as she was growing so quickly. Since Mother was too busy with her social life, I spoke with Lord Thorncliffe who happily parted with enough coins to buy what I needed and something extra for myself.

Early one morning, bundled warmly in hats, gloves and scarves, Janet and I climbed into the coach. Dan, the stableman, harnessed our sturdy old chestnut, Jake, and with a whistle and a flick of the reins, we started out.

It seemed that everyone was going to Wolstone that day. It took longer than usual to get to Wharferidge and from there it wanted another half-hour to navigate the narrow lanes into Wolstone itself. We left Dan and Jake in an alley some quarter mile from the market and set out on foot.

The village was vibrant and bustling with pre-Christmas stalls selling everything from bolts of brightly coloured fabrics, ribbons and buttons, to freshly killed meats, dried fruits, winter vegetables, clucking hens with eggs. It was loud, and stinking, and exhausting as people from places like Ilkley, Rippon and beyond, came to sell or buy. A troupe of players made music that was all but drowned beneath the cacophony of vendors shouting to compete with one another, and shoppers haggling for a bargain.

Janet and I held each other's hand tightly to avoid being separated in the jostling crowd. Our progress was slow round the cobbled market square as we were carried along by the crush of people and animals.

After a couple of hours, we rested in a tea house over a pot of strong black tea, before braving the crowd once more to make our final purchases.

I bought several lengths of cotton and wool for Meg's clothes, and for myself, a mother-of-pearl comb for my hair – ever hopeful I'd find some miracle that would tame my unruly curls, ever doomed to disappointment.

I slipped a coin to Janet who bought herself a spool of plum-coloured wool. It was so soft that I bought another for Clara.

By early afternoon, the marketers had packed their stalls and the lowering clouds brought a sprinkling of snow. Returning to the coach with a packet of toffee for Dan, we found the fellow sleeping, sheltered in a nearby doorway. Old Jake stood on three legs, the forth cocked restfully, head hung low in a doze.

I shook Dan awake and he looked at me sheepishly. "I falled asleep Mistress, but ole Jake 'ere's alroight."

"So he appears. Here – I bought you some toffee."

The man's black eyes lit up delightedly. He bustled us into the coach and clambered into the driver's seat: I heard the toffee packet rustling. "Gerrup Jake," Dan called, his voice suspiciously thick.

It was a slow drive back to Broughton Hall for the snow was heavier now and visibility was poor. Finally pulling into the drive, Dan navigated directly to the stables. Old Jake had done a praiseworthy job and it was time for him to eat and rest and be warm. Leaving Dan to take care of things, Janet and I, weighed down by our many parcels, entered the house by way of the kitchen.

Jemima leapt up from her favourite mat by the fire to greet me as I dumped my purchases on the table.

"Yer'll be moving them right quick, won't yer," Cook stated immediately. "That's my workspace, that is – shove off.

I enjoyed Cook's irreverent ranting, though I hated to think how Mother would respond had she overheard.

"Keep your pinny on Cook, I'm just passing through. Oh Janet, did you happen to bring my hat? I think I've left it in the coach."

"You were definitely wearing it when we left Wolstone – shall I fetch it?"

"No, no – I'll go. Jemima won't mind a trot outside – come, girl."

Jemima bounced along happily beside me, glad of my return. Though Jake was now warmly settled in the stables, the coach stood outside my hat still on the seat where I'd left it. I grabbed it and was about to return to the house when Jemima bounded off in pursuit of something in the kitchen garden.

"Bother!" I muttered, and followed.

The snow had stopped but night was falling quickly. I trailed along a brickwork path between the rows of winter herbs and vegetables.

What could have attracted the dog's attention here? I thought I could see Jemima in the dim light, but suddenly heard a low moan from somewhere nearby. It was so vague I could not be certain if I had imagined it. Standing still and straining my ears, I peered into the gloom and was about to move off when it came again; breathy and pained, and close by.

Squinting, I thought I saw a movement on the ground and cautiously crept over.

There, lying on the snow, was Jane Carter, the kitchen-maid.

"Good heavens! Jane …?"

I hunkered down beside her as she moaned and seemed to be gripped with some kind of convulsion for she lay curled on her side, her hands pressed to her belly.

"Jane, what is it?"

"Oh Miss … ahh …" She was rocking with the pain, and I felt my helplessness keenly.

"What's wrong? Can you get up? Here …" I took her arms and tried to lift her but she gave an agonised cry. I released her immediately and it was then that I noticed the dark patch on the skirt of her blue maid's uniform.

"Is that … are you bleeding?"

The maid began to sob. Clutching her stomach, her body convulsed and the stain spread.

Her hands clawed at the fabric of her skirt. "Please … miss … 'tis the baby … ahh … 'tis coming away."

"You're with child!"

Fortunately, I was still wearing my travelling cloak. Quickly, I removed it and threw it over her for warmth. "I'll be back, Jane. Don't worry – I'll be as quick as I can."

She groaned in reply and I turned and ran back up the path, knowing immediately to whom I would go.

I clattered through the kitchen, "What about these boxes?" Cook shouted after me, but I continued heedlessly up the stairs, round the corner, more steps, another corner and down the hall to the grand staircase.

Taking the stairs two at a time I was breathless when I exploded like a whirlwind into Simon's office.

Lord Thorncliffe looked up from his bookwork in astonishment. "Good grief, Alex! Got the Hounds of Hell on your tail?"

I gasped out my story and he reacted without hesitation. "Dear, oh dear," he muttered as we hurried downstairs.

A dreadful thought occurred to me and I knew instinctively I was right. "I think it is Simon's," I said soberly.

"Simon, you say?" he puffed. "Dear, oh dear – you Broughtons! Seems we'll be running short on staff the way you go on. I've only just done with Jeffrey, and now another."

"Hurry, please."

"Yes, I'm coming … dear oh dear, seems you're the odd one out Alex, who's it to be for you then? Master Baxter?"

He laughed heartily at his own joke and I glared at him over my shoulder. "Ugh that's not even remotely funny – hurry!"

In the kitchen he instructed Cook briskly, "Go and tell Dan to make all haste to Doc Edwards at Warferidge. Tell him to take the best horse and ride like hell. Tell him, don't come back without the doctor."

I led my stepfather to where poor Jane lay moaning beneath my cloak. The man never faltered. He scooped her into his arms, puffing as he carried her towards the house. Even in the dark I could see the back of her maid's gown was sodden with blood – did a body contain so much?

As he carried her into the servants' quarters, I held the door and shielded her lolling head. By now the poor girl was mercifully out cold.

"Best your mother doesn't know about this, Lass – at least not yet." I nodded, fully aware that Mother would be apoplectic should she find out.

Later, in the study I sipped a glass of Cook's plum wine while Lord Thorncliffe downed a Scottish whisky in one gulp then refilled his glass.

Doc Edwards had explained that it was common for medical students to supplement their incomes by performing abortions on those who found themselves in an unwanted situation. Most of their customers were serving girls or the occasional married woman with too many mouths to feed already. Mishaps were not unusual and Doc Edwards suspected Jane had been in Wolstone during the day – markets attracted all types of traders.

Where the procedure was unsuccessful, it was generally due to either infection or, as in Jane's case, too little care being taken with the steel hook they used, resulting in haemorrhage.

Doc Edwards administered a vile-looking brew in an attempt to slow the blood-loss and, once Lord Thorncliffe assured him all costs would be covered, he'd also given her a dose of expensive laudanum to ease the pain.

"Sleep's what she needs now," he said as Lord Thorncliffe showed him to the door, "but the bleeding cannot continue. If it doesn't slow ..." he left, shaking his head.

Jane was not strong, and was physically worn out from her ordeal. As I sat on the leather settee in Simon's study, I sipped my wine thoughtfully. "Father?" I'd said it before I realised, yet it felt natural.

He looked up, and though his eyes were tired he smiled. "Yes, Lass?"

"Should I write to Simon and tell him?"

"What for?"

"Perhaps he will do something to help her," I said, adding, "if she recovers."

He shook his head. "Alex, it is a sad fact that young men do what young men do. Your brother, and Patrick for that matter, are no different to any others their age."

"But she could be dying."

"As do serving girls every day when their young and handsome masters begin to feel their oats – does not mean it's right, mind."

I shook my head in dismay.

He continued. "You could write to Simon, but what would you have him do? Marry her?" He laughed humourlessly. "This is not the way of the world."

"But if Simon knew …" I stopped. I was being terribly naive.

"He may give her money, and none would even expect that. This kitchen wench is not the first – nor will she be the last – to be in such a predicament. They all fall for the handsome young lord of the manor."

I sipped my liquor, the flavour of last summer's fruit full-bodied in my mouth, and stared into the sinking fire.

"I think I'll go to bed," I said wearily. "It's past one o'clock."

"So it is. I shall finish this dram and retire myself."

I looked at this man, to whom, in the crisis this evening, I had immediately turned knowing he would do what was right; compassionately and discreetly.

"Good night, Father." I bent and placed a small kiss on the spot on his forehead where his hair was still thick and blond.

He took my hand and gently squeezed it. "Goodnight Lass. You did well coming to me tonight."

∾

Jane lingered, a pale husk on her little bed. Doc Edwards visited again but was unable to stem the flow of blood. All the following day she lay in delirium, weeping and calling Simon's name as her life drained from her. Finally, as the sun dipped behind the trees in the west, she slipped away.

By now, Mother had been informed and was appalled that such an event had occurred under our roof. She ranted and raved about servants bringing the family into disrepute, and then having the audacity to die — not even giving her employers the satisfaction of sending her home in disgrace.

Jane's brothers arrived to take her body home to bury in the local churchyard beside her grandparents. Lord Thorncliffe received them as distinguished guests, not the rustic siblings of a servant. He took them to Simon's study, called for brandy and when they departed twenty minutes later, their pockets were considerably heavier and their brows less furrowed.

The womenfolk of Broughton Hall watched from the parlour as the horse and cart departed with its sad burden. After seeing them off, Lord Thorncliffe came into the room.

"I don't believe it, Gerrard!" Mother roared so heartily I thought the ceiling would lift off. "How could you pay them money? She was a *servant*! A *nobody*!"

"She was sending money home to her family — they relied on it"

"So, they had their slice of her, why give them more?"

Lord Thorncliffe, ordinarily so quietly spoken, suddenly raised his voice. "Your son, Madam," he poked his finger at Mother across the fireplace. "Your son did this. And the girl died!"

"Oh Gerrard don't be so naive — as if Simon was the only one she's lain with. It could have been any of the male servants here

– or Patrick – what about your precious son? He's not fussy as to whom he beds – all over Wolstone I've heard – yet immediately you assume it was Simon's brat."

"Don't you bring my son into this!" Lord Thorncliffe warned with eyes blazing.

Anne, Maeve and I sat frozen in fascinated horror, afraid to move lest we remind our parents we were in the room and witnessing the scene. Mother jumped up from her chair and they faced off. "Well, why not? You said yourself he's lucky to still be allowed to stay at that university."

Gerrard shrugged, exactly the way I'd seen Patrick do. "The girl claimed it was Simon's child and that's enough for me."

"Those people, they breed like vermin. They –"

"Enough!" Gerrard declared. "It's finished … over. The girl is dead and her family paid." He suddenly looked tired. "It is done now." With that, he announced he had business in Leeds and needed to pack some things. We didn't see him again for a month.

CHAPTER 10

The apple and plum trees in the orchard were looking skeletal. It was a colder than usual winter and we gathered frequently round a glowing, hot fire. Mother had received a letter from Isabella renewing her invitation for us to visit Italy.

"I shan't go," Mother said, over the rim of her tea cup. "But you girls may if you wish."

"You could ensnare a nice Mediterranean count, Anne," Maeve teased.

"I prefer to aim my arrow a little higher," my sister retorted.

"Not in keeping with your dalliances in the woods," I muttered *sotto voce*.

"Like Patrick," she said and made a face at me.

Mother eyed her, thoughtfully. "So *do* you want to go to Italy, Anne?"

"Oh yes," Anne laughed. "Italy has more to offer than Mediterranean counts."

"Like what?" scoffed Maeve. "Other than men and money, what could possibly interest you anywhere?"

"The Colosseum," Anne replied looking affronted.

"That's in Rome, Isabella lives in Sienna," Maeve said.

"And they don't have horses in Italy?"

"Girls, stop it!" Mother interrupted. "I shall reply that you accept Isabella's invitation – it would be good for you. And I shall ask Gerrard to speak with his banker about an allowance for each of you."

"*Marvy!*" Maeve cried, clapping her hands, then sobered suddenly. "But what about Alex?"

Before I could respond, Mother said, "I don't consider it appropriate for Alexandra to go." She turned to me, "You are betrothed – your place is here learning to run a household. Don't look like that   it's not for discussion."

I sighed resignedly. I might have known Mother would see it that way.

❧

The first of the heavy winter snows arrived on the twentieth day of December. That same day, Simon arrived home for Christmas – alone.

I had been reading in the library, curled up in my favourite chair by the window above the front porch, when a much trimmer Oliver trotted up the drive. Simon offered a cheery salute when he saw me looking down and I quickly discarded my book to rush downstairs and greet him.

He looked well and relaxed, though mud-spattered from his journey, and he scooped me into a great hug. "Where're the others?" he asked, looking about and returning me to my feet.

"Mother is in Leeds visiting the Oxenburys. Maeve and Anne are practicing their singing with Mistress Banholme."

"Mistress Banholme?"

"Vocal tutor – apparently Anne shows great promise and Maeve is terrible." He laughed and took my arm as we went into the house.

Unable to endure the suspense, I asked as casually as possible, "Where's Patrick?"

"You don't know? Typical – said he'd write."

I shook my head, my heart sinking. "What don't I know?"

"He's spending Christmas in London with Grace."

My stomach lurched and Simon looked at me curiously. "You alright?"

"Oh yes. You hungry?" I quickly regained my composure. "Go and wash and change your clothes – you're filthy – I'll send for refreshments and let Father know you're here – he's just returned from Leeds for Christmas."

❧

Simon quaffed his brandy as one accustomed to strong liquor and refilled his glass. Turning, he held the bottle aloft in invitation. Lord Thorncliffe accepted and Simon said, "So …" as he returned the bottle to the sideboard, "What news? How's Meg doing?"

"She has Clara twined about her little finger," I said proudly."

"Not only Clara, by the look in your eye. And the tenants, the staff, anything I should take care of while home?"

Lord Thorncliffe and I exchanged uncertain glances and Simon frowned. "What?"

"Jane Carter." I said simply, waiting to see if he reacted.

"Jane? What about her?" His handsome face was open and unsuspecting.

"You *do* remember her, don't you?" I asked facetiously.

"Don't, Lass," Gerrard said gently. "She's dead, Simon."

My brother's face froze. "How … what do you mean?"

"You got a bastard on her, Son. She tried to get rid of it …"

My brother cursed softly and dropped heavily on to a chair, running his hands through his hair. I was gratified that he didn't question the child's paternity and thus tarnish the girl's reputation further. "Was it bad for her?" He addressed Lord Thorncliffe.

"Yes. And it was bad for your sister too. Alex found her in the garden. The poor girl lingered a day, then slipped away."

"I didn't know …"

"Of course you didn't, Son. And what would you've done if you did?" He placed his hand on Simon's bowed head. "But you can't go through life … well, you must be mindful, that's all."

"What about her … body?"

"Her brothers took her home. They were relying on her income, you see, so I gave them some money – a year's wages, from the estate's cash tin."

Simon nodded his approval.

"Simon –" I began but he rounded on me defensively.

"Don't say a word, Zan, just don't! I feel badly enough as it is."

Anne and Maeve were overjoyed that Simon was at home. Maeve, disappointed that Patrick hadn't returned, was nonetheless excited to learn that her brother was courting someone, "Even if it is quiet little Grace," she said.

On the other hand, Anne wondered loudly and derogatorily what Patrick could possibly find of interest in such a mouse.

The next day, when Mother returned from the Oxenburys, she was equally displeased by Patrick's liaison and demanded that Lord Thorncliffe write to his son. "You should make him aware that he is to be matched with Anne."

Her husband, reading a newspaper, seemed as surprised as the rest of us.

The paper twitched slightly and he said from behind it, "I didn't think the matter settled, Miriam."

Simon, tinkering quietly on the piano, did not falter but he wore a frown when he looked across at Mother. Maeve's face registered her surprise, but strangely, Anne's expression was quite composed and rather smug.

"Patrick may have other plans, Mother," Simon said calmly, his fingers moving easily over the keyboard.

"He is to inherit an earldom; it is not his right to have plans."

"Still, he may think otherwise."

Mother waved her hand dismissively. "With Alexandra wed to Elginbury in Scotland, and Anne to Patrick, the family will benefit immensely. Patrick has a responsibility to perform his familial duty. Isn't that so, Gerrard?" she challenged.

"Napoleon has divorced Josephine," Lord Thorncliffe announced irrelevantly.

"Gerrard, this is very important, you could at least pay attention," Mother said with irritation.

"Yes, yes – but listen to this …" Lord Thorncliffe scanned the article he was reading. "It was … somewhere … er … yes, as part of the prenuptial arrangement," he read,

> *the former Madame Bonaparte leaves the marriage with only her personal wardrobe which consists of the following; some six hundred and seventy dresses, nearly fifty court gowns, over four hundred pairs of stockings, nearly eight hundred pairs of slippers, two hundred and fifty hats, some sixty cashmere shawls and nearly five hundred chemises. The lady may find herself a divorcee, but certainly well dressed.*

Lord Thorncliffe folded the newspaper with finality.

"Hmph," grunted Mother, "and you thought *I* had too many gowns."

"That's probably why he divorced her," Simon commented dryly.

Lord Thorncliffe chuckled appreciatively.

"Gerrard, you *must* discuss your son's responsibilities with him," Mother pressed again. Eleanor, seated in the corner, was following the discourse with interest. We often overlooked her for she rarely spoke. Her face was pinched like one with a perpetual sniff and her almond eyes were sharp, missing nothing.

"Rest assured, he is fully aware of his responsibilities."

"We have an opportunity to maintain this family's fortune within our own, it should be —"

"Madam," Lord Thorncliffe's amiable face suddenly flushed, "when I peg it, the title, the inheritance, and the decision, will be Patrick's."

"But, Gerrard we've discussed this and —"

"I know we've discussed it — we've discussed it to death — but I'm not prepared to lock my son into a contract. Let an arrangement with Anne be a loose understanding for now — without contract." Mother opened her mouth but Lord Thorncliffe went on, "If Patrick chooses to marry Anne — by his own decision — he will have my blessing. Equally, if he chooses Grace or anyone else, he will have my blessing."

He rose, handing his newspaper to Anne who scanned it quickly for further news of Josephine.

But Mother was persistent. "You cannot be serious, we —"

"I could not be more serious. A loveless marriage? Shackled in a mismatched partnership? You may engineer such a future for your daughters, Madam, but you may not for my son. More strength to Napoleon, I say. Good night all."

Lord Thorncliffe returned to Leeds the next day and Mother went to York to spend Christmas with friends.

Thus Yuletide came and went and soon it was 1811. Simon and I spent many pleasant afternoons before the fire in the library simply enjoying the quietude. One afternoon, as he pored over a medical book, I watched his handsome profile as he studied the anatomical diagrams, and pondered what the future held for a man like my brother.

"Sime?"

"Hmm?"

"What will you do when you finish at the university? I mean, what's it all for? You don't need to work for your living."

He closed the book and thought for a long time before answering. Finally, he said, "I originally thought it would be a worthy vocation, to be a physician … help people. But I'm beginning to think that's a bit whimsical."

"Whimsical?" I gnawed the inside of my cheek.

"I want to contribute. I thought medicine would be a way of doing that."

"Isn't it?"

He shook his head. "I've been thinking about a different direction and … well Zan, you're not going to like it, but now is as good a time as any to tell you."

Feeling somewhat uneasy, I waited.

"I plan to enlist in the army as a medical officer."

It was worse than I expected. "Oh, Simon – *why*? You don't need to join the army to contribute – you can contribute here." The broad sweep of my arm indicated our estate and lands beyond.

"I don't want to treat upset bellies and children with running noses. I want to contribute to England's future. Medical officers are in great demand."

Breathing slowly, I modulated my voice to control myself. "What if I asked you to stay?"

He patted my knee affectionately as he rose from his chair. "Then I would be forced to disappoint you."

"Oh! Men and their wars!" I cried in exasperation, and he laughed and kissed the top of my head.

"See you at supper."

I stared into the flickering fire for several minutes before seeking distraction in taking up a discarded newspaper.

Turning to the social pages, I read an article about the Prince of Wales' latest favourite and a description of her gown when she attended a ball last week. I snorted derisively and scanned the opposite page – a single word leapt out at me, *Thorncliffe*. With my heart in my throat, I read:

… next in line to inherit the Earldom of Thorncliffe, has been seen often with the young lady around the theatres and more expensive restaurants in the Capital. The demure Senorina Grace Camelleri would seem an unlikely match for the spirited Lord, but the two young people seem to be enjoying one another's company, causing this observer to ask: is an announcement in the wind?

At Mrs Perceval's charity reception Monday last, an unidentified lady was overheard to comment on the First Lady's choice of centrepiece. Certainly the tables …

With my mind reeling and my mouth going dry, I sat thinking. Of course, Simon had told me about Grace and Patrick, but seeing it in print, their mutual interest publicly confirmed, gave me quite a jolt.

I was still staring into the fire when Janet called me to supper.

Simon departed for Oxford the next morning and later the same day Mother returned from York and dropped several of the latest Almack's editions – showing the fashion predictions for summer in Europe – on a table before Anne and Maeve. The two fell on them with cries of delight and immediately began planning their wardrobes for the trip to Italy.

Accompanied by Mother and Eleanor, they set out for a week-long shopping expedition, leaving me alone in the house, apart from Meg and the servants.

Rather than daunt me, I enjoyed the tranquillity of the house without Anne's unrelenting self-absorption and Maeve's boundless energy. The snows had now melted enabling me to wander the gardens, which were bursting into fragrant and colourful new life. And in Mother's absence, other previously *inappropriate* pursuits became available; like spending an afternoon floured to the elbows as I helped Cook to bake bread and cakes. Later, sitting round the battle-scarred kitchen table, Janet, Cook and I sipped hot tea and tasted the results of my efforts. It was unanimously agreed that my cooking skills surpassed my dancing skills – but only just.

The time passed pleasantly until the afternoon of the sixth day as Janet, Clara and I, with Meg playing happily at our feet, watched the spring rain dribble down the parlour windows.

We were each sampling a glass of Lord Thorncliffe's finest brandy from tiny crystal glasses, when Mother's coach rolled up the drive. My companions quickly returned to their work, while I sighed resignedly.

Anne and Maeve tumbled into the house, loud and excited and eager to show me their purchases and, despite my declarations of disinterest, my face turned a perfect shade of green as they modelled their neat little leather shoes, day-gowns, afternoon-gowns, ball-gowns, bonnets, and delicate lacy underthings. Mother had even engaged a maid to travel with them and assist with their clothing and personal needs.

Trapped and stifled by my inability to control my own destiny, I grumped through the house. If only I could take a horse and ride to London, or attend university like Simon and Patrick. Some women did go to university, but they were considered less than feminine and the best I could hope for was a ladies' finishing school – unlikely given my betrothal.

I missed Simon terribly, though it didn't compare with the way I pined for Patrick. I wondered why he'd never written – not even to tell me of his courtship of Grace. At the time of his leaving, the bridge between us had stood on firm foundations yet he'd told me nothing of his affection for Grace, and that betraying kiss hurt like nothing I'd experienced before.

As the corridors of Broughton Hall rang with my sisters' excitement, I saw my future stretch before me as a long, empty road. No forks to offer choice, no hills to challenge, no bends to intrigue, and having met Hamish and seen for myself that he was not possessed of two heads, I hardly dared admit, even to myself, that this marriage may well be my only prospect for diversion.

By arrangement, Isabella Camelleri's groom arrived to escort Anne and Maeve to Italy. They departed early one morning amid the bustle of scurrying servants and impatient horses. Missy endured the indignity of once again being crammed into a travel crate and placed on the seat beside Tilly, the new maid. Missy's mews of protest could be heard above the snorting of the horses and the energised chatter of the two travellers.

I stood on the porch beside Lord Thorncliffe, who'd returned from Leeds specially to see them off, and Mother stood on his other side.

When the coach disappeared round the bend in the drive, Lord Thorncliffe and Mother went indoors. Jemima came trotting round the side of the house – from where she'd been diverted with kitchen scraps from Cook – and we walked together down the stairs to the orchard.

The buds had burst and tiny new leaves were fluttering in the slight breeze. I strolled, oblivious of the early morning dew dampening the hem of my gown, following the stone wall dividing our land from Jackson's. A strong animal scent wafted across – a harem of black-saddled cows for the supercilious resident bull.

Once, I looked back toward Broughton Hall. It was just visible between the trees – pretty, pale-butter stone in the watery morning light. Though smaller than most homes of court ladies and gentlemen, it stood proudly overlooking prosperous lands, healthy tenants and beautiful fields. I loved this house – it was all I knew.

Yet I wondered why Mother and Gerrard did not live on Lord Thorncliffe's estate in Devon. According to Maeve, it was as enormous as a palace. I assumed Lord Thorncliffe was content to leave the running of the Devon estate to his steward, and to Patrick when he was there.

Patrick.

I sighed with the futility of what I recognised was an infatuation centred on my stepbrother – it was foolish and immature; evidenced my lack of worldly experience. If Patrick knew of my feelings, he would tease me mercilessly for an unsophisticated country rabbit, and he would be right.

❧

I turned 17 years that May and Janet asked Cook to bake my favourite honey cakes for the occasion. Simon sent a note from Oxford wishing me a happy day and a postcard arrived from Anne and Maeve in Sienna. My sisters described how they had settled into their new surroundings – which was to the delight of local swains eager to meet the two English girls. I could well imagine the bombardment of invitations to soirees, parties and balls, and Anne would be entirely in her element.

My envy knew no bounds, and then, unexpectedly, something exciting happened.

Lord Thorncliffe, Mother, Eleanor and I, were enjoying a balmy, late spring evening beneath the Great Oak when Lord Thorncliffe suggested we journey to Devon for the summer.

Mother wrinkled her small nose distastefully. "Good heavens, Gerrard. Why would we go traipsing over the countryside just as the summer is about to descend upon us?"

"Because, m'dear, I believe you'll find the warmer months rather more tolerable on the coast."

Mother sipped her plum wine and considered the idea for some minutes.

"I think it's a lovely idea," I said, hopefully.

"Well, there's certainly nothing to do here." Mother's expression was apathetic. "How long would it take to get there, do you think?"

"Good roads; ten days, perhaps less."

"Will Patrick pass the summer there?" I asked as innocently as I could.

Mother pursed her lips and studied me. "How you manage to get along with that boy escapes me."

Lord Thorncliffe ignored his wife. "I believe so. He's unlikely to spend summer in London."

"And Grace?" I ventured.

"I don't know. Maeve wrote from London before she and Anne left Southampton. She'd seen them together but he'd only said he was not returning to the university."

"You didn't tell me that!" Mother interjected.

"I don't tell you everything, m'dear."

"Evidently … so much for paying those exorbitant fees."

"It's his choice."

"The boy has too many choices. You must talk with him, Gerrard. The match with Anne – it's perfect."

"I did mention it once," her husband fingered his ear lobe. "I wrote. He didn't reply, but he's never been one to correspond."

I breathed evenly and adopted a look of disinterest.

"Well?" Mother persisted. "You must admit – it *is* perfect, the match with Anne."

"Ah yes, it would be an excellent match, but it's his choice – I've said it before. Besides, he's young – give the boy time."

"Time for what? For some peasant to hold a pistol to his head because his slattern daughter is pregnant with your son's bastard?"

"Shall we go to Devon?" I interrupted, looking hopefully at Lord Thorncliffe.

He too was eager to change the subject and turned away from Mother. She sighed petulantly, and he ignored her, "Pack your things. We shall leave at daybreak, the day after tomorrow."

∾

The trip was tedious. Made worse by the forced confinement and having to share the coach with Mother and Eleanor, and endure their incessant gossiping. I wished fervently that I could ride on horseback, or even atop with the drivers, Dan and Giles, enjoying the rolling midland countryside. Portly Lord Thorncliffe, growing ruddy in the sun beneath his hat, was astride Canto, a necessarily-sturdy chestnut thoroughbred.

I lowered the window and hung my head outside, breathing the scent of verdant pastures dotted with sheep and cattle, and swaying new wheat.

"Sit back Alexandra and show your breeding," Mother snapped, spoiling my small pleasure. I settled once more beside Janet, whose head lolled against the velvet headrest – mouth open, snoring.

Mother had demanded that Jemima should remain behind and already I missed her.

We stayed at inns along the way, where the innkeepers fawned over their exalted guests – an earl and his countess, no less – and provided excellent service. I was unused to such obsequiousness and was rather uncomfortable.

Our final night was in a small place called Taunton. The innkeeper sent a boy to Waterville on our behalf to herald our pending arrival. Rising early the next day, we broke our fast and set out on the last leg of our journey, finally approaching Lord Thorncliffe's grand house, as the sun moved beyond its apex.

I first glimpsed Waterville Place, glowing pink and gold in the westering sun, through the trees in the park. It took a full 15 minutes to drive from the gate to the house, and it took my breath away with its sheer size and beauty. The main section consisted of two storeys, and it had symmetrical three-storey wings. An enormous dome rose above the roofline like a jewel in a crown, glittering in the afternoon sun and hinting at a large cathedral-like ceiling. A leering griffin hung over the main entrance, keeping a check on visitors.

The gardens, on either side of the gravel drive, were closely clipped and ablaze in reds, pinks, yellows and oranges, and two or three armless marble statues in flowing Grecian robes were partially hidden behind shrubbery or trees.

Janet and I sat in open-mouthed awe, feasting on the splendour – I'd had no idea Lord Thorncliffe was this wealthy. No wonder Mother cast her eye on him!

Our coach looped a white marble fountain that chortled and bubbled welcomingly and, as we drew up, two liveried lads ran to assist with the horses. Lord Thorncliffe threw his reins to one of them as he dismounted, with a grunt of relief.

A footman opened the door and the steps were unfolded, and Lord Thorncliffe handed Mother down. Eleanor followed and I made a face behind her back that caused Janet to snort as we emerged beneath a fine, columned portico.

A pair of enormous iron-bound double doors, the height of the portico – some three yards – opened on well-greased hinges, as a stream of servants spilled out to form two neat rows. A butler was standing to attention at the head of one column. He now approached Lord Thorncliffe and spoke crisply, "Welcome home, My Lord."

"Thank you, Leonard," Lord Thorncliffe responded, then proceeded to walk the lines of his staff – there were at least twenty of them – like a general inspecting his troops. The males nodded, the females bobbed respectfully, and there were genuine smiles and murmurs of, "good day, My Lord", and "welcome home, My Lord".

He returned their greetings and chucked one thin, little maid under the chin. She blushed up at him and he grinned, "Hello Sylvie."

"Hello My Lord. It is good to see you, My Lord," she responded pleasantly. She tucked a stray silver-blond strand of hair beneath her cap, and I experienced the queer feeling of having seen her before.

Turning, Lord Thorncliffe formally introduced Mother to his household. The new countess acknowledged their bows and curtsies with an imperious air before gliding past, issuing instructions over her shoulder for someone to attend to her trunks.

Without waiting for Lord Thorncliffe's directive, Mrs Bath, introduced as the head housekeeper, wagged her finger at a pretty maid who broke ranks and hurried to follow Mother as she disappeared through the grand doors. Eleanor, as always close on

Mother's heels, levelled a frown at the girl, ensuring the maid knew her place.

Turning to me, Mrs Bath said, "This is Sylvie," indicating the pale-haired maid. "She will show you to your room and take care of your needs." She smiled at Sylvie and added, "Newly-elevated from below stairs, Miss, and still learning."

Sylvie dropped a little curtsy. "Please come, Miss."

I followed Sylvie through the large doors into an entry hall. The panelling on the walls was old and dark, and smelled of lemon and beeswax, and I breathed deeply, enjoying the fresh scent. Doors on either side led to formal waiting rooms and a small parlour but Sylvie pushed a weighty panelled door directly before us and stood apart to allow me to pass into a huge, circular foyer.

So unprepared was I for the magnificence of this room, that my breath caught in my throat. It was like being within a huge kaleidoscope. The walls were tiled with a million slivers of fractured mirror and multi-coloured glass. Palms and ferns in shiny enamelled bowls stood at intervals round the walls and a marble stand with a bust of some long-departed ancestor was the centrepiece. In awe, I turned a full circle, seeing myself reflected from a hundred shattered angles, and the candles – flickering in a chandelier suspended high above – threw a dazzling display of sparks. The ceiling was the great dome I'd seen from outside, though I hadn't noticed the colours before. Gazing up – as the afternoon sun darkened the greens, blues, reds and yellows – I drew in my breath and knew myself to be wondrously trapped in a prism of shifting light and colour. I could never have imagined such a magical, hypnotic room.

"They call this the atrium," said Sylvie softly, and her voice bounced sibilantly off the walls. She waited as I stared in wonder, before finally pushing open a mirrored panel between two palms to reveal an ante-room and grand staircase. "This way please, Miss."

This room was sparsely furnished but other rooms opened off it, through whose open doors I saw velvet-upholstered couches and chairs in the same wine-colour as the Thorncliffe livery. A great staircase dominated and I followed Sylvie as she ascended to the second floor, which was a long gallery running the width of the house between the two wings with windows looking north over the drive and formal gardens, and south over beautiful sweeping lawns punctuated with geometric garden beds. Sylvie turned towards the east and said over her shoulder, "Your room is in the guest wing."

I paused to take in the south view over the expanse of lawns and gardens. "There is a lake out there," the maid commented following my gaze. "I've seen the young lord swim his horse there. Follow me please, Miss Alex."

I liked this girl. She was relaxed and pleasant, respectful but with a quiet dignity of her own. Her speech was educated too, not touched with the loose accent common among the locals.

We arrived at the eastern end of the gallery before another flight of stairs. They led to the third floor wing that looked towards the front and side of the house and afforded a view of the lengthy drive and colourful gardens. Opening a door, Sylvie showed me into a lovely spacious room dominated by an enormous and most luxurious-looking bed. The posts were carved, dark wood, with a padded headboard of plush burgundy-velvet to match the curtains at the expansive windows, beside which a lounge chair and footstool, similarly upholstered, were positioned to perfectly capture the morning sun.

The room also contained a writing desk, an upright leather chair, and a wash-basin with a ewer of fine, white porcelain with pink and blue roses chasing round their rims.

A wardrobe stood against one wall, and adjacent were a chest of drawers and a dresser on which sat three delicate crystal ornaments; a trinket box through which I could see something pink, a gently ticking crystal clock, and a little vase containing a single apricot rose. Carefully, I opened the trinket box to find it full of variegated dried rosebuds.

"Will there be anything more, Miss?"

Quite spellbound, I merely shook my head.

Alone in that lovely room, I twirled with arms outstretched and laughed for sheer happiness. What a splendid house! What a beautiful room! I hadn't enough superlatives to describe it, but I was enchanted. Additionally, knowing that Patrick lived here brought a telling lightness to my heart.

The afternoon sun did not touch this room so it remained cool and pleasantly rose-scented during the warmer part of the day. I moved to the window and looked out. Just below to my left I could see the circular drive and fountain. My eyes trailed down the drive until it disappeared into an alley of trees skirting the woods. Beyond there, was the lumpy canopy of the forest we had driven through for the last hour of our journey.

A bowl of rose petals rested on the window-ledge that was wide enough to sit on. All in all, I'd never seen such grandness, such magnificence, and I breathed deeply and with great pleasure to know that this would be my room for the summer. I felt like royalty.

A knock startled me and my heart leapt – he'd come!

"Come in." I held my breath and prepared my smile.

"Over by the dresser." Janet marched in, instructing the burly men bringing my trunk. My disappointment must have shown on my face for she frowned. Closing the door after the men, she said, "My Lord Thorncliffe said the young lord is at Astor – some business or other. I heard him telling Lady Thorncliffe."

"You shouldn't listen to their conversation."

"If I hadn't, you'd still be waiting for him to knock on your door," she responded smartly and I glared at her.

"You're such a git sometimes, Janet."

She turned to begin unpacking my clothes. "They have an old French chef here. Grumpy as all-get-out, but apparently brilliant. Supper will be in two hours."

Suddenly heavy with fatigue, I yawned. "I think I'll rest. Can you wake me before supper? You'll have to show me the way, this place is like Versailles."

∽

"The dining room is only used when dignitaries visit," Janet told me pompously as she showed me into a cosy meals room. It was a charming room, with an informally laid table that would have seated a dozen people with ease. I couldn't imagine what the formal dining room was like. But this room had French-doors that were open to allow a breeze into the room. Outside was a tiled porch where rattan furniture and views over the gardens tempted diners to eat *al fresco*.

I caught a glimpse, in the distance beyond the gardens, of the lake that Sylvie had mentioned earlier.

Lord Thorncliffe was already tucking into a meal of vegetables and cold meats.

"Settled in?" he asked, with a full mouth.

"Yes, thank you."

"Your Mother is resting and won't be joining us – try the greens, they're delicious. Do you like your room?"

"Oh yes, it's luxurious. I love it."

"Excellent!" he said with his usual enthusiasm. "Do you know, in the mornings, that room is flooded with lovely golden sunshine – nice and warm when you get out of bed."

I nodded appreciatively and filled my plate from the variety of bowls and platters laid before me.

"And," my stepfather went on, "the last person to sleep in your room was none other than the Lady Margaret Salisbury when poor old Mad George and the court came here some years back."

I managed to look suitably impressed without knowing who Margaret Salisbury was. "This place … it's so beautiful. Why do you and Mother prefer living in Yorkshire?"

"It is your Mother's preference – she has her friends, her social life. But in truth, this house is Patrick's – passed to him when his Grandfather died."

I stared at him in surprise.

He went on, "The house, the village, the lands – all of it – belonged to his Mother's father. Place is entailed to the eldest male. When the old chap moved on, it passed to Patrick since there were no other males in the family. He's young still, so technically it's in my care until he reaches his majority, but he's sensible." He shrugged cheerfully. "He's also very responsible but don't tell your mother, eh." He winked and forked a piece of ham into his mouth.

"But your title?"

"Goes back a long, long way – back to the first kings. The lad will have my title, and my lands as well, of course."

I applied myself to my food, lost in thought. "Father, if this house never belonged to your family … I mean …" my voice trailed off uncomfortably, but he threw his bear-like head back and laughed heartily.

Recovering with a ruddy face he said,"You're wondering why I'm said to be so rich when I don't own this place?" He put his fork down. "There's more than this house, Lass. I have three houses in London; a factory and a row of shops, also in London; another house in Oxford, which is where Pat and Simon stay when they're at the university.

I also have lands and a draughty old castle in Scotland – legacy of a barbaric Scottish relative several hundred years ago, but currently inhabited by hairy highland sheep. There is a manor house with land and tenants in Cumbria, another in Essex with a village attached, half a dozen villages in the Midlands, another two down here in Devon, one of which is where Pat is now."

I tried not to look too overawed as the list went on, "There are businesses – a couple of trading ships sailing between London, the ports of Europe, and the africas; a half-share in a steel works up north, with a village housing the workers and their families," he nodded to himself, mentally checking off a list, "Oh and there are the two estates and land in Ireland that were part of my late wife's dowry, and will now be Maeve's portion."

"So, you are rich," I quipped brightly.

"Filthy," he said with no hint of the braggart, and we were both laughing as we returned to our meals.

❦

My first night at Waterville, I slept solidly and rose the next morning before the crystal clock on my dresser struck six o'clock. Washed and dressed, I slipped downstairs and made directly for the atrium.

Alone in that magical room, I allowed my senses to swim in a kaleidoscope of rainbow morning light. My heels tic … ticked brightly on the marble floor as I whirled in mesmerised delight with my arms outstretched, breathing deeply and engorged with colour.

At length, dizzy and euphoric, I moved on, emerging into the clean, crisp morning and inhaled the tang of the distant sea. The raked gravel drive was bordered by a box-hedge, clipped low enough to allow a view across the neat lawns and lush clusters of flowering shrubbery.

At the side of the house, a meandering path led to a high stone wall draped with climbing apricot-coloured roses. Their sweet, dew-damp scent lingered headily, and my footfalls on the gravel sounded loud in the silence of the morning. A wrought iron gate in the wall opened smoothly to reveal the kitchen garden. The soft fragrance of the roses gave way to the earthy, honest smells of herbs and vegetables; spinach, silver beet and carrots, cabbages and turnips, parsley, thyme, chives and sage, tempered by the peaty smell of damp soil and animal manure.

The door to the kitchens stood open nearby and I could hear the clatter of pans and a rhythmic chop-chop. Like a wild animal,

I lifted my nose to the tantalising aromas of frying onions, sausage, and baking bread hanging in the air.

A large greenhouse, its windows trickling with condensation, occupied a corner of the garden. A cheerfully tuneless whistle came from within, and not wishing to disturb, or be disturbed, I went to a wooden door set into the garden wall, lifted its latch and pushed, finding myself at the rear of the house.

Flawless as the finest handspun rug, the lawns sloped gently to where the lake lay partially hidden behind a tangle of greenery — rhododendron, hawthorn and dog roses. A stand of beeches framed the lake, above which a cloud of mist hovered hauntingly. Glancing over my shoulder, my breath caught in admiration of the wide expanse of this beautiful mansion with its tiled porch and large French doors and sunlight glancing off its gun-metal slate roof.

The lawns stretched further than they appeared and it was several minutes before I stood beside the lake. At the edge of the shrubbery, I followed a path through the overhanging branches and early-morning birdsong. Shifting and rippling, the surface broke with the movement of small, grey fish leaping to catch low flying insects, and as I watched, a cormorant dived into the water. His sleek body shimmered like a mirage beneath the surface until he emerged quite some distance away, with water streaming from his smooth lines, an unfortunate fish flapping in his bill. Continuing my walk, I ducked beneath the dripping strands of willow branches and stepped over the grey-green foliage of a catmint whose tiny blue flowers were spilling on to the path. Here, the walkway widened as it approached a pretty summer-house, complete with a wooden deck jutting over the water.

It was an octagonal, whitewashed wooden structure with blue shutters to admit a cooling breeze on a warm day. The door squeaked softly as I entered.

A padded bench lined its walls, affording a view outside, and a low table stood in the middle of the floor with a dried arrangement in its centre. A cabinet was against a wall with an assortment of books and London journals stacked on its shelves. From a window I could see a group of ducklings with their mother paddling through the rushes below.

Latching the door securely after me, I continued wandering towards the lawns, around the trees and shrubs. The hem of my yellow-cotton dress was already sodden and the new morning sun was not yet high enough to penetrate the trees. I hugged my pelisse closer against the cool air.

Without warning, the shrubbery exploded and a huge, gangly, blond pup appeared before me. I gasped in surprise and froze – providing the perfect opportunity for the animal to launch itself at me. Carried backwards by its weight, the air was forced painfully from my lungs as I hit the ground. Struggling to draw breath, I squirmed and flailed on the wet grass, unable to escape the hound's muddy paws and relentless tongue.

"Tess!" An old man growled raspingly from behind a screen of foliage, and was followed immediately by the appearance of a craggy, outdoor face. "Good 'eavens, Miss. Tess! Ger orf! Tess do as yer told, yer bloody flea-bitten cur!"

Finally the dog stood back, its tail slicing through the air like a whip. The old man offered a calloused hand and dragged me to my feet before retreating deferentially. I brushed at my gown and tried to catch my breath.

"Aw, Miss, good 'eavens, damn dog," he swore again. His face was wrinkled like old leather, and his black-pebble eyes were alert and merry. "You or-roight?"

"Yes … thank you."

"Too friendly by 'alf that pup. No need to be afeard. Wouldn' 'urt 'er own fleas but she's young an' disobedient."

"I'm alright. It was just the shock."

"Yer dress, Miss," he pointed with the stem of his pipe. "S'all ruint."

"Your Tess only finished what I began. I've been walking by the lake. Made a mess of it myself."

He nodded and returned the pipe to his mouth. "Sorry Miss," and touched his forehead respectfully. "Briggs, Miss, 'ead gardener."

I guessed he was somewhere near sixty, though his outdoor complexion made it difficult to tell. His hands were as lined and brown as his face but his wiry frame moved with a strength that suggested he was younger than he looked.

"Pleased to meet you, Mister Briggs," I said formally. "I'm Miss Alexandra Broughton."

"Guest o' the young lord, are yer?" We fell into step and Tess disappeared into the shrubbery.

"Ah, no. I'm his sister, or rather, stepsister."

He simply nodded, showing none of the annoying artificial respect people generally displayed when they found out who my stepfather was. I liked it.

"Didn't know the earl was in. When'd 'e arrive?"

"Last night. We're staying for the summer."

He nodded again and puffed on his pipe as we walked up the lawns toward the house. Though strangers, we were at ease, strolling in companionable silence until I asked, "Are you responsible for the kitchen garden?"

He emitted a plume of fragrant pipe-smoke and gave a tight shake of his head. "That be the cook's garden and none would int'fere else Chartrain skin us all. Got a lad … looks aft' it. Questions me 'bout this 'n' that."

"These gardens are beautiful. They're a credit to you."

"Yup. Meself'n four other from Astor. Don't do much o' th' back break m'self nowdays – young lord got me a lad for that." We were passing through an avenue of beeches that opened out on to the forecourt of the stables. Consistent with the grandeur of the house, the stables were a large, sturdy barn with doors wide enough for a carriage to pass through, and space to house several of them.

"'Ere." Briggs rummaged through his coat pocket and extracted a couple of short fat carrots. The dirt was still clinging to them. "Give'm to th'orse in there. Big beasts – gimme th' willies. But there's one … likes these an' all. Old Nella – white-faced and freckly. Give 'em to 'er. She's a good ol' girl an' Lord Thorncliffe 'as a soft spot for 'er too. I pick a couple each mornin' before me stroll."

"I'll do that each morning if you like – at least while I'm here."

He bobbed his head and let out a puff of smoke. "Aye, then. Pick 'em from th' kitchen garden but don't go lettin' Chartrain catch yer."

He whistled to Tess, nodded to me, and was gone.

The stables were clean and smelled of leather. A large room at the entrance contained a coach and two small carriages; the walls were hung with horse-harness, saddles and assorted work tools, and two great bins of feed stood in a corner. Six good-sized stalls ran its length, and as I moved down the line the scent of horse and hay filled the air. I could hear the snorting and nickering of contented animals.

Walking along the stalls, it didn't take long to find Nella – the only white among chestnuts and blacks, and she was old indeed. Though no judge of horses, I estimated she'd already seen 25 years. Once a beauty, she was now sway-backed and more grey than white. Her head hung inquisitively over the half-door of her stall; eyes alert, nostrils twitching to the scent of carrot.

"Hello, old girl." The other horses eyed me indifferently but Nella's lips quivered in anticipation. I handed over both carrots and the old horse accepted them gently, munching thoroughly while I rubbed her whiskery nose and promised to return the next day.

A pale-yellow river of light was streaming through the open doors as I emerged. I stood momentarily, taking in the supreme splendour of this beautiful place. The air was alive with birdsong and the humming of early bees and insects, and a soft breeze carried scents of rose, violet and honeysuckle. It promised to be a glorious day.

I returned to the house via the porch and a rear door that led to a back stairway to the gallery and guest wing. A corridor on my left meandered round a bend and I guessed it led to the servants' rooms, kitchen and scullery, judging by the distant sounds and smells filtering up.

So, now I had my bearings, I gathered the skirt of my sodden dress in my hands and took the stairs, two-at-a-time in most unladylike fashion, to change for breakfast.

Those first days drifted by in a haze of pleasant lassitude. I walked and I read, I explored the superb gardens and trawled the extensive library. I wrote to Julia and attempted to do justice to this magnificent place in my descriptions – the written word failing to paint that which I could not even describe in my thoughts. But I knew an uncommon serenity; such was the contagion of peace at this place.

Adopting a larcenous morning routine, I pilfered carrots from the kitchen garden, keeping a wary eye out for Monsieur Chartrain and his capricious humour.

After visiting Nella, my wanderings took me to the lake, through the morning-scented gardens, over the damp lawns and around the shrubs. Always, I was joined by Tess, and frequently by Briggs, puffs of sweet-smelling pipe-smoke trailing behind him.

The days were sunny and warm, and in the evenings a revitalising breeze blew in, off the distant sea. Lord Thorncliffe said the coast was only an hour's ride from Waterville and suggested a day visit.

"Chartrain can make up a picnic hamper. We can eat lunch and return in the afternoon."

"I shan't bathe," Mother said, wrinkling her nose to show her distaste. "I'm not one for the sea."

"Do you swim, Lass?" Lord Thorncliffe asked.

I shook my head.

"Alexandra, you would not enjoy bathing anyhow," Mother said dismissively. "The water, I'm told, is horrid. It makes one's hair sticky and salty."

"Nevertheless, a picnic sounds marvellous," I said brightly.

"Are there trees, Gerrard? Alexandra and I cannot be sitting in the sun all day."

"M'dear, 'tis a beach not a park. But I have a tent the footmen can erect to provide shade."

"That will do then I should think," Mother said. She'd been surprisingly agreeable since our arrival in Devon. Perhaps the opulence of our surroundings reminded her of her profitable marriage.

"Leave early … make a day of it, eh?" her husband suggested and when I nodded he added, "We'll need staff. Bring Janet, yes … and Sylvie too. I doubt the girl has ever seen the sea, though she's lived here all her life."

"Who cares if she has or hasn't. The scrawny waif's a servant, Gerrard."

Mother was back in form but Lord Thorncliffe ignored her. "They must have their work completed so they may join us."

ॐ

"But what if I can't finish my work?" Janet moaned.

"I'm certain you'll not be excluded. Sylvie is invited too."

"Oh!" Janet said, almost dropping the duster she held. "I cannot believe I forgot to tell you! Betty the scullery-maid told me."

"Blethering were you?"

"Don't you want to know?"

"Very well," I said with a weary sigh, though in truth I was always interested in below stairs gossip.

"Now I can't vouch for its truth, but Betty overheard Monsieur

Chartrain griping about how Sylvie was useless and would be thrown out of service anywhere else."

"But I expect Monsieur Chartrain would be difficult to please any time."

She rolled her eyes in wry agreement. "Anyhow, he said Sylvie was only kept on because she is Lord Thorncliffe's bastard and she could not be sent away."

I thought about that for a moment. "He does seem to favour her."

She wagged her head in agreement and wisps of brown hair escaped her cap. "I thought that myself. And then, there's that uncanny resemblance to Miss Maeve."

Janet's words hit me like a revelation. Of course – that's what it was about Sylvie I'd found strangely familiar. How could I have not realised it before? Her tiny hands, pixie-like face, the silver-blond hair – all an echo of Maeve's. I wondered if Mother knew. Would she even care? Doubtful – a bastard daughter was insignificant provided she knew her place and drew no unseemly attention.

So the morning of our excursion arrived, dawning with a lavender sky. Aglow with happy expectations, I put on a light cotton dress and tied my hair back with no regard for the comb. The house was very still though the doors had been unbolted and a servant was softly humming somewhere nearby.

I slunk along the hallway, heading toward Monsieur Chartrain's lair. Spying around the kitchen door, I spotted the cantankerous old chef sitting before a steaming cup. His elbows rested on the table, his fists supported his chin. Without his imposing chef's hat, he was nothing more than a frail-looking, wispy-haired old man with a downturned mouth and well-established frown. Retreating silently lest he transform into the cursing, cleaver-wielding tyrant of repute, I crept away to exit via a porch door.

Being early, Nella wasn't watching for me, but upon my approach she hung her head over the door to give a soft whicker of greeting.

"Hello girl, did I get you up early today?" I brushed the soil from the newly filched carrots and held them out for her. As she munched, I stood back wiping dirt from my hands and listening to the shuffling movement in the stall next door – the stall that was supposedly empty.

I held my breath for a second as realisation dawned.

Peering into the shadows, I made out a tall black horse standing with one back hoof tucked casually behind the other, and my heart gave a joyous leap for there was no mistaking the graceful legs and pretty head.

"Equus …?" My voice was low but the mare's ears flickered at her name. "Hello girl." I clicked my tongue and she turned expectantly. The thoughts tumbled through my head while my stomach churned with unexpected emotions.

He was home – finally.

∾

Lord Thorncliffe was already serving himself cold meat and pouring a cup of tea. He poured a second and pushed it towards me.

"You're up early," I said brightly.

"With good reason, we had an arrival last night."

"So I believe. I saw Equus in the stables."

He raised his bushy brows. "You've been to the stables?"

I helped myself to a slice of bread, fragrant and warm from the oven. "I visit every morning," then smiling sheepishly, "I nick carrots from Monsieur Chartrain's garden to give Nella."

At that, he threw back his great blond head and laughed loudly while I stared in bewilderment. When finally he calmed himself, he explained, "I do the same every evening. That old girl has us all bewitched, and Monsieur Chartrain the victim of serial theft."

"Well, she's a sweetheart and deserves it," I said, grinning.

"That she is. She's my dear late wife's favourite. 'Twill be a sad day when we lose her."

Ignoring good manners, I spread my bread with honey, rolled it with my fingers and bit into it. Immediately my mouth was flooded with the warm, sweet taste of summer. "So, what time did Patrick arrive?"

"Eleven or so. About time he came home. Bit of a wanderer, I'm afraid."

"Is he staying?"

I washed down my bread with a sip of tea. It was hot and I nearly choked on it as Lord Thorncliffe said, "Ask him yourself."

"Morning L'il Sis," said a familiar, if slightly deeper, voice behind me.

Overjoyed, in one fluid motion, I leapt from my chair and threw myself into his arms. He caught me, chuckling deep in his throat, his hands on my waist and giving a quick peck on my cheek.

Pushing me gently back, he looked me over and smiled. "Well, haven't you grown," he said in his slightly mocking way. "The extra year has polished off the ruffian to expose the young lady."

I laughed with sheer delight and plopped on to my seat as he released me.

Patrick and his father greeted one another amid much hugging and backslapping, before Pat took the empty seat at his father's right hand. The two launched into a vigorous conversation, punctuated with laughter and the industrious sounds of breakfasting.

Lord Thorncliffe asked questions about the estate's various business concerns, and Patrick responded with serious details and funny anecdotes. I sat spellbound, taking in not a word, picking at – but not tasting – fresh strawberries from a bowl before me, absorbing Pat's features.

At nearly twenty, he was a man, grown and old enough to run his own estate. The sun had bronzed his skin to a healthy glow and streaked his honey-coloured hair with gold. It sat cheerfully-tousled on his collar and his startlingly-green eyes danced with vitality. I watched him casually chatting with his father, one arm hooked over the back of his chair, his mouth curving often into the crooked grin I remembered so well. His soft white shirt was open at the neck, the sleeves casually rolled to the elbows, and tucked into dark blue trousers.

He looked relaxed, and handsome in a way I'd never known, never expected. He ate heartily and talked enthusiastically and now and then flashed me a grin that set my heart jumping erratically beneath my ribs, and I could not take my eyes away from him.

"So, the prodigal one has returned," Mother's acidic tone sliced through the amity.

Both men rose from their seats and Pat said with emphasis, "Greetings, *Mother*."

She took a seat next to him and opposite me, and poured a cup of tea for herself. "The place seems prosperous under your supervision," she said without looking at him. "And the maids are all a-twitter with excitement – the young lord is home again. Since your father is returned, it is fitting that you curb your behaviour – if such restraint lies within your capabilities."

"Er … Mim," Lord Thorncliffe reached for his ear lobe but Mother was on a roll.

"Thinking about taking a wife yet, hmm?" She stirred her tea, taking care not to clink the spoon in the cup. "You know; responsibility to the name, to the family, all that inconvenient stuff? I trust you've spoken with him about Anne, Gerrard?"

"Oh, here we go again," Pat said pushing his chair back. "We'll continue this discussion later, Father, when we're less likely to be distracted." He winked at me over Mother's chignon. The door gave a slight bang after him.

"Close your mouth, Alexandra, you look like a frog catching flies."

∽

Sylvie was tidying my room when I entered. I waved for her to continue and sat in the chair by the window to calm my thoughts. Pat was home – he was home at last and all I could think of was the way he'd smiled at me, and the feel of his hands on my waist. He had kissed my cheek. What, I wondered, would it feel like if he kissed my mouth – the way he'd kissed Grace? My cheeks flamed at the thought.

"You alright, Miss Alex?"

"I was thinking of our visit to the sea today. It's exciting."

She nodded. "Yes Miss," She flicked a dust-cloth over the dressing table, lifting the crystal pieces as she went.

"Sylvie?"

"Yes, Miss?"

"Has a young Italian lady by the name of Grace Camelleri ever visited this house?"

Sylvie paused, her dust-cloth held aloft. "Recently?"

"Has she ever visited? A guest of the young lord."

Sylvie answered without hesitation, "No Miss. I'm not aware of anyone by that name."

I smiled and ignored the curiosity she veiled quickly behind her servant's neutral face. "Thank you Sylvie. Now, hurry and get your jobs done. We're all going to the seaside – in case you've forgotten."

The maid grinned and there was no mistaking her resemblance to Maeve. "Of course, Miss. And certainly I have not forgotten."

For some reason, I'd assumed Patrick would be joining us, and was disappointed when our train of two carriages departed without him. The frilled edge on Mother's parasol fluttered in the breeze, and I tied the ribbon of my bonnet securely. Sylvie and Janet were opposite, giggling, and squashed against a less-than-amused Eleanor. The two shared conspiratorial glances, clearly enjoying Eleanor's discomfiture. Lord Thorncliffe, driving, sat at the front.

Davey, a lad of 15 years, was driving the second carriage. A younger boy sat beside him almost hidden by the pile of chairs, a table and a canvas tent. One of Monsieur Chartrain's trainees, a rather tormented looking fellow, had prepared a picnic of cheese, bread, cold chicken and beef, sliced cucumber and onions. There were fruit and pastries, and bottles of cider with which to wash it all down.

We lumbered along the drive and turned on to the road, and after half an hour, we cleared the Waterville forests and my head swung back and forth as I watched the passing farmhouses, stands of trees, and shifting, rolling paddocks with grazing animals. From time to time we pulled aside to allow a faster vehicle to overtake our little train – everyone, it seemed was on their way to the seaside.

The weather was glorious and the constancy of the blue sky was broken only by the gulls flying over head. As my excitement grew, it seemed the journey took much longer than the hour it actually did, and by the time we arrived at the bumpy, sandy lane that led to the shore, it was all I could do to sit still in my seat.

I heard the crashing of the sea long before it came into view, and then it appeared; grey-green and glittering with jewel-like drops of sun and I tasted the sharp zest of it on my lips.

The carriages bumped and ploughed their way along the beach and when finally we halted, I stared about me at the pebbles and shingle. The shore wasn't nearly as mysteriously beautiful as the water – it was perhaps even a little unpleasant. Seaweed lay in rotting clumps and created an almighty stink as it baked in the sun – Mother and Eleanor complained about it immediately. A cooling breeze blew off the water and raised goose-flesh on my arms, and fanned the smell over us. I took off my bonnet, letting it dangle from my hand and raised my face, like a worshipper of Apollo, to feel the sun's rays diffusing through my skin.

There were several other groups at the seaside. A veritable city of canvas pavilions had sprung up along the pebbly shore beyond the tide-line, and servants were scurrying back and forth carrying furniture and securing lines to hold up awnings and tents of every size and colour. Groups sat talking loudly, waving and calling out as they recognised friends and acquaintances.

"Commoners," Mother huffed derisively. "Can't they go somewhere else?"

There was certainly no tranquillity such as I'd imagined. Instead, it was a perpetual cacophony of sound; the raucous call of the gulls, squeals of excited children, warning shouts from parents, and everywhere people stood about, with arms raised against the glare of the sun, looking out to sea.

Sylvie, Janet and I slipped off our shoes and stockings and ran barefoot along the edge of the water kicking it up at each other till our dresses were sodden from the knee down. Even accustomed as I was to daily walking, I was unprepared for the difficulties of running on the lumpy sand. Before long, our feet and legs were caked with shingle and aching, and we were breathless.

There were several people in the water. Some had little bathing machines – brightly coloured contraptions like gypsy caravans with steps at the back. Burly servants with glistening brows dragged them over the shingle and pebbles into the water to where the feminine occupants could emerge and discreetly bathe.

"Miss Alex," Sylvie said and pointed behind me.

I turned to see Mother enthroned on a chair beneath the awning of our tent. Eleanor was approaching gingerly across the sand, her pointy face set disapprovingly. "The countess would have you return," she announced. "The food is being served."

Janet, Sylvie, Eleanor and the stable-boys, ate at one table while Mother, Father and I sat at another to enjoy our feast. The food and cider were distributed in an egalitarian fashion between the two groups, which, for the stable-lads, was as lavish as any Christmas feast.

We took our time over the food, and afterwards I reclined in my chair, letting my thoughts wander to Patrick and acknowledging the little flutter of excitement in the pit of my stomach. Lord Thorncliffe shook out a newspaper and settled in for a good read, while Mother and Eleanor pored over Mother's latest Almack's.

The afternoon passed thus and eventually fat white clouds began to pile on the horizon. The water darkened and Lord Thorncliffe squinted up at the sky. Pulling out his fob watch, he instructed the servants to begin packing. "Would you agree m'dear?"

Mother nodded congenially. "Yes, I think so. It's cool now the clouds are coming in."

Finally, our fully-loaded carriages joined the exodus towards the road. I glanced over my shoulder to see the seagulls swoop immediately, shrieking discordantly, and battling one another for scraps.

The food, the fresh air, and the rhythmic rocking of the carriage did their work, and, after what seemed like only minutes, Mother was nudging me awake.

I allowed a footman fresh from the house to assist me down and wearily dragged myself to my room, calling for warm water on the way.

Bea, a maid recently employed by Mrs Bath, arrived with herb-infused water and a thick towel. "Would you like me to help you, Miss?" she asked.

"No Bea, thank you, but I would kill for a cup of tea."

"Right away, Miss Alex." She bobbed and closed the door softly after her.

Exhausted, I hunched over the bowl and inhaled the soothing peppermint and rosemary scent of the steam rising off the basin. The skin on my face felt tight and my legs ached from running along the beach. I'd read about a tribe of natives in Africa who could run all day without stopping and wondered at how strong they must be. Hitching my skirt up above my knees, I placed my feet in the warm water and released a long, blissful sigh.

A tight rap on the door jerked me from a doze. "Yes," I called without opening my eyes. "Just leave it on the desk, thanks Bea."

"Er … should I come back later?" My eyes shot open and my heart leapt through my ribs.

Patrick was leaning casually against the door jam, smiling with arms folded over his chest and his shirt-tail hanging from the back of his trousers.

"Oh!" I said in surprise, quickly pulling my skirt over my legs. "I was expecting a pot of tea."

He grinned ruefully and showed his empty hands, "Sorry. Sore feet?"

"Hmm – I'm trying to soothe them."

"You might want something for your face as well. Looks like you've caught too much sun."

I touched my nose gingerly. "It feels hot. I haven't seen it yet. Will I be shocked?"

He regarded me speculatively. "Depends how easily shocked you are. But if it's sore now, it'll be worse by tomorrow."

I groaned.

"And then it will become dry and flaky." He sat on the edge of my bed and nodded soberly. "Yes, I believe you will be shocked."

I groaned again.

"So, did you enjoy your visit to the sea?"

"It wasn't too bad, but too many people were there. Probably not worth all the preparation and lugging of furniture and everything." I wriggled my toes in the water basin beneath my skirt. "And all I have to show for it is a red face, sore legs, and my toes have shingle stuck between them."

"Did you bathe?"

"No, I don't swim. In any case, I don't think I'd enjoy that sticky smelly water all over me. It has bleached my skirt where it got wet so it mustn't be good for your skin."

"On the contrary, it's very good for the skin. I can teach you to swim in the lake here if you like." My doubt must have shown on my face for he added, "Not sticky, and certainly not smelly."

"I don't know," I said hesitantly. "And even if I wanted to, I don't have a swimming costume."

"We could find you something, though Maeve swims in her shift."

I knew Mother would be outraged were I to swim with Patrick, more so if I were wearing only my shift, but the idea was tempting nonetheless and I relented slightly. "Perhaps, if it gets very hot, I may consider it."

He shrugged and reclined on my bed resting his head on the bolster. "The offer's there."

"What have you done today?"

"Oh, not a lot," he said. "Though I spent some time with Briggs."

"I know him …"

"Funny old chap – that bloody pipe always in his mouth. Anyway, I plan to build an arboretum by the porch – train roses to climb over it. Might make a pretty walkway in the spring and summer." He talked slowly, visualising, and wasn't looking at me so I hiked my skirt and finished washing the shell from my feet and legs.

Pat had left the door open and now Janet entered carrying a tray with a silver tea service and fine china tea cup, and her eyes narrowed disapprovingly as she saw him on my bed while I pulled on clean stockings. She glared significantly.

"Please just put it on the writing desk, Janet," I said, finishing my task and smoothing down my skirt. "And take the basin downstairs, please."

Pat sat up suddenly. "Janet! I didn't know you'd come all the way down here as well."

"Hello, Master Pat," she clasped her hands respectfully before her but angled another critical glance in my direction.

"Do you like it here?" he asked cheerfully.

"Yes, Master Pat. It's like I'm on holiday."

"Excellent, but tell me, did the worthy Eleanor find her way here as well?"

"Yes." Janet and I chorused and this time when our eyes met we both laughed.

"Good God, your face is all red too! You'll suffer for it tomorrow as well. Go see Mrs Bath. She'll give you a salve, alright?"

Janet tried to smile but the tightness of her reddened skin turned it into something of a grimace. "Thank you Master Pat. Is there anything else?"

"Would you mind bringing an extra cup and some cake?" Pat asked.

"Monsieur Chartrain said he wouldn't make cake because the pudding he made last evening was not eaten and his talents were not appreciated."

My eyes widened disbelievingly but Patrick laughed. "Sounds like Chartrain – tyrannical old bastard. I only keep him on because he's good. Just the cup then, thank you Janet."

Janet bobbed and deliberately pushed the door so that it stood fully opened against the wall.

"So how was the journey from Yorkshire? Did you see the standing stones?"

"The journey was painful with Mother and Eleanor gossiping like fishwives the entire way. What standing stones?"

"Huge stones … ancient. Nobody knows how they came to be there or what they represent but they're worth seeing." He lay back on my bed again and stared at the drapery. "They're near Amesbury in Wiltshire. You would have come through there."

I shrugged. "We didn't see them. What should I put on my face?"

"I don't know. Mrs Bath will though. Go and see her."

"I shall. But right now – about that tea …"

Sitting up, he raised his hand delicately, "Shall I pour?" he said in a perfect imitation of Mother, complete with a little moue.

"If you would be so kind," I responded in like fashion, as Janet arrived with the second cup. She eyed me archly but I pointedly ignored her and she departed again.

Pat poured the tea, adding a slice of lemon to both cups and I joined him on the edge of my bed.

"Do you like my house?" He seemed to be in a rather expansive mood and a wave of contentment washed over me as I sipped my tea. It was remarkably soothing after the day's exertions. I took another restorative sip before answering.

"I do. Why did you never tell me it was yours?"

"Does it matter?" We drank our tea in companionable silence for a while, then he said, "I didn't know you were here, you know. I'd have come home sooner had I known. So, I'm guessing you've not had the guided tour."

I shook my head.

"Right then."

He took my empty cup and returned it to the tray, then grasping my hands pulled me to my feet. "Most of the good stuff is in the residential wing. You, on the other hand, are accommodated in the guest wing. So let's go."

Hand in hand, my fatigue forgotten, we spent the hours before supper wandering from room to room, my eyes fairly popping at centuries of accumulated artefacts of unimagined splendour. This house was an Aladdin's Cave of exquisite works of art, and beauty of immeasurable proportion. I was transported to wonderful, mysterious lands by the treasures collected by Patrick's ancestors during their travels. Mirrors, cabinets, desks in dark wood – polished to enhance the knots and veins in the natural material – painstakingly carved with animal heads, feet and legs.

Feathered head-dresses and fearsome wooden masks from the Caribbean; glass and brass ornaments from the africas; delicate, ancient pottery, silk paintings, and exotic artwork from the orient – I was spellbound.

"Maeve and I used to spend days roaming this house. It's been in the family for centuries so there are treasures collected from all over the world – there's more in the attic."

"Like your Strad," I interrupted.

"Like my Strad. Every owner has added his touch, changed something, built something, pulled down something – it constantly evolves."

"So whose idea was the atrium?"

"That was my grandfather's idea. He'd seen something similar in Morocco. It's fantastic isn't it?"

I nodded vigorously.

"When it was first completed, the King and the whole court came to see it. Not this King, of course, though he also has visited. I remember being unimpressed by all the court goings-on."

"What goings-on?"

He grinned slyly, "I don't know that I should share those grisly details with such an innocent as you."

"Such gallantry," I said shooting him a glare, but he laughed.

"Really, it was all deceit, bed-hopping, jostling for position … I didn't like it then, and I didn't like it when I went to court myself. Come on, there's still more to show you before supper."

"Our parents each have their suites along this corridor, and Maeve's room is here too," then as we paused before a door at the end of the hall, he stood aside and opened it with a flourish. "*Entrez.*"

Books were piled on the writing desk and a shirt was flung over the back of a chair. The room, though clean, was a study of clutter and disarray, yet to my surprise, on the window-ledge in a little porcelain pot, was a lush geranium complete with vivid, red flowers.

"Your room," I said solemnly, recognising immediately the sanctuary he'd created here.

"You can tell?"

"Wild guess," I said, forcing lightness into my voice as I walked around the room. Time seemed to slow and a burgeoning intimacy with him consumed me. This was where he grew up; this was the very heart of him and I saw now that his room at Broughton Hall was merely temporary.

A true reflection of its owner, this room was casual and unkempt, intellectual and reserved, and the disorder was tempered by an unexpectedly gentle touch. The room smelt of the citrus and clove fragrance he had about him, offset by the more pungent smell of horse coming from a riding jacket and boots strewn on the floor.

I felt so comfortable in this room I wanted never to leave. It was furnished in the same heavy style as the other nine bedrooms we'd explored, but it also included a tall, packed-to-overflowing bookcase against one wall, with additional books piled on the floor beside it.

The huge four-poster bed was unmade, the blue velvet counterpane turned down at one side, a hollow shape in the pillow. I suppressed a longing to snuggle into it and took a deep breath as I turned abruptly. He was watching me intensely, his eyes dark and inscrutable.

"You ought to have your room cleaned," I said cheerfully, attempting to insert some buoyancy into the solemnity of mood that seemed to fall over us.

He smiled. "I know. But I told Mrs Bath not to clean here. I've been reading, and drawing up plans for the arboretum. When I'm finished she may send someone in." He took my hand again. "Come, there's one last place to show you – you'll love this."

Out in the hall, the earth began to rotate once more. We emerged to find Sylvie approaching with an armload of linen. Her face lit up prettily when she spotted Patrick but he furtively grasped her arm and pulled her into his room.

"What are you doing?" His voice was a gruff whisper.

"Mrs Bath asked me to make up your bed with fresh sheets," she explained. "Don't worry; I shan't touch anything else – she warned me."

"Why you?" he whispered hurriedly.

"She asked me to," the maid responded simply.

He ran his hand through his hair distractedly. "This is ridiculous – get someone else."

"It *is* my job, My Lord."

"Don't call me that!" he snapped, and as I feigned disinterest, he took the linen from her and dumped it on the bed. The rapport between them was honest and private and, though I felt like an intruder, I could not turn away. "Find someone else and tell them I said so."

She shook her head, "It is my job," she repeated, softly. "You will make things difficult for me."

"I'm talking with Father."

She put her hand on his arm, "Please don't, it will make things worse. I'm happy Pat, truly I am."

He stood looking down at her, and the resemblance between them was plain. His expression softened affectionately. "Shit Sylvie, only because you look at me like that – I'll make it up to you, I promise."

He moved aside as she slid into the room and set about her work. Turning to me, he said, "You know, don't you?"

"I don't know anything," I responded quickly.

"Very well."

I sensed his humour had changed, and as I followed him down the hallway, he seemed lost in thought, though typically he gave no hint as to what he was thinking. Rounding a corner, we continued along a narrow corridor that wound into the nethermost regions of the house. There were no windows to provide light and I felt along the wall for guidance. We were in almost complete darkness when we reached a tiny spiral staircase that led high up into the roof space. I groped uncertainly along the handrail to the top where

I stepped on to a small landing. Pat pulled a ladder from the ceiling and climbed up to a trap door. Pushing it up, a torrent of afternoon light cascaded over us. I waited as he disappeared through the hole amid floating particles of dust and then his face reappeared in the hole.

"Come up."

Bunching my skirt in one hand, I held the ladder with the other and climbed. At the top, he handed me through the hole into a small, perfectly circular room. The walls were made entirely of glass panes and arched over our heads with the eerie feeling of being within a protective bubble.

"Another room my grandfather designed after his stay in Morocco. It's a feat of engineering and was to be his observatory." Patrick sat on a bench that ran the perimeter of the room and I took a space next to him.

"In Morocco, they are keen astronomers. My grandfather caught the interest from them and built this room so he also could study the pathways of the stars. Unfortunately the skies here are not always so clear."

The room gave a perfect 360 degree view from the roof of the house. I could see the park and the lake, the Tuscan terracotta roof of the summer house; grey-slated stables, the bright patchwork colours of the gardens in summer bloom. I followed the neat driveway as it snaked up to the house, like a river cutting through emerald pastures, and there was the protruding coloured dome of the atrium. I could even see the sea – a crouching grey-green smudge in the distance.

"Grandfather planned to install a telescope but became ill and never managed it. He barely used this room at all."

"A pity …" I murmured, spellbound.

"It's breathtaking during a storm, and then at night when the sky is clear …"

"Next time the stars are all out, could we come up?"

"Of course."

We let the silence stand for some time while I walked slowly around the entire perimeter, soaking up the view from each angle. The sun was just beginning to dip below the shifting green forest of trees, tinting the sky gold and burnt orange.

"Have you heard from your Lord Whatsit?" Patrick asked, unexpectedly.

In dismay, I turned and looked at him. "Why did you have to mention him?"

He shrugged, unrepentant.

"He visited shortly after you left last year. I haven't heard from him since."

"But the betrothal still stands?"

"I've heard nothing to the contrary." I eyed him curiously. "And no line of suitors beating a path to my door."

"There ought to be," he said, softly. He watched my face closely. "You're rather appealing when you're not being a thorough bitch."

It was a compliment disguised as our usual banter and I flushed self-consciously. "Don't tease me. Who'd wed a country-rabbit with messy hair and narrow hips? I'm not built to be a brood mare, nor am I glamorous court material. Aren't they the qualities one desires in a wife?"

"Not necessarily. Do you go to balls and parties often?"

I was beginning to feel uncomfortable. "Of course," I said firmly, "but Mother is proud of the match with Hamish, and consequently, everyone knows I'm spoken for. What about you?"

"What about me?" He seemed somewhat affronted that I should ask.

"Mother would have you married to Anne in a blink if she could." I realised, suddenly, I was on dangerous ground and turned away quickly, ostensibly to admire the view.

"She is old enough," he mused, and my stomach dropped.

"So you would marry Anne?" I attempted nonchalance but

slanted a cautious glance at him. He was watching a falcon wheeling in the sky above the moving canopy. "She is beautiful and intelligent enough to be a worthy bride," I fished precariously.

"Yes, she is rather decorative," he agreed at last. "And there's a lot of pressure being exerted. I cannot resist forever; eventually I must marry and produce a string of brats. It would be constructive to marry one of you Broughton girls, and since there's only one available …"

I frowned and wondered at his use of the word *constructive*. But he was watching me now, and I was certain he could hear the thudding of my heart.

"Come," he said, and his eyes glittered with amusement. "We'll be late for supper – and don't worry, I was only teasing. I've no intention of marrying Anne."

"At least not while you're courting Grace," I rejoined smartly without thinking. He stopped abruptly and stared at me.

"What makes you say that?"

"Well, you've been escorting her around … everyone's talking … I just thought –"

"Don't think!"

CHAPTER 12

Our conversation in the observatory wasn't revisited, but over the following weeks I observed my stepbrother and learned a lot about him. He played an active role in the management and maintenance of his domain, regularly riding out to inspect the estate and surrounds. He worked tirelessly beside his tenant farmers; shearing sheep, repairing fencing and homes, adjudicating in local disputes, and so much more. Often he returned exhausted at the end of the day, glowing bronze from the sun, his clothes work-stained.

Other mornings, he closeted himself in his dark-panelled office where he looked over the accounts. Those were the days he appeared at the dinner table and chatted socially with his father, until finally turning to me.

"Well, Li'l Sis, what plans have you for this afternoon?"

Thus Patrick and I spent many long, summered afternoons together. Invariably, he suggested various pastimes and we might be found meandering through the forest – he on Equus and me perched on the back of a placid, little, brown gelding called Gloaming. Sometimes we visited his village market or we called at a local inn to share ale and a plate of bread and cheese with his tenants. Patrick was feted as the district's much admired *Young Lord* and, as his sister, I was treated accordingly – a rather humbling experience since I was no such celebrity.

Always, he was relaxed and gracious, and when it came time to pay, his coins were firmly refused, though he left more than adequate beneath our plate when we departed.

Patrick as a boy had enchanted me with his quick humour and sense of fun. Now, as a young adult, he captivated me with his pragmatic sense of duty towards his position and tenants. He seemed unaffected by his vast wealth and maintained an earthy regard for his responsibilities. Whenever we happened upon any of his villagers, he listened to their concerns and acted on promises immediately. The pleasure with which he was received was sincere, and he, in turn, responded with respect and genuine interest.

For me, he provided witty and agreeable diversion, and I delighted in the afternoons spent in his company – even on the odd occasion when the weather turned inclement and we were forced indoors.

On such days we might pit our wits against each other in a suspense-filled game of chess. Other times he brought out his Strad and I sang along to his playing. The gallery vibrated with our music and the hilarity afforded by my ineptly-performed dance routines. Any passing maid or footman was shanghaied into our happy chaos, only to be released breathless and laughing at the song's end.

So the weeks passed in pleasant indolence. When alone, I spent long meditative hours lying in the grass beneath a tree with the humming of bumble-bees in wildflowers gently lulling me. Other times, I could be found in the summer-house, reading or daydreaming while the sheer curtaining at the French doors billowed with a breeze that whispered of cool forests and nearby seas.

One such afternoon, I reclined on a couch in the summer-house pondering my world. I was in love – with this house, the gardens, and the halcyon life I was living. I could linger here forever.

But too soon the forest would be ablaze in bronze, red and gold, and I would be sipping Cook's plum wine before a leaping fire in the parlour at Broughton Hall, anticipating another cold winter.

I pushed the thought away lest it spoil my slow, contented afternoon, and returned to my book – a play by Forsythe Burchall, the latest darling of the *au courant*.

The air was stagnant and muggy and I could feel the dampness under my arms and breasts. The humidity was potent and I was drunk on it, unaware that my eyes were closing in a delicious, half-sleep until I heard, with detachment, my book fall to the floor.

"Is this where the prince awakens his true love with a kiss?"

I roused with a start. "How long have you been there?"

"Not long." Patrick squatted to retrieve my book. "Burchall – any good?"

I stretched luxuriously, "Good enough, though I've read better." I could feel the perspiration at my nape and knew my face would be flushed with sleep and warmth.

He looked at me speculatively, "So what about it? Fancy a dip in the lake?" He raised his eyebrows challengingly.

"I don't think so," I replied, though the thought of immersing my sticky body in cool water was tempting. "May I have my book? I'll leave you to your privacy."

"It'll wake you up."

"I can't swim and I've nothing to wear."

He shrugged dismissively. "Maeve swims in her shift."

"So you've said." Involuntarily my eyes slid to where the lake could be glimpsed through the open window. The water sparkled tauntingly with jewels of light dancing on its surface, broken occasionally by a hovering dragonfly. It was certainly inviting, but how could I strip down to my shift before him?

Correctly interpreting the expression on my face, he said, "There's no-one to know."

I hesitated and while I considered, he arranged his face into a semblance of propriety, entirely belied by the mischief dancing in his eyes.

"I'll not see a thing you don't want me to – I swear."

With a rush of recklessness, I grinned. "Oh, why not?"

"Good." He rose lithely and strode to the door. "I'll be outside." He exited, throwing over his shoulder, "and if you want my advice, you'll take your underthings off so your bloomers are dry when you get dressed again."

My blush owed nothing to the humidity and I was grateful he'd already gone. Left alone, I rolled down my stockings and stuffed them into my shoes. Next I began the struggle with the row of tiny, bone buttons at the back of my dress, which Janet had helped me with that morning. Several I could reach, but most were in a spot I could not.

"There's a lot of grunting going on in there," Patrick called through the window, sounding amused.

"I … I can't … reach these … rotten buttons." Twisting this way and that, I muttered an unladylike oath of exasperation and heard him chuckling before his bare feet padded across the floor behind me.

"Stand still," he commanded, throwing his own clothes in a pile on the settee.

I held my breath, intensely aware that he may well be naked behind me. Deftly as Janet, he undid the remaining buttons. "There now … get on with it." I remained with my back turned until I heard him leave.

Doubts resurfaced, but I pushed them aside and eased the dress from my shoulders before I could lose my nerve. It dropped significantly to the floor. Then reaching beneath my shift I tugged down my bloomers and bundled them into a tight ball and buried them discreetly under my dress.

By the door, feeling quite exposed, I called out, "You're not in the altogether are you?"

His soft laughter mingled with the hum of insects in the still afternoon air. "No, you're quite safe."

I relaxed only slightly and stepped outside. He was sitting on the edge, his feet dangling in the water, naked but for his underdrawers. His body was lean and muscular, and tanned to the colour of honey. He looked up as I approached and the way his eyes ran over me evoked a little shiver.

Self-consciously I dropped to sit beside him and hugged my knees.

"See that bird over there?" He pointed to a long-legged grey bird with a swan-like neck. "It's a heron. They sit for hours … patiently, waiting for a fish or frog or something."

I understood that he was trying to put me at ease, but I'd not seen a male in such state of undress before and was distractingly aware of him. Patrick's body glowed with vitality and, against my will, my eyes were drawn to his chest with its sprinkling of gold hair and his flat abdomen. His skin looked so smooth that I longed to trail my fingers over it as one would quality velvet.

My eyes drifted to his face and to my acute embarrassment he was watching me. Heat flooded my cheeks again but he merely slipped into the water. "It's a bit cold but you quickly get used to it. It's not deep."

I let my legs dangle in the water, testing its temperature. It was cooler than I expected, and my skin tingled with it. He stood waist-deep before me. "Just scoot forward on your tail a bit – that's right."

Balanced on the edge, I took a deep breath and … gasped in shock as my shift ballooned around me and I experienced the not entirely unpleasant sensation of cold water hitting my naked skin. I pushed my shift down to stop it floating and stood chest-deep before him. Mud squelched between my toes and I made a face of distaste.

"There's nothing in the mud that bites is there?" I asked with trepidation.

"You're bigger than they are. They'll get out of your way."

"That's not very reassuring."

He grinned and took my hand, leading me out to where the water reached just below my chin. "You alright?"

I nodded. I was becoming accustomed to the temperature. Abruptly, he released my hand and dived under to glide effortlessly below the surface, the sun making shimmering dapples on his back. He surfaced about 10 yards from where I stood and shook the wet hair from his face. "*Whew* … that feels good! Now, what about you? Can you float?"

"I don't know."

He ducked again, cutting gracefully through the water, and bobbed up before me with water streaming over his shoulders and a disarming grin; and in that instance I'd have walked hot coals for that grin – it lit his face, transforming his usually reserved expression into something open and inviting, the likes of which would rival Simon's for beauty.

His eyes glittered like emeralds and he pushed his golden hair, darkened by the water, from his forehead. "Give me your hands," he instructed, and I complied unquestioningly. "Now, I'm going to pull you forward – just let your legs float up naturally, understand?"

I nodded.

"Ready?"

"Yes."

He stepped back and pulled gently. My feet left the mud and I let them drift weightlessly as he continued moving backwards, towing me along.

"Good! Can you kick your legs? No – like a frog. That's good – you're doing it!"

He dragged me up and down in front of the summer-house while I practised my kicking. It was immensely pleasurable this gliding through the cool water. Part of my hair had come down and was clinging wetly to my face, and my sodden shift was tangling awkwardly around my legs, but I didn't mind, so refreshing was it.

"Now, can you feel that weightless feeling?"

"Yes."

"Good. I'm going to release your hands. Just keep floating and move your arms out and around."

"No … I'm not ready!"

"I'm right here."

"No!"

But he let me go and I flailed and sank immediately. When my feet touched the mud my head broke the surface. "You beast!" I gasped, spluttering gracelessly. "I told you … wasn't ready, now … hair's all wet!"

He stood laughing at me and it was infectious. An irrepressible grin spread across my own face and with a sweep of my arm I pushed a wave over him.

It doused him thoroughly and it was my turn to laugh, but his expression sobered me immediately. "Right, now you've done it," and he leapt after me. The game was on.

We splashed and laughed and frolicked like children, and when I bettered him he came for me, lifting me effortlessly and tossing me so that I plunged into the water.

Having administered his reprisal, he was very amused, but I'd swallowed a mouthful of water and came to the surface coughing and wheezing far beyond necessary, and when he approached with a little furrow of concern on his brow, I played it to the hilt. Waiting until he was close enough, I charged at him. The buoyancy of the water lifted me high enough to add strength to my weight and I shoved him under. My vengeance was sweet, if short-lived.

I'd planned my offensive well and immediately lunged for the decking. With my hands on the boards, I tried to heave myself out, but my wet shift clung restrictively. He reached me easily and dragged me back into the water. Turning me to face him, he grasped my wrists, and held my arms wide, pinning me in place.

The water swirled around us. I could feel his warmth through the wet fabric of my shift and my stomach lurched strangely. We were both laughing and breathing hard with our exertions, and in that moment – that giddy, breathless moment – an expression I'd never known crossed his face.

It was surprise, and wonderment, and something unnamed. He stared at me. His green eyes had grown soft. His lips were full and half-open, and instinctively, I closed my eyes, tilted my head, and waited for his kiss.

Painful, uneventful seconds passed.

He dropped my hands and moved back, and my eyes snapped open. His face had hardened and he said gruffly, "Come on, I'll help you out."

He climbed on to the deck, then reached for my hands and pulled me after him. The tense set of his jaw told me clearly what he thought of me now and I cursed my foolishness. Immediately, he turned his back and disappeared into the summer-house.

I stood irresolutely, a puddle forming around my feet, arms covering my chest, completely shamed. He reappeared promptly with a scowl and a blanket. Turning away, he threw the blanket in my direction. "Cover up – your shift is practically transparent." He returned to the summer-house.

I wrapped the blanket about myself like a cloak and followed him. His face had that shuttered look he used to get when we were at odds years ago.

"Could you turn your back please?" I asked quietly.

"I'll leave you in peace." He scooped up his clothes and stalked past me.

Oh God, Alex, you fool … you fool, I berated myself, but there'd be time enough to explore my humiliation. For now, I quickly peeled off my sodden shift and pulled on my dry bloomers tying the string at the waist – glad I'd taken Pat's advice. I dropped my dress over my head, stuck my arms through the little summer sleeves and paused.

I could hear him dressing outside and called meekly, "Could you help with my buttons?"

He strode through the door grimly and wordlessly; he roughly grasped my shoulders and turned me around. Starting at the base of my spine he attended each button, brusquely and with great care to avoid touching my bare skin.

My embarrassment was complete and I itched to escape. I wanted to hide, or mount my brown Gloaming and flee to Yorkshire where I belonged. Tears of self-pity and recrimination prickled my eyes and I pressed my lips together for control.

His hands dropped away when he'd finished and I gathered up my wet shift. He was silent as I left.

∾

That evening at supper, I ate distractedly as Mother, absorbed as ever in gossip, chatted incessantly. From the gist of it, she was trying to decide whether she and Lord Thorncliffe would be well received if they returned to court. He didn't seem to care.

As usual, Pat and I sat opposite each other, but the tension between us was like static before a thunderstorm. I kept my eyes fixed on my plate, miserably spooning tasteless food into my mouth.

Generally, these informal mealtimes were the only occasions the four of us spent together, where we fell into easy banter. Pat and I ordinarily teased and poked fun at one another while even Mother put aside her grudges.

But this evening the mood was strained. Lord Thorncliffe glanced once or twice from me to Patrick and back — no doubt assuming we'd had a falling out — but his wife seemed oblivious. At the first opportunity, I excused myself and retreated to my room to hide out like a criminal.

I lay on my back gazing at the drapery hanging around my bed — the dark red velvet had a swirly pattern I hadn't noticed before and, if I stared long enough, it seemed to have faces in it. It gave me the chills so I looked away and watched the darkening sky through the window as night came down.

At length the room was shrouded in thick darkness. I made no move to light a lamp and when a knock sounded at the door I gave no reply. The door opened slightly. "Miss Alex?"

"Yes, Sylvie."

"Would you like a cup of chocolate? Mrs Bath has made a pot."

"No, thank you."

"Are you unwell?"

"I have a headache." It was true.

"Can I bring you anything?"

"No."

"Thank you, miss." The door closed softly.

I must have drifted into sleep, for I was startled by another knock at the door.

"I said I don't want any chocolate," I called out grumpily.

The door opened. "Then it's good I didn't bring any," Pat's voice filtered through the dark.

My heart leapt in my chest and I held my breath. The door closed quietly and he cursed softly as he bumped something in the dark, then the bed dipped at the edge "Can we talk?" he asked.

Oh yes, I wanted to resolve this and obliterate my embarrassment. But it was done and nothing could reverse it. I remained silent for I knew not what to say.

"Alex?"

I shifted uncomfortably. Then, with acute embarrassment I whispered, "I thought you were going to kiss me."

"I know," he said, gently.

"Then ... why are you here?"

"Because we must talk about the difficulty between us now."

"I feel foolish." My voice was barely audible.

"Why?"

Thankful for the near-perfect darkness that hid my burning

cheeks I said, "Because … because it was silly. I've embarrassed you, and myself. You must think … you must hate me now."

"No." His voice was caressing. He sighed and found my hand in the dark. "I don't hate you at all – far from it. Would it help to know that I almost *did* kiss you?"

"But you didn't," I persisted. "I was the one stupidly pursing my lips at my brother."

He laughed kindly. "We were caught up in the mood. Don't think you didn't look tempting all wet and eyes closed like that. And there would be no crime in it – there's no common blood between us. But it wouldn't be right, that's all."

"Because of Grace?" I held my breath. I hadn't planned to say that, but I hadn't planned any of this.

"You're jealous of Grace, aren't you?"

I bristled. "Of course not! But everyone –"

"Have I ever given any indication that Grace and I are courting? Besides, I've no intention of marrying just yet – despite your mother's best efforts."

"It has been in all the papers. Everyone has talked about it. You're a fine catch, Patrick Washburn," I was unable to disguise the edge in my voice.

He thought for a moment. Then, "Can you keep a secret?"

I responded petulantly. "I suppose."

"Shove over." He released my hand and moved beside me, propping his back against the headboard, his legs stretched out beside me.

"The truth of it is, Grace was courting a young fellow from London. Isabella would never have approved this chap, and when the Camelleris were to return to Italy after the season, Grace opted to remain in London, ostensibly to be with me. We knew the social pages would report on us, but what the gossip-mongers failed to notice, was that Grace and I were always accompanied by George. He has no money, no name, and not even looks, but is one of the nicest people I've ever met. They were secretly married a few months back. Grace is with child, and very, very happy."

Relief washed over me but the irresistible picture of their kiss flooded my memory. That was not the kiss of a friend; that had been a lover's kiss – even to my inexperienced eye.

"What about that kiss? In front of everyone, you kissed her, and she was giggling."

His response was immediate. "That kiss – the only one we've ever shared – was entirely contrived." His teeth showed white in the darkness as he grinned with the memory. "She was giggling because I said we'd give them something to gossip about. It was all a stunt for your mother's and Isabella's benefit."

"Why?"

"To substantiate Grace's decision to stay in London. We also hoped that if your mother thought I was involved with Grace she'd stop banging on about my responsibilities."

"But she hasn't."

"No, sadly. She's terrified I'll marry some peasant and squander the family fortune."

Silently I absorbed all this information and was satisfied that he'd sought me out to resolve things between us, embarrassed as I still was.

"So," he said, easing off the bed – I could just make out his silhouette in the darkness. "Are we friends again?"

"Yes."

"And we're not going to be silly because we nearly kissed?"

"No."

"Good. Did you enjoy your swim today?"

"Yes, thank you."

"Then I shall see you tomorrow evening. I'm riding to Astor tomorrow for something Father wants me to do."

I nodded, though in the dark he probably couldn't see me.

"Goodnight then, Li'l Sis."

❧

He was to be home in the evening but he wasn't. Nor did he appear at breakfast the following morning. Had something happened? Perhaps he'd been accosted on the highway – summer seaside visitors attracted thieves and vagabonds to the roads. I mentioned my concerns to Lord Thorncliffe but he merely shrugged leaving me little choice but to continue my restless wait.

By breakfast the second day, I was very worried. I strolled the gardens seeking Tess, needing the distraction the dog invariably provided. I was wandering by the rear porch when he finally arrived. He rode up the gravel path and trotted towards to the stables looking tired, his clothes rumpled and clearly slept-in. Yet when he saw me, he gave a cheerful wave and I changed course to meet him. He didn't look well and my anxiety increased.

As I approached, he slid with uncharacteristic clumsiness from Equus' back and I saw with dismay that his eyes, normally bright with intelligence and mischief, were dull and red-rimmed. His hair was lank and he smelt of stale wine, tobacco smoke, and … cheap perfume. It quickly became evident that if he was ill, it was his own doing, and instantly, both my pleasure at seeing him, and my concerns for his wellbeing evaporated in a surge of anger and unwarranted jealousy.

He sensed my withdrawal immediately. "What?" he demanded, arms akimbo, a scowl quickly appearing.

"You stink to high heaven. Where've you been?"

"Er …" his ordinarily quick mind failed him and the best he could offer was a pained look. He ran his hand through his unkempt hair. "Father's man … Wheeler, had me at … some tavern and …"

"Forced you to drink and wench, did he?" I challenged, furiously, unreasonably resentful, and maddened that I'd worried over nothing more than an episode of rampant debauchery.

"And you're my keeper?" He found his tongue and his anger ignited immediately. "Christ Alex … every time I turn round you're like shit clinging to a blanket. So what if I was delayed – it's none of your bloody business anyway!"

I stared aghast. "That's so unfair," I said quietly, aware that the lads in the stable had stopped work to follow our argument. Embarrassed and shocked by his attack, I turned on my heel and stalked away but he wasn't finished with me yet.

With a cruelty he'd not subjected me to for years, he shouted after me, "Perhaps if you lived in the real world rather than a land of lovers and fantasies, you'd not be so involved in my life. Go find yourself some other unfortunate swain to level your adorations on."

I froze mid-stride and remained very still. That really, really hurt. It was a dagger thrown at my back and it hit its mark with precision. Forcing my legs to move, I stomped on without looking back, a painful lump clogging my throat. I would not weaken where he could see me.

I marched briskly, head up, eyes straight ahead, determined I would not cry – conveniently ignoring my unreasonable questioning of his whereabouts that had been my contribution to this turn of events. At the edge of the lawn, I plunged into the woods and, shrouded by beech, silver birch, and pine, I broke into a run fuelled by anger, hurt and humiliation.

The undergrowth was thick and clawed at my skirt. I wrenched it free impatiently as I ran on, stumbling over fallen branches and uneven ground. The pain in my heart made me reckless; so familiar was I with our forest at home, I took no care of my surroundings.

Every gasping breath rasped my lungs and, with a cramp gripping my side, I finally slowed to a brisk walk, gulping air in dry, hacking sobs. I continued aimlessly for a long, long time. Eventually, my legs ached and my feet were sore in their thin, summer slippers and, as my anger finally cooled, I rested on a fallen log to catch my breath.

My throat ached with thirst and unshed tears but I breathed

deeply – he wasn't worth it. He'd been intentionally cruel, attacking me in a raw wound. Why? That was not the behaviour of a friend.

I sat on that log for a long time. A squirrel scurried up and down a tree, and, as I watched, two parent birds taught their youngsters to fly. A hare came quite close to my feet, his little, tawny nose twitching nervously before he moved on. And still, I sat.

The cathedral ceiling of branches above my head obscured the sun so it was only when I grew hungry that I realised it must be late afternoon.

I should return to the house; though I seriously hoped Patrick had taken himself back to his whore so I would not have to face him. I brushed bark and dust from the back of my skirt and looked about. I had sat for so long I was uncertain as to the direction I should be taking. I tried to see the position of the sun through the trees, though gathering clouds made it almost impossible. I made a guess, and set out.

My feet were bruised and ached mercilessly in their thin slippers – the delicate things had not been made with such abuse in mind – but I trudged on despite the tenderness of my feet and the stiffness developing in my calves. In my anger I had covered a lot of ground and it was impossible to know how long it would take to get back. But when hunger really set in, I knew I had a long walk ahead of me.

Gradually, the air cooled and, as the pitch and tone of insect and bird life altered, I realised that evening was settling over the forest. Exhaustion and screaming muscles were slowing me. Nothing seemed familiar. Surely the house could not possibly be this far? I was picking my way through the matted undergrowth when I heard the rush of water.

I'd not passed a river this morning, of that I was certain, but I gratefully slaked my thirst, then tried to remember the lay of the land around Waterville. Would I be upstream from the house, or down? Or was I completely off course? I had walked for hours, I could be anywhere and it was now almost dark. The thought that

I might spend the night alone, wandering this infinite labyrinth became a real possibility.

Think Alex …

Leaning against a tree, I tried to clear my head, to rationally think out my situation. There was a lake at Waterville. Did that suggest the house was downstream? Since I did not know what else to do, I pushed away from the tree and followed the flow of the river.

It was tough going. My body was bleeding, bruised, aching. I was hungry and exhausted, and now I was cold as well. The trees and shapes in the dark began to play with my fatigued mind and a night in the woods loomed with terrifying images.

Suddenly I froze. I'd heard something. It was there; a careless crashing through the undergrowth – doubtless an animal.

Holding my breath and listening intently, I thought the sounds were coming closer and knew with mounting terror that I'd never have the strength to run. Were there fearsome creatures in English forests? Did we still have wolves? My stomach knotted, my hands grew clammy and my heart thudded in my breast. Urgently, I began looking for somewhere to hide – something, anything …

Don't panic, Alex … and breathe …

I was chilled but perspiration broke on my brow. The sound was coming closer, gaining momentum. It moved quickly and noisily – definitely animal – a large one by the snapping of branches and pounding of its footfalls. And it had scented me – I knew it!

Terror gripped me and I couldn't move. My breathing was short and erratic. The sound grew louder as the creature drew closer. It smashed through the foliage. It was almost upon me and cold sweat trickled down my back.

With a crash the undergrowth shattered and a great shadow exploded from the dark and was upon me. My scream was cut off by my chest being crushed as I was pinned to the ground.

I thrashed and cried, kicking, screaming, wrestling for my

very life. Yet all the while, my fear-fogged brain was trying to register something – something not right, and it was with stunned incredulity that realised I was not being mauled.

My face, neck and hands were being thoroughly and enthusiastically slobbered over by a relentless tongue. Its owner joyously straddled me, expertly resisting all efforts to eject it.

"Tess?"

The animal flopped beside me, wagging her tail furiously. My relief was so intense that I immediately burst into tears. Sprawled on a decaying pile of forest litter, I held the huge dog close and sobbed from fear, fatigue, relief and the echo of harsh words.

Tess whined and snuggled her long body close. She was warm, her fur coarse, and she smelt like a stable-blanket, but she was as welcome as a duck down quilt.

We were lying thus when I heard their approach through the undergrowth. First I heard the voices, then I saw their shapes in the dark. Recognising Briggs by the friendly orange glow and the scent of his pipe, the other I knew by his tall silhouette.

"Good dog, Tess. Yer a good girl, eh?" The dog abandoned me returning proudly to her master, while Patrick knelt beside me.

"Are you alright?" he asked gently.

I hated him for seeing me this way. I hated him even more for what he'd said that morning, but I nodded and wiped my nose on my sleeve.

"Here, I'll help you – let's get you home."

Stubbornly, I slapped his hands away and gritted my teeth, attempting to stand but the effort was too much and my knees buckled.

Without a word, he scooped me into his arms. Too relieved to fight, I buried my face in his neck and wept again.

To my surprise, following downstream had been correct. After about ten minutes of walking, we emerged behind the lake. It was well past dusk and the stars glittered like crystals in the sky.

Briggs walked beside us and Tess cantered cheerfully ahead. Lamps were bobbing down the lawn toward us, carried by Lord Thorncliffe and Janet, Mother was there as well. Pat restored me to my feet, supporting me with an arm about my waist. Janet arrived first followed by Mother. Each put a solicitous arm around me as they guided me up the porch steps.

"See to it that gardener is rewarded, Gerrard," Mother said over her shoulder as we entered the house.

I could not remember a time in my life when I had been as exhausted. Mother was stiff with contained anger. Her thinly-plucked eyebrows were set in a straight line as she instructed the maids to fill a bath with hot water and turn down the bed. "And bring some food," she ordered as an afterthought.

"We were worried," she said, watching as Janet stripped off my filthy dress. "You did not appear at the dinner table – so unlike you."

Janet threw the dress on the floor and Mother crinkled her nose in disgust. "Well, that's the end of *that* gown. Take your shift off." She rummaged in my dresser for a nightgown. "Heavens, look at the state of your feet! And when you didn't appear for supper that no-good brother of yours – still in bed nursing a morning-after when Gerrard roused him – went out looking for you."

I relaxed into the great iron bath, steaming with delicious rose-scented water while Mother sat by the window, tapping her fingers on the arm of the chair. Janet lathered and rinsed my hair and, when at length I emerged from the water, she wrapped me in a warm towel.

Mother dropped the nightgown over my head then dismissed my maid. She waited for Janet to close the door before turning to me.

"At least Patrick had the good sense to get that gardener and his dog involved," she said grudgingly. She studied me for a moment, with something similar to concern on her face. "You gave us a scare today, Alexandra," she said, finally.

"I gave myself a scare too," I said attempting a small smile.

"What were you doing? We thought you'd fallen into the lake … got yourself drowned."

"Just walking, I became lost."

She appeared to consider that for a moment, then said, "The stable-boys reported that you and Patrick had a rather loud disagreement this morning. Said you marched off in anger. Is this true?"

I stared at my hands clasped before me.

"Well? Did you argue?"

"Yes," I said, contritely.

"What about? What could you possibly argue about that would see you go off into the woods like that – for an entire day?"

I threw my mind about for something reasonable.

"I'm waiting," Mother said.

"It was … quite silly really." I thought hurriedly. "Something about … Gloaming, the horse. I'm so tired, I can't even remember now."

She looked unconvinced, but Mother, never overly concerned with the associations of others – unless it involved an opportunity to her own advantage – was already disinclined to pursue the matter.

"Perhaps you've been spending too much time with him, Alexandra. You'll learn that he is not the stuff from which good companions are made. He's too arrogant … too self-interested."

She rose and stood with her hand on the door-knob. "In any case, your supper will be here soon. Try to eat, and get plenty of rest tonight. We are leaving for Yorkshire tomorrow at daybreak."

The door closed and my shoulders slumped wearily.

We were going home.

Part of me rejoiced at the thought of seeing Jemima again, and while I was saddened by what had happened between Patrick and me, I would certainly enjoy the tranquillity of Broughton Hall, with no-one to set my emotions a-jangling as he did.

My thoughts were interrupted as Sylvie brought in a tray of cold meat, roasted vegetables, bread and tea.

"Oh, Miss Alex," she said, as she placed the tray on the desk. "We were all so worried – even Master Pat."

I snorted derisively and hoped he was riddled with guilt.

"Did you know you are leaving tomorrow?" she asked as I fell ravenously on the food. "I have already packed most of your things. I shall finish while you eat."

She busied herself laying out my travelling costume and fresh underthings for the journey and said over her shoulder, "Master Pat would speak with you. He was in the kitchen and he asked me to tell him when you were dressed."

"I'm not talking to him."

"He seems anxious to talk to you," she insisted.

"He can stay that way!" I snapped and immediately felt guilty. I sighed. "I'm sorry, Sylvie. I've had a … I've …"

"That's alright, miss. I'll finish the packing if you don't mind."

I did not sleep well. I tossed, fretfully running my argument with Patrick through my head. His cruelty was unforgivable, yet in truth, I had no right to question his whereabouts. An unjustifiable if compelling jealousy had released my tongue. A more mature woman would have curbed her behaviour. Any wonder he would forever regard me as his *Li'l Sis*. Finally, after much soul-searching, I resolved to speak with him before our departure and attempt to make amends.

When Janet woke me an hour before daybreak she helped me into my travelling clothes and thrust a plate of oat cakes before me. I ate while she buttoned me up.

Dabbing at my mouth with a napkin, I said, "I must speak with Master Patrick. I'll meet you at the coach."

She frowned. "He's not here."

"What do you mean, he's not here?"

She shrugged. "Apparently when you wouldn't see him last evening, he said some rude words, then he stamped off to the stables."

"Blast!" I swore, but almost immediately decided he may have come in during the night. There was one way to be certain. I hiked up my skirt and, despite my aching muscles and bruised feet, left the room at a run.

The servants' stairs led outside by the quickest route. I plunged down, nearly bowling over one surprised footman on my way, and stumbled outside into the pre-dawn gloom, then sprinted to the stables.

It was black as pitch inside and the smell of hay and horse hit me, seemingly stronger in darkness than in daylight. I went immediately toward Nella's stall. She recognised me and approached hopefully.

"Sorry, old girl, no carrots this morning." I rubbed her nose as I passed to the next stall. It was empty. I could feel its emptiness through the dark, and heard its hollow sound when I said, "Equus?"

He was gone – probably returned to his slattern – and the knowledge, along with a sense of my own stupidity, cut deeply.

The coaches stood ready in a splash of light from their lamps. The horses shuffled and stamped impatiently in their harness. I flopped despondently on to the padded, velvet seat, exhausted from lack of sleep and the previous day's exertions, and now my head ached dully. Mother could be heard inside the house issuing a string of imperious instructions.

Lord Thorncliffe sat astride Canto supervising the loading of our luggage. As he manoeuvred to the side of the coach I hailed him and opened my face innocently. "Pat must be still abed. I'd thought he would come to say goodbye."

He gave me a brief, preoccupied glance, "Did he not say his

farewell last night?" I shook my head and he continued. "He said he would see you after you were settled. He was returning to Astor for the night."

My fears were confirmed and my stomach turned over but my step-father's attention was distracted. "Gordon, be careful with that, will you," he pointed at a trunk with his riding-crop. "And did my horse get a good breakfast this morning? Not that he needs it really," he said as an aside. "Look at the condition he's carrying after summering out in that paddock. Don't you think this horse is fat, Alex?"

"You'll ride it off him on the way home."

"Yes, probably you're right. No, Gordon – lengthways. Patrick said something about Wheeler's mill needing repairs before the harvest … I don't know … Gordon! Must I climb up there and do it myself?"

Miserably, I sat back in my seat as Mother appeared, buttoning her gloves and trailed by Eleanor.

"Where's Janet?" Mother asked.

"I don't know."

"Why not? She's your maid. Go find her."

I suppressed a sigh and stepped down just as Sylvie rushed up and grasped my arm. "Miss Alex!" she said breathlessly, skilfully avoiding Mother's glare. "Please come, quickly!"

"What is it?" I demanded once we were out of Mother's earshot, but she lifted her skirt almost to her knees, and ran through the house. Following behind, I nearly bumped into her when she stopped abruptly at the door to the rear porch. Moving aside, she pushed it open and jerked her head, urging me through. I caught my skirt up in one hand and stepped outside.

A swirl of mist hung above the lawn and dew-dampened, late summer lavender scented the air. In the shadows, his silhouette stood on the grass, Equus beside him, her head bowed as she cropped the lawn.

"Pat?"

"I could not let you leave like this." His voice was disembodied in the dimness of dawn. "I can't tell you how rotten I feel for the things I said to you yesterday."

I barely heard his words. Fairly flying down the steps I ran at him and he caught me. We stood together, arms wrapped around each other, my face buried in his neck, breathing in his wonderful spicy fragrance.

He took my forearms and put me away so he could peer into my face. "Now listen well, Alex," he said earnestly. "I am sorry I hurt you, though in your prideful way you marched into the woods and got yourself lost – it was my fault. I ask you to forgive me."

"Of course I forgive you," I cried throwing myself against his chest again and feeling his arms go about me.

"Miss Alex!" Sylvie said in a hoarse whisper from the porch. "The countess is calling – you must go."

He was the first to break away. With his hand on my waist, he led me up the steps. "I came home early … I didn't want you leaving with us on bad terms. We are both too stubborn for our own good."

On the porch, Sylvie grabbed my hand and tugged me towards the door, but I looked back to where he stood with the first gold traces of morning streaking the sky behind him.

"Safe travels, Li'l Sis," he whispered.

I faltered.

With a small cry, I broke away from Sylvie. Taking him completely by surprise, I flung my arms about his neck and kissed him decisively on the mouth.

His lips were warm and soft and, though I had no experience of such things, I knew instinctively that my kiss was not unwelcome, for in that splendid moment, his lips moved on mine and his mouth opened. His hand reached up to cup my head while his other slid about my waist and drew me against him.

But it was all too brief. Sylvie wrenched me away, and we ran towards Mother's voice, raised in anger, demanding my presence in the coach.

CHAPTER 13

My eyes were closed. I was feigning sleep. The motion of the coach had long since rocked Janet and Mother into slumber. Only Eleanor sat rigid and watchful.

Hugging the memory of Patrick's farewell to my heart, I replayed our kiss in my mind, over and over. He'd come home – of the same mind as I, not wanting our parting to be on bad terms. He'd said once he would never apologise for anything – yet he'd apologised to me. Did the rogue have a conscience after all?

Then I was struck by a thought. The morning we'd quarrelled he had positively reeked from his night's activities. But this morning, I'd buried my face in his neck and there'd been no such odour. He had been out all night and yet he hadn't been drunk, and only his usual spicy scent clung to him, mixed understandably with that of horse and leather.

Perhaps he had, in truth, been conducting business. Regardless, he had returned. He cared – despite himself – he cared!

I sighed happily, wrapped in the memory of his arms and wonderful mouth, and lulled by the swaying of the coach, I drifted into a happy sleep.

⌒

The journey was uneventful and tedious. Mother and Eleanor gossiped and I gathered that our early return to Yorkshire resulted from a falling-out Mother had had with one of the local ladies of influence – a feisty duchess, no less.

In any case, it didn't concern me. The only point that mattered was that by the third day of our journey I was missing Patrick terribly, and forced to admit that my feelings were nothing to do with friendship – they were more.

Yet, I knew they would ever be unrequited. Oh, I'd no doubt he enjoyed my company, but I was to Patrick nothing more than his Li'l Sis – which was why he hadn't kissed me at the lake; why he always held me at arm's length. My infatuation had shown me for a foolish and inexperienced girl, and I should thank Patrick for not taking advantage of my raw innocence. I smirked inwardly – so much for the image of the unscrupulous libertine he so carefully cultivated!

⌒

Our coaches lumbered up the driveway of Broughton Hall and I alighted, stretching my jolted muscles with relief. Amidst the chaos of arrival, I was handed a letter. It was from Hamish, requesting a visit to pay his respects. He mentioned that the senior Lord Elginbury was desirous that his son visit regularly in order that we two became better acquainted. He awaited our earliest response.

My feeling that all was good with the world evaporated immediately and I was plunged into depression. Easy to pretend that my betrothal was a malicious fiction when my contracted husband was out of sight, but, with the receipt of his letter, he was suddenly made flesh and blood again.

Mother, clearly delighted, sent a welcoming response immediately.

❧

"That one there looks like a castle," Julia said pointing to the fat, white, non-threatening cloud that drifted in a duck-egg blue sky. My friend and I were lying in the lush grass at the edge of the park. We had removed our hats and shoes, for warm summer was yet to give way to cool autumn, though the trees abutting our park were already turning gold and russet.

"See," Julia continued. "There's the turret and that bit there's the drawbridge."

"It's a frog, and your turret is one of his legs."

"Well, what about the drawbridge?"

"That's his head."

She was unconvinced, but in the time we'd been debating, the cloud had rolled and churned and now we both agreed it resembled a horse with a too-long neck.

The bees had noted the imminent arrival of autumn and the air hummed with their final pollen gathering. The afternoon sun was soaking deliciously into my bones through the yellow-striped cotton dress I wore and, when I closed my eyes, dapples of orange and red danced through my eyelids.

"I have something to tell you," Julia said, and her voice was heavy with import.

"What is it?" I didn't open my eyes, but was quite alert.

There was a slight pause as she drew breath. "I am betrothed."

I sat up quickly and stared at her. Her pretty, freckled face was aglow with happiness and her eyes shone brightly.

"You're *happy*?" I said in astonishment, and her vigorous nod caused her burnished curls to bob.

"Do I know him?" I asked.

"You know *of* him. Deon Morehead. You've not met him, but you will – he's Adrienne's brother."

If she had a fancy for this Deon she'd been quiet about it. But now she gushed, "Oh, Alex, he's so handsome and such a nice person. Just wait until you meet him – what?" her face fell.

"Well, it's just that you've never mentioned him before."

She gripped my hand earnestly, "I haven't said anything because I never dreamed … but I've fancied him for so long – it's a dream come true."

"Then I *am* happy for you, Jules."

She grinned delightedly, "I did so hope Papa could arrange it. I think Mama wanted someone with a title, but Papa said it was more important that I be happy. He said that since we were wealthier than the Moreheads, it should not be difficult to come to an understanding." She winked slyly, "And it wasn't."

"Do you think you will have a long betrothal?" I said, thinking of my own arrangement with Hamish.

"I'm seventeen, quite old enough to be married. Mama agrees but said it couldn't possibly be arranged until next year – she's planning something big. I don't mind either way. With everything agreed, it's like we're married anyway."

"I think there's more to it than that," I said knowingly. Having been betrothed for some time now, I considered myself quite the expert. "For starters, you'll have to … you know … share his bed."

She smiled archly. "Oh, that won't be so bad. We've already kissed, and I know I like that – a lot."

My eyes widened, gleefully scandalised, "You've *kissed* him? What was it like?"

She stared at me in surprise, "*What was it like*? You've kissed Hamish, haven't you?"

I recoiled indignantly, "Of course!"

"Really?" she sounded sceptical and I flushed self-consciously.

"No," I conceded, "not really. Not unless you count a quick peck on the cheek … like a brother."

She nodded with satisfaction. "As I thought – I can't imagine Hamish being … you know … like *that*."

"Like *what*?" I demanded, piqued.

She grinned. "Passionate. It's not a real kiss if his lips don't move."

I thought about that for a moment. "Hmm, I don't know what I'd do if Hamish wanted to kiss me like that."

"That's not good – I simply *adore* kissing Deon."

In truth there was only one person I wanted to kiss, but … she was watching me.

"You don't want to kiss Hamish," she guessed shrewdly.

"Julia," I said with significance, "can you keep a secret?"

She rolled her eyes, indicating the foolishness of my question.

"There's only one person I want to kiss, and … I *have* kissed him."

Her eyes popped and suddenly she was grasping my hands eagerly. "Do tell!"

"You must never –"

"*Yes*! *Yes*! I shan't say anything. Just tell me before I burst."

I felt a silly grin spread across my lips. "Patrick."

"Saints alive!" my friend squealed in delight. "You kissed *Pa* –"

"*Shush*!" I hissed savagely, glancing over my shoulder.

Her eyes were shining with delight. "Oh Alex! Tell me all about it." She knelt before me, heedless of the grass staining her skirt, "How? When? In Devon, I'll wager!"

I nodded and began with the near-kiss in the lake. "And later, when we talked about it, he admitted he was tempted to kiss me."

"Ohh," Julia fairly swooned with pleasure. "He must have a fancy for you, Alex … oh, how utterly *romantic*!"

I waved my hand dismissively. "Stop it – he doesn't have a fancy for me, Jules. He said I had looked appealing in the water that's all … he also said that I was his little sister and it would be wrong. In any case, he went off with some other girl."

Julia's mouth turned down. "Another girl?"

"He didn't come home one night and … he'd been with this other girl. We quarrelled about it."

"So how did you come to kiss him?"

"It was just as we were leaving to come home. I hadn't seen him since our quarrel but he sent a maid to fetch me so he could say goodbye."

"He fancies you," Julia sing-songed and I made a face at her.

"He didn't kiss me – I kissed him. He apologised for our disagreement and hugged me – that's all. *I* kissed *him* – on the mouth."

"Ooh what did he do?" She was visibly squirming now.

"He kissed me back … but I had to run because Mother was calling. It was only for a few seconds."

"Did his lips move?"

"Well, it was so quick," I said, recollecting, "but his mouth opened."

"*Ah!*" Julia shrieked. "That's even better!"

"Is it?"

She nodded enthusiastically. "And was it good?"

"Oh, Jules," I said, rapturously, "it was wonderful, *he* was wonderful, his lips are so soft, and he smells so good."

"Saints alive," my friend breathed, sobering suddenly. "You're in love!"

"Don't be ridiculous!" I snapped.

"Oh yes you are. But don't worry Alex, I'll not tell a living soul."

"You'd better not else I'll deny it and tell everyone it is your own fancy."

She smiled mysteriously and lay back languidly on the grass. "You wouldn't be far off."

"What does that mean? I thought you loved Deon?"

"I do, but that doesn't stop me from … you know … having thoughts."

I looked at her quizzically and she said, "Oh come on, Alex, you know what I mean. There's something about Patrick that … makes a girl think about … things."

"Things?"

"Things … you know … *doing things* … with him. Heavens, do I have to spell it out?"

No, I didn't need her to spell it out. I knew exactly what she meant and the blood in my cheeks burst into flame, which caused her to hoot with laughter.

∾

A letter arrived from Italy. Isabella wrote that Anne and Maeve were doing well and therefore, unless their Mother expressly preferred it, she welcomed their continued company and requested her friend's permission for her daughters to remain indefinitely.

Other news conveyed was that Catarina was affianced to an Italian nobleman and Grace was in London. Isabella's youngest was refusing to return home and Isabella prayed fervently that her daughter continued her liaison with Patrick.

Mother's reply explained that we had recently visited with Patrick in Devon and regretfully, there was no mention of Grace. Mother also granted permission for Anne and Maeve to remain in Italy, provided they were not inconveniencing their hostess, and made arrangements to extend their allowances.

∾

As autumn progressed, the squirrels scurried about collecting acorns from the Great Oak. These mornings, Jemima ran like she'd been released from a cage, and I too felt my heart overflowing with vitality. We bounced along the terraced gardens and trotted down the stone stairway to the orchard, startling rabbits who industriously gnawed on grass and fallen apples. Jemima considered it great sport to chase them but, as her agile quarry darted through narrow gaps in the stone wall, she stood on her rear legs, staring after them, her great, pink tongue lolling out.

Meg was walking freely and conducting garbled conversations

with everyone. She adored Jemima, often wrapping her pudgy arms about the endlessly tolerant dog. Life was relaxed, the weather mild, the days pleasant, and, into this agreeable environ, Hamish arrived.

He rode in one afternoon on his smart bay gelding. I was positioned where the afternoon sun slanted across the porch, mending a skirt-hem. At the sound of his approach, I shaded my eyes to see two riders and a pack horse draw up before me, and I rose and descended the steps while Hamish dismounted and swept off his hat in a flamboyant genuflection.

"Greetings, Miss Broughton," he said, in his Scottish burr.

"Greetings, My Lord," I responded, immediately and unreasonably irritated by him.

"Get back, dog," he said, wrinkling his fastidious nose as Jemima drew close.

"Jemima, come here!" I said, quickly. "Have your man take the horses to the stables, My Lord, then he may see Cook for something to eat."

Hamish turned to the young, and rather handsome, man holding the horses. "Hear that Grahame?"

The groom nodded.

"Off you go, then." Turning to me he said, "It is good to see you again."

"And you, My Lord."

"Och now, if I'm to be your husband," he waved a be-ringed hand, "best you call me Hamish."

I recognised his gesture as an effort to be pleasant and smiled as I led him into the house where Lord Thorncliffe was thumping down the stairs. "Hamish, lad, how are you?" He gave the young Scot a hearty backslap and Hamish visibly winced.

"Very well, thank you My Lord, and you?"

"Excellent, excellent. Just give your hat to Sarah here – there's a lad." He turned to a young maid waiting quietly behind him. "And Sarah, please bring refreshments to the drawing-room."

That afternoon Lord Thorncliffe, Hamish and I, sipped tea and exchanged news, and in the evening, Mother joined us for supper – Gerrard's favourite hare pie. Hamish patted his soft paunch, and stated firmly that he'd never enjoyed better. He helped himself to a second serve, and Patrick's firm torso – tanned and glistening with water – sprang unbidden to mind.

When Gerrard called for brandy, Mother and I rose and left the men at the dining table.

In the parlour, Eleanor waited with Mother's embroidery frame. Taking up her work, Mother spoke contemplatively, "He's quite nice, don't you think, Alexandra?"

"Perhaps."

"Are you more accepting of your betrothal now?"

"Given a choice I'd rather not marry at all." A frown creased her brow and I added quickly, "but I expect I could do worse."

"You could do considerably worse, couldn't she Eleanor."

"Indeed," her witch responded dutifully.

❧

Over the next week, contrary to polite practice, Hamish and I spent much time alone together. We talked as we strolled through the park, played games and even discovered several common interests.

But the seasons were turning and one afternoon we sat beside a glowing fire while the rain pattered against the windows. I was stitching buttons on a little jacket for Meg when he said without warning, "It was my father's arrangement, this betrothal. I'd seen you only once – here one summer – and I confess, I didn't want to consider marriage."

I was taken aback by his directness but was glad of the opportunity for discussion. He shrugged and went on, "I must be practical. My father is unwell, you see, and I've been forced to assist in the running of his business interests. Unfortunately, there's a price to pay for my father's previous excesses – being at the English court – our wealth all but drained away. Besides that though, Father desperately wants to see my own heir before he dies. So …" he sighed dramatically. "I must marry."

I thought about Mother's constant theme and wondered if she was perhaps right? She had arranged this marriage, and in her position, I too would probably arrange to marry Anne and Patrick – it tied everything up neatly.

Anne, I knew, would favour wealth and position over a love match any day. But I'd rather marry for love. I looked at Hamish. He wasn't possessed of unpleasant looks, for all his flaccid, sedentary physique, and he dressed fussily – any wonder Anne found him attractive. But then I thought of Patrick's cynical, masculine face, his unkempt hair and casual manner and exhaled regretfully, for the man I was to marry sat before me now, one leg crossed neatly over the other, trousers tucked up at the knee, stroking his new moustache.

"What ails your father?" I asked to distract myself.

"His doctors say he has a growth in his gut. Nothing they can do. There are days when the pain is so great he cannot rise from his bed or even eat."

"How terrible," I responded, sincerely. "To be so debilitated …"

"Aye. It worsens and he knows he will die of it. Father says others our age are wed already – he is anxious that we produce an heir."

"Perhaps, but I have many child-bearing years before me."

His laugh was short and derisive. He had a gap between his two front teeth that I'd not noticed before. "You must know … you would not be my choice. You are rather … *unrefined*. Perhaps in time … Perhaps when you're … twenty?"

My relief shadowed my annoyance. The man was simply too pompous, but his clear reluctance to marry me – despite his father's urgings – pleased me. I nodded and forced a smile.

"Good – I shall advise my father."

Hamish departed the following day. He kissed me coolly on each cheek and promised to write, and I was happy enough with this.

❧

Only a day after Hamish's departure, Simon arrived unexpectedly. He looked relaxed and happy and taller than his last visit. He scooped me into a tight hug that lifted me off my feet, and planted a smacking kiss on my forehead.

Washed and changed from his travel-stained clothes, he joined Gerrard, Mother and me in the parlour. Gerrard poured brandy for the two men and plum wine for Mother and me, and Simon cheerfully regaled us with stories from Oxford and his friends. He asked after Maeve and Anne, and Meg was brought down from the nursery. Then, quite without warning, Simon announced that he and Patrick had decided to join the war in Europe.

It was all so sudden. My face grew cold as the blood drained from it and the wine turned sour in my mouth. Mother rose from her chair, her face taut. "Without consulting your family?"

"The British are launching a new offensive in the spring. They're calling for young officers – "

"That's not what I asked," she said through thin lips.

Without waiting for his reply, she lifted her chin and drew a long breath through her nose, then stalked from the room.

Simon watched her leave then turned to where I sat staring at him in astonishment. "You've made up your mind?" His nod answered my question and tears spilled on to my cheeks.

"I have enlisted as a doctor."

"How can you?" I cried. "You've not completed your studies."

"I've completed nearly three years. It's enough – they're desperate and it is a rare opportunity. I should learn more there in a month than an entire year at the university. I came home to say goodbye."

Thus far Lord Thorncliffe had remained silent. Now he muttered, "More considerate than my son."

"He is in Devon, Sir," Simon defended quickly. "Securing everything and making arrangements for the estate's management in his absence. He has written a letter – it should arrive any day."

"Well good for you!" I stood up so abruptly my chair jumped. "Good for you both! You'll go get yourselves killed and for what? I hope you enjoy yourselves." I strode from the room slamming the door after me.

Later, when Janet came to attend me, she said, "Oh you're already abed. You've no need of my help."

When I didn't respond, she counselled, "Miss Alex, men go to war. It's what they do."

"I know that!" I snapped impatiently but then began to cry. "But … oh why do they have to go? And … and he just comes out with it … *I'm going to war* … as if he's going to a garden party."

"I'm certain it wasn't meant like that."

I turned my face into the pillow and sobbed. "And … Patrick … he didn't even write … didn't tell me … at all."

Her voice was sharp. "Why would he write to *you*? He's writing to his father, isn't he?"

With a shuddering breath, I controlled myself and swiped at my tears with the sleeve of my nightgown. My betrothed had only recently left our house, and I'd almost resigned myself to the marriage, yet the mere thought of Patrick obliterated all good sense.

"You're right. I'm being silly," I said with a weak smile, but her expression remained grim as she left my room.

❧

Mother had evidently considered her course of attack, and when Simon joined us for breakfast the following morning, she launched her offensive, berating him roundly for his lack of familial regard.

"You're so ready to abandon your inheritance, your tenants your family – you ought to be seeking a wife, breeding heirs. And Patrick – how typically irresponsible of him – the last of the Washburn line. If he were killed – either of you – with no heirs, what do you expect would happen?"

"The estate will have enough income to support you, you need have no worries about that," Simon said with a heavy dose of sarcasm.

"That's not the point," Mother argued and turned to her husband. "The males in this family have no concept of responsibility. The blame lies squarely with their fathers. Dudley was never a proper father to Simon," she said, conveniently forgetting her own parental failings. "And you, Gerrard, had you applied more discipline to that boy of yours he would not be running amok now."

Lord Thorncliffe cleared his throat. "I'd hardly say he's running amok, Miriam."

"I would – straying across the countryside like a dog on the scent, chasing anything in petticoats – what would you call it? What did you call it when that filthy farmer came to your door claiming –"

"I'm anxious to receive this letter and see what he has to say," her husband interrupted decisively.

Thus far I'd been invisible, but now Mother turned to me, "What do you think, Alexandra? You could hardly be happy with your brothers going to war."

Three sets of eyes bored into me as though our very fates hung on my response. I replied immediately, "No, Mother, I'm not happy, but since when has a woman's thoughts on war ever been considered?"

"Hmph," she grunted, with reluctant admiration. "You see, Gerrard, even Alexandra knows it is foolishness."

"That isn't what she said."

"It doesn't matter," Simon interjected. "Pat and I are decided and there's an end to it."

Later that morning, Patrick's letter arrived and confirmed what Simon had already told us. Mother's fury was renewed. She berated Simon for conspiring with Patrick behind their parents' backs, but my brother merely smiled and shrugged.

∾

Since it was pointless to argue, I decided to enjoy Simon's company as much as I could. In an echo of our childhood, we wandered through the woods with Jemima at our heels, we pilfered from the kitchens, and played games before the fire in the parlour, only stopping short at our more juvenile pursuits, like spitting competitions and tree climbing.

We took a day trip to Wolstone market and visited friends we hadn't seen for a long time. Elspbeth was still there working magic with her needle. She greeted us enthusiastically as we admired her work. Some of the older ladies competed shamelessly for Simon's attention and I was puffed with pride at the effect Simon's looks had on these work-hardened women.

Jasper and Samuel's mother, the fishmonger's widow, offered us our choice of the freshest trout. She told us that Jasper had married a nice girl from Rippon but she still had Samuel on her hands.

"What's a worthy woman t'do?" she moaned. "Widowed eight years 'n' more, how'm I t'find a man t'take me on wi' 'im lurkin' about?"

"Now Mistress Fish," Simon teased, pinching her plump cheek. "What man with air in his lungs could resist you?"

As we moved on, her wistful sigh was audible.

"Tell me again why you want to leave all this behind and go to war?" I said and he laughed and draped his arm casually across my shoulders as we drifted along the cobbled lanes of the little farming village.

∾

Simon departed the following Monday. Though she'd barely spoken to him since his announcement, Mother made an appearance in the silvery morning to bid her son farewell. They spoke quietly and she dabbed at her eyes with a lace-edged handkerchief.

He shook hands with Lord Thorncliffe, embraced Janet, Clara, Cook and little Meg, then turned to me.

"Please take care of yourself, Simon — and Patrick too," I said with a tremor in my voice. "Don't either of you do anything stupid or brave — just come home safely."

He hugged me tightly and kissed my cheek. "Don't worry. Pretend we're in Oxford and we'll be home in no time."

I was growing weary of goodbyes, but this occasion was sharpened by fear — what if they were wounded? What if they were never to come home …?

∽

That winter the snow piled deep around our house. It lay thick and weighty on the sagging branches of the trees in the park and forest. The water in the horse trough froze each night forcing the stable-boys to chip it away with mattocks and refill it each morning. Deer and other creatures ventured to the edge of the park with their young, hunger bettering their natural timidity. They dug at the snow with their cold hooves looking for acorns and roots and, in Simon's absence, I took it upon myself to direct the stable-boys to distribute bales of hay where the hungry animals could find them. I could not remember a winter as cold and I busied myself in the nursery beside a hearty fire with Clara and Meg — my sewing was showing a marked improvement — and I tried not to worry about my brothers in Europe preparing for a spring campaign.

Meg turned three in February and, several weeks later, spring arrived in a parade of snowdrops and crocuses. They pushed their way through the frozen earth as the melting snow slipped in great lumps from the trees making dead thudding sounds.

It was around this time we learned that Sir Arthur Wellesley was pressing an advantage in Spain. His armies had besieged Cuidad Rodrigo in January and embarked upon a furious orgy of rape, pillage and drunkenness. Naturally, we English did not believe a word of it – that barbaric style of warfare was doubtless a proclivity of the Scots, but our own troops – gentlemen to a man – would never conduct themselves so appallingly.

Nevertheless, the newspapers continued their reports claiming that Wellesley was powerless to curtail such behaviour and allowed his men to eventually grow too tired or too drunk – whichever came first – and cease rampaging of their own accord.

Notwithstanding, the siege of Cuidad Rodrigo was successful. In April 1812 they marched on to Badajoz. One in eight British troops were killed or wounded, the survivors again reportedly enjoying a frenzy of theft and rape that lasted several days.

I had no idea where Simon or Patrick were, whether they were involved in these sieges, or whether they were even anywhere near each other. Simon's letters were brief and infrequent – Patrick's were non-existent.

I remember it rained a lot that spring. I could often be found in the library with only Jemima for company, watching rivulets of water stream down the windows and seep through tiny gaps to pool on the ledges. One afternoon, I sat very still and watched *the lady* drift silently along the rows of books. She took her time reading their titles, and when she turned she saw me watching – our eyes met in some timeless, spaceless connection that sent a shiver along my spine.

Her mouth was moving, she was trying to speak, but I could hear nothing. At length, she simply evaporated.

Spring advanced through May and it was my birthday. I was now 18 years old – 18 years and on the brink of a painfully predictable future. Marriage to Hamish, babies and … nothing …

As the days lengthened towards summer, I lingered out of doors with Clara and Meg. We lay in the grass playing games and laughing as Jemima and the little girl chased butterflies. It was serene, peaceful and mind-numbingly habitual. I could not believe that more than a year had passed since the summer we spent in Devon – since I'd last seen Patrick.

Mail arrived from Hamish – his father insisted that he visit again and I acquiesced; prepared to welcome any relief from the daily monotony.

He arrived on a warm spring evening. The past months had altered him only by adding to his paunch but he was, as always, immaculately and fashionably dressed.

Each afternoon we shared a jug of lemonade and conversation of no more weight than the weather and the latest plays being performed in London, and gradually we grew to know each other well enough that when Janet delivered a crumpled and travel-stained letter addressed in Simon's hand, Hamish noted my anxiety.

"I shall leave you so you may read it," he said immediately.

"Thank you," I responded, but he remained seated.

"Alex?"

I looked up and he made a small smile of apology. "Alex, my father … he has … he is asking about our nuptials."

My heart leapt into my mouth. "But, we agreed – we both agreed we'd wait."

"True, however … my father's illness … he feels we shouldn't wait any longer."

He watched my face closely as I threw about desperately for an excuse to postpone our marriage. Eventually, coming to my rescue, he said, "Look, I want this no more than you but we shall have to discuss it in more detail. For now, I shall leave you to your letter."

As he stood I said, "Please tell your father … explain that my brothers are at the Peninsular War. I would await their return."

"My father is dying and would see an heir before it's too late," he insisted.

I rose, sighing, and touched his arm in what I hoped was a conciliatory gesture. "I know and I have agreed to marry you, Hamish, but —"

"You think I want to marry you?" His chin jutted out petulantly and he wrinkled his nose like he'd stepped in dog's turd. "I am in honour bound to my father. Under other circumstances I would never even *talk* to the likes of you, and now you place me in this difficult position."

My mouth fell open in surprise, so unprepared was I for such overt hostility, and I stared at him. Finally, he exhaled with a sulky, "*Hmph*. I shall leave you to your beloved brother."

8 May 1812
Dearest Sister,

I trust this letter finds you well as I am, if not in spirit, at least physically. I'd only been in this place a week before I found that war is not as I expected even for a medical man. Long, unpredictable hours and inclement weather (either too hot, too cold, too dry or too wet) make for a most unpleasant environ.

I cannot begin to describe my professional experiences over the months here. Suffice to say that my medical training, albeit incomplete, in no way prepared me for these horrors. The hospital to which I have been assigned does not deserve the title, so poorly manned and ill-equipped is it.

We are mostly men working here, though there are several women. The older staff have seen war before and are better able to cope, but there are some younger ones … they simply should not be here.

Then there are the soldiers. I clean their wounds, I cut and stitch, yet I cannot ease their pain, I cannot repair their limbs and often I cannot save their lives.

The worst part, good God Alex — the worst part is that they are so young — some as young as you. I feel nostalgic for our childhood and the lives we led, blissfully unaware of the atrocities man can do unto man. I think about the fierce battles fought on our own soil in years gone by and pray such a scourge never again comes to England.

I know you must wonder at this, but despite all, I do not regret my enlistment. My greatest joy is to save the life of a young man, and my greatest grief is to see him return to the very place he received his wounds, to take his chances yet again.

I apologise, dear sister, for the depressing tone of this letter, but have felt of late that I needed this release, so unlike me, though I remain,

Your loving brother
Simon.

It was indeed unlike him — Simon, my carefree brother, who had always treated life as good sport populated with games, laughter and lively company — though I'd ever known there was a more sensitive, less playful side to my older sibling. My loose Christian upbringing prompted an apology to God for my laxity before I prayed for protection over Simon and Patrick, and their safe return.

The descriptions in Simon's letter brought the war closer to us here in this tranquil corner of the world. I passed it to Gerrard and Mother — the latter appeared quite shaken, and for the first time in my memory, seemed worried for someone other than herself.

But life continued, summer rolled on and Hamish thanked Lord Thorncliffe for our hospitality and returned to Scotland. Mother was growing bored with Yorkshire and, since King George had officially been declared insane back in 1810, the Prince of Wales had been made Regent and she was eager to return to her former life.

"Oh, Gerrard," she grasped her husband's sleeve, "we simply *must* go to London next season. And we must begin planning now."

"We won't be received, m'dear," he replied, patiently.

"Of course we will. It's Prinnie – if we don't go he will be insulted."

"Nonsense, that chapter of our lives is over. Prinnie's set is much younger. We will be terribly out of place."

"Hmph," Mother folded her arms indignantly. "I think you're wrong."

"I know you do, and there we are." Lord Thorncliffe shook out a newspaper and disappeared behind it.

No further mail was received from Simon, and certainly nothing from Patrick. The end of the year was fast approaching and it was October 1812 when Mother wrote to Anne suggesting my sister should return home. Mother was certain she could attain a court posting for Anne and, when the war ended, Anne's marriage to Patrick could be arranged.

Anne's reply arrived as the first autumn leaves were fluttering to the ground. She confirmed that while marriage to Patrick was definitely desirous, she preferred to remain in Italy – with Mother's blessing, of course – until Patrick was home.

Mother raised her eyebrows. "Could this Anne possibly be the same Anne as my daughter? The same one whose expressed ambitions included going to court?"

I shrugged, though I wondered the same thing myself.

The curious letter then switched to more interesting matters. Apparently, Grace had married some penniless, nameless fellow and had borne him a child. Isabella had begged her daughter to return to Italy, abandoning this George someone-or-other – even extending the magnanimous gesture that Grace bring her child with her. Only Isabella was surprised when Grace's curt refusal arrived.

༄

Molly Morehead, an acquaintance of Mother's, was holding a Christmas ball and Janet was helping me into my new ball gown –

a fabulous creation in gold velvet, trimmed with black Venetian lace – when Mother strode into my room. "Janet, ensure you dress your mistress' hair so that little ringlets sit at her neck – it suits her well that way. Alexandra, you shall wear my obsidian earrings."

She opened a little box to reveal a pair of gleaming black stones caught in fine gold so they looked like black teardrops captured in gossamer nets. I gaped at her, surprised by her uncommon gesture. Only as we arrived at the ball did I realise her attempt to outshine the Morehead's daughter, Adrienne – rumoured to be a beauty.

Adrienne stood between her parents and her brother, greeting their guests. She was dressed magnificently in rich lavender silk with a glittering silver Grecian design, chasing a line beneath the bodice and along the hemline. Her glossy, blue-black hair was piled high on her head and sparkled with scattered diamonds. "Hired," Mother asserted scornfully. "I doubt their finances would support ownership."

Her complexion was like perfect alabaster, contrasting mystically with her dark hair and sapphire eyes. She stood straight and slender, and something in those eyes raking over me unnerved me in a way I could not fathom. She moved deliberately, as one accustomed to attention and the slim hand she extended wore a creamy, opalescent glove. Her voice was low and breathy when she said, "So nice to meet you, Miss Broughton. Thank you for coming this evening."

Deon shared his sister's fascinating looks and could certainly have challenged Simon for his title of Catch-of-the-County, though with some small bias, I preferred Simon's open cheerfulness to Deon's heavy-lidded pride.

"Deon is Julia's betrothed," I whispered to my parents as we passed into the ballroom.

"Young lad's done well then," Lord Thorncliffe commented.

"Done his duty," Mother added dryly. "And what was Molly thinking with those names – French and pretentious."

"Seem to suit those looks – that girl ... *glorious* ..." Lord

Thorncliffe enthused and would have continued but for his wife's silencing glare.

"Cadaverous – girl needs colour and some meat on her bones."

An attendant took our coats and another tied a dance-card to my wrist, while a blue-liveried waiter offered glasses of champagne and explained that food was available from the *buffet* in the next room.

"All the rage in France," Mother explained, contemptuously regarding the guests standing about with plates in their hands. Much as we, the English, despised the French, we seemed to appreciate their style.

Savouries and every kind of sweetmeat imaginable were laid on a great table. Mother snorted at this also since sugar was such an expensive commodity, only the wealthiest – or those desperate to impress – would countenance the extravagance. Guests walked along the table placing tiny portions of food on their plates. An adjacent table was laid with crystal goblets and bowls of wine-punch, all glittering beneath a thousand candles in crystal chandeliers.

I gazed around, overwhelmed by the sights and sounds; the music, the ladies' gowns and sparkling jewels, the fragrant array of food mixing with the scent of perfume. Mother tapped my arm with her fan. "Don't gawp, Alexandra – it's so common. This is nothing like the *buffets* we enjoyed at court. But then, Molly wouldn't know about that."

Mother was tireless in her critique of this one with the false hair, or that one with the badly-fitting bodice and suddenly, like a saviour, Julia appeared before me. She was wearing a tawny-silk gown, overlaid with a sheer veil of bronze gauze. Her hair was gathered in a knot at her crown, and she wore pearls in her ears and around her neck. "You look beautiful," I breathed.

"As do you," my friend responded while we hugged. Julia's mother was in conversation with mine, and Lord Thorncliffe was distracted by a roving waiter bearing glasses of wine. "Here's your chance to escape." Julia took my gloved hand, "Come, Alex. Let us have some champagne. Then, I shall properly introduce you to Deon."

As Deon rose from an elegant bow, he said, "So Miss Broughton, *you're* the Alex I've heard so much about. I should have known when you arrived with Thorncliffe."

I wanted to ask who'd been speaking of me, but Julia was presenting others – so many names to remember – and one gangly, but pleasant enough, young man asked to have his name placed on my dance-card.

Much later, having danced with an impressive number of young men, I returned to where Lord Thorncliffe waited with a bored expression while Mother gossiped with a crony from Leeds. My stepfather's nose, beacon-like at the best of times, had grown rosier as the night progressed. "The wine does not suit you," I said pointedly, with a smirk.

"Where's your respect!" He snapped with mock annoyance. "It suits me well enough … 'tis the lighting in this place does not."

Suddenly a man's voice cut in. "Thorncliffe, old boy! Don't believe it … never thought to see you so far north."

Amid much backslapping, I was introduced to Lord Hammersby, whose wife was talking with Mother. "So what brings you here – and don't say your horse for I doubt any could carry you with that newly acquired padding you've grown."

The grandfather clock in the vestibule struck one as I drifted away from the men, and I realised I was exhausted and rather tipsy. The room felt clammy and close and smelled sickly-sweet with perspiration, candle-smoke and perfume, and little beads of sweat were dampening my hairline.

French doors at the end of the ballroom stood open and inviting and a soothing breeze lifted the tendrils of hair at my nape as I stepped outside. Lanterns, swaying gently at intervals along the pathways, illuminated the clipped gardens and a gurgling cherub in a fountain.

Nearby a group of women whispered to one another.

Despite a sudden wooziness, I followed a path wending through shrubbery, and the sounds of merriment faded behind me as I quickened my pace past a couple entwined on a bench, and drifted across a carpet of lawn glittering prettily with a fine dusting of early snow. A sliver of moon lit my way as I approached a tall hedge silhouetted boldly against the night. I trailed along it for some distance before finding an opening like a gaping black mouth.

I was starting to feel unwell when I found myself in a small garden room. It smelled wetly of peat and pine and had a bronze statue of cupid, poised on one leg, his arrow aimed at the sky. It was icy-cold beneath my light touch as I circled it, and, when the clouds scudded across the moon creating a blackness that was almost perfect, I left its stability to grope through space until my fingertips brushed foliage. Then, my knees buckled and I let myself drop drunkenly to the ground where I could brace against the hedged wall.

My head was beginning to ache dully. Abandoning decorum, I pulled my knees up letting my forehead rest upon them.

The silence here was unspoiled by the distant party affording me an opportunity to still my head spinning and, as the cloying dizziness of the drink began to subside, I floated into a light sleep, making no effort to stop myself.

Minutes later, startled into wakefulness, I sat uncomfortably in the dark wondering what had woken me. The taste of stale wine in my mouth brought a rush of nausea but at the sound of a smothered groan and rustling of silk, I stiffened.

"Shh!" It was a man and I shrank further into my hedge.

"Won't they miss us?" a woman asked. Her voice was unfamiliar, and thick with champagne.

"Mmm, not if we're quick. Help me …"

I listened intently. I knew his voice, but could not place it.

"No … let me," she said. "Mama'll kill me if that gets torn."

"Then hurry up."

"Deon, wait … slow down."

My mind jolted in the darkness. Deon! But that girl was not Julia …!

"What? You were willing enough before. Surely –"

"I know … it's just that …"

"Oh, come on Cee, I need you … here, feel how much I need you …"

There was a soft feminine moan, and I shifted with difficulty – my bottom was growing numb from the cold. Pressing myself further into the shadows, I could hear their rapid breathing and sense the increasing urgency in their movements.

Abruptly there was silence.

"What? What is it now?" Deon demanded with impatience.

"Nothing … well … everything."

"Come on, Cee." He was wheedling now. "You know how I feel about you … you feel it too, I know you do."

"Yes perhaps, but … you're to wed Julia."

He gave a low chuckle, "That's what they tell me, but it is you I'm going to fuck."

She moaned again followed by a plaintive sound at the sound of tearing fabric.

"Mama's going to kill me … *oh! Oh my goodness …!*"

A pair of lace-trimmed bloomers was dropped to the ground and lay like a puddle while the pale moon darted among the clouds and, as the sounds of their lovemaking grew to a crescendo, their cries hung in the raw, night air.

❧

The next day, Mother suggested I invite Adrienne and Deon Morehead to an afternoon tea the following Sunday. Dismayed by Deon's behaviour in the garden, I was uncertain, but Mother inaccurately guessed my reluctance and said, "Invite your friend Julia too, and anyone else you think."

I sighed. "Very well. It could be nice."

"Imagine Alexandra, if we invited them to Waterville. Their eyes would pop clear out of their plebeian little skulls."

I shrugged, unimpressed by her snobbery but she carried on obliviously, "And think; when Anne marries Patrick how green Molly Morehead will turn."

"Shall I ask Cook to prepare a tea cake?" I said covering my irritation.

"Oh yes, and sugared fancies, and pastries with the custard and fruit in them. They'd never have had those before, I'll wager."

Despite my misgivings, as Sunday approached I grew excited, and when the day arrived I watched the parlour clock until the carriages rolled up the driveway exactly three minutes late. Hurrying downstairs, I arranged my pretty, red skirt as I'd seen Anne do and positioned myself calmly by the fire.

My guests, six in all – Deon and Adrienne, Julia and her friend Celia, and two young fellows I had danced with, Thomas and Jonathon – waited as Mrs Grainger announced their names. Then, I realised with a surge of dislike the identity of *Cee*. Celia was standing beside Julia, smiling sweetly, nauseatingly, and my stomach churned as I recalled Julia had asked Celia to stand with me as bride's maidens at her wedding.

Pushing aside the disturbing memory of Deon and Celia gasping together in the dark, I turned to Adrienne. Intrigued by my own betrothal she was bombarding me with questions about Hamish. Was it a love match? No? Well then was I happy with it? When will the marriage take place? And on it went. Mrs Morehead was planning to launch her daughter in a London season next year, in the hopes of finding a suitable husband.

"If I had my way, I would not marry at all," she said in her velvety voice.

"Rubbish!" her brother declared. "If you had your way you'd race Alex's brother to the altar in the blink of an eye."

"Simon?" I asked in confusion.

"Not Simon," Deon said with a sly wink. "The other one – Patrick."

"Pat?"

"I reckon she'd do better with Simon, though. Steadier of the two at Oxford – he'd make a loyal husband I should think, less inclined to wander."

Ignoring the irony, I said placidly, "Is Oxford where you know them from?"

"Simon was studying medicine. God alone knows what Patrick was about – the only studies he made were dissipation and the bottom of his jar at the – "

At Julia's hiss, he broke off immediately but appeared unapologetic.

"Patrick's heart wasn't in it. That's why he left," I said, sharper than I intended. "He and Simon are at the Peninsular War – they enlisted."

"In the war?" Deon's voice was incredulous. "Simon perhaps, but Patrick? More like whoring his way across Spain –"

"*Deon …!*" Julia was aghast.

A flush of anger started at my neck, rapidly moving upwards. "Unlike some, Patrick has a conscience. He bought a commission and is an officer. That he had no interest in study does not mean he is irredeemably entrenched in debauchery."

Deon sat back regarding me warily while his sister watched me with interest. Her blue eyes missed nothing, and a little furrow marred her smooth brow. After considering my defence of Patrick's rather dubious virtue, she asked, "Are you close then, you and Patrick?"

Before I could think up a suitably casual response, Deon said, "Don't worry about my sister, Alex. She's been panting after Patrick since the first time she saw him. She'll interrogate the motives of anyone he spends time with – even his sister."

"I would not!" Ugly splotches of colour disfigured Adrienne's porcelain complexion and she glared at him.

Fearing an unbecoming row between the siblings, I quickly changed the subject. "My betrothed, Hamish, is visiting in the new year. I thought to hold a gathering so you could all meet him." I'd been planning nothing of the kind but it served to distract them.

"That sounds lovely, Alex," Celia said smoothly.

"Perhaps Patrick will have leave by then?" Deon asked, his dark eyes glinting with mischief. "What …?" He was all innocence as we stared at him incredulously.

Deon's playful question proved to be prophetic, for only a week later Lord Thorncliffe received a letter. The scuffed envelope bore Simon's handwriting and was dated a month back. I held my breath nervously as my stepfather read the single page, his ordinarily ruddy complexion paling as his eyes darted back and forth along the lines.

Finally, he looked up. Mother and I waited as he drew breath and advised that Patrick had been wounded – a deep gash to his leg – at Salamanca, and ended up on Simon's operating table. He had been recovering well enough until he contracted a fever that had been spreading through the hospital. For a week his life had hung in the balance but he was now mending satisfactorily.

Since it had been decided to rest the troops until launching a new campaign in the summer, Patrick opted to return home to complete his recovery, and Simon was writing to advise our brother would soon be discharged from the hospital. He could be expected at Broughton Hall early February.

CHAPTER 14

As the winter progressed, I had become a fixed member of the popular young set that frequented various soirees, parties and dinners; and the more I saw Julia with Deon, the more disheartened I grew. True, he did and said all the right things: dancing with her as appropriate, bringing her food, placing her wrap solicitously over her shoulders, but I knew what it meant when his eyes strayed in Celia's direction, and I noticed how often they did – and I was not alone.

More than once I caught Julia following her affianced's gaze, a little frown spoiling her pretty features. One evening, while at a gathering hosted by Celia's parents, in trying to locate the ladies withdrawing-room, I found myself in the library and discovered Julia sitting alone in the dark.

"Alex! Come, please sit with me." She patted the divan beside her and I saw at once she'd been crying. Her apricot and cream complexion was flushed and swollen, and I knew it was because Deon had danced with Celia most of the evening.

"He can hover about her all he likes but in the end it is you he's marrying," I said firmly.

"Is it?" she said, dabbing at her eyes with an inadequate scrap of lace. "Whenever I suggest we choose a date … he … he …" She hid her face in her hands and wept. "And now everyone … is talking about … the way he … dances with her …"

I sat with my arm about her shuddering shoulders, feeling helpless and unable to refute her.

"I don't know what to say, Jules." It was the truth.

She took a deep, shaky breath. "You would not, I suppose. You don't know … what it feels like to love someone … who does not love you in return."

I sat very still and thought about that. Patrick's departure for Europe, his injury, and impending return, had all occurred without his writing a single word to me, and had effectively dashed any fanciful daydreams I might have had. Even Julia had admitted she'd been mistaken, and agreed that it had only been one kiss; and what man would not have responded favourably? But if my fantasies were crushed, my heart was not. My feelings for him had grown despite their futility, and therefore she was wrong – I knew very well how unrequited love felt.

"Come on," I said gently. "Clean yourself up – we must rejoin the group downstairs."

"Oh, I won't be missed," she said miserably.

"Yes, you will." I forced her to follow me to a washroom where she bathed her face and smoothed her hair. She was looking better by the time we emerged, and miraculously, Deon was standing at the foot of the stairs watching in apparent concern as we descended.

"I've been looking for you all over, where've you been?"

"Oh," I responded breezily, "a pin came out of my hair and Julia was helping me with it." Recalling the silky falsehoods that slipped from my tongue when Simon and I had been up to mischief as children, I congratulated myself for my continued talent.

ॐ

I had written to Hamish and invited him to visit since I was holding a gathering of my friends. He replied that his father suggested he ought to attend, and it was about this time that I noticed Janet becoming increasingly distracted. The reason became evident when she began twittering like an excited sparrow and asked if My Lord's valet, Grahame was to accompany his master. Worn out by her constant prattling, I wrote to Hamish seeking his thoughts. He replied that Grahame was equally tiresome and suggested that Janet return with him to Scotland. Though I would miss her greatly, I thought this might be the best solution.

Unfortunately when I approached Janet on the subject, her eyes grew round with fear and she pleaded with me not to dismiss her.

"Of course I'm not dismissing you. We thought you'd be happier with Grahame."

She hesitated before answering. "I would, of course. Would this mean you and Lord Hamish are to wed soon?"

"Lord Hamish and I have not agreed on a date."

"But if only you would. I, that is, Grahame and I … we don't understand why you've not …"

"It is not your business to understand," I snapped. Back in my room I regretted my harsh words, but pooh to it all! Our desires are not simply handed to us. I exhaled grumpily through my nose, for February was nearly over and there'd been no sign of Patrick.

From time to time Julia and I visited Leeds with her mother. We attended a performance of *As You Like It*, and occasionally we dined at a restaurant owned by Julia's uncle. Mother would have been appalled had she known, for my friend's uncle greeted us at the door. In Mother's opinion, people of quality may *own* a business but they most definitely did not *work* in it. How conveniently forgotten was her own father's wool business that had fed, clothed and provided substantial dowries for her and her sister.

Suddenly spring arrived in a flood of melting snow and an explosion of colour. The roses, pruned to stumps before winter, now trembled with new leaves and clusters of buds. Daffodils, hyacinths, irises and snowdrops lined the walkways along the terraces. Jonquils and freesias began appearing at the edge of the forest and, as the sun made weak, watery appearances, the bees emerged from their winter hiding and buzzed about excitedly. It was pleasing to watch the garden opening into life after lying dormant for months beneath the frozen earth. The blossoms on the fruit trees filled the garden with their sweet scent and early each morning, Jemima and I strolled down the half-dozen steps into the orchard through a cloud of pungent fragrance.

As I walked, my thoughts wandered to my friends. My knowledge of Deon and Celia's affair weighed heavily on my conscience for I had said nothing to Julia and held on to the hope that once married, Deon would reform his faithless ways.

This morning however, my thoughts centred on Simon. We hadn't heard from him since his last letter and there was no way of knowing where he was or how he fared. We knew from the papers that Wellington, allied with Spain, was planning to resume his march into France in the warmer months around June, and I could only pray that the offensive was quick and successful, and returned all those men to their loved ones as soon as possible.

And I'd have thought Patrick would be home by now. Perhaps he'd decided to go to Devon rather than travel up north, but then why hadn't he advised his father?

Thoughts of Patrick made me sigh. They also reminded me that Hamish would be arriving any day soon. Even as his visits were becoming rather frequent, I could not envision myself married to this man.

My stomach gave a protracted rumble. I called to Jemima and turned towards the house.

Hamish arrived the next morning. He greeted me coolly and

admired my new hairstyle – scooped up and clipped at the crown with ringlets at my neck and ears. It suited me to have my unruly hair held off my face and I was surprised that he noticed.

I'd begun dressing my hair differently in recent months – a comment about my maturity I supposed – and Janet had demonstrated a talent I didn't know she had. Besides, I'd grown tired of my hair looking like I'd been pulled through a hedgerow backwards.

I remember Anne, who'd always been immaculately turned out, declaring that a girl could never know who might be waiting to fall in love with her.

"Were the roads kind to you, Hamish?" I asked, watching Grahame and Janet greet each other enthusiastically from the corner of my eye.

"Aye, not too bad, though there is still much snow further north."

We looked at our respective servants. "We must talk about this," I said simply.

He nodded his agreement. "We shall discuss it after dinner under that oak tree."

"Very well," I said. "I'll have Cook make up some lemonade. You quite like it, don't you?"

Hamish lounged in a chair beneath the Great Oak but rose politely as I approached. Jemima flopped at my feet panting and we both watched her for a moment. "I wonder if I could have her sheared like a sheep. She does struggle with the warmth – and yet, it is only spring."

"If you didn't mollycoddle it so, it would not be so fastidious."

I frowned but Sarah was coming across the lawn with our lemonade. The maid poured a cup for each of us before bobbing and returning to the house.

Hamish took a sip and pursed his lips in a way that reminded me of Eleanor when she was sizing things up. "Did you speak to Janet about moving to Scotland? We could find work for her, though we probably don't pay so well as the *Washburns*."

He said the name with contempt but I chose to ignore it. "She is opposed to the idea."

"Without you there?"

"That's what she said."

He hesitated, then with transparent reluctance, offered tentatively, "We could bring our wedding forward."

"No!" My response was sharper than intended. "I mean … I'm not ready, and certainly not to further the romance of a maid, however loyal she may be."

He must have been holding his breath for he seemed to let it out in a rush. "Aye," he nodded emphatically. "Grahame has been very loyal too, but I agree."

"Good," I said.

"Good," he repeated.

We sat quietly for a minute or two until finally, I said, "We're right back where we started."

"Then, they must await our convenience."

"I can see no other way. Are we agreed?"

"We are," he said firmly.

The contrary female in me questioned his obvious reluctance to marry me almost peevishly, while my more pragmatic side accepted that our marriage was as forced upon him as it was me. I didn't like him, but hoped that in time we might develop some friendship. I knew I could never feel love for him – and certainly nothing approaching the style of feeling I secretly harboured for Patrick.

Patrick … Another time, another place; had we met as friends, perhaps things could have been different. I was drawn to him, like a moth is drawn to a flame; an attraction that may well be the moth's undoing yet was impossible to resist.

The pointlessness of my infatuation was made abundantly clear by his continued silence however sweet our parting last time I saw him – almost two years ago now.

The sun moved behind a cloud and a shiver ran through me.

"You're cold," Hamish said. "Shall we return to the house, *dear*?"

He'd taken to calling me *dear* lately. It was strained and didn't sit comfortably with him – nor did it with me. We were acting the roles we'd been assigned – though not very well. And now he was distractedly admiring his reflection in the polished pewter cup he held and I rolled my eyes.

"Don't call me dear."

The next morning, I rose earlier than normal for my walk. I wanted to think about Hamish. He was clearly disdainful of me, but it was apparent that our marriage would be going ahead, so I needed to work out how I could improve relations between us.

It was cold, being early March, and I poked at my fire to revive it. I dressed on my hearth, struggling as usual with my buttons, before pulling on my thick walking boots. My hair was quite long now and not so difficult, curling down my back in soft waves. I combed it hurriedly with my fingers and called to Jemima.

We left the house by the front door and crossed the gravel drive. Everything was white – touched overnight by a crystalline frost. I breathed deeply, feeling the frigid air burn my lungs and I lifted my arms above my head in a long luxurious stretch.

Turning to the left I stepped cautiously on to the icy terraces where I paused here and there to inspect flowers and shrubs. I was becoming expert at naming the different plants we grew and I enjoyed watching them come to life after the cold winter.

Tomorrow was Sunday – the day of my soiree. I was feeling quite grown up about hosting my own gathering. Lord Thorncliffe planned to welcome my guests but would then discreetly withdraw.

From where I stood on the terrace, I could see down to the orchard. The plum and apple trees had exploded into white and soft-pink blossoms. Soon the baby fruit would follow, though for now, the trees were resplendent in their delicate new beauty.

Jemima suddenly stiffened and gave a small woof, startling me. Following her line of vision beyond the rose garden, I could just make out a horse and rider coming up the drive. Thinking perhaps it was Hamish out for an early ride, I turned away, but something was out of place. Hamish's horse was a bay. This one was black and slender, and as I watched, broke into a canter to take up the rest of the drive.

I knew that graceful, rocking-horse motion could belong only to Equus and my mouth grew dry.

The rider was wearing the red coat of the British army with a long sword hanging at his hip, and as he drew closer, I could better see his features. The blond hair was longer than I remembered, and the lines of his profile had firmed with adulthood.

He hadn't yet seen me. With supreme control, I walked sedately back along the path.

Jemima barked again, and then she bolted flat and close to the ground in sheep-herding style, across the crisp lawns to the drive. The horse shied, dancing to the side and the soldier looked around to see the dog barrelling towards him. Controlling his mount, he watched as the black and white creature halted in a scattering of gravel, bouncing, squirming and twisting double with joy.

Dismounting, he dropped to one knee to greet her, though his eyes, dark and unreadable, were levelled on me as I crossed the lawn.

The memory of our last parting was in the forefront of my mind setting my heart a-hammer and, as I approached, he gave Jemima a final pat and slowly rose. He had filled out, the cut of his red jacket and tight fitting breeches defining the shape of his broad shoulders and long legs. He was a man now I realised with surprise, and had attained his majority.

He continued to watch as I walked, but as I drew close, I paused uncertainly. Then, with an unexpected explosion of movement, he breached the gap between us. Snatching me into his embrace he pulled me hard against his chest, holding me with a desperate ferocity that took my breath away. With his face buried in my neck, he clung to me, breathing deeply as if to absorb me, murmuring words I could not discern, and I wondered what kind of hostilities experienced in war-torn Europe, could result in such uncharacteristic behaviour.

My arms instinctively went around him, and I cleaved to him as though I were drowning. He smelled of sweat, horse and leather; and I felt the scratchy wool of his coat against my cheek. I needed release to breathe but could not move, for the strength of his arms around me and my own need to hold him. Time slowed so as to have no meaning and I have no idea how long we stood thus, wrapped wordlessly in each other's arms.

Finally, we became aware of Equus stamping and snorting impatiently. Our hold on each other loosened and we drew apart, shyly, arms falling to our sides. Only as the morning breeze touched my face did I become aware of the tears on my cheeks.

Examining his face, I saw now that he wore a gold moustache and beard. He had little crinkles at the corners of his eyes from the sun, and he was stamped with a maturity that hadn't been there when last I'd seen him. The green eyes I loved so well were distant and glassy with fatigue.

"Are you hungry?" I said inadequately – my first words and it was all I could produce. It seemed, however, to break the spell hanging over us.

He shook his head. "No, I'm tired though. I need to rest."

"We didn't know you were arriving this morning – I'll have a fire made up in your room." There were so many questions I wanted to ask, and it was with a superhuman effort that I contained them.

"I'll take Equus to the stables," he said and I nodded mutely, my arms hanging empty and useless. He gathered the horse's reins and took a few steps before he paused. Without turning, he said, "It is good to see you, Alex."

∾

My morning routine irretrievably interrupted, I returned to my room and lay on my bed. I could still smell him, could still feel his embrace such was the intensity of my emotions, and I knew with certainty that this was no mere infatuation.

I was in love with him.

But he had been altered by experience. He'd been to war, he'd been wounded, he'd nearly died, and he had clung to me without words, so desperately and so painfully.

Oh, how I longed to go to his room for no reason other than to look at him. I had no words for him; I simply wanted to be near him, and the wanting was so fierce, it ached in my chest and called to life a primitive urge deep within my core that pulled my emotions tight like bow-strings.

At length, I climbed sluggishly off my bed, straightened my clothes, and went down to breakfast.

Hamish and Gerrard had almost finished their meals. They rose as I entered.

"You're late this morning, dear," Hamish commented resuming his seat. "Did you oversleep?"

He'd called me dear again and I bristled with unreasonable irritation, snapping involuntarily, "I've been up and walking for some time, if you must know."

Lord Thorncliffe raised his eyebrows at the edge in my voice but said nothing. Watching him closely as he applied himself cheerily – as he did all tasks involving food – to the buttering of his toast, I broke the news.

"Father, Patrick is home."

Knife suspended in mid air, he stared at me uncomprehendingly. Hamish was the first to recover from the surprise.

"Well, that is good news, Alex. My Lord, you must be pleased."

"Where is he?"

"Upstairs. He's —"

The sound of his chair scraping back cut me off. "My son's back from a bloody war he shouldn't have been involved in — please excuse me."

"You must be relieved, dear.

I glared across the table. "Don't call me dear."

Later that morning, Gerrard came to me as I wandered through the kitchen garden. I was collecting sprigs of herbs to make a centre-piece for the dinner table and the mixture in my hand was blending into a pleasant fragrance.

"How did you find him?" I asked as he offered his arm and we walked together.

"Physically? Simply exhausted. That fever he contracted in the hospital wore him out. Spiritually? Well that's another matter. Do me a service, Lass. Introduce him to these friends of yours, get him involved in a normal routine again. He's made of strong stuff — he'll be alright."

"He could attend my gathering tomorrow," I suggested, doubtfully. My concern was that Adrienne would be there.

He patted my hand where it rested in the crook of his elbow. "Yes, that would be perfect."

With infuriating timing, Hamish approached. He was dressed up in buff trousers that hooked as stirrups beneath his tan boots; a crisp, snow-white shirt under a rich, green-silk waistcoat. His frockcoat was forest-green and he carried a walking cane with a solid-silver knob.

"Oh joy, he's become a dandy," I muttered and my stepfather

chuckled softly. "Are you going somewhere?" I asked as my intended paused before me.

"Perhaps …" he said coyly. "I thought we could take a carriage ride into Leeds, enjoy a nice dinner and look at the shops." He swept me a courtly, and somewhat exaggerated bow. "What do you say?"

My annoyance with him was mounting. "Your timing is appalling," I said with an edge to my voice. "How –"

"Forgive me – you're right," he apologised quickly.

I groaned inwardly and said with effort, "I'm sorry Hamish, it's just that –"

"No, forgive me. My suggestion is inappropriate. Your brother is returned home and you should spend time with him, of course." He paused for a heartbeat then brightened. "If you have no objections, perhaps I'll go anyway – I have some friends I may call on."

"Do whatever you want, Hamish, just remember the soiree tomorrow." He nodded cheerfully, and I knew instinctively he'd planned his day without me all along. He would no doubt have his reasons, but I didn't care to examine what purported to be some kind of ploy.

Watching from the lawn as Hamish rode way, Gerrard turned to me. "That was rather too easy wouldn't you say?"

I nodded but sighed in relief – happy to be rid of him for the day.

∽

After dinner I sat on the lawn soaking up the pale afternoon sun. Jemima, ever the perfect companion, reclined at my side. The weather was beautiful, as it had promised to be earlier this morning. The sky was clear, and a soft breeze stirred the tendrils of hair curling at my temple. With a feeling of liberation, I decided to do a most unladylike thing: I sprawled out, flat on my back, arms and legs splayed in starfish fashion, and closed my eyes.

The touch of the sun was heavenly. I could feel its warmth seeping through my pink, woollen dress and into my bones, and I knew a true sense of peace and wellbeing.

My breathing slowed, I was relaxed and floating above the lawn. In the distance, the voices of newly-hatched birds announced their hunger, and rose, lavender and honeysuckle hung in the air.

A shadow crossed my face, the change visible through my closed eyelids. Somewhere in the back of my mind I remembered the sky being cloudless. I opened one eye, squinting against the light.

Patrick was standing above me looking down. His long hair was falling about his face and the sun shone through it like a halo.

"Mind if I join you?"

I smiled lazily though my pulse quickened, and patted the lawn beside me. He sat and stretched his legs out before him, leaning back on his elbows. He was clean and freshly shaved and his skin was pale where the beard and moustache had been. Jemima went to lick him and he avoided her tongue by ruffling her fur. Satisfied, she lay beside him and immediately closed her eyes contentedly.

He'd changed out of his soldier's garb into casual, blue trousers and a white shirt, which was open at the neck and rolled up loosely at the sleeves. The contrast between Patrick's relaxed air and Hamish's fussy style could not be more profound.

"How've you been?" he asked.

"Oh, you know how it is around here," I said brightly. "Something new and exciting everyday. More to the point; how are you?"

"Simon filled you in on the leg and fever. Other than that …" he shrugged, "I haven't had the best of times, but I've had it better than others."

"I'm glad you're home, Pat." I said cautiously, then in a rush of honesty I added, "I've missed you so much." Suddenly self-conscious, I closed my eyes again as though by not seeing him, he could not see my embarrassment. I was in danger of laying my heart bare, and I must never expose myself in that way.

There was movement beside me and I was aware that he was lying in the grass, his head resting in his hands. "I've missed you too," he said, so softly it blended with the breeze.

I wondered at the lack of ease between us for I felt quite awkward and unsure of myself. My carefree childhood was gone, we were adults – though he'd been through more, seen and experienced more – we were no longer children. Innocent looks, touches and jokes held a different meaning now, and there was the lingering distraction of our last parting – that kiss – all compounding my discomfort.

Suddenly I needed to lighten the mood, return to our easy banter, tease him into laughing the way he used to. I rolled on to my stomach and turned to him. He opened his eyes and I struggled to gather my thoughts.

"How about those whiskers you arrived home with? Trying to look all grown up were you?" I tweaked at his chin, bereft now of the goatee. Quick as a flash he rolled over, flung me on my back, and straddled me as he had when we were young and uninhibited. Pinning my arms above my head with one hand, he flicked at the curls about my face with the other.

"I could say the same of you … expecting royalty perhaps?" I squealed and struggled, trying vainly to unseat him. "And what about these …" he deftly unhooked a dangly earring from my lobe and held it against his own ear, "I'm Hamish, I'm Hamish …" he sing-songed.

We both laughed at that and he relaxed his grip on my hands but remained sitting on me, a knee either side of my middle.

"Get off me, you great lump, I can barely breathe," I gasped.

He slid to one side and pulled me to a sitting position. Dropping the earring into my palm, he said, "Seriously Li'l Sis, you are looking very grown up these days."

"Hmph," I snorted, threading the wire through my lobe. "That's because I am all grown up."

"How old?"

"I'll be nineteen in May, and haven't you been told it is impolite to question a lady's age?"

"And what a ripe old age that is. I see your Lord Whatsit has been educating you in the ways of feminine attire. I was quite surprised to see you in a dress this morning. I expected you'd have graduated to long pants by now."

"Very funny. I'm quite the statement in elegance — and I have a whole group of new friends."

"Have you indeed?" he looked impressed but he was mocking me, and I was glad we'd fallen into our old ways. "Anyone I'd know?"

"Yes, as a matter of fact. You know Deon Morehead —"

"Christ," he swore, "who within five yards of any tavern in Oxford does not know Deon Morehead?"

I made a disgusted face. "Deon is affianced to one of my friends — you remember Julia? Typical male philanderer though he is," I added derisively.

"That's what Oxford was all about; cavorting and drinking. Why do you think I dropped out and went to war? I was exhausted." He grinned wickedly and my heart leapt in my breast.

"Deon said you went to the taverns, but he never said he drank there himself."

"Was his Mother present?"

"No, but his sister was."

"There you go. He's not about to say anything incriminating in front of Adrienne, is he?"

"Then you know Adrienne too?" I probed innocently and watched his face.

He nodded. "Of course. When Deon's family visited, I made it my business to meet Adrienne."

The jealousy was so sharp my face must have turned pea-green. "She's very beautiful," I fished perversely.

"She's intoxicating," he agreed, and I glared at him.

"Your father described her as glorious."

"True enough."

"She's coming here tomorrow."

"Is she?"

I nodded. "I'm having a gathering tomorrow for my friends. They haven't met Hamish yet and —"

"Is he here too?" Surprise and annoyance flickered for the briefest second across his face before being replaced with his normally shuttered expression.

"I thought you knew. He knows you're here," I said, equally surprised by his reaction. "With all the carrying on … the earring … I thought …"

He shook his head. "Where is he?"

"Gone to Leeds for the day."

"Without you?"

"I didn't want to go."

"Can't say I blame you."

"It's not that … rather … I was worried about you. I was waiting for you to wake … to see you were alright."

He studied my face for a long moment, and I supposed he was weighing up whether to tease me or not. Finally, he smiled and touched my cheek gently, "I'm alright, believe me."

I reclined on the grass then, happy; if intensely aware of his presence beside me. "Will you be staying, or will you go to Devon?" I feared the answer for I hoped very much he would choose to stay at Broughton Hall.

He rested on his elbows, "Those of us who were wounded were sent home to recuperate. I shall be returning to Europe in time for the summer."

I sat upright so quickly I felt the blood drain from my face. "What are you saying?" My stomach tightened and my heart began to pound. "You can't, Pat, it will kill your father, and what about the rest of us … Oh God, not again; haven't you had enough?"

He held his hands up as if to ward me off. "Alex, I have to … I'm a soldier – it's not over yet. Wellington sent us home for a spell, but we're still needed."

"Of course it is over. The French are out of Spain, Napoleon's starving his troops in Russia – what more is there?"

"Please – I didn't come here for this." He stared at me, uncharacteristically unsettled, his face imploring, but I scrambled to my feet.

"Then why'd you bother coming at all?" I gathered my skirt in my hand and ran up the lawn towards the house.

◦◦

Supper that night started as a subdued affair. Gerrard's initial joy at his son's return had been tempered by the knowledge that the visit was only temporary. Janet told me, once she'd torn herself away from Grahame long enough to perform some of her duties, that Lord Thorncliffe and Patrick had sipped wine in the library for some time deep in conversation. Supper was announced and I entered the dining room alone, for Hamish had not yet returned from Leeds. I should have been concerned but I wasn't.

The two men rose as I took my seat and Gerrard poured me a glass of wine. They were discussing the war and Napoleon's doomed march into Russia.

"Such foolishness, all those men starving," Gerrard said. "Pass the bread please, Lass … thank you … bread, Son?"

"No, thank you. Overzealous, Napoleon. They say he's mad with power."

The conversation continued and I, having nothing to contribute, remained silent. Occasionally Patrick's eyes met mine and I thought I saw an appeal in them, but since he was ordinarily a closed book, I decided I could not.

Cook had laid out a feast for Patrick's return but I had little taste for the food and could hardly eat a thing.

"Did Alex tell you she is having a gathering tomorrow?" Gerrard asked.

"She did," Pat said, taking a sip of wine. "Seems I know some of the guests."

"So you'll be attending, Lad?"

"I shall – if permitted." Again, he looked at me strangely.

My heart sank. Patrick and I had quarrelled, and the last thing I wanted was for Hamish and I to be hosting our first reception as a couple, while enduring Adrienne's flirtations with Patrick. The thought of him welcoming her approaches was sure to make me entirely ill.

"Don't feel obliged!" I snapped.

"Would not miss it for the world," Patrick returned with a savage glint in his eye and too late I remembered his talent for cruel repartee when he added derisively, "You and your Lord Whatsit, publicly displaying your happy togetherness – so quaint."

Gerrard glanced narrowly at his son but said nothing. Patrick, as usual, had caught me right where it hurt the most. I glared at him sulkily, but he merely cocked a facetious eyebrow in response.

"Besides," he continued, turning to his father, "I understand the beautiful Adrienne will be in attendance."

"Oh ho! Yes indeed, *glorious* girl." His father raised his glass in a toast. "To the glorious Adrienne."

"Oh!" I scoffed. "You two are disgusting – she's my age!"

"A young filly – easy to break, easy to train." Patrick drawled lecherously, at which father and son erupted into sniggers like naughty children.

I flushed furiously. "I can't believe you're talking about our visitor like that. *My friend*," I added for emphasis.

Gerrard sobered. "Cheer up, Lass, we're teasing you. Your brother's home and we must enjoy his company while we can. Here – have another wine."

Patrick's interest in Adrienne rankled but I sighed resignedly.

I didn't know how long Pat would be staying, but if he was going to be like this he could leave tomorrow.

Nevertheless, my glass was refilled with a ruby-red Italian variety and, almost in spite of myself, I relaxed.

Patrick and his father were in fine form and the evening's festive tone was contagious. Draining my glass, I poured another, and before long my tension melted and the smile returned to my face.

We called for another bottle and talked into the night; and I heard Hamish return and take himself directly to his room, for which I was keenly grateful. I couldn't have tolerated his cocksure behaviour.

Much later, I was quite drunk and Gerrard dozed in his chair. Pat appeared only slightly less influenced.

"I must … go t'bed," I slurred. "My friends … tomorrow …" I rose, swaying and holding hard to the back of my chair. My feet seemed made of lead and my head wanted to loll on my neck.

"Here, I'll help," Patrick said. It was slow going, stumbling up the stairs, giggling and shushing one-another like schoolchildren. We staggered along the unlit hall, his arm about my waist, and I could feel the heat of his hand burning through the silk of my dress, branding my skin. Oh God, how good it felt to have his arm around me – Hamish's wooden touch was never like this.

At my door we halted and he fumbled in the dark for the latch. I leaned heavily into him, and breathed his scented skin at the opening of his shirt, but everything began spinning and whirling, and unexpectedly my knees failed me.

I was aware of Janet's voice – a conversation was taking place, and I was gently lowered to the enveloping comfort of my bed. Soft lips lingered between my closed eyes, and then all was quiet.

❧

The morning of my soiree, I awoke feeling so ill I could not believe it. My head pounded and I felt sick in my stomach. I moaned and rolled over. Someone had already opened the drapes and the morning sun streamed glaringly into my room. I pulled the counterpane over my head and groaned in pain.

Janet was in the room. Hearing my pitiful sounds, she approached the bed. "Miss Alex, are you unwell?"

"Leave me alone," I gasped from beneath the bedclothes.

"It is nearly nine. Lord Hamish has been asking for you. They've already broken their fast. I could bring something up?"

Bring something up? That's exactly what I would do if she didn't shut up. Every word was crashing in my head and the blood was rushing in my temples. Simply listening to her was more effort than I could manage.

"No … I'm sick … go away."

"Your friends are coming today …"

"Go away …"

The door closed quietly as she left the room and I lay in misery, riding violent waves of nausea.

Oh God, what was I going to do? Of all the days to become sick.

I lay on my side, hugging my knees while the bed spun dizzyingly, and I had the foulest of tastes in my mouth.

The door opened abruptly and purposeful footsteps crossed the room. Too heavy to be Janet's, the footfalls stopped beside my bed. When Patrick's voice sounded, I groaned anew. "Janet said you weren't well."

"Whatever did Cook do to that fish last night? I feel terrible," I whined from under the counterpane, nearly in tears.

Suddenly he laughed like he'd heard the funniest thing. "It's a little unfair to blame poor ol' Cook," he said with the laughter still thick in his voice. "You were well and truly foxed last night. Now you've one hell of a hangover by the sounds of it and it serves you right."

"Why does it serve me right?"

"Restitution for all those times you raged at Simon and me."

"That's mean; I feel like I'm dying."

"That's right, your head's throbbing and your tongue's swollen and furry."

"I have friends coming today," I wailed.

"Not going to be looking your best, are you?" He laughed again.

Beneath the bedclothes I'd started to sweat. It was stuffy, and the air was putrid from my breath. My mouth began to water and I felt my stomach shift ominously.

"Uh-oh …" I gagged, and with a speed I never suspected I had, I leapt from the bed, heedless that I was wearing only my nightgown, and flung myself on all fours before my chamber pot. My abdomen heaved painfully while I belched up the entire rancid contents of my stomach.

Barely able to breathe for the violence of the contractions – even when there was nothing left – I strained and gasped. Pat stood over me, holding my hair away from my face, making soothing noises and assuring me that it was better out than in.

Finally, I sat back on my heels, humiliated, and just as I thought it was over, my stomach rebelled and I lurched over my pot yet again.

When at last I curled on the floor, weak as a kitten and weeping, Pat brought water from my night stand and bathed my face. I was trembling from my exertions and he knelt beside me, rubbing my bare arms to ward off the shivers.

"How do you feel?" he asked, gently. "Are you going to be ill again?"

"I don't know … I … don't think so."

"Then, you'll soon be feeling better now you're rid of all that."

"Doubt it."

"Oh you will. Believe me; I'm exceedingly experienced in these matters. Now you need something nourishing to put in your stomach."

"I'll be sick again."

"No you won't – you'll be surprised."

He scooped me up and carried me to the bed. With selective clarity, I suddenly remembered the kiss before I slept last night, and could not imagine it had been Janet.

"Did you kiss me last night?" I asked as he tucked the bedclothes around my shoulders.

"I did," he responded simply.

I was feeling slightly better now, and was growing drowsy. I smiled up at him, my eyes drooping.

"You looked very appealing," he continued, "I couldn't help myself. Do you mind?"

"No."

"Good. But you'll not be getting another now; you're all sticky and smelly. I'll let you sleep for a while, then I'll bring you some food. You'll be ready for your friends. Don't worry."

I must have been asleep before he even closed the door, for the next thing I heard was a tray being placed on my desk and Pat saying, "Thank you. I'll take care of her now."

The door closed quietly.

"C'mon you ol' drunkard, time to face the day," He was infuriatingly cheerful. "Hungry?"

My head wasn't throbbing so much and my stomach felt empty. I nodded.

"Then look what Cook has prepared for you – the morning-after feast." He lifted the lid off a plate with a flourish. "Scrambled eggs, bacon and a big pile of spinach in butter."

I sat up gingerly, pulling the counterpane decorously to my chin – though he'd already seen me in all my glory. The food smelled heavenly and I watched eagerly as he brought the tray over.

"Christ!" he declared, "you're still looking a little grisly but you'll soon be feeling better."

"What time is it?"

"Just after one – you've plenty of time."

He sat on the edge of the bed and watched while I ate. He had changed quite a bit in the last couple of years. Adulthood had defined his looks and etched character into his face. His emerald eyes were bright and sparkled with amusement and his lips were full and …

I studied my food to hide my blush. I was thinking that he was not handsome in the classical way like Simon, but he was extremely attractive, carrying himself with confidence, exuding a charisma that was undeniably alluring. I was not surprised that women like Adrienne flocked to him.

He was also capable of cutting cynicism, but was possessed of an extraordinarily gentle side. I had, in the last day, been on the receiving end of both.

"Why are you feeling no ill effects this morning?" I asked, my mouth full of bacon.

He shrugged. "They say if you take a small amount of poison each day, gradually increasing the dose, you begin to build up immunity, until eventually it has no effect."

"So you've regularly dosed yourself, have you?"

He responded with a smile. "Are you finished?"

I wiped my mouth with the napkin. "Yes, thank you."

"Good." He removed the tray. "Now, I'll send Janet to help you get ready for your guests."

At the door, he paused and grinned, "Just wondering though …"

"Yes?"

"What price my silence?"

"You are no gentleman!" I announced, glaring.

"Ah yes, but a real lady would not know that!" I heard his laughter receding down the hallway.

CHAPTER 15

Lord Thorncliffe had hired a string quartet to provide the music. They arrived promptly at three o'clock, set themselves up in the entry hall and proceeded to tune their instruments.

Meg was beside herself with excitement watching the musicians organise themselves, following Cook and Mrs Grainger as they directed the maids, and generally getting under everyone's feet.

Finally, she asked if it was time for her to put on her favourite dress and it was difficult to explain that the party was for the big people. When Clara took her hand, the child's face collapsed and I relented, agreeing that she could watch the guests arrive; but she must be silent and polite, and remember her best curtsy.

Cook had outdone herself. A trestle covered in white linen was brought into the parlour and laid with an assortment of pastries, meats, fruits, custards, a cream-filled gateau, marchpane and cakes.

Ice wines from Germany were to be served and the chilled bottles waited in readiness. Mother would have been pleased had she been here.

Standing in the parlour, I awaited my guests' arrival. I wore a beautiful new blue-silk gown that was scooped low at the bodice. Mrs Gladstone had inserted some kind of stay that lifted and shaped

– rather daring for me – the rounded swell of my small bosom. Janet had caught up my hair at the crown to allow a cascade of curls to tumble about my shoulders, and I had sapphire teardrops dangling from my ears. Being ill had lent my skin a rosy tinge and, though my eyes looked somewhat over-bright, I conceded the result could have been a lot worse.

Hamish stood at my side, elegantly and fashionably attired in spotless, white trousers, pale-blue-silk waistcoat over a crisp, white shirt. His neckcloth was starched and stiffly tied and he wore a coat of rich, dark-blue brocade, the points of its collar brushing his cheeks.

If he'd stopped there I could not have faulted him, but being Hamish, he could not resist overdoing it. He wore a ring on each finger, and he had a huge blue and white enamel pin in his neckcloth. His top hat was black to match his polished boots but had a blue silk ribbon around it with the lengths hanging down his back. That last, I thought, looked foolish and I eyed it warily wondering if perhaps it was I who was out of touch with the fashions.

"My friend in Leeds yesterday said it is all the rage in London," Hamish said proudly. "D'you like it?"

"Looks intriguing," said Patrick coming in behind him. "How are you, Elginbury?"

Hamish spun around awkwardly and his mouth worked with agitation. Quickly gathering himself, he countered, "Well, your opinion counts for nought. Look how you present yourself."

Patrick executed a courtly bow. "I'm well, thank you, and thank you for asking," he said pleasantly and I wondered at Hamish's sudden discomfiture around my brother.

"It is Alex's get-together. Are you happy with my attire, Li'l Sis?" Pat performed a dandified pirouette – much to Meg's delight – and I heard Hamish's indignant intake of breath.

My brother was wearing black trousers with brilliantly polished knee-high boots and, although his shirt was snow-white, he was typically without a neckcloth and his shirtsleeves were rolled to the elbows. He was wearing a magnificent purple and silver brocade waistcoat, and had neatly tied his hair back with a cord.

I hesitated, aware that if I said the wrong thing I might well end up deflecting Hamish's sulks all evening. I sighed wearily.

"I think Pat looks suitable, though a neckcloth and coat would perhaps …" My voice trailed off uncertainly and there was a momentary silence as Hamish looked triumphant and I wondered how Pat would react.

"Consider it done!" my brother declared cheerfully, and disappeared immediately.

"Why did you defend him?" Hamish complained, his voice a child-like whine.

I blinked with surprise. "I didn't. And why did you antagonise him?"

"He was always like that; always belittling, never serious."

"You could simply have said, hello." I put a hand to my temple to soothe the dull ache that was returning.

"Are you feeling alright, dear?"

I responded with deliberate patience, "Yes, Hamish."

Patrick reappeared with Meg proudly holding his hand. He had donned a silver frockcoat and a black neckcloth. The cut of his coat unavoidably showed the strength of his shoulders, demanding comparison with Hamish who relied on his tailor for such form.

At that moment, a footman positioned at the door announced formally that Mr Deon Morehead and Miss Julia Chapman had arrived, followed immediately by Mr Jonathon Merriday and Miss Adrienne Morehead. Pat was behaving very agreeably. He stood inconspicuously aside holding Meg's small hand, and allowing Hamish and me to receive our guests.

A tall, bookish youth, with spectacles perched at the end of his nose, was introduced as Mr Charles Chatham, Julia's first cousin. Charles was visiting from Northumbria. "Not exactly protocol," my friend said with a wink, "but I hoped you would not mind. I could not bear to leave him at home alone with Mama."

Of course I didn't mind, and once Charles was introduced he immediately acquainted himself with the beverage table.

Adrienne, as always, was perfectly turned out. Her white, porcelain skin contrasted delightfully with her pink-silk gown embroidered with white rosebuds. Her hair was held back with a band of wrought silver, allowing ringlets to frame her face, and she had garnets in her ears and about her neck.

More guests were arriving, including Celia. They lingered in the entry hall where the musicians struck up a gay tune and others spilled into the parlour, where Gerrard's ice wine was an instant pleaser.

Julia and Hamish had already met during Hamish's previous visits, so I introduced him to those he didn't know and polite conversation ensued. Hamish seemed intrigued by Deon's exotic looks and his eyes often slid in Deon's direction. Charles, gangly and ill at ease, sipped his wine and followed Adrienne over the rim of his glass. Glancing at Patrick, I saw his eyes also rested on her. She did not immediately see him against the wall, for he was bending to kiss Meg's cheek as Clara collected her charge.

It was obvious when she did notice him, for a quick, excited flush suffused her cheeks, and I watched with a mixture of interest and annoyance as she chewed her lips to bring the colour up.

Turning to me she said breathily, "Oh Alex, you didn't say your brother was home."

"Only arrived yesterday," I said, checking the edge in my voice.

"Charles … *that's* Patrick – the one Adrienne told you about," Julia whispered appraisingly to her cousin.

Deon patted his fiancée's hand where it rested on his sleeve. "No, my dear, *that's* the devil incarnate."

Charles dipped his head slightly and peered at Patrick over the top of his spectacles. "He seems only to have eyes for you, Miss

Adrienne," in what I thought was a rather pompous accent for a country gent.

"Excuse me, my sweet," Deon released his betrothed and sidled to where Patrick stood and the two shook hands and slapped each other's backs like the old alehouse chums they were.

Julia remained beside me with Adrienne while Hamish's eyes followed Deon with an intensity I found disconcerting. Brushing it aside, I turned to Julia. She was dressed beautifully in mint silk with a silver thread running through it. Her abundant auburn curls were swept into a modish, Grecian style, but, with her unfashionably freckled face and soft figure, she would never be the girl that men clambered over one another for. I knew that Patrick thought well of her and hoped he would spend time with her and not devote himself entirely to Deon – or Adrienne, who even now was edging her way towards him.

My attention was drawn once more to the door, as the footman announced further arrivals and Lord Thorncliffe appeared and greeted those he knew. I presented to him those he didn't and many were in awe of his title; but the earl was friendly and open, and his calm manner relaxed my guests. He moved about the room with social ease and, after delivering a short speech of welcome, encouraged everyone to enjoy the refreshments, before taking his leave.

Hamish and I stood awkwardly and silently together, and it was painfully obvious that we had nothing in common. His attention continued to be focused on Deon and it was starting to annoy me. I took the opportunity to look around the room, and was delighted that there were some two dozen people milling about, enjoying Cook's fancies and sipping the ice wine.

The music from the quartet in the hall was a perfect background to the laughter and conversation and at last I relaxed, feeling quite the young lady of fashion holding my first serious gathering. The house was alive with the gay sounds of clinking glassware and vibrant chatter.

But as time wore on, the numerous pins holding my hair in place were beginning to tell on my scalp. Hamish had drifted away to talk with someone and I was struggling to concentrate on Charles' critique of a play he saw in Leeds. When a young lady I'd met briefly at Julia's house chipped in with her opinion, he turned to her and I was free to slip away.

I leaned discreetly against a wall and placed a hand to my forehead. It was hot and slightly damp and I felt decidedly unwell.

"Thirsty?" I started in surprise. Patrick was beside me with a glass of lemonade. "I had Cook make it up. You should stay away from the other," he indicated the wine with a nod of his head and a sly smile. "May not agree with you after your recent … bout of illness."

I grasped the glass eagerly and took a long and very unladylike swig. Moving so that Patrick shielded me from my guests, I wiped my mouth with the back of my gloved hand causing him to laugh out loud. "Oh, I needed that," I gasped gratefully.

"Evidently."

"Wine, dear?" Hamish appeared offering a glass of the German grape. He shot a glare at Patrick and, though I definitely didn't want the wine, neither did I want any problems with Hamish. Hiding my reluctance, I took the wine and even managed a smile. "Thank you Hamish."

He nodded imperiously, took my arm and rudely turned his back to Patrick, leading me to where Julia and Deon were talking with Andrew, Celia and Beatrice.

The hall clock struck seven and the wine was still flowing. I had managed to leave my untouched wine on a side table and poured another glass of lemonade to quench my raging thirst. A pair of footmen milled about carrying plates of food. I cornered one and asked him to throw open the French doors leading onto the balcony and direct the quartet to move outside. Beatrice and Andrew were dancing and bumping into rattan furniture.

Deon took Celia by the hand and they joined in.

Perhaps my observations were sharpened by my knowledge of their affair, but as I watched them dance, I found it difficult to fathom that others could not detect a certain intimacy between them.

I glanced at Julia, who simply shrugged and cleverly started up a conversation with Hamish about his beautiful enamelled pin, instinctively targeting his favourite topic – his clothes – and effectively winning him over.

My gaze swept the room searching vainly for Pat and it was then I noted Adrienne's similar absence. Inappropriate jealousy needled me, distracting me from my guests and prompting me to wander on to the porch ostensibly to watch the dancers, and it was there I spotted them immediately – strolling like lovers, her hand on his sleeve, heads inclined towards one another, along the top terrace beyond the rose garden.

"She's been waiting for such an opportunity ever since she met you," Julia whispered at my shoulder following my gaze. "She speaks of little else."

"It's none of my affair," I said dispassionately and turned away, feigning indifference. My headache was pounding furiously.

"I've seen the way you look at him – no, hear me out – when I first met Hamish I knew he wasn't right for you. But that one …" she nodded towards the couple who had stopped walking and were deep in conversation. "I've always known it, and …" she leaned close to my ear, "you've never recovered from that kiss."

"He's my brother," I said irritably, feeling fatigue fall on me like a net.

"No, he's not – not really." She patted my arm, "and I've seen how he looks at you too, when you don't realise it. Your affections are not one-sided, but keep your secret if you will," she slanted me one of her cunning winks before moving to join a group by the food table.

What secret? I thought grumpily. I ought to be so lucky as to have one.

When finally the footman closed the heavy front doors behind the last of my guests I plumped wearily on to the settee. Hamish stood looking down at me.

"Are you unwell, dear?"

"I have a splitting headache, Hamish. Have had all day."

"I wasn't aware."

"Oh, Hamish," I sighed and stood with effort. "I'm exhausted and not feeling very well. I'm to bed."

He kissed my cheek as though he felt he ought to, and I thought how wooden and cold his lips were. Not soft and warm like –

"Good night, dear."

"Good night," I responded lifelessly and dragged myself up the stairs by the banister.

CHAPTER 16

The morning dawned sunny and crisp. Jemima and I made our way downstairs past the beckoning smells from the kitchens: fresh bread, fried onions, roasting meats. My stomach rumbled appreciatively.

On the porch, I extended my hand towards the east. The sun was about my thumb's width above the horizon and a few gold-bellied clouds hung in the sky. The smell of new day and damp earth, was carried on a breeze that set the flowers a-tremble on their dewy stems.

As was her habit, Jemima galloped joyously along the top terrace and down the steps into the orchard while I strolled sedately behind. There were only a few blossoms left on the trees now and the petals drifted on the grass like translucent snow. Bright young leaves were springing forth and I slowed my steps to admire them as Jemima bounded between the rows and disappeared from sight.

The path sloped gently down towards the stone wall at the end of the orchard and as I neared, I heard a low voice. Rounding the row of trees at the very end, I came across Patrick, crouching with Jemima.

"What are you doing up so early?" I said, pleased to see him.

"Good morning to you too," he replied, grinning. "A couple of years in Wellesley's troop and it becomes habit. Mind if I join you?"

"No. How did you know I'd be here?"

"Didn't – just lucky perhaps." We fell into step beside the wall separating the orchard from Jackson's property. "You're looking considerably better than yesterday morning," he continued.

"I feel like I look better."

"Did you enjoy yourself with your friends yesterday? Have they approved your Lord Whatsit?"

"You shouldn't call him that," I responded testily. My relationship with Hamish was irritating me immensely and I didn't need Patrick adding to it.

"I'm not the one going to marry him; I can call him what I like."

"Thank you for that little *aide memoire*. Anyhow, yes I did enjoy myself. You seemed to be having a nice time too."

"I was. I had forgotten how much I enjoyed Deon's company. No doubt we'll down a few ales before I leave for the continent."

"And no doubt re-acquaint yourself with the *glorious Adrienne*. Pair of lovesick poodles you were yesterday." I rolled my eyes mockingly. Laughing scornfully, it took only a moment to realise that he wasn't beside me.

I turned and looked back at him. "What?"

He sighed. "This jealousy of yours is quite tiresome."

I flushed to the roots of my hair and my mind flew unbidden to my unreasonable questioning of him in Devon two years ago, and knew we were on the edge of another such disagreement. This time I would not turn and run.

I balled my fists on my hips imperiously. "Just what …" but he was walking away, between the rows of trees towards the house.

"Forget it Alex," he threw over his shoulder.

"Don't you walk away, Patrick Washburn," I called and my voice echoed in the still air.

He rounded on me. "Shut up! Do you want to wake the whole house?"

"Then don't say something like that and walk away like a coward. I don't want to have that old argument with you again but –"

"Really? Then why is it you're constantly rolling your eyes and sighing petulantly every time that girl's name is mentioned?"

"Probably because her name is mentioned *all the time*. And the things you and your father said about her the other night – plain disgusting."

"You're jealous."

I glared at him furiously. "How conceited you are."

"Jealous and ridiculous. Just look how you're carrying on now." He stood before me and we were snarling at one another in hoarse stage-whispers.

"How dare you! Sometimes you're so hateful," I hissed ferociously.

"Then what's it to you if I spend time with Adrienne?"

"Everything," I cried hotly, my outrage rising further. "It has always been the same: those girls in Leeds, Wolstone, Astor … God knows how many in between."

"And why are my activities your concern?"

"Because now it's my friend … I won't have you treating my friend like one of your slutty conquests."

His face hardened. "She's no friend of yours, but you can't see it because you're so worried I might return her fancy."

"Oh, that's the least of my worries! You … return someone's fancy? You're nothing but a philanderer, a rake … too shallow to have a fancy for anyone. I'm not jealous of Adrienne – I *pity* her!"

"Such a noble defender of virtue, aren't you," he sneered. "Well what about you? Always interfering … poking your long nose into everything I do – who I see, where I go. If you don't like it – keep the hell out!" He made to walk away but changed his mind. "And besides, she was hanging around me!"

"Oh that's rich!"

"You ought to know. Every second … in the parlour, walking in the garden … watching, lurking like a spider … every-bloody-where I went."

"Don't be ridiculous! I had a roomful of guests." But the truth caused me to waver.

"Ridiculous you say?" He squared up to me and we stood two yards apart eyeing each other like spitting cats. "That's a great steaming pile of horse-shit and you know it." His voice was low and dangerous and the fight drained from me in a fearful rush as relentlessly, he went on, "You think what I do and where I go is your business … following me around like a hound on the trail, I don't answer to you … *Jesus Christ!* … I'm sick to death of this whole farce …"

I stood staring at him in horror as he raged on, his every word spelling out his contempt for me. I knew the cruelty he was capable of, and knew also that this was going to hurt – a lot.

"*Leave me alone for sweet sake!*" he continued his tirade, his voice taut with fury.

I could not bear his scorn. I should not have provoked him … should not have challenged him … should have let him walk away when he was about to. I clamped my hands over my ears, chanting, "*No! No! No!*" but I could still hear him.

"This has to stop – I'm stopping it right now because I've had enough, Alex – d'you hear me? It's over … why can't you be honest with yourself?"

He lunged toward me and grasped my wrists pulling my hands from my ears. His face was flushed with anger and I recoiled fearfully.

"Answer me!" he demanded.

"I …"

"It's all a façade … a sham!"

"Pat … *please* …"

The gulf was widening between us, my feet teetering on the

edge. I tried to wrench my hands free but he held firmly. I prayed he would stop before it was too late but he went on, each word pummelling me, "Come on Alex, be honest for once. Tell me why you're so jealous of every female within ten paces. And how about Hamish! Admit you can't marry him. And while you're at it … tell him why! How about the truth? Now there's a novel idea!"

I gasped fearfully, "Pat, please don't …"

"Instead of all this jealousy and resentment – tell *me* the truth. Tell *Hamish* the truth – that you can't marry him because you're in love with me!"

Oh God, he said it!

My head began to spin – oh *dear God*! I stared in shock and the tears welled in my eyes.

It was over.

He released my hands and stepped back, breathing heavily, glaring at me, his green eyes dark and flashing, while my own anger was replaced with grief. I was as naked before him, childishly infatuated with my own stepbrother. Forced to confront my wishful imaginings and, now that fantasy was flung in my face, leaving me humiliated.

In the distance a cow lowed. Her world hadn't changed in these last minutes, but mine had – irrevocably. Her world still rotated on its axis, but mine had been thrown off balance and nothing could ever be the same again.

Hiding my face in my hands, the tears streamed down my cheeks. Why did he continue to stand there? Oh why didn't he just go away – back to Spain, to Devon, to Adrienne, to *hell* … anywhere but here? Involuntarily, I gave a ragged sob.

After a long moment, he spoke in a whisper, his voice pained and tight with emotion, "Sweetheart … don't cry. I never wanted it to be like this – I should have gone while I still could. I can't be strong for both of us."

Slowly, as his tone sunk in, I lowered my hands.

He stood before me, arms at his sides in defeat.

"Oh, Alex … my darling girl," he said softly. With abrupt decisiveness, he moved towards me. In confusion, I retreated, coming up hard against the unyielding trunk of a tree, but he grasped my shoulders, and pressed me against the damp and fragrant bark, and kissed me.

There was nothing brotherly in that kiss. It was compelling and full of pent up passion, though his lips were warm, soft, and moved on mine as if he would drain the life from me. And instinctively, my mouth opened beneath his, my arms curled about his neck, and I clung to him.

I felt his need in that kiss, similar to the need in him the morning of his arrival when he'd embraced me with such intensity. Now he kissed me like he would never let me go – and I kissed him back. His arms clasped me to him desperately, and I felt he drew out my soul and exchanged it for his own.

It was a long time before we breathlessly drew apart, both of us shaken and transformed by the release of long held secrets. My heart was thudding and my lips burning. The emotions finally became too much and he folded me against his chest, cradling me to the ground, as I wept.

He loves me … he loves me … my heart sang disbelievingly. At last I raised my tear-stained face to him and whispered tentatively, "You love me?"

He nodded. "I do – have for a long time. And you've loved me a long time in return."

I bowed my head in agreement.

"I knew it when you were at Waterville," he said, "and I was hard pressed then to keep you at arm's length. Now you're all grown up and I saw immediately that morning I arrived home, your feelings hadn't changed – and neither had mine."

"Yet you are leaving again? Do you have to go?"

He nodded. "I'm committed to Wellesley, anything less would

be desertion." He sighed, "Let's see if I can explain. When I was in hospital in Spain, they thought I might die – *I* thought I might. I suppose it makes you think about what's really important – like my feelings for you. I had to know if you still felt as you had that summer, or if you'd grown out of it.

"But this war is important too," he went on. "I have a purpose – I'm not just some self-absorbed nobleman taxing my tenants and arranging my next party. I *want* to do this. They gave us leave over winter but we're expected back before the summer – hopefully to finish it off. I decided to come here … see if you still felt as you did … now you're older. I needed to know."

"And if I had changed?"

"Then I'd have returned to Spain and you would be none the wiser. But you hadn't changed – I saw that straight away."

He pressed his lips to the top of my head, lingering there and warming my hair with his breath. Then, raising his head, he continued, "But though you hadn't changed … with Hamish here and relations continuing … I decided to keep my distance."

"Even knowing how I felt?"

"You're to wed your Lord Whatsit … you seemed to be in accord and accepting of your fate. I resigned to leave it at that and make my future in the army. Alex, to be together we'd have an almighty struggle on our hands. It would perhaps be kinder on both of us had I left without making such a declaration."

I adjusted my position, snuggling closer to him, breathing his heady scent. He held me tightly and I revelled in the rapid *volte-face* of my life. To be loved and to love in return – eclipsed all worries, and nullified any trials we'd have to endure. At that moment I felt there was nothing I could not face and conquer.

He trailed his fingers along my jaw. "I've been worn out these last days with our squabbles and planned to cut my stay short. I hadn't intended to make this confession, my love, but it would not be the first time you've forced my hand."

I wriggled around so I could look into his face. His eyes were smoky with emotion and his hair hung loosely over his forehead. He smiled slightly – those warm, full lips, such sweet-tasting lips. "Are you regretting it then?"

"No. I'll never regret it."

"Then what do we do now? I mean, I'm still betrothed to Hamish."

"Is the date set?"

"No. We've agreed to wait until I'm older, but Hamish's father is ill … he's desperate for an heir before he dies."

He nodded, thinking it over, then he said, "Your Mother plans to marry me to Anne. If she suspects anything she'll see her lawyers and try to find some way to lock me into a contract. Then, no doubt, pack you straight off to Scotland. I suggest you hold off Hamish and when I return from Europe we can discuss it with my father."

"Is the war nearly over? Will it be long?"

He shrugged. "I'm a soldier – I know only what they tell me."

We lingered thus for a long time with Jemima sleeping beside us. He was propped against the tree, and I sat across his lap cuddled into his chest. I began to chuckle with a distant memory.

"What?"

"That day in the lake at Waterville. You really were going to kiss me, weren't you? You were angry with me and let me make a fool of myself."

He laughed lightly. "Guilty. You were so delightful – all wet and nymph-like – I wouldn't have been able to stop at a kiss. I was angrier with myself than with you."

"I'd have denied you nothing," I said softly.

"I know. That's why one of us had to show restraint."

I shook my head. "Your behaviour was so mysterious, and you were furious with me that morning I met you coming back from Astor."

He took a deep breath. "I'd been dealing with some associate of Father's … there were several of us at supper. One of the guests – a girl – watching me … making her availability quite obvious – so …" he shrugged. "I took up her offer. For some inexplicable reason, being with Kat made me feel such guilt – all I could think about was you. I lashed out at you, deliberately hurting you, for no reason other than the fact that such remorse was foreign to me. I didn't know how else to react."

"I'd worried when you hadn't come home that night. When I realised you'd been out whoring I was livid."

"I could see that. Do you know, when you stormed off into the woods I decided I didn't like the way I felt about you – all that guilty-conscience and anger. I thought to cut you out of my life. Then Father dragged me out of bed because you were missing, and instantly I forgot my new resolution and was desperate with worry."

"And I refused to speak with you," I interrupted giggling.

"You were a bitch!"

"But you came home to bid me farewell and I held it to my heart," I said. Sneaking a look at his face I added, "Along with the kiss."

He smiled reflectively, "Ah, that kiss. Yes, it was worth the argument to have it end in a kiss like that. For the record, I hadn't seen Kat again. You suspected I had."

"I knew you hadn't."

"How?"

My smile was mysterious. "I could tell."

"Well, listen to me now. I never wanted to love anyone. I promised myself I never would … determined to steel myself – walk away if I had to – and I planned to. I'd planned to leave here tomorrow … put you out of my life for good. But there's no going back now. I do love you, Alex, and I'm happy and relieved to admit it. And now I've made my confession, I'm yours and I'll save myself for you only. My whoring days are over – gladly."

"What about Adrienne?"

"An interesting diversion, and never anything more. And to save you enquiring – as is your wont Madam Treacle-Beak – nothing more than a kiss on her fingertips has ever passed between us."

I gestured to brush away so insignificant a detail and he laughed, unconvinced. "Which leads me to another thing."

"Yes?"

"Had you been anyone else looking at me with such adoring eyes, I'd have thrown you down and lifted your skirt years ago. But I want to marry you Alex, with our family's blessing. It won't further our cause if you are with child – particularly if I'm in Europe. You'll be packed off to Scotland so fast poor old Hamish won't know what hit him. I think it best we wait until we're wed before we … become lovers."

I flushed coyly, relieved and yet disappointed. "Oh, the sacrifice! You'd do that for me?"

"For both of us – just imagine our wedding night," he gave a bawdy chuckle.

"You haven't asked if I'll have you."

"Shall I present myself on bended knee, then?"

I snorted inelegantly. "No, it's not necessary – oh, there's something else. Julia – she suspects us and only yesterday said she believed we had feelings for each other."

"How could she know?"

"Apparently by the way we look at each other."

"Then others will notice too."

"Particularly Hamish – I think he's jealous of you anyway."

"With just cause as it turns out – not a situation I'm happy about, incidentally."

I nodded and rested against him and breathed deeply the spring scents on the air: the new hay growing in the fields beyond the wall, the flowers, the budding fruit on the trees, and wanted to cry again for the beauty of our love, bursting suddenly into life like the world around us. I wanted to imprint this moment forever in my mind, but the earth had resumed its rotation and I knew we had to return to the house.

"They'll be at breakfast wondering where we are," I said softly.

He was quiet for a moment. "Then you go back and tell them you got carried away on your walk. They'll think I overslept – I'll come down later."

"Aren't you hungry?"

"Ravenous, but I'm on special terms with Cook. Up you get Jemima!"

Rising, he pulled me to my feet with him and we faced one another. He looked different – less guarded somehow and I closed my eyes as he cupped the back of my head and bent his face towards mine.

CHAPTER 17

It was like a dream. I wondered if I'd imagined the whole thing. I floated into the breakfast room on a cloud.

"My dear, we were about to send out a search party."

And the cloud evaporated dropping me to earth with a thud.

"It's such a beautiful morning, Hamish, I quite lost track of time." It was a version of the truth.

"I was planning to search for you myself once I have finished here."

I tried not to roll my eyes. "I was perfectly safe and happy," I said honestly. I helped myself to fruit and cold meats, and contemplated going for a ride this afternoon with Pat, or possibly laying under a tree with Meg and reading poetry or –

"What would you like to do today, dear?" Hamish cut across my reverie.

"Er … I've not given it any thought."

"Perhaps we could take a carriage to Fountain's Abbey. I haven't seen it and Mrs Grainger tells me it's worth a visit."

"It is lovely," I agreed, trying to hide my dismay.

He took that as acceptance and rose immediately. "Good. I shall ask Cook to prepare a picnic."

Gerrard continued to read the paper and seemed oblivious to my presence. When I touched the napkin to my lips, they felt rather puffy and bruised and I knew a rush of pleasure, even as I hoped the swelling was not evident to others. I pushed back my chair.

"If you don't want to go picnicking with Hamish, you ought to say so," Gerrard said from behind his paper.

I paused. "Is it so obvious?"

"You were humming to yourself when you came in. Now you're frowning and silent as the grave. I'd say it's obvious, though I don't think he noticed."

"I don't know what to do," I said with sincerity. "I just don't like him."

My stepfather folded his paper and placed it on the table beside his plate. "Take my advice, Lass. Get used to him – you're marrying this man." He took up his cup and studied it thoughtfully before continuing. "You have known for some considerable time now the contract is in place, signed, sealed, and for all purposes delivered. We cannot back out now without a serious financial impact to both families."

I felt my palms go clammy and resumed my seat. "Financial impact? When was all this done?"

"About a year ago."

"Well, thank you for telling me." I said sarcastically. "Did anyone think that I might want to be told?"

"No," he said simply. "Consider yourself fortunate that I'm telling you now. Traditionally the happy couple have no involvement at all. We are wealthy people, people with rank. Only those without money, without position, may marry where they choose, for so much less rides on it. If you marry the wrong person, the results may be disastrous to the family name and fortune."

"You sound like Mother." My eyes shifted past him to the garden where Hamish could be seen inspecting a new daffodil.

"Your mother and I are pleased he visits regularly. You must resign yourself to this match. You could have done a lot worse, you know."

Suddenly I was angry. "I didn't *do* any of this," I said. "And that sounds very much like I should be grateful that he's not elderly and ugly."

"We've been all through this, Alex." He sighed wearily. "Your mother – "

"Yes, my mother – if ever there was a more self-serving person on earth … It is not too late to break the contract."

"The settlement has already been paid, Alex," he said flatly, and as I sat back in surprised disbelief, he continued, "That's what I'm trying to tell you. Your Mother has already made her investment. It is complicated and unconventional, but Lord Hamish has struggled financially for some years. Your Mother offered to pay his debts in their entirety – no small amount, I might add – considerably more than most dowries. Now, Lord Hamish was concerned by your reluctance, and extracted a guarantee from your Mother that you would go through with the marriage, since if you didn't, he could not afford to repay the money and stood to lose his business interests.

"But more than that, it seems that through some well-intended gesture of appreciation for your papa's military services, the taxes on this estate were substantially reduced. Your mother is out of favour these days and if the balance of those taxes was called in now, your brother could well be ruined. Since Lord Hamish's English cousin is related by marriage to the Prime Minister … I'm sure you see where I'm going …"

I certainly could, and having been so full of hope for the future only minutes ago, I now felt the room was washed of its colour. As I absorbed the information, I understood that ethically, legally and financially, I was most assuredly trapped.

✷

In my room I examined my face in the mirror. Was there evidence of Patrick's kisses? Did I look different? I certainly looked strained and shadows of worry haunted my eyes. I could see no way clear, no way of breaking the contract with Hamish's father, no way of being free to be with Patrick.

I decided I would tell Hamish that I didn't feel well and couldn't picnic with him – and it would be the truth. It wasn't difficult to find him. He was sitting on a wrought iron chair under the Great Oak, leaning back with his hands behind his head, staring into the ancient boughs above.

He rose as I approached and pulled out a chair for me.

"I'm not staying," I said and continued to stand. "I came to tell you I shan't be going for a picnic today. With all the excitement yesterday I … I don't feel quite myself."

He regarded me thoughtfully. "Tell me what's going on?"

I faltered. "I don't understand."

Hamish scoffed. "I'm sure you do. Ever since Patrick arrived home you've been different – distant. Has he … I mean … he does not like me very much."

I was surprised by his insecurity. "Don't be silly Hamish. He's never said any such thing."

"We've delayed our marriage plans for some time now. I agreed only because you are young, but my father is a dying man and would see us wed before it's too late."

"You've been as happy to delay our marriage as I," I said challengingly.

"True, but I've received mail from my father's valet – arrived yesterday. Father's health has taken a downturn … we must set a date."

"Not now, Hamish," I implored. I was beginning to feel claustrophobic. Surely it can't happen like this … could God be so cruel as to grant my heart's desire and then remove it again within the space of a single morning?

Almost on cue I spotted Patrick strolling toward the stables and my heart skipped a beat. As if he felt my eyes, Patrick glanced over and doffed his hat cheerfully. I waved back, but Hamish remained unmoving.

"You'd go riding with him," he said grumpily.

"Don't be ridiculous," I lied firmly. "I told you, I feel unwell. Why does my friendship with Patrick concern you?"

"It would not if I thought it was merely friendship. But the change in you over the last few days has been marked – he's your brother, it's not natural. Even when your guests were here yesterday, your eyes … always following."

"Nonsense," I said with bravado.

"I saw you."

"What are you worried about Hamish?" I demanded, suddenly losing patience. "You know I'm bound to marry you. I've been locked into a nice little bargain between your father and my mother. Is your concern for me, or for the money you'll have to pay my mother if I don't marry you?"

He had the decency to look embarrassed. "You know about that?"

"Thanks to my stepfather – he told me this morning."

"I was only recently told of that myself. That's why I … that's why I agreed to this visit. My father insisted we … improve our relations."

I stood staring at him. "I don't want to decide on a date yet simply because my morally bereft mother and your father have boxed us into a tight corner. I –"

"Shut up, damn it!" Hamish suddenly hissed.

Shocked, I stared at him, "You speak so and we're not even married! Imagine if –"

"I said *shut up*!" He was watching over my shoulder and I swung around and saw the object of his attention – Equus, clopping lazily across the grass toward us, Patrick seated casually in the saddle.

"Greetings young lovers," he said, smiling as he approached. The irony in his words was not lost on me, but I was in no mood to participate in a private joke at Hamish's expense.

"Sit down," Hamish commanded *sotto voce*. I feigned deafness.

"I'm to my room – I feel quite fatigued. You may entertain one other." I marched away angrily.

"The unfathomable humours of women," Patrick observed, attempting a cheerful solidarity with Hamish, who was having none of it.

∿

I slammed my door and stamped my foot like a petulant child. Hamish's suspicions rankled and I wished he would go home. Then suddenly guilt flooded over me for it was not Hamish's fault – none of this was.

But neither was it my fault, nor Patrick's. I still had no idea how long Patrick planned to be here before returning to Europe. I needed to be with him, to explore our new feelings for each other. I felt like a plant long deprived of light finally brought into the sun and, though I knew it was grossly unfair to Hamish, I was in love and incapable of suppressing my feelings.

I watched Patrick from my window, riding with his customary ease, perfectly attuned to Equus' graceful stride, down the driveway towards the lane and wondered where he was going. I threw myself into the overstuffed chair by the window, and gasped as I looked directly into the face of *the lady*. She hovered six inches above the floor – serene and silent, and watching me with her lovely hazel eyes.

"I can't marry Hamish," I said aloud. "I can't, for I love Patrick. Would the greater crime lie in sacrificing the family's name and fortune, or being untrue to myself?"

Her gaze seemed to shift beyond me for a second and then she faded into nothing and I was alone.

∾

Later that afternoon, Meg and I tossed a ball between us, trying to keep it from Jemima. Being with the child enabled me to put my adult concerns aside, and I enjoyed her company. She chortled delightedly whenever I missed my catch and Jemima won the contest, forcing us to chase her down to retrieve the ball, all slippery and sodden. Holding the dreadful leather thing aloft in revulsion, I called off the game and we fell happily to the grass in the shade of a spruce tree.

Before we could regain our breath, Meg leapt to her feet again. "Pat!" Both dog and child charged off to where Patrick on Equus was trotting along the gravel drive. I followed and arrived before the tall horse as Pat dismounted and handed the reins to Meg.

"Can you hold this great, unruly beast for me, Midget?" he asked, knowing full well that Equus was too obedient to go anywhere.

"Yes," the girl declared solemnly.

"And have you enjoyed your day?" he asked me, as he unbuckled his saddle bags.

"Do you really want to know?"

He laughed and I longed to touch him. Knowing that he returned my regard and knowing that I was free to express my feelings – if only to him – my heart soared.

"What about you?" I asked.

"Not bad. Father asked me to ride into Wolstone this morning to find a carpenter to build some new stable doors. They need replacing before they rot off their hinges." He continued to fiddle with his saddle, and added under his breath, "May I taste your sweet lips before supper tonight?"

I flushed with pleasure. "You may. Shall we say the library at four o'clock?"

"Done!" he said in his normal voice. "The carpenter cannot come until next week. I expect they'll hold until then."

He dragged some articles wrapped in cloth from his saddlebags, "A bag of onions and a wheel of reeky cheese for Cook," he said cheerfully holding them aloft and pulling a face that caused Meg to giggle. "The menial things I do for that woman – I'm reduced to buying staples from the market like some common hausfrau."

He retrieved the reins from Meg. "You did a marvellous job keeping this monster under control, Midget." The little girl fairly glowed with pride. Turning toward the stables, he threw over his shoulder, "Four," and I waved happily.

"What's four?" asked Meg.

"You," I replied. "Come, let's get you out of that dress – it has grass stains on it and Clara will be quite upset."

∽

At five minutes before four o'clock, I crept into the library. My hands trembled with anticipation as I closed the door softly behind me. Hamish would be nowhere near the library, preferring to ride his bay gelding in the late afternoon sun. I stood in the window overlooking the drive – the very place from which I'd seen Maeve and Patrick first arrive. How I'd resented their coming. How I'd railed against Patrick. And now, how I loved him.

The door clicked behind me as he slipped into the room and turned the key in the lock.

"You look pensive, my darling girl." He came up behind me, his arms going around my waist and his chin resting on my head as his gaze followed mine down the length of the drive to where it disappeared around the bend and was swallowed by the trees in the park.

"It's all a big mess," I murmured.

"What is?"

"You, me, Hamish. It's all Mother's doing – hers and Hamish's father. Did you know the betrothal has been financially settled already?"

"Come and tell me." He led me to the two wing chairs facing each other across the empty fireplace and I repeated the story his father had told me that very morning; the same morning we had acknowledged our love for each other – a lifetime ago it now seemed.

He listened without speaking and when I was finished he said, "Then we must be doubly cautious lest our secret be known and Lord Whatsit's father has you wedded and bedded to his son before either of you can draw breath."

"Hamish is suspicious of you. He thinks I've been behaving differently toward him since you arrived."

"Have you?" he grinned maliciously.

"I didn't think I had but … why don't you like him?"

"I'm sure he's a nice enough fellow – though he's not for you. I don't think he'd make a happy wife of you."

"Why do you say that? What do you know that I don't?"

"Nothing that would alter circumstances – come here." He pulled me across the space between us to share his chair. Settling me on his lap, he applied himself diligently to kissing me. In his embrace, I forgot all concerns, all fears, and could only breathe, and feel, and respond.

I loved the way he tasted and smelt. My heart swelled and my pulse raced, and I moved with the stirrings of an animal urgency deep within. When finally he drew away, we were both breathing rapidly. I nestled against his chest with my head on his shoulder, my eyes half-closed as he recited:

> *Come hither Womankind and all their worth,*
> *Give me thy kisses as I call them forth.*
> *Give me the billing-kiss, that of the dove,*
> *A kiss of love;*
> *The melting-kiss, a kiss that doth consume*
> *To a perfume;*

The extract-kiss, of every sweet a part,
A kiss of art;
The kiss which ever stirs some new delight,
A kiss of might;
The twaching, smacking kiss, and when you cease
A kiss of peace;
The music-kiss, crotchet and quaver time,
The kiss of rhyme;
The kiss of eloquence, which doth belong
Unto the tongue;
The kiss of all sciences in one,
The kiss alone.
So 'tis enough.

"Lord Herbert of Cherbury," I supplied dreamily.

"The very one."

"It's lovely."

"So now you've had a half-day to ponder, how do you feel?"

"I feel honoured that you love me."

"The news about your dowry will make it even more difficult for us to extricate you from your contract."

"Surely there's something we can do — but you sound doubtful yourself."

He shook his head and said soberly, "There'll be a way. Only, remember that I won't be here to help you. The pressure to marry Hamish will be great, but you will always have a home in Devon, even if I'm not there — if you find you cannot remain here."

I nodded. "Thank you, but hopefully it won't come to that, not if we're careful. But there's something we've not yet discussed."

He cocked his head enquiringly.

"How long will you be here? When do you leave for Europe?"

"I must be in Belgium before the end of May."

"So we have about two months," I calculated.

He lazily trailed his lips along my jaw, sending a tremor up my spine. "More or less, allowing for travelling time," he murmured as he found my lips.

And as the afternoon grew late, we talked quietly, laughed, and found an entirely new pleasure in each other's company. The crunch of horses' hooves on the drive outside signalled Hamish's return and we reluctantly drew apart.

"I feel like the unfaithful wife," I grumbled.

"And I, the secret lover … it's delicious." At my look of rebuke, he quickly removed his grin. "One day we'll be open about our love and shall be together, free from the dictates and expectations of others."

"Patience," I said.

"A virtue – of which, I mentioned to you once before, I am bereft, but I'm expecting you to have in abundance."

He eased me off his lap and rose, turning me to face him, gently brushing aside a lock of hair. He pressed his mouth to the hollow beneath my ear causing my breath to catch with the thrill of it, and he gave a low chuckle, leading me a slow, rapturous dance across the rug to the door.

Pat and I sat across the supper table from one another and I kept my focus firmly on my plate, fearing that if our eyes met my heart would be laid bare for all to see. But he and his father discussed the work that the Wolstone carpenter would be doing, then moved on to some of the changes they wanted to make at Waterville. Gerrard opened a bottle of wine and Pat smirked knowingly at me as I declined his father's offer.

Hamish had been quiet throughout the meal and, as our plates were cleared, he invited me to walk with him in the garden.

He'd evidently given some thought to our quarrel earlier in the day and apologised for pressuring me. I accepted graciously, and we walked on as though nothing incidental had passed between us. As we turned towards the house he paused and touched my shoulder, "Alex, I shall be leaving earlier than planned. First light tomorrow – since my father is so unwell."

I stared at him, my thoughts in turmoil. Naturally, I was happy to be left alone with Patrick, but I did not enjoy deceiving Hamish and hated this situation, for if anyone suspected my involvement with Patrick, it would not go well – not even Gerrard would support a breach of my betrothal contract.

And when Hamish arrived home to a failing father, would he be required to solidify the relationship – name a date?

Janet and I rose early to farewell Hamish and Grahame. I hugged my betrothed with as much affection as I could muster and even kissed his cold, powdered cheek. We walked together down the drive until we reached the bend and then the two men mounted their horses and trotted out to the lane, before turning towards the north.

For several days, Janet was distraught and, when I caught her eyes on me, I read the accusation there. She blamed me for delaying my marriage and subsequently delaying her own. But Hamish had made it clear that she was welcome in his home – it was her own doing that she lingered here.

Later that week, Mother returned to Broughton Hall with even more trunks and boxes than when she'd departed. Her groom unfolded the steps and handed her down, but since Lord Thorncliffe and I arrived too late to meet her as she considered befitting, we were treated to her icy glare.

"Oh, there you are," she commented caustically as we greeted her. "I was beginning to wonder."

"Hello, Mother," I said brightly.

"Hello," she responded absently. "Gerrard, organise someone to carry these," she indicated her trunks with a wave of her gloved hand, "No Eleanor, bring that with you. I'm exhausted, Gerrard, simply done in – I'll be in my rooms. Mrs Grainger, has dinner been served yet? No? Good. Have it delayed an hour – I must rest."

Gerrard shot me a look that said, *Here we go again*, and called for a footman to arrange a pair of sturdy fellows to haul Mother's luggage upstairs.

Dinner was served on the back porch overlooking the lawns, for the day was warm. A soft breeze lifted the corners of the white linen tablecloth as we seated ourselves. Mother expressed surprise when she learned Patrick was home. Her eyes appraised him appreciatively as he took his seat at the table and allowed Emily to pour him a glass of wine. And while she clearly admired the young man he'd become, Mother's words spoke differently. "So he finally arrived, did he?" she said acidly to Father. "Taken him to task yet for his filial disobedience, hmm?"

"How now my Regan?" Patrick responded in good spirits. "It is well I've been seasoned at war else I'd not have the stomach to sit at table with your fine self."

"They say the military has a way of making men from boys, but I can see our good Arthur Wellesley has a way to go with this one," Mother countered.

I groaned audibly and Gerrard said, "Leave it alone you two."

"Well she started it," Pat threw in childishly, with a jaunty wink in Mother's direction.

"Hmph …" she glared over the floral centrepiece at him.

"Leave it," Gerrard repeated, uncommonly irritable. "You're both very tiresome, sniping at each other like this."

"You could have told me he was returned before I sat," Mother persisted.

"What difference would it have made?"

"I could have taken my meal in my room."

"It is not too late," Patrick pointed out pleasantly.

"Oh!" she pushed her chair back indignantly and stormed out of the room, muttering to herself, "all vengeance comes too short!"

"Ah!" Pat saluted her receding back with a raised glass. "She appreciates the Regan moniker."

"Now, why did you do that? Life has been pleasant here of late, when you weren't trying to get up Hamish's nose, that is – doubtless you had something to do with the boy going home early – and now this."

Patrick shrugged, "She could simply have said hello," he said reasonably.

"Mother is quick to ignite at the best of times, Pat," I said. "Why could you not have let her be?"

He turned to me. "Why do you tolerate her?"

"Because she's my mother."

"Which gives her leave to be as rude as she pleases? Well, you might choose to roll over and wait submissively for her kick, but *I* shan't."

"I wish you would. It would be all the better for the rest of us," I muttered to my plate.

"Then you'll have to be disappointed. Pass the bowl, please Father."

As always, Gerrard's irritation wilted in the face of his son's indifference to his remonstrations. He reached for the bowl of steaming, spring vegetables, running with melted butter and fresh parsley. Pat served himself and turned to me. I nodded, and he spooned a serve on to my plate. I inhaled the delicious aroma and we ate in silence until finally Gerrard said, "Your sister's right, Son. It would be better if you could put aside your disagreement."

Pat took a sip of wine and regarded his father solemnly before answering, "It is not a disagreement."

"Then, whatever it is, it has to stop. I'm going to Leeds immediately after I've finished my meal. Try not to provoke a disturbance while I'm gone."

"How fascinating," Pat commented dryly. He leaned on the table and casually pointed his knife toward the door Mother had disappeared through. "Your beloved wife has only today returned from Leeds and you're racing back there as fast as your overworked nag can carry you."

"I have business to attend to.

"Oh yes, I know all about your *business*." Pat sounded tired. "Don't lecture me on my position with your wife when you can't wait to remove yourself from her sight."

I'd kept my eyes on my plate throughout this exchange but at his last comment I raised my head in surprise. Father and son were sizing each other up and some wordless dialogue seemed to pass between them.

In the end, Gerrard uncomfortably returned to his meal, eating hurriedly and excusing himself, leaving the two of us at the table alone. We continued to eat wordlessly and a short time later we heard Lord Thorncliffe ride out, his valet cantering behind.

"I'm sorry," Patrick said into the silence. The apology surprised me. I looked up at him as he went on, "I know it upsets you."

"Look, it's just that ... you two are always baiting each other."

"I know – you're right. I'll try for the remainder of my stay to be agreeable. I want you and I to enjoy our time together ... not be at odds because your mother and I can't get along."

"What is it between you? I don't understand."

"It's no matter."

"It obviously is – I want to know."

He took a deep breath. "It's difficult to explain. You've not been to court."

"You knew her at court?"

"Briefly, before I returned to Devon."

"So ..." I prompted.

He shrugged. "There's not a lot to tell. You have to understand what it's like there. Depraved, debauched, and any other adjective of that ilk you wish to apply – that's what it is."

"But the king – he would never approve –"

"He didn't know the half of it – all going on under his nose and he, locked in his insanity. It was the prince's set … parties and dancing every night. And among the ladies and gentlemen, it was sport to … ah …"

"Just say it!" I snapped impatiently.

"Your mother … she worked her way through a considerable number of men … rising higher with each. She wasn't alone, of course, they all do – it's about greed and ambition.

"I arrived at court quite young, but with a reputation – I was wealthy, or rather my father was. I held a position in the Queen's stables and enjoyed it, and occasionally I was permitted to attend various events as befitted my age and station. There was a group of us – Hamish was there but he's older and had his own set – many of the wealthier young men were picked off one by one by the ladies of the court."

"But you were *fourteen!*" I cried aghast.

He shrugged. "Exactly so, and consequently managed to exclude myself from much of this. But the older lads welcomed it. It happened with the maids too – ladies in waiting … your mother would have been one of them in her time. Sex is the most efficient form of career advancement and goes on in all the courts across Europe – has for centuries, think of Henry the Eighth."

"But we've moved on from those days, surely?"

"In some respects, but not all. Often the young fellows believed themselves in love and loved in return. They lavished gifts on the ladies – expensive things, money and jewels, and received little more than bragging rights in return."

I held my breath in dread. Images from my childhood rushed at me unbidden; a secluded garden, Mother, a young man in a shiny, grey coat.

He hesitated and chose his words carefully, "Your mother singled several of the lads out … obviously worked out their financial worth. I'd seen her flirting and manipulating with the best of them, sending notes of assignation via Eleanor. You see, these young men represent a tidy income for a widowed lady."

I drew in my breath quickly. "What about you? Did she … did any of the older ladies …?"

He smiled, quick to reassure me. "No. I was largely excluded by age, but it was only a matter of time before she moved in on my father – although older than the other fellows he's no less gullible. I was fully occupied with the *young* and pretty Mary Whitmore. It was she who introduced me to the sins of the flesh, though I was certainly not *her* first."

"So then, what did happen between you and Mother?" I asked, cautiously.

"She and my father began a courtship, although she hadn't abandoned her … *business enterprises*, and knowing her greed for wealth and status, I told him what I'd witnessed. It caused a terrible stink and my father broke off his liaison with her"

"Not what she had in mind?"

"Not exactly, no. Your mother despises me for interfering; she'll never forgive me that. But she had an ace up her sleeve and therein lies the problem for it was around that time she discovered she was with child and my generous and forgiving father accepted that the child was his."

"So here we are."

He smiled ruefully in agreement. "Life at court is corrupt and perverted, and the perversion is contagious. The King deplores it – he won't tolerate it – but has little influence among his own people. Your father's death, accident though it surely was, was a timely event for your mother. Her ambition has run amok ever since."

I was satisfied by his explanation for I'd seen enough corruption when Mother's friends used to visit here.

One question still remained though. "What of Hamish? Was he involved with these older women?"

"Hamish …" Patrick thought for a moment. "Now, he had his

own affairs going on." He smiled then. "Do we have an end to it?"

I smiled in return, relieved. "Yes, but please, for my sake, can you try to ignore Mother's barbs?"

"For your sake? Very well, I'll try."

∾

Several days later, I sat alone in the morning room. Patrick had ridden to Bolton and wasn't due back until the afternoon. I was attempting to finish a tapestry I'd started during the empty winter months and while I worked, a bell sounded at the front door followed by Mrs Grainger's heavy footfalls in the hall. Cocking my head to listen, I thought I detected Adrienne's sultry voice.

I waited, needle poised and then the door swung open and the housekeeper announced, "Miss Morehead and Miss Chapman for you, Miss Alex. Shall I show them in?"

"Thank you. And could you bring lemonade?"

Adrienne and Julia were in high spirits, chattering excitedly about my recent gathering and what a success they considered it.

"And did you notice," Adrienne said tamping her fan on my forearm, "Lizzie Botham's slippers? Oh they were so exquisite. Her father *must* be buying from the French."

"Do you think?" Julia feigned shock. Anyone wealthy enough to pay the smugglers' exorbitant costs was buying from the French, though none ever admitted it.

"Where else would you get slippers like those?"

"Well, I for one would not wear anything those Froggies made," said Julia.

"Bull's wool!" Adrienne snorted. "You'd be first in line if you thought you could get away with it."

Julia tapped the side of her nose and winked. We were laughing as Mother appeared in the doorway. I felt a twinge of annoyance for Adrienne's head turned abruptly, her expression expectant, before falling with transparent disappointment. She recovered quickly and received Mother's courteous greeting – the latter ever flawless when observing correct social behaviour.

I invited Mother to take a glass of lemonade with us, but she politely declined. "Only came to fetch my bible," she said collecting her Almack's from a table. "Are you girls staying for dinner?"

Julia immediately framed an apology, ignoring Adrienne's dark look. The other girl waited until the tapping of Mother's wooden heels faded down the hall before turning on her friend.

"It would have been nice to stay."

"If you'd hoped to see Patrick," I said caustically, "you'd have been disappointed. He's gone to Bolton."

I watched the frustration flicker momentarily across Adrienne's beautiful face but she laughed gaily. "Oh, you silly. *You're* our friend. We came to visit *you*."

"How easily falsehoods drip from your tongue," Julia commented dryly. There was a moment's hesitation before the conversation took a different turn and by the time the hall clock struck eleven, Julia rose and gathered her gloves and reticule, forcing Adrienne to reluctantly follow her lead.

The girls were waiting for their carriage when Mother appeared and suggested Adrienne's mother call by for afternoon tea one day the following week.

"I have the most delicious news from Leeds. Your mother will simply burst when she hears what I have discovered. Tell her I have my at-home on Thursday afternoons."

Adrienne nodded, smiling. "I shall, it all sounds so –"

She broke off as Patrick rode up the drive. The delight on Adrienne's face was clear for all to see – including Mother, who was not in the least impressed. Neither, for that matter, was Julia who looked sharply at me. As their carriage was brought around, I composed my expression appropriately, and took Julia's arm, moving towards the carriage as I did so. "It was a most pleasant visit, thank you both so much for coming."

"Oh ..." Adrienne floundered, searching for words. "It would be rude to leave without greeting Patrick."

"Stop it!" Julia hissed and judging by Mother's snort, she'd been overheard. Pat dismounted and took Equus' reins and walked towards us.

"Greetings ladies." He took off his dusty hat and whacked it against his thigh as he approached. "What a fair welcoming party."

The midday sun shot highlights through his honey hair as he brushed it from his face, and Adrienne was immediately beside him, blushing delicately and extending her hand. "If we'd known you were on your way up the lane, we'd have lingered a little longer over our lemonade," she said in her low, breathy voice.

"Had I known you were here, I'd have been home sooner to share a cup," he replied gallantly, bowing over her hand.

She lowered her lashes coquettishly, "You oughtn't tease me so ... "

"I never tease young ladies who so prettily greet me upon my arrival," he looked past her and grinned at Julia and me.

"Oh, you're too kind," Adrienne simpered and I had to contain an unladylike sound.

"Too kind, indeed," Mother snapped. "This young man is an incurable flirt, Miss Morehead, you mustn't let him turn your head. One would never have guessed he's betrothed to my daughter, Anne."

My stomach twisted painfully and Adrienne's black brows shot up in surprise. Only Julia and Pat remained composed.

Mother immediately took charge, leaving no room for reaction. She bustled our guests towards their carriage, talking rapidly all the way; bidding them farewell ... thanking them for coming ... hoping to see them again soon. She shut the carriage door firmly behind them and commanded, "Move on, driver!"

Patrick and I remained frozen where we stood until the carriage had disappeared round the bend. Then Mother turned to him. "What?" she said, innocently. "Surely you didn't think we'd sit by and let you make your own life … drinking and whoring … squandering your father's money?"

"I won't marry Anne," he said firmly. He was gripping his hat in a white-knuckled hand and his face had grown ashen beneath its tan.

"Well, you're not marrying Alexandra – she's betrothed to another," Mother responded flippantly, "and since I have only the two daughters, you must settle for Anne. Your father agreed that we see our lawyers in the coming weeks to draw up the paperwork, but you may as well get used to the idea now."

"Madam," he said, dangerously low, "you will not dictate the terms of my life. May I remind you that I'm of age and beyond your influence?"

"We shall see about that, for legally I'm your mother and I am morally bound to ensure you make a good match – to protect you against your youthful folly, to safeguard the interests of this family. Considering the style of life you enjoy, you are clearly in no position to make any such decisions for yourself. I'm sure my legal man will agree."

Turning then, she swept victoriously into the house, her back straight, her chin thrust out.

I'd been paralysed with alarm, but now as I took a step towards him he stayed me with a raised hand. "We're being watched. Let me deal with this. I'll be back in a couple of days."

He turned to Equus and seconds later, the gravel sprayed behind him as the horse's long elegant legs measured the drive at a gallop.

Patrick did not return the next day, or the next. Anxiety saw me drifting restlessly around the gardens and the house, and by the third day, my uneasiness had become anger for he was throwing away the short time we had before he was due to leave.

He finally returned during the third night. I had fallen into a restive sleep and awoke to Jemima's low growl. I shimmied to a sitting position and could just make out a silhouette edging towards me. Jem's growling was suddenly replaced by the thumping of her tail so I was not afraid when I asked quietly, "Who's there?"

"It's me," said the voice of my beloved. In an instant, my anger was forgotten and I was out of bed and in his arms. He caught me awkwardly and we stumbled and crashed against my washstand. Holding each other tightly, barely breathing, we listened for any stirring within the house. There was no sound and I could stand it no longer.

"My God, where've you —"

His lips found mine hungrily and I gave myself over to this most wonderful, and still so new, expression. When at last we parted, he took my hand and led me to my bed. "Get in, you must be freezing."

He was right, for the stone of our house cooled quickly — despite the thick rugs on the floors. I scrambled beneath the bedclothes and he sat on the edge. Jemima jumped up and he fondled her ears absently as he talked.

"I went to Leeds to see Father, to find out what he knew about this contract for me and Anne."

"And?"

"Apparently it had been discussed but Father's position hasn't changed. Though his preference is that I make my own choice, he did concede that a match with Anne would be excellent. He's quite reasonable — he reminded me of my responsibilities, and agreed that provided I demonstrate discernment, there will be no formal contract drawn up."

"And what is meant by discernment?"

"I am to be seen in the *right* company … appropriate young ladies of suitable marriageable quality. All other … *improper dalliances* must be kept extremely discreet."

I snorted. "Would I be considered an improper dalliance, since I am betrothed and consequently considered unavailable?"

"Undoubtedly," he said, and I could hear the grin in his voice.

I sighed. "This is becoming quite unbearable. It seems that every day there's some new hurdle. The fates are conspiring against us." I pressed my forehead into his travelling coat, recoiling suddenly, "Pooh, you smell like a sweaty horse."

"Not surprising. I have worn these same clothes for three days!" Laughing lightly he took off his coat and flung it to the floor then carelessly kicked off his boots.

"Better?" he asked and pulled me to his chest where I snuggled close.

"Couldn't we run away? Elope? We could marry over the anvil in Gretna … live at your house in Devon?"

"I wish it were that easy. My love, I'm not a free man – if I don't rejoin Wellesley I'll be a deserter. They shoot deserters – you'd be a very young and wealthy widow."

I was in no mood for humour. "But we could marry … I could return to Europe with you – many wives do, I've read about them."

He shook his head. "It's no life. No, I don't want us sneaking off in the night and I don't want you in Europe where I'll only worry about you. When the war is over, we'll marry without hindrance, preferably with our parents' blessing."

"But …" I began, but he silenced me with a finger on my lips.

"We love each other – that's not going to change. As long as you refuse to marry Lord Whatsit – and remember, they can't drag you to that altar – wait for me … that's all I ask, and we shall marry then."

"But what about my contract? It could be very bad for Simon should I –"

"Alex, darling girl, listen to me – I don't care about any damned contract. I do, however, care very much about Lord Hamish's parliamentary influence and I would not jeopardise Simon's position. We shan't be stroking Hamish's fur backwards, but we are an influential family and I am not above buying his acquiescence. Through Father's lawyer, I could make an offer to buy out the contract."

"You'd pay him a bribe? You'd be *buying* me." I pretended outrage.

He paused to yawn. "Yes, but be assured I'd haggle a bargain." He was grinning and I relaxed against him. He made it sound so easy.

Now the initial excitement of his homecoming had dulled, I found myself growing drowsy. He tucked the counterpane around us, and after a time, I slept.

We both slept.

The sky was lightening when I awoke, curled on my side with Pat spooned behind me. He was still fully clothed, but snuggled beneath the bedclothes with one arm around me, holding me against him.

I lay for a moment, revelling in his soft breathing against my hair, and my heart swelled with love and happiness. Though it was still early, I was conscious of the need for him to go to his own room, yet I hated for him leave. Just a few moments more … but already he stirred behind me and pushed on to one elbow. Turning, I smiled. He had a crease mark on one cheek from the pillow and his face was shadowy with several day's growth.

"I'd best go to my own room."

I nodded resignedly but he leaned down and gently touched his lips to mine. I sighed languidly and curled my arms around his neck holding him to my mouth. He shifted his weight and was half laying on me and we kissed until our hearts pounded against each other.

When at last he pulled his head back his green eyes were dark and intense. "How I love you," he whispered.

I smiled dreamily. "I wish you could stay with me."

"So do I, but I'm afraid if I don't leave now, I shall be tempted to something that's beyond my powers of resistance."

Suggestively, I trailed my hand down his throat to the opening of his shirt. "Would that be so terrible?"

He caught my hand, "You wicked, shameless harlot! Now I am most certainly leaving before we are discovered and my reputation tarnished forever."

He sat up and I wriggled in beside him. "How could your reputation be tarnished?" I questioned pertly. "I doubt your contemporaries would bat an eyelid were you discovered in my bed – though trouble for me would certainly ensue."

"*Au contraire ma belle*, I would have a great deal of explaining to do should it become known that I spent the night in a lady's bed with nary a sigh between us."

I snorted through my nose and he kissed me quickly. "Tempting as you are, I must leave, for if I pause any longer, we may be discovered and accused of something we have only thought about."

I groaned. "Then if we are to be accused of it … "

"We haven't yet – and it's unwise to tempt fate."

"Drop the question what tomorrow may bring, and count as profit every day that fate allows you," I recited sagely.

He grinned. "'Tis unlikely either of us will see tomorrow should your mother discover we shared a bed, and quoting Horace won't save us." He slid out of my arms and padded across the room, quickly blowing a kiss and closing the door softly behind him.

CHAPTER 18

I love watching storms. I stood at my window as slate-coloured clouds filled the sky and rain splattered against my window. A maid came in to change the water in my ewer and I turned to her. "Did you see the size of those raindrops, Emily?"

"Yes, Miss. Me mum always called 'em thunder spots 'cause they big enough to carry the thunder in 'em."

A well-timed thunderclap rattled the windows and I shivered. "I think your mum was right." I turned and started slightly. Janet was standing by the bed, glaring at Pat's discarded coat and boots. Deliberately, she bent to retrieve the coat and hung it over the back of my desk chair and paired the boots beside it.

Returning to the storm, I could feel her eyes boring into my back, and when Emily left the room she came forward.

"Master Pat's clothes are in your room. This is why you delay your marriage to Lord Hamish."

The bitter look on her face took me aback and for a moment I had no response. Fear that Patrick and I had been discovered caused my pulse to roar in my ears but I spoke calmly, "I don't answer to you, Janet. But if you need an explanation, Master Pat arrived home last night and came to talk with me."

"And left his boots by your bed and his clothes on your floor?"

"It was only his riding coat. He removed it because it smelt –
why am I even bothering with this conversation? Go about your
business."

The thunder crashed again and the room grew dim. The
window was leaking. A dribble of water was working its way along
the ledge. Funny how leaks that need repairing are only thought
of when they're in the act of leaking – like a boot with a hole. I
shivered involuntarily.

Janet continued to stare at me. Ignoring her, I went to the door
but she spoke again.

"It all makes sense now," she said tightly. "Not only are you
duping Lord Hamish – cavorting with your own brother – but
Grahame and I must await your convenience. You think only of
yourself – no-one else."

Rage exploded within me and I rounded on her. "You keep
your filthy thoughts to yourself before you find yourself looking
for a new position!"

Startled, she staggered several paces backwards and her face
registered shock, followed closely by fear. She looked to the floor as
I went on, "You've been told, more than once, that you're welcome
in Scotland to be with Grahame. Don't make me your excuse for
lack of gumption. I have my own reasons for not marrying Lord
Hamish and they do not involve Master Patrick – nor do they
involve you!"

Breathing hard, I pointed to the door. "Now get out!"

She scuttled to the door and closed it quietly behind her while
I slumped into a chair, shaking with emotion.

In reality, I could not dismiss Janet for Mother would demand
the reason. Even so, she may decide to betray me from spite. And if
I sent the woman – my maid and confidante for as long as I could
remember – to Scotland, she may tell Hamish.

I clung to the knowledge that Janet needed this position and hoped she would not jeopardise it. The only solution was to convince her that my relationship with Patrick was entirely fraternal.

I breathed deeply trying to calm myself until the thunder faded into the distance and the rain eased. Though, given the heavy-bellied clouds lingering above the trees, any break would be only temporary.

A swift movement caught my eye. Barely within view from my window was Patrick, wearing black breeches, boots and a loose hanging shirt. He was practicing his sword skills against an invisible foe. Lunging and slashing, dodging, weaving and thrusting; he moved, despite his recently healed wounds, with effortless grace and agility, and I, knowing nothing of what differentiated an expert warrior from a poor one, prayed that his ability proved greater than any opponent's.

After the earlier ebbing of the storm, it returned with a vengeance; fiercely, relentlessly pounding on the roof and against the windows. The wind rose to bend the trees in the park and buffet the house, finding sly gaps through which to blow icy drafts. Trapped indoors and feeling the restriction keenly, I passed my time in the nursery with Clara and Meg, mending clothing, singing songs and sharing gossip from the village.

As the persistent clatter of the rain seemed to slow, I looked out at the sodden park. A young deer was sheltering beneath a fir at its edge, some fifty yards away. Deer were not normally so close to the house, the storm must have caught her by surprise. She sniffed the air and disappeared into the forest.

"Pat!" Meg suddenly cried, excitedly. I wheeled around happily as Patrick lifted Meg on to his shoulders.

"Morning ladies," he greeted us.

The heat rose to my cheeks with the pleasure of seeing him. How my love was growing – now I could allow it.

Meg grasped a handful of his hair and he yelped in exaggerated pain as the little girl squealed joyously.

"Hey, Meggie, that hurts!" he scolded and swung her to the ground where she stood with her arms wrapped lovingly around his thighs.

"She's getting taller," he remarked to Clara.

"That she certainly is, Master Pat."

"Mother mentioned the other day that she would soon engage a governess for her." I said.

"Is it time already? Surely she's too young." Pat said, assessing his youngest sister.

"I told Mother I thought that – even Eleanor agreed." I shook my head in bewilderment. "Eleanor with an opinion different from Mother's – wonder of wonders."

He laughed. "Never have you said a truer word. Where's your dolly, Meggie?"

Meg ran to her bed and grabbed a little porcelain doll with scruffy, matted hair. "Clara make dress," the little girl's lisp was vaguely similar to her half-sister Anne's. "See?"

Pat sat cross-legged on the floor and examined the doll's outfit with great seriousness. Clara and I joined him forming a circle on the rug, and we talked softly like we used to before Pat and Simon went to war, before Maeve and Anne went to Italy, and before I knew myself to be in love. All the while, Meg kept up a steady stream of childish chatter about her doll.

So, the afternoon passed pleasantly and when Clara left the nursery to fetch afternoon tea for us all, Patrick kissed his finger and pressed it to my lips, evoking the memory of a long ago gesture that had thrilled me even then.

Perhaps it was that day, as he sat his horse and touched me so, that the first stirrings of sentiment had awoken within me.

I laughed lightly, self-consciously, and he smiled, his brilliant-green eyes glistening. "You're beautiful," he whispered and the blood rushed to my face. I was saved from further embarrassment by Clara returning with a tray of lemonade; milk for Meg, and bread and cheese for us all.

"Come here petal, and have your milk," Clara instructed, and as we ate, Patrick chewed thoughtfully, then very slowly, as he sought the words, recited,

> *As rain from high falls to the ground,*
> *It scatters faeries all around*
> *They love to frolic in flower beds*
> *Garlands of petals 'round their heads*
> *And beads of dew dripping from their sleeves*
> *Playing hide and find among the leaves*
> *For faeries like to dance and play*
> *And mostly at the end of day*
> *They come at night time dark and deep*
> *But that's when little girls should sleep*

"Not one of my better ones," Pat said, then shrugging, "What about this,"

> *"Thee, Mary, with this ring I wed,"*
> *So, fourteen years ago I said —*
> *Behold another ring! — "For what?"*
> *"To wed thee o'er again — why not?"*

"I like that — it is better," Clara said, laughing.

"Considerably, which proves it's not one of mine. Samuel Bishop wrote that. It's quite long. One day, if so inclined, I shall recite it in its entirety."

❧

In the month that followed, Patrick and I explored our new intimacy. Like a long-caged creature newly released, it burst to life, flourishing and growing freely. We learnt things about each other that could only be revealed through familiarity and trust, and I discovered that behind his reserved façade, Patrick was profoundly passionate and capable of great love, surprisingly demonstrative; he sometimes lifted my hair to affectionately caress with his lips a little mole at the base of my neck.

We spent lazy afternoons beneath the Great Oak, he propped against its trunk playing pretty tunes on his violin, as I lay in the grass reading or dozing. We never touched during these languid hours for fear of onlookers, but the feeling between us was such that I fancied it rippled the air like a heat-haze over the paddocks in summer.

More intimate moments found us hidden in the grotto, where – observed only by Our Lady smiling benevolently down from her plinth in her pale blue cloak – we kissed and embraced, our whispered promises hanging between us on the spring-scented breeze.

We spent so much time together that I became anxious lest we occasion comment, though naturally our parents were too busy with their own affairs to bother themselves overly with us. Thus, Janet remained my only real cause for concern. She watched us obsessively, to the point where I could feel her eyes on us even when it was impossible. I had, of course, told Patrick of my encounter with her and his attitude was that she be dismissed immediately. But I could not do it.

"She's not being loyal to you," he reasoned.

"True," I agreed as we strolled through the orchard one morning. "But she's in love with Grahame. Love changes people … it makes them far more selfish than they would ordinarily be."

"How wise you are, my darling girl."

"Not wise, just selfishly in love. I want to greedily grasp every moment with you … every kiss and breath, and to hell with anyone else."

Though neither of us mentioned it, the passage of time hung over us like an ever-increasing weight. With the coming of April, we had at best, four weeks before he was to leave.

"In any case," I continued, "I'm afraid that she might tell Mother or Hamish. Without you here to add your voice to mine … if they called in the contract, all would be lost."

Patrick didn't respond. He squinted into the distance where Jackson's bull, aged and cranky now, stood scowling at a tree stump, and I could almost read my beloved's thoughts; he was returning to war where he would need his wits and concentration to survive, and he needed to know there was someone waiting for him.

I smiled and added, "But I can withstand anything if I know you'll be coming home to me, and that we will grow old together."

The progress of spring brought longer days and warmer evenings. Mother, Eleanor, Patrick and I, ritually shared a decanter of plum wine beneath the Great Oak and watched the evening sky turn gold, then orange, then indigo.

When Patrick told Mother of his meeting with his father and confirmed there would be no contracted match with Anne, Mother had turned white in her fury and shook down the wrath of the heavens. Never being one to dwell overlong on situations that displeased her, she settled into reluctant acceptance which saw a return to her sarcastic jibes, which he successfully ignored. When she failed to get a rise out of him, Mother refrained from throwing her lures altogether and the household breathed a sigh of relief as they established a wary truce.

Eventually Lord Thorncliffe returned home and joined our evenings beneath the Great Oak and, aside from Eleanor's perpetual sneer, the company was relatively pleasant.

Father and son frequently discussed the war and agreed that Wellesley was planning a fierce campaign for the summer that would hopefully bring an end to it all. I hated these talks, and more, I hated having to pretend that I felt no more than a sister's natural reluctance for her favourite brother to join the fighting.

It was during one of these pleasant evenings that Gerrard took out a letter he'd received from Simon, explaining that it had arrived that morning and he'd saved it for our evening gathering.

It seemed that Simon had met and fallen irretrievably in love with a Spanish girl who worked in the hospital with him.

Maria Therese Cardoza was, according to Simon's description, a beauty with long, black hair and kind, brown eyes. It was Simon's intention to marry the girl and sought his parents' blessing.

Gerrard read from the letter:

I know the circumstances of this request are unusual, Father, but in the present situation, being that I cannot introduce you to Maria until this blasted war is over, I am forced to ask your blessing in absentia.

Maria has no family of her own, so it is important to her as well as to me, that you favour us with your approval. We wish to hold a small reception here with some of our friends, but upon our return to England, we may conduct a second ceremony in the little chapel in Wolstone.

Mother, listening in tight-lipped disapproval, interrupted. "Gerrard, you must tell him it is entirely out of the question. A Spanish girl — no name, no family! She could not possibly marry a person of Simon's standing."

Gerrard hesitated, weighing his words carefully before answering. "I think, m'dear, that under the circumstances we should not judge the girl too harshly. Simon appears very much in love and —"

"*Love!*" Mother cried, shattering the peaceful evening. "Since when is *that* relevant? He has a responsibility to this family," she indicated Pat with a nod of her head, "as does he – and, God knows Gerrard, you're too liberal with *him*. Simon cannot marry this nobody. I won't allow it, and there's an end to it."

"Many Spanish girls work in the hospitals over there – caring people, often of suitable pedigree," Patrick commented with a hint of sarcasm. "And some indeed are very beautiful."

"I shall write tomorrow to give my approval," his father said defiantly, though he fondled his earlobe.

Mother snorted indelicately. "I said, I won't allow it and I'll not discuss it further."

Gerrard, uncommonly bold, bridled. "In Simon's absence, I am head of this household, Madam, and consequently I make the decisions. Patrick may decide whom he marries – within reason of course," he added, throwing a significant look at his son. "I don't believe Simon should be any different. Give them credit for being level-headed young men, fully aware of their responsibilities."

Mother leapt to her feet in outrage. "Credit! *Credit for what*? While your son services every slattern from Landsend to Newcastle, my son falls prey to some penniless social-climbing peasant!" She wagged a finger at Patrick's bemused look, "You have a lot to answer for, young man, a *hell* of a lot."

She stormed across the lawn in a flurry of hissing silk while Eleanor all but twisted an ankle in her haste to follow. We watched as the two disappeared into the house, the heavy, studded door slamming behind them.

"I think she genuinely wants the best for the family," I offered generously.

"Your mother wants only what is best for her social and financial position," Patrick said cynically.

I turned to my stepfather. "What will you do?"

"Exactly as I said – I shall be giving Simon my blessing. I trust I may add the good wishes of his brother and sister?"

Pat and I nodded as one, for who were we to deny anyone their love?

We sat silently after that, watching the early-evening sunlight lengthen towards the nearby forest, from which a gentle verdant breeze cooled the balmy air. Into this pleasant setting, Clara arrived with Meg tottering happily at her side. The nurse accepted a glass of plum wine while her charge played in the grass at our feet. The evening was calm but for the birds roosting in the distant trees and Meg's solemn discussion with her doll.

"I don't like that doll," Patrick said decisively. He was sitting forward on his chair, elbows on his knees, regarding the doll's porcelain face with an expression of distaste. "It looks so smug. Whoever painted it did a dreadful job."

The doll's vacant, blue-glass stare had never appealed to me either, but now I studied it – clay-white face, two pink cheeks, superior rosebud mouth – and said, "It's the smile."

"It's not a smile at all," Gerrard said. "It is a smirk … almost a sneer. Very self-satisfied."

"I've never liked it either," Clara said.

Patrick dragged his eyes away from the toy as though he didn't trust it. "Then Meggie must have a new doll."

But Clara shook her head. "She loves this one, Master Pat. Only the Lord above knows why."

"Next time I'm in Leeds I shall buy a new one," Gerrard said and we nodded in consensus though Clara looked doubtful.

With an abrupt change of conversation, Patrick turned to Clara, "Have you been to Fountain's Abbey?"

"That I have, Master Pat, and can vouch for its beauty."

He reclined in his chair and smiled, "Then I suggest we go for a drive tomorrow. What say you, Father?"

"Excellent idea! Tomorrow promises to be good weather too. Have a picnic made up for us all, Clara – and pack everything Meg will need for an outing."

The nurse agreed enthusiastically, clearly delighted at the prospect of an excursion.

Gerrard rose and stretched with a noisy yawn. "I shall leave you now. It grows late and I must complete some paperwork … free up my day tomorrow. Clara, please bring that small tyrant with you – it's time she went in."

Clara scooped up the reluctant child, settling her on one round hip. Lord Thorncliffe bent to pick up the ugly doll, grimacing with the stiffness in his back, and the three departed, leaving Patrick and me alone beneath the tree.

He stretched his long legs out, crossed at the ankles, and leaned back in his chair to gaze into the branches of the mighty oak, through whose boughs the first evening stars peeped.

We'd not been alone together in many days and I ached to touch him. Would ever a time come when I could openly do so?

"So thoughtful," he said. I sighed wistfully and he smiled through the gathering dusk, needing no response. "Care to walk?"

At the word *walk* Jemima jumped up expectantly and stood before him, tail swaying from side to side.

He rose and bowed elegantly offering his arm but I quickly shook my head. "What? You can't promenade with your brother?"

"If Janet should be watching …"

"She'd need to report more than an innocent stroll in the park." He cocked his head, "Or do you tempt me into providing evidence of something more?"

A flush of pleasure suffused my cheeks and a delicious tingle of longing stirred in the depths of my stomach. A welcoming night breeze, gently fragranced with freesia and jonquil cooled my face and resolutely, I took his proffered arm.

We strolled in silence down the lawn towards the park, my hand resting formally on his sleeve, our steps unhurried and companionable. Jemima galloped ahead of us into the darkness, returning every so often to make sure we followed. At the edge of the park we tracked a winding path through low, thick shrubbery into the forest.

Screened by the privacy of the woods, Patrick dropped his arm and turned me to face him. "I've needed to do this for days." He bent his head towards me.

We kissed for a long, long time. With a need that bordered on desperation, I moved up to him and instinctively pushed my hips to his.

Groaning, he eased me back to an ancient birch and pressed against me. Parts of me were hurting with want. I drew my breath in through my teeth as he unbuttoned my bodice. The cool night air touched my breasts and he closed his lips over one nipple causing my senses to reel. His tongue was hot and fluttering, and my head spun deliriously.

But abruptly, he stopped.

Pushing away, he ran his hands through his hair and paced out his ardour. "I'm sorry, Alex," he whispered huskily. "I don't want this to get out of control."

I sighed, and nodding with resignation, buttoned my dress, all the while aching with disappointment. I said, "Surely it would be worse if we did not experience each other – what if you are wounded again or … to never know love with you …"

He blew out his breath and regarded me through the dark. "We can't run the risk of your getting with child."

"I may not."

"But you may. And then what? Your Lord Whatsit will not want you. You'd be wed to the first man with pockets empty enough to blind him to another's child."

"If you did not return, I'd not care," I declared with bravado.

"Easy to say now. Our best chance to be together is to wait until I return. Then we can tell them. An unexpected babe will not further our cause."

I went over to where he stood and took his face between my

hands. "I love you," I said solemnly. "And if you were not to return at least I would have something of you."

"But it's more than that. Alex, I don't want our first time to be some hurried coupling somewhere, hidden and fearful of discovery. My world is a history of drunken, meaningless encounters. I don't want to do this with you and then disappear from your life like it never happened. You mean so much more than that. What I feel for you is pure and honourable. Our first time together … your first experience *must* be special, do you understand?"

I stared at him, touched by his depth of feeling, but even so, I couldn't bear the thought of him leaving me.

"Yes, I do understand," I murmured, "but despite everything, and all the risks, I want this. I'm the one left behind when you go."

He held my gaze steadily for a long moment and, just as I thought I saw capitulation in his eyes, he tensed.

"Wha –?"

"Shh …" He quickly bundled me behind a broad pine trunk. "Listen …"

I held my breath. It was a moment before I heard it; a soft laugh, whispered voices, the snap of a twig.

"Where's Jemima?" he breathed.

"I don't know."

The sounds drew closer and we waited, intensely alert as the moon's pale light revealed Emily and one of the footmen, picking their way along the same trail we'd only passed minutes earlier. The footman bent and whispered something to her at which she groaned and coiled her arms around his neck and fell back against a tree.

He growled into her breasts then searched out her lips and from where my would-be lover and I hid, I had an unavoidable and perfect view. My passions flamed voyeuristically as the man dropped to his knees and vanished beneath Emily's blue servant's skirt.

Unable to tear my eyes away, I watched as Emily writhed and

strained against his moving head. My body throbbed with longing and I struggled for control as Emily's need grew and as her cries became more demanding, her partner frantically unbuttoned his breeches. Grasping himself, his hand worked urgently, and almost immediately, he gave a violent jerk, gasping, and shuddering, his whole body convulsing.

Weak with desire my knees threatened to buckle, and into my turmoil Patrick exhaled in a soft, "Shh …"

Just then, Emily bucked and cried out in breathless agony. The pair collapsed to the ground, and seizing the opportunity, Patrick clasped my hand and undetected, we slipped away through the trees.

Emerging into the full glare of the moon, my senses were reeling. With great difficulty, we resumed our slow, innocent stroll towards the house, and I wondered at Patrick's apparent calm. But as we arrived at the door we paused and he seemed to read my thoughts. Shaded by the overhang of the library window above, his humid breath touched my lips as he whispered, "No, my darling, I am not unmoved. Sleep easy and dream fondly of one whose need for you will see him hot and sleepless this night."

The following morning, I examined the dirty birch-smudge stains on the back of my gown sustained in last evening's passionate tryst. The incriminating dress was bundled into a bulky ball and I deviated from my usual route, to visit Mrs Grainger. Though the fearsome woman was no taller than I, her disapproving scowl shrivelled me to half my height.

"If you've been climbing trees again … high time you grew out of such hoydenish pursuits, young Madam," she grumbled but for once, I was impervious to her reprimand for the stains were my token of last evening's delicious torment, and she was no gossip — knowledge of Miss Alex's dirty gown would go no further than the scullery – regardless of how she thought the stains had been acquired.

Later, as Emily served breakfast with her usual quiet efficiency, I was hard pressed to keep my mind from replaying the picture of our respectful maid in the throes of passion with another of our staff on the soft, mulchy forest floor. Mother, I knew, would immediately dismiss them both.

When Patrick took his seat across the table, his eyes locked heatedly with mine and I quickly looked away, but not before seeing the mischief lurking there.

"Good morning, Emily," he said cheerfully as the girl poured tea into my cup, before moving to Gerrard.

"Good mornin', Master Pat," she responded politely.

"You're looking very well this morning, Emily"

The maid flushed prettily beneath his compliment but didn't falter in her task. "Thank you, Master Pat." She moved around the table to pour Patrick's tea and he pushed his cup helpfully towards her. "Nice rosy cheeks … isn't she looking well Father? Plenty of fresh air, I'd say."

"Hmm," his father responded absently for he was applying himself to his breakfast.

"Yes," Patrick continued, "now's the time for it though…nice balmy evenings … sunsets … perfect for strolling in the woods with a friend – *whoops!*" Pat leapt to his feet, grinning and holding his trousers, wet with scalding tea, away from his skin.

"*Oh My Lord forgive me …!*" Emily cried in horror. "I'm so sorry … are you burned … ? Here … let me … just a moment … oh my goodness … *I'm so sorry* … I'll fetch a cloth … oh dear …"

The sight of Patrick, flushed with mischievous merriment, with a spreading tea-stain on his lap was too much. Lord Thorncliffe and I exploded into loud laughter.

"That was unnecessarily cruel, Pat, and you got your just desserts," I said wiping my streaming eyes.

"I've no idea what just happened, Lad, but I've no doubt the fates have punished you roundly and deservingly," his father said.

Emily reappeared with a stony-faced Mrs Grainger behind her. As the unfortunate maid attempted to press a dry cloth to Patrick's lap, the housekeeper slapped her hands away. "Don't you touch the young lord!" she cried. "Haven't you done enough without manhandling …"

Emily burst into tears. My laughter halted immediately and I glared significantly across the table at my stepbrother, who had the decency to attempt a penitent expression.

"Mrs Grainger," Patrick spoke placatingly, "there's no call to be so harsh — it was not Emily's fault."

"But the girl is hopeless —"

"It's alright — it was an accident and I assure you the future generation of Washburns has avoided a poaching."

This time it was Mrs Grainger who coloured. Grasping Emily by the elbow, she marched the girl back to the kitchen.

Patrick shot a mutinous grin in my direction.

"You'd best change your clothes," I said.

"Later. It looks worse than it is." Turning to his father, "So are we heading out to this Fountains Abbey today?"

"We certainly are," Gerrard responded, moving on as though nothing had happened. "I believe Miriam may come, though I've not spoken with her yet."

"If you're talking about Fountains Abbey — I shall pass," Mother announced, coming into the room, trailed as always by her poker-straight shadow.

"Good morning Eleanor," Patrick said brightly and I groaned inwardly. "Looking particularly attractive today, you are. Better not sit next to me — I doubt my youthful urges could withstand such temptation."

"Son …" Lord Thorncliffe adopted a rather impotent warning tone.

"My apologies, Eleanor," Pat said with apparent sincerity. He indicated the chair beside him. "Come, sit by me, I shan't bite – *unless you want me to* – alright Father, don't look like that. Eleanor come, your tortured virginity is entirely safe –"

"*Son …!*"

Patrick made a tutting sound and offered Eleanor a conciliatory smile. Wavering momentarily, she finally sat and reached for a slice of toast.

"Alexandra, have you collected your mail today?" Mother asked.

"I haven't. Is there something?"

"There's an invitation, and one for you as well." She nodded in Patrick's direction as the second maid for the morning poured her tea. "I assume it's from the Moreheads – same stationery as one Gerrard and I received."

"What's it to?" asked Pat.

"A dinner. They have relatives over from Wales who will be guests of honour."

Patrick jumped suddenly in surprise. "Eleanor!" he declared in outrage. "You have exactly *twenty minutes* to remove your hand from my thigh!"

"B … but I … " the woman stammered in confusion, her face hot and both hands clearly in view above the table.

Even Mother, who always enjoyed another's discomfiture, laughed at that.

"I'll ring for Emily to bring the mail," Pat suggested reaching for the bell.

"*No!*" both his father and I cried in unison and I dashed out to retrieve the mail myself.

The letter was, as Mother predicted, an invitation to a dinner from Adrienne's parents requesting the presence of Miss Alexandra Washburn and Lord Hamish Glendenning – interesting since Adrienne knew that Hamish had returned to Scotland.

Pat's invitation bade him bring a guest. "Wherever shall I find myself a suitable lady?" he wondered aloud, looking slyly at Eleanor who seemed uncharacteristically fidgety.

"I shall have to find myself a substitute Hamish," I said.

Mother looked at me over the rose and ivy centrepiece. "I don't suppose there's any point in asking him to come. He could stay for the summer."

"Hmm," said her husband. "I doubt the boy would be keen to journey back this way so soon after his recent experience."

He took a bite of sausage and avoided looking at anyone, but I knew the point he made. Deliberately misunderstanding, I said, "I agree. He won't want to be away from home while his father is so ill."

Mother said, "What is it that ails him Alexandra, do you know?"

"I understand there is a growth in his stomach … causes much pain and the doctors have thrown up their hands in resignation."

"There is such a lot we don't know," Gerrard pondered. "I'll wager in fifty years they'll have answers to everything. But for now, it must be very frustrating for men like Simon."

Patrick pushed back his chair. "If we don't finish here and be on our way, it'll be fifty years before we get to Fountains Abbey." He stood up. "Over Skelldale way, isn't it?"

"What on earth did you spill on those trousers?" Mother was staring in horror at Patrick's lap. "Is that how you present yourself at a dining table? Perhaps you'd do well to decline the Moreheads' invitation – save us all from your unsocial conduct."

"My unsocial conduct has been studiously cultivated over a very long time."

"Well, please spare us the fruits of your studious cultivation."

Patrick grinned and clapped his hands over his heart. "O Regan, she hath tied sharp-toothed unkindness, like a vulture, here." He winked then and swept Mother a courtly bow.

An hour later, Meg, Clara, Janet and I were all settled in an open carriage with rugs, picnic baskets and umbrellas strapped to the back. Dan, the coachman, sat in the driver's seat while Gerrard on Canto, and Patrick on Equus, opted for the freedom of horseback.

We were a merry gang setting out that morning with a gentle wind lifting our hair and the sun sending filtered light through the trees to warm our skin.

As we picked up speed on the road, Gerrard took a deep breath. With his right hand on his heart, he sang, or rather, bellowed,

> *Ooooh, would you pity give my heart*
> *One corner of your breast*
> *T'would learn of yours the winning art*
> *And quickly steal the rest*

"My Lord, isn't that the end of the song, not the beginning?" Janet asked.

Gerrard laughed. "It certainly is Lass, but I don't remember the beginning."

The mood was lively and infectious. I began to sing something Simon played occasionally on the piano,

> *Pack, clouds, away, and welcome day,*
> *With night we banish sorrow;*

The others joined in and our voices rang out across the fields, raising the heads of sheep and cattle as we went.

> *Sweet air blow soft, mount larks aloft*
> *To give my Love good-morrow!*
> *Wings from the wind to please her mind*
> *Notes from the lark I'll borrow;*
> *Bird, prune thy wing, nightingale sing,*

To give my Love good-morrow;
To give my Love good-morrow
Notes from them both I'll borrow.

Meg clapped her small hands delightedly. "More! Sing more!" she demanded.

We complied, our three feminine voices blending prettily, the men, including Dan – who lent a lower harmony that was altogether more cheerful than talented. Gerrard's booming, tuneless voice drowned us all and we laughed gaily at the sight of his jovial face fixed in concentration, arm outstretched like an Italian operatic performer.

Wake from thy nest, robin-red-breast,
Sing, birds, in every furrow;
And from each hill, let music shrill
Give my fair Love good-morrow!
Blackbird and thrush in every bush,
Stare, linnet, and cock-sparrow!
You pretty elves, amongst yourselves
Sing my fair Love good-morrow;
To give my Love good-morrow
Sing, birds, in every furrow!

Pat sat relaxed on Equus' back, leaning forwards in the saddle, his hat tilted back from his forehead, his hair, the colour of dirty straw, pushed away from his face.

All young men of the day were wearing their hair cut short in the Brutus style, but Pat applied no such efforts to his appearance, making only reluctant concessions when attending a social engagement. On days like this, he was as carelessly casual as the boy I'd first met – rustic, indifferent to the pretensions of the station he was born into. Likewise, his father was dressed as a country gentleman in brown woollen riding breeches, linen shirt and wool coat.

I smiled in pure enjoyment of the uplifting, life-giving, spring day. From time to time Pat's eyes met mine and the velvety cloak of contentment wrapped about me. I loved him, *oh God, how I loved him*! My spirit soared and my engorged heart throbbed with it.

Watching him now, muscled legs encased in leather boots and tight, beige riding breeches, rocking gently back and forth with the graceful ease of the habitual horseman, the motion of his hips tuned to Equus' stride, was … delightful, and I drew in my breath longingly.

We arrived at Fountains Abbey before the sun reached its apex and made our way to a spot that would be shaded by the ruins as the sun dipped westwards in the warmest part of the day.

This was a hauntingly beautiful ruin, undisturbed and hidden by a wooded valley through which ran the River Skell. Built in the bold and severe manner of the Cistercians, it relied on size and proportion for impact. I read from a visitors' guide-book, " 'The Cistercian monks were known as *The White Monks* due to the colour of their habit, an uncomfortably coarse garment made from undyed sheep's wool.' "

We were sprawled on thick woollen rugs beneath the ruins of the eastern window. Our picnic spread included wine from Burgundy, in honour of the Cistercians who originated there. I continued my reading, " 'Cistercian Monks committed to extended periods of silence, consequently, they developed their own language of gestures.' Any wonder this place is so peaceful," I observed.

Clara and Meg were strolling towards the river, each carrying chunks of bread to feed the black-and-brown, speckled ducks paddling among the reeds. Dan unhitched the horses and they joined Equus and Canto, loosely tethered to a tree where they could feast on the sweet spears of new grass.

Patrick stood bouncing a tennis ball on a racket. "Anyone for a game?" He had stripped off his boots and coat. His shirtsleeves were rolled up and his arms and feet were tanned.

While Janet accepted Pat's challenge, I removed my shoes and stockings, luxuriating in the thick grass springing between my toes.

Meg and Clara returned from their walk. The hems of Clara's skirt and Meg's frilly pantaloons were wet and the nurse carried their shoes and stockings.

"The water is lovely, Miss Alex," the nurse said. She flopped heavily beside me, her face was damp and ruddy from her exertions.

Meg skipped over to Pat, "May I play … may I?"

"Very well Midget, let me show you."

Janet hit the ball and Pat stood behind Meg. As the ball approached, her older brother swept the child off her feet and yelled, "Hit it!"

Obediently, Meg gave a wild swing of her racket, almost decapitating her brother. "The *ball!*" he cried. "*Hit the ball.*"

The child soon caught the idea and was lifted and flung about, yipping with delight. She wielded the racket like a deadly weapon, her flapping skirts showing an unseemly amount of grass-stained pantaloon.

Eventually the players fell red of face and breathless to the rug. Gerrard poured two mugs of wine and passed them to Janet and Patrick. "A little re-invigorator."

Pat raised his mug in salute, "To good company, good times, and good wine. May they flow a-plenty."

Meg cried, "What about me?"

Anticipating a childish outburst, Clara quickly poured a mug of lemonade and gave it into Meg's eager hands. "Don't gulp! Oh dear, don't come running to me if you bring that up, young lady."

We dined like kings and drank like seamen and finally, stuffed full, reclined on the rug replete and lethargic. A weighty sleepiness overtook me and lulled by birdsong and the distant burble of the Skell, I allowed myself to drift into a contented doze.

A bug was tickling my cheek. Reluctant to stir from my bliss, I swiped at it. Annoyingly, it persisted, expertly avoiding my swatting. Exasperated, I opened my eyes.

Patrick was leaning on one elbow, a wildflower in his hand, a playful smile twitching his lips.

Now that he had my attention he put the flower aside. Cautiously, I glanced around. Dan was on his back, his flat-cap over his face and a suspiciously-rhythmic rumble coming from beneath. Janet slept, curled on her side, around a contentedly breathing Meg. Gerrard and Clara were walking by the river some distance away.

"I love you," he mouthed and I smiled drowsily in reply. "Come down to the river," he said in his normal voice. He got up and offered his hand.

My neck was stiff and I rubbed it as we walked. Gerrard stood ankle-deep in the running water. His trousers were rolled to the knees exposing legs that appeared too skinny to support his portly frame.

"Hullo chicken-legs!" I called as we approached.

"Shouldn't you put those away before someone takes offence?" Patrick said.

His father saluted jauntily. "Come in, it's very nice."

Pat grasped my hand and we ran to the edge of the river like a pair of children. I tucked the hem of my skirt into my waistband. The water was crisp and colder than I expected and I gasped in surprise but inched deeper until the water swirled about my calves.

"Come on, Clara," I called. "Ooh there're fish in here!" I had just spotted a swift brown streak darting over and around the rocky bed.

"Fish?" Clara said doubtfully. "Lucky I didn't see them before. I'd much prefer to explore the ruins."

"Excellent idea!" Gerrard declared, leaving the water. He offered his arm to his daughter's nurse and Pat did likewise to me. I determinedly avoided glancing to where Dan, Janet and Meg still slept, even though in the context of the day, my hand on Patrick's arm should occasion no comment, I was nevertheless wary until we made our way into the magnificent ancient ruins and disappeared from view.

But for the fact that three of us were barefoot, we strolled as elegantly as any courtiers exploring the gardens of Hampton Court. We meandered along the length of the nave, pausing in the presbytery to read the lichen-covered headstones of abbots who long ago served in silent dedication at these now crumbling altars. When we arrived at the cellarium, we gazed in wonder at the cavernous intertwining arches and ceiling with its criss-cross beams, and magnificently austere beauty.

Pat released his breath in a reverent sigh. My hand continued to rest on his elbow, but now it fell to my side and his arm encircled my waist pulling me against his hip. Such affection I realised, in this spiritually charged milieu, did not seem out of place, and I leaned into him, revelling in his nearness.

We stood respectfully silent for some minutes, remembering the history and envisioning the monks who had lived here, and died, tilled the fertile earth, and worshipped, in tranquillity.

Finally, by unspoken agreement, we continued our wordless explorations. Gerrard and Clara drifted slowly down the north aisle, while Patrick and I followed, making our way towards the great east window, beyond which the leftovers of our picnic were.

Pat had dropped his arm from my waist and I reached for his hand. Unseen by our companions, he pressed his lips to my palm, causing sparks of sensation to shoot through me.

The remains of the day were cast in long shards of sun as it made its downwards sweep towards the horizon. Shadows had darkened the grounds by the time we stepped over a collapsed wall and found Meg, bewildered and tearful, sobbing into Janet's bodice. Apparently in her childish reasoning, our absence meant that her beloved brother had deserted her.

She turned and flung her little body into Patrick's arms and bawled out her tale of woe.

"I explained, Master Pat, that the horses were still here, but she'd have none of it," Janet said.

Fortunately, Meg's distress helped dissipate the lingering, emotion-fuelled current between Patrick and me, but not before Clara's eyes caught mine in unspoken question. I carefully ignored her, arranging my face to appear entranced by our intensely serene surroundings.

"She's all better," Pat said, stroking the tears from his little sister's unhappy face.

"I'll take her," said Clara holding out her arms. "Come to Clara, Lamb."

Meg obeyed, scrubbing at her eyes with her small bunched-up fists and, cradled by her nurse, she was carried to the carriage.

The evening air was cooling by the time we settled within the carriage and Dan clicked the horses forwards. The steady clopping of hooves drifted into the distance and we slept – Janet and me leaning against each other, while opposite, Clara snored with her head against the back of the seat, mouth wide open, and little Meg pillowed across her broad lap.

CHAPTER 19

In the library, I had Meg enthralled in a fable of Aesop – the one about the greedy dog. Patrick's voice floated up from where he stood with a pair of Simon's tenants. They'd come to enquire about the cutting of our hay at the end of summer. In Simon's absence, Patrick was discussing the number of men needed and how much we'd be paying.

He broke off at the sound of a horse being ridden too fast. Peering from the window I saw him clap the men's backs, their conversation over, before turning towards the horse and rider.

Recognising Julia's horse at once, I shushed Meg's indignant demands that I continue with the tale and watched as my friend dismounted inelegantly and ran towards Patrick.

He hurried her forwards, with his hand resting consolingly on her shoulder and, as Mrs Grainger appeared on the porch, I heard him say, "Bring refreshments to the morning room, please, Mrs Grainger, and advise Miss Alex that Miss Chapman is here."

The morning sun was a warm puddle on the floor and the scent of violets drifted in through the open window. Oblivious, Julia was standing in the middle of the room. She had her riding-crop tucked beneath one arm and was agitatedly stripping off her leather gloves when I came in. She turned to me with wide, tear reddened eyes and her face crumpled.

"Julia …!" I drew her to me as she collapsed in great, gusty sobs.

"Good heavens, what is it?" I cried. I steered her to a couch, but her weeping was so violent she was unable to speak for some minutes and all I could do was rock her in my arms like a child.

At last, she blew her nose on an inadequately-sized scrap of linen. Emily had discreetly left a tray of tea and biscuits. Easing myself from the couch, I poured a cup of tea for each of us and added a slice of lemon with Mother's silver tongs.

At length, Julia calmed and I asked gently, "Can you tell me what's wrong?"

Her chin quivered and her face, ordinarily so bright and cheerful, was pale and drawn with sorrow. She drew a shaky breath. "It's Deon," she gulped loudly and I stiffened. Since the night I'd discovered his infidelity, I'd known this moment would come. "I … I think he's having a liaison with Celia."

"You *think*?" My heart pounded in my breast and my mind was working furiously. "Do you know this for certain?"

"Almost certain. He'll not marry me – I'm certain of *that*."

I took her hand, "Julia, please don't be upset. You don't know for –"

"Oh Alex!" she snatched her hand away angrily. "You've no idea what I'm going through … all this time …" her anger retreated and she began to cry again. "All this time … I've loved him … all … th-this time and … he's … n-never … loved me. It has always been … her … *oh*!" She buried her face in her handkerchief, her heart breaking.

I watched miserably, grieving for my friend and my head aching with my dilemma; should I tell her and confirm her pain, or should I keep my peace and give her hope? What would *I* want in her place?

"Oh Alex, wh-what shall I *do*?" she ended on a wail and I

quickly pulled her to me as much to muffle her loud cry as to comfort her. "Saints alive … I love him so much … but he … they … oh, I cannot bear it!"

We were sitting thus, my arms about her shuddering shoulders when the door slowly opened. I looked up, anxiously praying Julia's cries hadn't alerted Mother. As Pat's head appeared around the door, I sighed in relief. Assessing the scene, he quickly slipped into the room closing the door behind him.

"What's all this about, then?" He touched Julia's hair gently, his eyes on my face.

Reading his silent question, I grimaced helplessly. "She's upset about Deon – "

Suddenly Julia turned and threw herself against Pat's chest, he caught her and eased himself on to the couch, which was now overcrowded having been designed to seat only two.

"Oh Patrick!" she cried into his shirt. "You're his friend … talk to him … t-tell him how … m-much I love him!"

"First tell me what's going on," he insisted.

I filled him in while Julia snuffled wetly in his arms.

"There now, you're only guessing … you don't know for sure …" Pat said, when I'd finished.

"That's what Alex said, but … I do … I *doo.*'

"Have you seen anything untoward?" I asked precariously.

She shook her head.

"Has he broken your betrothal?" Pat questioned.

Again she shook her head.

"Well, then …" I rubbed the spot between her shoulder-blades; her face was still buried against him. "If you've seen nothing and heard nothing …"

She sat up so abruptly that Pat's face registered surprise and she turned to me, her pretty autumn complexion blotchy and swollen.

"That's just it … there's been nothing … n-no word, no letter … n-nothing … you can't *possibly* know what that f-feels like."

"But I rarely hear from Hamish, I —"

"*Ha!*" She made a sharp, derogatory sound like a bark. "Don't be ridiculous! You don't c-care for Hamish and … he doesn't c-care for you. It's you two … you and P-Patrick who are in love …"

Pat's eyebrows shot up and his eyes caught mine over Julia's head. I shook my head, equally surprised while Julia turned in Patrick's arms to look from me to him and back again. "It's obvious … your f-feelings for each other … l-look at you Alex … like a cat with a robin … I've nothing like that with Deon and … *what?*"

I widened my eyes innocently but she sneered contemptuously. "Oh come on for heaven's sake! Don't pretend there's nothing going on … first time I saw you together I knew."

"Jules …"

"Well if there isn't — there should be …" she made a snorting noise, which was about as much of a laugh as her stuffy nose would allow. "Of course, if you must have your little secret …"

I shot a questioning look at Pat and he answered with a resigned shrug.

Taking her hands, one of which clutched her sodden handkerchief, I said, "Please Julia, Pat and I … you *must* promise not to tell anyone. *Please* promise for if anyone knew I'd be packed off to marry Hamish so quickly I'd leave an eddy in my wake. Pat is going back to Wellesley, but when he returns …"

She attempted one of her bright grins, though managed only a grimace. "Alex, you know your secret is safe with me and believe me when I say how happy I am for …," she didn't finish for she'd erupted into a renewed storm of tears, her handkerchief pressed to her mouth.

"He will not marry me … I know it," she cried and turned to Pat, her eyes pleading. "Please Patrick, I beg you, *please* t-talk to him … you're his f-friend … m-make him see I love him … *oh how can I bear this?*"

She continued her sobbing and Patrick, disarmed in the face of such feminine distress, found himself in uncharted territory – he didn't know what to do.

In any other circumstances, I'd have found Patrick's expression of alarm terribly funny. His eyes drifted longingly towards the door and, as I hugged Julia to me, I indicated with a nod that he should escape. Standing, he touched the girl's shoulder. "I'll ride over tomorrow, Julia," he said gently. "I don't know what good it will do, but I'll try."

That evoked another flood of tears accompanied by a snorted, "*Thank you.*" With a final glance at me, he slipped gratefully out the door. Eventually, possibly through exhaustion, Julia sat back and reached for her, now cold, cup of tea.

"Will Patrick really go over and speak with him? Is he true to his word?"

"If he says he will, he will."

"He's a good man – you're so lucky Alex." She looked ready to cry again but gulped her tea and the moment passed.

I nodded and she gripped my arm with a sudden spark of her old mischievous self, "And it will be such fun to watch Adrienne flirt with him, never knowing it is all for nought."

I stared at her in surprise. "That's cruel, Jules. I thought you liked Adrienne."

"Oh I do … most of the time. But she's never approved of Deon's betrothal to me and throws Celia in his path at every opportunity." She sipped her tea thoughtfully. "You know the only reason we're all invited to the Moreheads' dinner is so Adrienne can get her claws into Patrick. After that day in your drive … Adrienne and her aunt have plotted ways of spending as much time with him as possible before he returns to the war."

"I didn't know …"

"No, you wouldn't. But Adrienne told me herself. You and Hamish were invited because otherwise it would be too obvious. Observe the seating arrangements. Adrienne will be beside Patrick."

"I thought she'd relent after Mother's comment."

"She considered it. But she's out to snare him, Alex. I only hope Patrick proves truer to you than Deon has to me."

∾

That evening, as the boughs of the Great Oak extended strong and enduring above us, Patrick asked, "Did you manage to calm Julia in the end?"

Lord Thorncliffe lowered his newspaper and looked on with interest. "Was that Chapman girl here today?"

I nodded.

"Nice girl, that one. Better than her friend."

"What? The *glorious* Adrienne!" I threw a teasing look at Patrick. He'd ceased being touchy and now winked at me slyly.

"Mmm, glorious she may be, but I was watching her at your gathering, Alex. A rather elevated opinion of herself, that one – she has aimed her arrow firmly in your direction, my boy."

"There you go," I said brightly. "If you're not keen to marry Anne, there's a nice alternative."

"Begging your pardons – Father, Sister – but I'll make my own decisions on that score. I may well run away to some silent, celibate ashram in India."

"Off you go then," I said, playfully.

"So quick to dismiss me? What if I traded one sister for t'other and married you?"

I blushed, thoroughly enjoying the dangerous ground we were on. "Why, is *that* a proposition, brother?"

"Could be. What say you, my esteemed and most generous father? May I marry my sister here?"

His father had been watching our exchange with indulgent amusement but now he frowned slightly. "Well, for starters, your sister here is spoken for elsewhere. But should you feel inclined to follow the incestuous theme, Miriam has already written to Anne to garner her thoughts. As I understand it, a positive response was returned. She's yours for the taking."

My mouth grew dry and I stared at Pat but he continued off-handedly without missing a beat. "No matter. One sister's pretty much as good as the other. Anyhow, to my original question, how's Julia?"

Gerrard lost interest and returned to his paper, turning the page and folding it into a readable size.

"She only stopped crying because she'd worn herself out. She's convinced Deon has been courting Celia and that he won't marry her."

"I've no doubt she's right," Pat said flatly. "Deon has no intention of marrying Julia. He was forced into the betrothal by his mother."

"That's terrible …!"

"Indeed. A woman so ruthlessly ambitious," he quipped archly. "Have you read King Lear?"

"Stop it!" I snapped, impatient with his flippancy. I'd been thinking of confiding in him for a long time, and now saw an opportunity to share my burden. I said, "I saw Deon and Celia together."

He frowned. "What do you mean, you saw them together?"

"I *saw* them *together*," I said emphatically.

At his quizzical look, I described how I'd wandered away from the party, and how Celia and Deon had been unaware I was there.

Gerrard's newspaper twitched and he gave a little snigger behind it. "Any wonder you returned to the party all flustered."

My cheeks grew hot and Patrick cocked a suggestive eyebrow. "From what I understand of it," he said, "Julia took a fancy to him; and her parents, ever ready to indulge their only daughter, made the arrangement. The Moreheads saw an opportunity to increase the family's wealth and social standing and there you go — a match made in heaven."

"You will talk to Deon tomorrow, won't you? You promised."

"I will, though it's pointless."

"But you will talk to him …?"

"I said I will, but don't expect miracles – particularly in view of what you witnessed."

I sighed in frustration. "Julia loves him."

"So what if she loves him? If I said Hamish loved you, would that alter your reluctance to marry him? Don't pout like that – it won't change anything."

"I feel sorry for her, that's all. It isn't fair."

"Life isn't fair, Lass." Lord Thorncliffe placed his paper on the grass at his feet. "Best you get used to that yourself before your own wedding. Have you heard from Hamish since he went home? No? Then, I suggest you write to him, patch up whatever disagreement you had. Your mother is planning to write to Lord Hamish and suggest a date. December, I believe."

I stared at him, dumb with surprise. It could not be possible. December was only seven months away. I looked at Patrick who was casually swirling wine around his glass, seemingly fascinated by it. Why didn't he say something?

"But, I am not ready yet. I thought … that is … we …" I searched my stepfather's face hopefully.

He fondled his ear lobe and avoided my eyes. "It is neither yours nor Hamish's decision to make."

I turned to Patrick in desperation. "I can't … Patrick tell him … And I want Simon here …" The panic was mounting, making my throat tight and my voice rise. This was the destruction of all our plans and Patrick was saying nothing. Why did he just sit there like that while his own plans were threatened?

"This wedding will be going ahead, Lass – there is no way around it. You know the financial situation and I explained to you long ago that you've –"

"I *don't care* about the financial situation, don't you see? This is *my* life! What about what I want?

Lord Thorncliffe sighed but spoke calmly. "We've had this argument many times. Our position hasn't changed."

"Neither has my position changed. I will not do it, do you hear? I will not go through with this." I stood up, poised to flee, hoping one last time for a show of support from Patrick. I glared down at him. "And what have *you* to say about this? You're vocal enough when they try to force you into an unwelcome marriage, but you say nothing to defend me."

"What do you expect me to say?" he asked, infuriatingly unruffled.

"You know *exactly* what you could say," I hissed meaningfully. Though he was leaving in two weeks he could initiate dealings with Lord Hamish before he left, surely, *surely* if he loved me … I stared at him and he met my eyes defiantly and kept his silence.

"Don't involve your brother, Alex. I don't know what you think you've cooked up between you, but the contract stands."

I glowered at the two men – the one I loved and who angered me so, and his father, who could not meet my eyes and who, over the years, had appeared as displeased with the match with Hamish Glendenning as I.

I needed Pat's support desperately yet he remained remote and eventually broke my stare by returning to his wine glass. His failure to back me cut deeply. I turned quickly and the little wooden heel on my shoe dug into the soft earth. I stumbled and nearly fell, corrected, and ran towards the house.

I sat still in the dark, perched stiffly in an overstuffed chair by the window in Patrick's room, waiting for him to retire for the night. It was some time before his footfalls sounded outside the door. He came into the room carrying a candle and closed the door behind him. Going directly to his writing desk, he sat, elbows on the polished hardwood surface, chin resting in his palms.

Seated outside the candle's arc of light, I assumed he was unaware of my presence and was about to speak when he said, "What was all that about, Alex?"

"You're asking *me*!" I exclaimed incredulously.

"Hush! Keep your voice down – yes I'm asking you."

"I could ask the same of you." I rose and went to him, sitting on the edge of the desk. He looked up at me, his mouth grim.

"Well?" I demanded.

"Alex," he sighed and leaned back, one hand reached out to touch mine where it rested beside my hip. "You should not have tried to involve me. You might have given us away."

I pulled my hand away. "You could have spoken up for me," I huffed, adding dismally, "You let me down."

He laughed without humour. "You very nearly let us both down."

"How? I only asked that you stand up for me."

"You don't understand, do you? We cannot do anything that will draw attention to us. As soon as this damned war is over I'll make Lord Hamish an offer to tear up the contract."

"It is not that simple ..." I could feel my frustration rising.

"It *is* that simple. If you –"

"It's not!" My anger was making it difficult to be quiet. "It's seven months away. How will I hold this off? If you love me ... *truly* love me and want to marry me, you'd make your intentions known – you'd make an offer now."

He shook his head firmly. "Not now. If I make an offer now, I won't be around to see it to completion and your mother would have stepped in straight away to bring your wedding forwards. Remember, we don't even know if Lord Elginbury will accept an offer – it will doubtless involve a lot of heated discussion."

I sulked. "Then you don't love me enough to start the negotiation." I knew I was being churlish but my fear was growing as his departure date loomed.

"Ah now, that's not fair and you know it." He got up and stood in front of me, taking my two hands in his. "We must be patient until Wellesley finishes this."

"And by that time I'll have Hamish's ring on my finger and babe hanging from my breast."

"That can only happen if you let it. They can't force you to the altar. As soon as I'm back, I'll see the family lawyer and have an offer drawn up."

"You *do* truly love me, don't you? You're not just playing games?"

"How can you ask me that?"

"You have a *reputation!*" I cried in a stage whisper. "How do I know that you're not amusing yourself – just like with all the others?"

"Alex …!"

"How am I to know?" I repeated, sadly.

"You must trust me."

I wilted wearily. "And I imagine you told all your other doxies to trust you too."

"Oh Alex," he sighed and pulled me into his arms. "I'm in love like I've never known. Just please be patient and hold the wedding off. I'll write and let you know how the campaign progresses. It may be easier for you to delay proceedings that way."

I nuzzled his neck, scratchy with the day's stubble, and breathed his spicy fragrance. "You're a woeful correspondent."

He laughed lightly. "Agree on that score, but will attempt to mend my ways – if it makes it easier – if it means you'll wait."

"You keep saying *if*. Don't you see … I would wait forever, but it is not up to me."

"Christ!" he stepped away from me irritably. "Have you not heard a word I said? Just keep delaying. Do *anything* just delay it."

We were going round in circles and I was growing tired of it. I nodded in reluctant acceptance though in my mind the subject was only temporarily closed.

"Good. And now, you'd better be off to bed." He bent to kiss me briefly before I made my way back to my own room, to fall into bed and an uneasy, anxiety-filled sleep.

∾

Mother was arranging cut flowers in a bowl on the dining table when I found her. It was the day of the Morehead's dinner and I was still uncertain as to what I should wear. She was pale and seemed strangely distracted, but asked me to show her the two dresses I had in my arms so she could give her advice.

I held up the first, a pale-green, watered silk with a low neckline and blood coloured bows on the sleeves and under the bodice. It was a new gown and cut much lower in the bodice than anything I'd worn before.

She stood back with her hand on her chin. "What jewels would you wear with it?"

"I don't know really, so I thought of this one." I held up the alternative, a midnight-blue-satin gown with a tiny matching jacket which scooped just under the bodice and buttoned with little pearls giving the wearer's bosom a nice shape.

"My pearl choker would look nice with this," I suggested.

Mother shook her head. "It's quite warm tonight; I think you'd be better in the green. You may borrow my ruby earrings and pendant if you like. They'll look nice."

I turned to leave but she spoke again. "Take a seat please Alexandra, I must talk with you."

I couldn't imagine what she would want to talk about but I pulled up one of the leather dining chairs and watched curiously as she sat on a second. We faced each other.

"Alexandra, I understand from Lord Hamish that you and his son have discussed delaying your marriage, is this true?"

I nodded, fearing her next words.

"May I ask why?"

"We both believe I am too young."

"You both, or you?"

"We talked about it and —"

"For him to agree to that, I suspect you may have exerted some influence over the boy." I opened my mouth to protest but she held up a hand and continued. "Lord Hamish is not a well man and believes his time grows short. It is his wish that his son marry and an heir be produced while he is still on this earth."

"But Hamish agreed that —" again the hand was raised.

"Alexandra, no contract was signed by Hamish Glendenning or you. The agreement is between his father and me, therefore any decisions made will be made only by us. The question of your age, by the way, is irrelevant. You are well into your marriageable years, quite old enough to produce a child."

Pat's voice echoed in my head warning me to adopt all pretence in going with Mother's plan. Though it grated on me, I bowed my head, feigning acquiescence though I was screaming inside and gripped my hands together in my lap to still them.

"In any case, I suspect that the Glendenning boy is reluctant also and shall write to his father with my suggestion that we plan a December wedding."

She was prepared for my objection and seemed pleased when I remained silent. Nodding with satisfaction, she went on, "Now, the real reason I wanted to talk with you. We received a letter from Simon today. He is discharged from the army and will be returning to take his place as the head of this house."

My heart leapt joyously. "Simon is coming home?"

"Yes," she confirmed, but I began to see her earlier distraction was in fact anxiety, and I deflated and waited uneasily while she seemed to be trying to compose herself.

Finally she said, "He'll be home in October," and added, holding my gaze, "There is something you must know and become accustomed to before he arrives."

I was genuinely worried now for this was more than simply a tirade of derogatory remarks against Maria, whom I assumed had wed my brother by now. "What is it?" I prompted in a small voice.

"You've always been close to your brother and he'll need your support – you must not cause him any distress. You must behave yourself and embark upon your marriage without causing a fracas."

I was truly alarmed now. "What …?"

"Simon has been wounded."

"But he's a doc –"

She waved dismissively. "There was a report of some villagers injured after a skirmish – troublesome rebels or something like that. Simon and another fellow went to tend them. When they arrived, they found the village deserted. They searched but found nothing. Then, as they were about to leave, there was an explosion. The French probably hoped a whole troop had been sent rather than just two physicians. It was a trap: they walked straight into it."

Mother's hands were trembling now and she dabbed at her eyes with her fine Venetian-lace handkerchief. Her sorrow was, for the first time in my experience, genuine.

"How bad is it?"

I waited while she struggled to gather herself. "I suppose we won't know the full extent until we see him, but … I do know … he has lost an arm and … his face …" her features contorted as she fought for control – and failed. "His beautiful face …" she covered her mouth with her handkerchief and wept softly.

I'd never seen my mother cry. In fact, I'd never seen her behave in any way remotely maternal. Now, I slumped in my chair numb with shock for Mother's honest grief added weight to the horror of her words. I could not reconcile the pictures in my head of laughing, disarmingly-handsome Simon with the image Mother's description had produced. Gentle, mischievous Simon – cruelly deceived, disabled and disfigured.

I sat in stunned silence as Mother blew her nose and worked to collect herself. Finally she said in a voice raw with anguish, "The other chap was killed. Simon at least survived. He will be a patient in his own ward for some time yet, then they're sending him home."

Rising, she replaced her chair under the table, then smoothed her dress and touched her hair. "Alexandra, you have a fine life ahead of you with Glendenning. Accept gratefully that you are able-bodied, intelligent and rather pretty in your own way. Your brother's life will never be the same. His Spanish girl will be with him, which only confirms my belief that she's set her sights on his fortune."

"Mother, you're a cynic," I said sadly, shaking my head. "If his injuries are as bad as described, her support must be such a comfort to him."

"When you've seen the things I have, you'll realise I'm right to be cynical."

I didn't argue. "Does Father know yet?"

"Yes, and he's telling Patrick at the moment. The staff will also be told. I shall write to Anne tomorrow. She ought to be home. Her brother will need his family about him. Regardless, Isabella tells me Anne's only interest these days is painting – of all things! I must see her betrothed to Patrick before she decides to become an artist and live in an attic, or whatever it is they do. You shall both be married and I'll be damned if I'll put up with any nonsense from either of you!"

Mother's brief flirtation with her human side was quickly forgotten. She drew in her breath, straightened her back, and left me bewildered, dry-eyed, and afraid.

❧

I remained there for some time. Jemima, probably having searched the house, finally wandered in and lay at my feet. By the time Janet appeared in the doorway, I had been there more than an hour. Her face was etched with sorrow and she looked at me from eyes that were red-rimmed. "Miss Alex," she said quietly. "'tis time to prepare for the dinner."

I nodded and rose stiffly. The maid gathered the dresses I'd laid across the table and followed me in silence.

The hall was empty and I could hear the sounds of the household moving about downstairs – it was safe. I rapped quickly on his door.

"Yes?"

I turned the handle and pushed the door open a crack. "It's me," I whispered. The door was jerked open and he grabbed my wrist, dragging me inside.

Patrick stood naked from the waist up; naked, sun-browned and muscular. I made to avert my eyes but was pulled hard against his smooth chest and his mouth closed over mine in an aggressive but brief kiss. He released me abruptly and I slumped against the wall.

"I presume you're not in the habit of visiting the bedchambers of men so you must have heard about Simon?

I nodded. "I can't believe it. It's so … I can't believe God could be so cruel."

He sighed sadly. "God had nothing to do with it – damn Frogs! All the more reason for me to get back there – sooner the better!"

"You can't punish them all. Oh Pat …" I began to cry.

"Shh …" He pulled me to him and I rested my forehead against his naked chest while he gently stroked my hair. His skin smelled wonderful.

I reluctantly pulled away so I could watch his face. "I also came to tell you Mother is writing to Lord Elginbury to confirm the date of my wedding."

"When's it to be?"

"A day in December."

"I'm asking a lot of you," he admitted dismally. "Time is against us."

"I know, and I'm afraid."

"I can see that, but try not to be." He touched Mother's ruby at my throat, "Is this what you're wearing? You look lovely."

"Shameless flattery won't distract me. Pat, what if something happens to you? Oh, why do we deny ourselves? We love each other … there's no shame in expressing it."

He moved away and reached for a crisp, white shirt. I watched as he slipped his arms into the sleeves and buttoned the shirt before reaching for me again. Our lips came together, gentler this time but quickly deepening, becoming demanding and urgent. When finally we drew apart, he smiled ardently and his eyes were deep, green pools. Sliding his hands between us, he cupped my breasts. "Mmm Alex, this gown … rather daring for you – I love it." His voice was gravelly with desire and, lowering his face, he whispered against my mouth, "Christ, how I long to love you."

"Then –" A thumping on the door caused us to spring apart guiltily.

My would-be lover pressed a silencing finger to my lips and called casually, "Who is it?"

"It's Janet," came the reply, and my heart dropped to my stomach. "I am searching for Miss Alex." My maid's voice was muffled behind the heavy wood of the door. I looked fearfully at Patrick and wondered how long she'd been standing there, but he seemed unconcerned.

"I'm dressing for dinner. Why would Miss Alex be here?"

There was a short silence from the other side of the door. Then she spoke again, "Forgive me, Master Pat … I … my Lady Thorncliffe asked me to find her."

Patrick grimaced and replied with undisguised annoyance, "Well, I'm certain she didn't suggest you look here, so if you'd be so kind as to afford me some privacy …"

"Yes, Master Pat." We waited as her footfalls died away down the hall.

I released my breath and ran my hands down the skirt of my gown.

He grinned. "A timely interruption."

"Depends how you look at it," I replied sulkily. "We must talk about this."

"We've nothing to talk about. I was but a kiss from throwing you on that bed. We mustn't."

I sighed, my pulse was returning to normal. "I just wish –"

"I'm glad she interrupted us – no, let me speak – I love you Alex, and I want you so badly it hurts, but we cannot … we *must* not. Do you have any inkling as to what would happen if you became pregnant? And what if I didn't return from the war? What would you do?"

"I would have something of you … bad things happen – consider Simon." I reached for him but he pulled away and went to his wardrobe, examining its contents.

"Don't make it more difficult."

I sighed heavily. "I wonder what Mother wants. I suppose she wants to look me over – make sure I shall make a suitable impression on our social inferiors. She's relentless. After the news about Simon, you'd think she'd have other things on her mind."

"Anyone else might, but not your mother." He tucked his shirt into the tight black trousers he wore while I sat on the bed feeling wifely. There was a black waistcoat with claret coloured stripes hanging over the back of a chair, which he now slipped into.

"You know if you are caught here there'll be hell to pay," he said over his shoulder, while doing up buttons made of polished Whitby jet.

"No-one saw me come in. You'll have to check the hall is clear when I leave. I only hope Janet didn't hear us."

He reached for a starched, white neckcloth. "Doubtless we'll find out soon enough. Can you hold this?"

He stood facing me and I held the cloth where he indicated.

He executed a series of loops bringing the edges forwards and tying a large knot, then tucked the ends into his waistcoat.

"Thank you." He studied his handiwork in the mirror and snorted deprecatingly. "It will do – it's not as if Brummell's going to be at this thing."

"Who's Brummell, or does that make me sound like a country rabbit?"

He smiled at me in the mirror. "One of Prinnie's chums. Self-proclaimed leader of fashion. Makes every gentleman's life a misery, he does."

"I know you hate the pretension of it, but I do love the way you look in evening dress."

He turned to face me. "Thank you, and I love the way you look. You don't realise how you attract attention, and not just from the men. Women, I can tell, are envious of your pretty little body."

I blushed self-consciously. "You're embarrassing me."

"Why? You have inherited the Broughton good looks." He turned me to face the mirror and I saw myself: high-cheekbones, straight nose, soft brown eyes, shining hair, above a slim, well-proportioned figure. He stood behind me. "You're beautiful. You're everything, and more, that I thought you would be when I first met you. I was attracted to you despite your prickles and obstinacy. You showed that passion and loyalty lurked within."

My eyes dampened and I blinked the tears away. "I feel so blessed that you love me like this," I whispered. "And Simon's Maria is standing by him, he's also blessed."

"We're all blessed, darling girl." He turned me to face him. His eyes, a cloudy dark green with the intensity of his feelings, searched my face. "Simon is alive, he's coming home … don't be sad. He'll need you – more than anyone – to be strong for him."

I wiped my cheeks miserably, "I know and I'm frightened. I'm also frightened of losing you to the war, and what if it happens without us ever knowing each other properly? I can't lose you,

Patrick, and it can happen so easily. Who would've thought that Simon, a physician …?"

We watched each other wordlessly for some time until finally he took a deep breath and moved away. Crossing to the wardrobe he took out a high-collared brocade coat in a deep forest green, the perfect partner to my gown. Shrugging into it, he stated flatly, "Beau Brummell hates these coats, but he's not the final word on everything."

∽

I was seated beside Mr Crabtree, an ageing gentleman whose constant sniffing tempted me to offer him my handkerchief. On my right was a skinny youth with slicked down hair who introduced himself as Mr Dickie Long; causing Julia, seated on Mr Long's other side, to titter delightedly into her napkin.

As predicted, Patrick was placed alongside Adrienne, though Julia's hope that Patrick proved more steadfast than Deon was far from my mind as my would-be lover met my glance. The indecent glitter in his eye brought a telling blush to my cheeks, at which he cocked a significant eyebrow. The very air between us seemed to shimmer with feeling and I wondered that the party gathered round that lavishly-laid table remained unaware.

"Would you agree, Miss Broughton?" Mr Long and several others were looking expectantly at me.

"Oh … I'm sorry …?"

"Indeed," laughed Julia knowingly, "you had quite floated away on a magic carpet. Mr Long believes that the new dance from Europe is improper, though I tend to disagree."

"What new dance is that?" I asked aware that I was showing myself up for the country rabbit I was.

"Why the waltz, my dear," said a spherical lady with impossibly-pink cheeks, across from me. "The Imperial Waltz, fresh from Vienna. Have you not heard of it? The lady is held rather close to her partner for the length of the dance. Exceedingly suggestive and quite indecorous." She shook her head adamantly making her corkscrew curls bob and her jowls wobble. "Too much contact inflames the passions," she added in a menacing voice.

"The steps are quite basic, Georgina, don't you know," said Mrs Morehead from the top of the table. "No technicalities whatsoever, any farmer could do it."

"Vulgar!" continued Georgina Bradbury from behind her fan. I now realised she was Adrienne's aunt. "It is simply an excuse for gentlemen to touch ladies immodestly. I've heard all about it — popular at Almack's but young ladies must seek approval from a patroness before they may dance it. It's quite obscene — further evidence of the decline of our times." Her chins jiggled with the effort of fanning herself with indignant vigour.

Mr Crabtree contributed with a sniff, "Precisely why it attracts the working classes — uneducated as they are — we, on the other hand are capable of much more complex routines."

"Quite so, Mr Crabtree," Miss Bradbury agreed enthusiastically. "'Tis why they breed so prolifically — all that indiscriminate touching."

Suddenly Pat gave a derisive shout of laughter causing a dozen heads to swivel in his direction. "You all, until your recently acquired wealth," he said smoothly, "were no closer to the aristocracy you covet than the working class you disparage." I stiffened in alarm as a series of gasps and indignant murmurs echoed around the table. Recognising the mischievous glint in his eyes, I cringed inwardly as he went on, undeterred. "Have any of you actually witnessed the dance being performed, or is your information grounded merely on the kind of ignorance and aspiring snobbery that typifies you middle bourgeois?"

Miss Bradbury's fan was so overworked that its ribs were creaking in the silence that followed. Stealing a quick look at Mother, I detected a distinct gleam in her eye and the tension about her mouth belied her attempt to restrain a smile, though anyone less familiar with her would have seen only a blank mask.

Mrs Morehead's nostrils flared and a flush crept up her neck. She rose from her seat, creating a commotion, as every male at the table respectfully stood. "If the ladies would be so kind as to follow me, perhaps it is time we leave the gentlemen to their brandy."

In a rustle of silk and satin, the ladies joined their hostess, and I smiled as I saw Mother discreetly shoot Patrick a rare and grudging nod of approval. Julia, a member of Patrick's middle bourgeois, arched her eyebrows at me as we joined the train of ladies trailing our hostess into the parlour.

Mother and two companions occupied a couch while some ladies sat on chairs. Others drifted elegantly around the room conversing congenially – or not, judging by the heads bent together and the furtive glances in Mother's and my directions.

"Perhaps Adrienne will play for us," suggested a lady in lavender. "She does play so beautifully."

Adrienne smiled demurely and arranged her skirt prettily on the piano stool. She commenced to play as another young lady sang in accompaniment. Their recital concluded to polite applause. They nodded in acknowledgement and began another song.

At length we were joined by several of the men, Patrick among them. He perched casually on the arm of my chair beneath the affronted scrutiny of the many narrowed eyes that slid towards him. I wondered how he dared show his face and said as much.

"With an overt lack of remorse. Don't worry," he added sardonically, "my father's rank will smooth their ruffled feathers. They would never dream of remaining insulted for fear of his refusal of future invitations. I will say good evening to you, my dear, and to thank our disgruntled hostess before taking my leave."

I watched Deon and Julia in order to distract myself. They seemed to be rather happy together and I realised to my discredit, that I'd been too concerned with my own affairs to know the outcome of Patrick's discussion with Deon. I assumed all was well since there was Julia now, gay as a flower in springtime, with her betrothed standing beside her.

"Have you enjoyed the evening?" Patrick asked, breaking into my thoughts. His brandy scented breath tickled my hair pleasantly.

"It was rather civilised until your outburst," I replied tightly but with a serene smile knowing we were being observed. "It was very uncouth of you to insult our hostess and her guests."

"Pompous fools – it's all they deserve. You're glowing tonight," he whispered and warmth flooded my cheeks. He laughed lightly and continued, "You far outshine anyone else here – is it the wine?"

"That was a lovely compliment you just ruined," I rejoined.

"And you do blush so prettily. I wonder … how pink would you become if I were really to tease you?"

"Shh! Are you drunk?"

"Intoxicated – by your proximity, my love. Oh, God help me," he groaned as though in pain. "Do you have any idea what I would like to do to your breasts? I can see right down between them from here and they look delicious."

I shot up from my seat, my face flaming. "You're impossible!" I hissed and his laughter caused several heads to turn in our direction.

"Well, old boy," Deon interrupted suddenly. He and Julia were standing beside us and Julia was eyeing me with a suspicious little smirk. "You've accounted for yourself rather charmingly tonight. I'd best stay on the right side of you, or am I too bourgeois for you to even bother with?"

"Perhaps you are, Morehead, but wed this lovely here on your arm and I'll reconsider my opinion." Patrick winked at Julia who smiled brightly. "Anyway," he continued, "your coin's as good as any other's when we're in the tap-room."

With that, Patrick executed a series of courtly bows before approaching Mrs Morehead. I turned away as Deon hailed a friend and left Julia alone with me.

"What did I tell you about the seating arrangements?" she said in a low voice. "Georgina Bradbury's making an obvious play for your brother on behalf of her niece."

I shrugged. "It would be funny if it wasn't so annoying. I take it things are resolved between you and Deon?"

"If they appear that way, it's because I'm turning a brave face on it. You see, Celia is always light-hearted and carefree. So, if that's what he's attracted to, that's what I shall be."

I frowned. "You can't go through life pretending to be always light-hearted and carefree – it's not real."

Her eyes snapped angrily and she hissed, "Don't rain on my picnic, Alex. Things are well for now. Just be happy for me."

Adrienne finished playing and we joined the audience in another round of dutiful clapping. "Let's find the ladies' withdrawing room," Julia said returning to her cheerful mood. "I'm about to burst."

As I rose to follow, I saw that Adrienne had left the piano, crossing to where her Mother seemed to be talking rather amiably with Patrick. Immediately latching on to his elbow, Adrienne hooked her hand through his arm and whispered something at which he laughed. I paused, noting that Miss Bradbury had done likewise, a little smile of satisfaction turning her painted mouth into a plump heart-shape.

"Do you trust him?" Julia asked following my gaze.

"Of course!"

"Then, come on."

∽

Mrs Morehead suggested we return to the dining-room for the servants had cleared the remains of the meal and left plates of fruit jellies. Miss Bradbury, cheerfully smug, was leaning back in her chair, telling my mother how only a few short years ago her dance-card was always full.

"I was quite the most engaging creature," the ageing spinster asserted haughtily. "And Adrienne inherited my charms, you know. All the young men vied for my attention."

"Oh, Georgina, you're adorable," Mother said melodiously, "You almost had me believing you."

Miss Bradbury pursed her lips in annoyance as Mother sailed away, her condescending laugh pealing gaily behind her.

The older lady turned her attention to me. "Your brother has quite an unrestrained tongue Miss Broughton – obviously gets it from your Mother. I understand he is not yet spoken for – any wonder. Nevertheless, he and my niece would make a delightful couple, don't you think?"

My smile was forced. "Patrick is my stepbrother, Miss Bradbury – not my Mother's son." I spoke automatically, somewhat distracted for Adrienne had not yet returned to the dining room. And I was not the only one to notice, for her aunt's eyes slid frequently to the door, no doubt counting the minutes of her absence.

"Alex, try the jellies," Julia held a plate before me and I helped myself to a pink one.

"My sister's cook makes them with fruit purée," Miss Bradbury said proudly. "Aren't they simply divine?"

I nodded, without enthusiasm.

"Miss Broughton – Alexandra if I may," Miss Bradbury continued in a tone of obsequious companionship. "I shall overlook your brother's outburst earlier for I understand he's young and, of course, men of such high birth tend to be rather tightly-strung. In any case, he must learn to curb his tongue since this family adheres to a rather strict social etiquette. Your brother's youthful impetuosity – let's call it that – may be somewhat off-putting, but I shall, all the same, stamp my approval upon any match between him and my niece." The older woman sat back and folded her chubby arms over her bosom with a self-satisfied sigh. "Ah yes … the roughest diamonds become the finest jewels!" She giggled like a girl and I could stand it no longer.

"Men of such high birth! And you know this from your vast experience in such matters!" The words spilled forth before I'd realised they were there. The lady's eyes widened in surprise and her mouth worked foolishly. Beside me Julia stiffened with contained laughter. Impossible as it was to retract my words and, perversely delighting in the moment, I continued, "After all, how would *you* know? What could you *possibly* know of the charms of men of *high birth* since your closest contact with them has been in the nursery reading to their children!"

A moment passed when I truly feared I had done Miss Bradbury an injury for she clutched her bosom and the blood rushed up her neck to suffuse her already pink cheeks. A sheen of perspiration broke on her brow and she snapped open her fan with a violent flourish. Sucking in a breath to deliver a piece of her mind, she was momentarily distracted, as Adrienne, similarly agitated, stormed like a whirlwind into the room. She threw herself into a chair beside her mother, two large ugly blotches of indignant colour marring her alabaster cheeks.

CHAPTER 20

I was preparing for bed as Mother stalked in and dropped into the chair by my window. Patiently she waited as Janet, unabashedly curious, reluctantly closed the door on her way out.

Contrary to my expectations, Mother was not angry, though she spoke without preamble, "I understand you were quite rude to Miss Bradbury this evening."

A denial was futile. I nodded solemnly but made no effort to look remorseful.

"What exactly did you say?" Encouraged by her mild tone, I told her truthfully, and to my surprise, she laughed with genuine abandon.

When eventually she regained control she said, "Well done girl! I didn't know you had it in you. Now, tell me what provoked you so?"

"Her attempts to pair Patrick and Adrienne were annoying me," I said honestly.

"Yes. I was similarly annoyed. Obviously that colourless girl has a fancy for him. Georgina Bradbury arranged the seating tonight, you know." Mother sighed wearily. "The woman is getting on my nerves."

"I believe Mrs Morehead is playing the same game."

"I'm a seasoned campaigner, Alexandra, not much goes by me. Your brother's wealth and position make him irresistible to those … *people*. If only Gerrard would agree to a contract with Anne – it would solve everything. Instead, the boy prowls the county like an oversexed tom-cat."

She studied the sickle-moon hovering above the park before continuing, "That clumsy, fat spinster would be laughable if she were not so irritating. Fancy the likes of Georgina Bradbury thinking to marry her niece into *this* family! Good heavens – we are *quality*. Gerrard's line is descended from kings! Never would we dilute such a bloodline with a gaggle of jumped-up merchants!"

A short time later, as I climbed into my great over-stuffed bed and pulled the counterpane to my neck, I shuddered to think of Mother's reaction should she suspect my behaviour owed nothing to preserving the integrity of the family pedigree.

But I drifted to sleep, my smile fading as I recalled her description of Patrick; *prowling the county like an oversexed tom-cat.*

I knew he had led a rather sordid life for one so young, knew also his considerable local exploits – for servants could never keep their mouths shut. Yet he had promised me his fidelity. Could I trust him, or was he cut from Deon's cloth?

Towards the middle of April, Patrick began preparing for his departure, scheduled for the following week. He had taken out his uniform – the red, woollen coat had been brushed, the white breeches had benefited from Mrs Grainger's vigorous washing, and the black, knee-high boots gleamed.

I went to his room and found him grumbling that his breeches had grown tight about the girth.

"Perhaps you've been eating too many of Cook's lemon biscuits, Butterball."

He stared at me as if I'd said the sky was pink with green spots. "Don't be absurd! And what's Butterball?"

"That's what Simon used to call Anne. She was a chubby little girl."

"Hmph! I'll ride it off on the way to London – if I can sit my horse without bursting my seams."

"London? I thought you were leaving from Hull?"

"I was. But Father wants me to check his house in Cheapside. He thinks the tenant's up to no good. Military ships leave from Dover every day – passage will be easy to obtain. If I can, I shall pay a quick visit to Waterville too."

I shrugged. It made no difference to me, he was leaving either way. He examined his shirts for holes and missing buttons and made a pile on his dresser for packing.

"I trust you're not here to watch me pack," he said.

"Mother has written to Lord Elginbury. They have agreed on December fourteenth for the wedding."

He paused momentarily. "I see."

"What shall I do, Pat?"

Continuing his work, he said, "Nothing. Think about it – Simon will be home soon. He's marrying a woman for whom there'll be no approval yet he's following his heart. Did you ever ask his opinion of your betrothal to Hamish?"

"No."

"If Simon does not become our greatest ally, I'll eat that shiny Hessian over there."

Of course, Simon! He of all people surely would defend me.

"I hadn't thought of that," I said softly. I felt a rush of relief. Simon would be home in October – we could reopen the contract negotiation. "It will mean telling him about us."

Patrick took his baldric from the back of his wardrobe. Hanging it over the bedpost, he withdrew the sword from the scabbard with a metallic hiss. Tilting it to the light and examining the blade he said, "Simon won't be surprised. He always said you and I quarrelled so regularly we should be married."

"He said *that*?"

"He was only half joking. Perhaps he sensed something between us."

"Julia guessed."

"Hmm …" Somewhat distracted now, he grasped the sword and executed a series of cuts and slashes, the blade slicing the air with an evil swish.

I cringed. "I don't like that."

He looked contrite. "Sorry … I wasn't thinking. We were instructed to practice four times in a sennight but I've been lazy – hence the paunch." He ruefully patted his still-hard abdomen.

"Then, I shall leave you to it." I gave a weak smile.

Clicking his heels, he offered a formal salute with the beautiful, deadly blade.

∽

Beneath the Great Oak that evening, Lord Thorncliffe poured plum wine into four glasses. Mother turned to her stepson. "As I think of it, what did you say to Adrienne Morehead the other night that left her red-faced and puffed up like an affronted pigeon?"

Patrick's eyes glittered merrily. "She admitted a certain fondness for me and said that her parents would not oppose my calling on her. I merely explained I was not the marrying kind but rather enjoyed a bevy of mistresses. I then indicated my interest should she be possessed of any unusual talents."

Mother's brows arched in surprise but Gerrard chuckled as he handed the wine to her.

"A *bevy*? Exactly how many do you keep?" she asked.

"Talents, eh?" his father remarked, passing a glass to me. Patrick winked suggestively in response.

"Any wonder she was outraged," I commented.

"And so she was. Particularly when I kindly offered to introduce her to some of my doxies, stressing the need for them to rub along nicely together. She delivered a fair wallop – right across the ear – nearly took all the fun out of it."

"If I thought you were keeping a bevy of mistresses, Patrick Washburn, I'd wallop you too," Mother said, at which he grinned disarmingly and she smiled despite herself, adding, "in any case, regardless of whether you marry Anne or no, that girl is definitely not a suitable match."

Patrick raised his glass in Mother's direction. "For once, Regan, you and I are in complete accord."

In the days remaining to us, Patrick and I played like children; frolicking in the park, or running through the woods where, hidden from the house, we acknowledged our love in promises and kisses. We wandered the park and the forest, often accompanied by Meg and Clara, the latter becoming our unacknowledged and self-imposed chaperone. She was too discreet to comment with aught but her eyes, but she was clearly aware of the intimacy between us and I trusted her discretion.

We were ever mindful that our time was drying up like a puddle in the sun. Many afternoons were spent lying in the park; the heady scent of April wildflowers crushed beneath our backs hung in the air. Laughing, reciting poetry, or simply reading in silence, with Patrick, I knew a contentment I'd never imagined possible.

It was April 15, the morning of Patrick's last day, and Jemima and I rose earlier than normal – earlier than the stable-boy, for the stables were silent and dark when we arrived. Patrick emerged from the shadows, greeted me with a quick embrace, and I followed as he led Equus by the halter into the pearly dawn. She wore no saddle, but he slipped a bridle over her ears and the bit into her mouth, then he threw the reins over her head and leapt on to her bare back.

I stood on the mounting block and reaching down, he pulled me up behind him.

Jemima seemed aware of the gravity of the occasion. Normally so excitable, she padded sedately beside Equus' elegant walk through the park. I wrapped my arms around Pat's waist and, with my head against his shoulder, pressed as close to him as I could, matching the rhythm of our movements with Equus' smooth gait.

The woods loomed deep and dark before us. As the first gold and pink shafts of light streaked the eastern sky, a sense of magic infused the air and I would not have been surprised to see forest sprites dancing behind leaves or swinging from flowers as we rode by.

Equus strolled loose-reined, picking her own way through the matted morning-scented undergrowth. Jemima paused here and there, no doubt catching rabbit or fox or deer scents, but nevertheless, she stayed with us.

A gentle mist floated just above the ground, shrouding us in a verdant perfume and Patrick tilted his head back to reach me with a lingering, emotion-charged kiss. When our mouths separated I lay my forehead where his tousled, blond hair brushed his collar and, with my bosom pressed to his back, I could feel his heartbeat, his flesh, muscle and bone – warm with his life and spirit – moving beneath his shirt. I breathed him in as though he was life-giving, aware that it must strengthen and sustain me for his leaving.

At length, we entered a small clearing where the boughs of aged hawthorns formed a cathedral ceiling of pretty, white flowers above our heads. Pat slipped to the ground landing softly in a mulch of fallen leaves. Lifting me down, I remained momentarily leaning against the mare's warm side, my arms about his neck, as we kissed tenderly.

"Here?" he asked, finally drawing away. His voice was a reverent whisper – the first spoken word of the morning.

I glanced around at the naturally occurring room emerging

from a veil of mist and nodded. Immediately, he set to work. Taking a dagger from his belt he began clearing the forest floor of loose leaves and twigs; centuries of forest debris. He carved into the ground, scraping and digging, shaping a heart – the span of two octaves on a piano.

While he worked, I took a candle and tinder-box from the pocket of my skirt and, after several strikes of the flint, I lit the small square of char-cloth that I touched to the candle. With no breeze, the candle burned steadily, shrinking our little clearing to the circle of its light.

Patrick sat back on his heels and watched as I extracted from my other pocket a small bag of iris bulbs. Untying the drawstring, I up-ended it, tipping its contents into the centre of the heart.

Together we planted them, placing the little nubs along the scratched outline and filling the centre. We worked in enchanted silence by the light of the candle and witnessed by all manner of faeries and dryads.

The forest was coming to life around us; the first birds were singing their morning hymns accompanied by a rustling in the undergrowth. The clearing had brightened, its boundaries broadened and ringed by the uneven trunks of pale birch and craggy hawthorn.

When finally it was done, Patrick's eyes were dark and intense with emotion. He reached for my hand and quoted deferentially,

Let not thy divining heart
Forethink me any ill;
Destiny may take thy part,
And may thy fears fulfil;
But think that we
Are but turn'd aside to sleep;
They who one another keep
Alive, ne'er parted be.

His reciting Donne brought tears to my eyes. He brushed them aside with his thumb before we kissed, sealing our pact, and wordlessly we watched the day begin to slide her fingers of sunlight between the branches, removing the last wispy traces of dawn.

"It's too late in the season for them now," Pat whispered, "but, my darling, *darling* girl, we shall come next spring to behold our first irises."

He dug a little hole in the centre of the heart and stuck in the candle packing the earth around it, then pulled me to my feet.

Equus was dozing with her nose bobbing towards the ground. As we approached, she raised her head and nuzzled Patrick's shoulder. He took her reins in one hand, his other still holding mine, and we retraced our steps with Jemima following close behind. Reaching the ring of trees, I paused to glance behind and shuddered as a shadow crossed my heart.

"What is it?"

"I … I'm not sure." The candle was a soft halo in the centre of the trees, but as I watched, a breath of wind rippled through our clearing. Nearby leaves fluttered and the pale yellow glow flickered and died.

"The candle went out," I said gravely.

His eyes widened in mock horror. "Ooh – a portent of misfortune?"

"Don't …" I squeezed his hand. "You mustn't scoff. I feel strange … like something is wrong."

"And so it shall be if we will it. C'mon, I'm after my breakfast and I believe our worthy four-legged companions are too."

∾

For much of the day Patrick was closeted in Simon's study with his father going over paperwork presumably relating to Waterville. I spent the time of his absence in the still-room with Emily labelling and sealing in clay jars, the herbs collected and dried from the kitchen garden. And as cruel as time can be, the day passed with the speed of a runaway horse.

That evening, against Mother's strict sense of propriety, Gerrard had decided that we would eat in the servants' dining room and that Mrs Grainger, Eleanor, Janet, Cook and Clara, would join us for a special farewell supper in Patrick's honour. He contributed not two, but three of his jealously guarded bottles of Bordeaux, along with several lesser-revered offerings.

The spring evening sky blushed pink and rose, and long shadows slanted through the windows as, despite the sorrow of the occasion, we made a pleasant party around the table, toasting Wellesley's health and a quick end to the war.

Though Cook had prepared the meal earlier and left its service in Emily's hands, she nevertheless made frequent visits to the kitchens to ensure all was going to plan.

"Relax and enjoy yourself this evening, dear Cook," Gerrard said refilling her cup. "You're wearing a trench in the rug with all this to-ing and fro-ing – care for another, Janet?" He brandished the bottle before the maid, who was already flushed and glassy-eyed. She declined politely, and Gerrard, undeterred, turned to his son, "Not like some, eh, my boy? I know *you* won't say no!"

Pat grinned and held out his cup. "Certainly not! Disrespectful, Janet, that's what you are, not paying due homage to the god of wine and plenty."

"Ah – to Bacchus," his father toasted, and drained his cup.

Though Patrick's departure lurked like a storm on the horizon, the evening progressed gaily. Even Eleanor's normally pallid face was rosy with rare cheerfulness and she, seated beside Mrs Grainger, was engaged in unlikely conversation buoyed nicely by copious amounts of Gerrard's wine.

Caught up in a celebration of food, wine and family, I was becoming quite tipsy and thoroughly enjoying myself, so it was with something of a rude and sobering jolt that I remembered the reason we were all gathered was Patrick's imminent departure. Watching him now, telling a tale from a childhood visit to Ireland, his face animated and engaging, my heart ached, and suddenly, I knew a desperate need to freeze time, to suspend this moment forever.

If, I reasoned in my wine-fuddled mind, I could have stoppered the fissure through which the seconds had first begun to trickle, I could now stand against the unavoidable torrent of minutes rushing by, gaining momentum, leaving no time for the things I needed to tell him. Like how he made my blood beat through my veins when he smiled just for me, how I loved to watch him with Jemima and Equus and imagine him with our children, how I loved him so much I could cry, how I wish we'd made love.

There was a burst of laughter from around the table and Patrick said, "Knocked him out cold. I doubt Aden has fished since."

"I've heard tales of this Aden," Mother said. "A very likeable young man by all accounts."

"And so he is," Gerrard confirmed, "but not a proficient angler."

The story continued, and though inconsequential in itself, it was the style of the telling that held his listeners captive, for Patrick had a magnetic personality and wondrous turn of phrase. That he could love me humbled and filled me with inexpressible joy, while such love rendered me immensely vulnerable.

The hall clock chimed the eleventh hour and Mother stifled a yawn. "Good grief, the night has flown by. What time will you ride out?"

"Before light. I intend to put some miles behind me before midday," Pat replied.

"Then I shall wish you Godspeed now for I'm to bed."

They both rose and came together in an embrace that for all their past conflicts appeared genuine. "Farewell and return in one piece, and may this whole business be done with soon," she said. He accepted a brief kiss on each cheek and thanked her.

Eleanor stepped forwards and dropped an unsteady curtsy. "God will you safely home, My Lord."

Mother and her woman left the room then, and Janet looked questioningly at me. I'd had no intention of retiring yet, but it was now apparent, with Mother's departure, that it was expected.

Gerrard spoke. "I'll see you off in the morning, Son, though it may be too early for others."

"Not too early for me. I'll have a sack of food ready for your ride." Cook hauled her bulk upright and bustled off to the back of the house.

It was now my turn. I took a deep breath and rose from my seat. "Well, this is farewell, brother." I could hear the tremor in my voice and fought to control it. Clara stood beside me and I felt her hand discreetly touch my back, lending her strength.

I stepped towards him. I longed to feel his arms go about me, but he took both my hands in his and said, "Kiss me quickly, Li'l Sis and go to bed. I shall be home before you've missed me."

I raised my face to him, his lips looked inviting, but I leaned towards his cheek and placed a chaste kiss there. How I wanted to melt against him and beg him not to leave, and I quaked with the effort of keeping myself together.

He felt it, and squeezed my fingers lightly in support before releasing me to turn to Janet. His face set with meaning, he said simply, "Loyal helper, until we meet again."

She dropped a small curtsy and rose, not meeting his eyes. "Farewell, Master Pat."

And then it was over and I was alone in my bed. I lay staring at the drapery above while slow, fat tears rolled into the hair at my temples, soaking miserably into my pillow.

Jemima stirred in her basket on the floor and whimpered in response to my sorrow. She sat up and peered at me through the dark. "Lie down, Jem," I whispered and she obediently circled two, three times and flopped down with a sigh.

I longed for oblivion, but sleep proved elusive, abandoning me to restlessness as the moon moved within sight.

We hadn't enough time – it had all been too short. Yet in the brief time we'd been allowed our love had ripened and bloomed into this marvellous, beautiful thing.

Suddenly my body heaved convulsively and I began to sob as I thought about our lost opportunity, for I hadn't given myself to him – and he hadn't asked me to, preferring to await a time when we could be open. A time so distant it may never be, for nothing was guaranteed – nothing set in stone save this blasted war and my looming marriage to another.

Now, in the cold reality of farewell, I saw how regretful was this denial of ourselves – for our love to remain unconsummated was simply … foolish.

And then I knew what I had to do.

Fired with determination, I slipped from my bed and drew a silk wrap over my nightdress.

The hall was in darkness and the house silent save for the comfortable creaking of it settling after a long day. I padded on bare feet down the hall runner, feeling my way along the panelled walls. Finally, I came to his door and without hesitation I turned the handle and gave a small push.

The door moved with the soft groan of heavy, old wood on oiled hinges. I slipped inside.

The blood boomed in my ears while I paused and turned the key in the lock. His furniture gleamed like polished silver in the moonlight, and from his rhythmic breathing I knew he slept.

I crept to the side of his bed, and let my wrap fall to the rug where it lay like a shimmering puddle. He was lying on his back, one arm flung out in the abandonment of sleep. I knelt beside him and whispered, "Patrick …"

It sounded hoarse for my throat was constricted with tears. He stirred drowsily.

"Mm-hmm?"

"Pat, wake up." I touched his cheek lightly.

"Mmm? Alex? What are you doing?"

"What do you think, you idiot?" My voice caught and the unshed tears still clinging to my lashes now spilled over.

"Oh my darling," he breathed. He held open the side of the bed and I slid in beside him, my arms going about him, and discovering, to my surprised delight, that he slept naked.

"I can't let you leave like this … without knowing me … without me knowing you …" I wept into his neck. He cradled me lovingly and wrapped thus in his arms, pressed against his lean nakedness, the emotion of goodbye and the physical need of him were nearly drowning me.

I shook with silent sobs and he held me tightly, his face buried in my hair, murmuring unintelligibly.

Instinctively, I moved against him and heard his quick intake of air. "Please Pat," I beseeched, "I want this …"

"And if we should create a child this night, what then?" he whispered, and his voice was low and gravelly with desire.

"Then I shall go to Devon and wait for you."

"Good idea – they'll never find you there."

"Stop it! I love you and I want you to make love to me." I felt his body's reply against my hip and moved wantonly. "And if you don't return … I'll have this one night. I'll know what it is to be loved by you."

"I won't be here for you if –"

I pressed my lips to his, effectively cutting off his words. Fuelled by all my pent up passions and fears, I kissed him and he replied with equal fervour.

Finally we drew breathlessly apart and I squinted through the dark to see his face. Since declaring our love, he'd not shuttered his expressions from me as he had in the past, and during this enchanted spring, I'd learned to understand him and loved him all the more for his trust in me. Now, I read a mixture of wonder and delight as he gazed back at me.

"I too," he said at last, "have hated the thought of leaving without loving you, though it is undoubtedly the safer course. And now, my darling girl, how could I not accept your precious gift when offered so persuasively."

With unfailing dexterity, he untied the ribbon at the neck of my nightgown and pulled it over my head. He tossed it to the floor and his arms coiled about me drawing my nakedness against his own, and as his hands caressed my body his lips sipped at mine, tongue probing and exploring, igniting such flames that I writhed with need. When he lay half over me, his knee between mine, I felt his desire for me against my groin.

I boldly trailed my hands over the topography of his back, his firm buttocks and hard thighs, and he kissed and stroked and brought me to the brink of delirium.

Finally, shifting on to his elbows he leaned over me, searching my face through the dark, silently questioning.

My voice was ragged when I whispered, "Yes!" and he pressed forwards.

The moment of first penetration brought an unexpected stab of pain. I gasped in surprise and he lay still. "Tell me when it stops hurting." His voice was a breath on my mouth, his lips slid along my jaw, and as my body accustomed itself to this new sensation I felt whole, physically, emotionally, spiritually.

I pressed my nose to the hollow of his throat, breathing deeply of his wonderful masculine scent.

"You alright?" he whispered and I nodded.

He began to move slowly, in long rapturous strokes, and finally I knew — I understood what it meant to be truly loved and to love in return.

The emotion between us that night, our love for one another and anxiety for us both, lent a desperate edge to our passions.

I wound about him like a serpent as he initiated me with all the tenderness and compassion I knew he would.

Later, when at last we lay still, allowing our breathing to return to normal, we kissed gently. I tasted sweat on his lip and revelled in our silken nakedness while drifting into a floating, sated sleep, the salt of my tears drying on my cheeks.

We slept in a tangle of limbs and bedclothes, and awoke while it was still dark. Our bodies instinctively came together, and this time there was no pain of initiation, only delight and pleasure, tempered by the knowledge that we would soon be parted. I soared above the dawn and my heart sang for joy as we knew each other again. And as the glow of the new day hovered just beyond the horizon, I reluctantly slid from his bed.

He stood naked and beautiful by the door while I dropped my nightdress over my head and tied my wrap. I approached and he opened his arms to me and we kissed again, swearing our love, renewing our promises. Then, with my heart breaking, I drew away.

Like a shimmering sprite, glowing and replete; and already grieving, I returned to my room.

CHAPTER 21

I could smell him on my skin. I could feel the discomfort and dampness at the junction of my thighs. It was real. I rolled over, hugging myself. *It was real …* We had finally loved one another, and committed to each other, and nothing would take that away.

My heart swelled with the force of it and I lay for a long time, watching the sky lighten.

I didn't hear him leave. But I knew the moment he did for I felt it. Like a small bird fluttering within my breast – a magical sensation of lengthening, gradual distancing, while maintaining connectedness; together and apart.

I placed my hands on my belly. *And if we should create a child this night.* I will treasure it, bear it with pride and raise it in love, for that was how its parents came together.

∾

Each day, my first thought upon waking and my last thought before sleeping were centred on Patrick. I felt his departure keenly and prayed for his safety. The physical distance between us grew daily, though spiritually I felt closer to him with every breath I took, and each morning I stroked my abdomen hopefully.

But two weeks later nature confirmed I was not pregnant. I was immediately disappointed, for in some foolish fantasy-place I believed that had I proven with child, Mother would force us to marry. Foolish indeed since Mother was bound to honour my betrothal and Hamish would have found himself wedded before the month was out and anticipating fatherhood, though unaware of the child's true parentage.

I sighed. It was for the better.

June came bringing warm days and balmy nights. Meg caught a summer fever and was gravely ill for several weeks. I sat by the little girl's bed for long hours listening as she rambled in childish delirium. She also missed Patrick terribly, relentlessly asking for him during her convalesence. I met her pleas with my own sadness.

By July, she had recovered but remained pale and listless. Those warm summer afternoons Clara and I passed with her beneath the Great Oak hoping the outdoors would return some colour to her face, but as July progressed to summer's hot apex, even shaded by those ancient boughs, the days were too warm. These we spent in the morning room, which, by design, received the morning sun but avoided the heat of the afternoon.

The news arrived in the middle of July, several weeks old; Wellesley, now Viscount Wellington, had taken his well-rested force and launched an attack on Burgos. Victorious in only two days, they marched on to Vitoria where they again proved triumphant – twice in a month. Wellington's forces, now at the edge of the Pyrenees, were threatening France.

Reading this, we naturally hoped the successes translated into an early end to the conflict. I prayed our troops remained safe, and the reported victories were welcome news since I considered a victory might more likely result in their safety.

Consequently, I trawled through every newspaper and journal I could lay my hands on for any mention of the war. Each night I watched the moon draw its bow across the sky and concentrated my thoughts on him, trusting that by such meditations, he would feel me as I felt him.

While studying the progress of the allied forces, I learned that before they could march into France they must take control of the Fortress of San Sebastian. Situated on the Atlantic Coast, between the united armies of Spain and Britain, it was a valuable communications centre and Wellington's focal point. I searched for it on the world globe in Simon's study, training my attentions there when I watched the moon at night.

Though Wellington's forces were quite outnumbered by those at Napoleon's disposal, the papers reported the Viscount's strategic genius was unmatched, and accordingly, I placed my hopes.

I'd given up trying to sleep and was sitting by the open window in my room. Even for late July, this night was extraordinarily hot and sticky. A stretch of searing days with no evening respite had rendered the garden dry and wilting. The stone of our house seemed inordinately predisposed to absorbing the heat of the sun thus ensuring uncomfortably-warm nights.

No relief stirred the trees in the park and the lonely hoot of an owl in the nearby woods fell flat in the thick night air. The moon was a hazy disc high in the sky and I gazed at it, trying to make out the shapes and shadows on its surface.

Was Patrick also watching at this moment? With my hands flattened on the warm sill, I leaned from the window, the better to fully immerse myself in soft moonlight. It was then that I heard it: a sibilant, urgent, whispering in the garden below.

My window faced the east side of the house, but the voices were distinctly coming from the porch to my left — two, no three of them. Listening intently, I made out Mother's clipped sentences, and Gerrard's lower tones. But there was a third — a female I didn't recognise. The door closed firmly and silence followed.

Lighting a candle, I checked the time – half-eleven – strange hour to receive a caller, but before I could consider it further my door was unceremoniously flung open and Janet burst in.

Brimming with news, her manners forgotten, nightcap askew, she gasped, "You'll never believe who's here!"

"I heard someone. Who is it?"

"Miss Anne – your sister – she's home!"

"Anne?"

She nodded vigorously. "Downstairs … the parlour … with Lord and Lady Thorncliffe."

"Fetch my wrap," I said hurriedly.

My maid shook her head. "You can't see her – the countess instructed Eleanor not to let anyone in."

I frowned. "Why?"

She shook her head again.

"Nonsense! Get my wrap."

I tied the belt at my waist while descending the great staircase, jumping the last two steps, and turning sharply to the right towards the parlour. I could hear the voices, angry and raised before I arrived.

Eleanor, stationed outside, was listening avidly, but at my approach stepped innocently away. The shouting alarmed me and forestalled my entry, so as Janet and I joined Mother's woman, we three cocked our ears to the door in unlikely solidarity.

It was a tight squeeze and I pressed against an ornately carved hall-stand. An antique Grecian urn stood in its centre, its arrangement of roses and lavender gave off a powerful scent. With great care, I moved it aside ensuring I'd not bump it.

On the other side of the heavy door, feminine footsteps tapped briskly back and forth across the wooden floor, and Mother was failing to keep her voice low, "I cannot believe it! *How* could this *happen*, Anne? I can-*not* believe you could be so foolish!"

Gerrard's soothing entreaty failed to calm her. He added, "Hush, Lass, your mother and I will sort this out –"

"Sort this out!" Mother cried. "Just tell me who did this so I can sort *him* out – with my bare hands!"

Eleanor, Janet and I, united as never before, exchanged scandalised looks. Anne's response was pitched too low for audibility, and Mother said, "Can't or *won't*."

"Miriam, you're not making this easier for the girl."

The sound of rapid footfalls was followed closely by Anne's yelp of surprise, and I well imagined Mother grasping my sister's shoulder and giving her a good shake. "Now don't mess with me, girl. I want a name and I want it now. Was it that Italian nobody painter Isabella wrote about?"

There was a muffled response and I strained my ears further.

"*Then where!*" Mother shouted so loud I envisioned plaster falling from the ceiling. Sobbing, a whispered answer, then Mother spoke, her voice was hesitant. "When were you in London?"

There was a span of several moments during which Anne haltingly spoke, and we at the door could not make out her words.

Suddenly Gerrard's voice broke in, "But that can't be right –"

"Gerrard, listen to the girl – she's been in London these last three months – how far gone are you?" Mother's voice sounded exasperated.

Anne's response was muffled but a cold shadow passed over me. I shivered involuntarily.

"When were you in Devon?" Mother's voice was low and menacing and I felt Janet's eyes settle sharply on me. I refused to look at her. My hands were clasped before me, they felt clammy yet cold on this warm night, and my stomach stirred sickeningly.

"I see. Well the dates add up. So what are you saying?" Mother was gentler now, wheedling, and Anne responded.

We three eavesdroppers held our collective breaths, and finally Lord Thorncliffe spoke. "That *cannot* be right."

"Oh don't be so naïve, Gerrard – you know what he's like. And he's the only one you've been with, Anne?"

My sister made a sound of affirmation and broke into noisy sobs again.

"I won't believe it —" her stepfather began but suddenly Anne's voice, unmistakable though thick with tears, interrupted.

"There has *not been* anyone else!"

Mother sounded triumphant. "Well, so much for his sense of responsibility, eh, Gerrard! His philandering ways have finally caught up with him. He's marrying her now, that's certain. You get down to Devon the minute he returns — no, no, that's too late — write to him — immediately!"

Cold sweat broke on my face and I leaned my suddenly boneless weight against the hall stand for support. *It can't be him … it can't … please God don't let it be …*

But Mother's voice continued, her every word a knife to my heart, "He's with the thirty-second isn't he — there couldn't be many Patrick Washburns —"

A vile wave washed over me and my companions' faces swam beyond focus. Groping blindly, I clawed desperately for something to hold to and heard the breaking of fine porcelain as my knees hit the rug, heavily …

❧

I was being carried.

My face was pressed against Gerrard's brocade night-robe and he had one arm under my knees the other around my shoulders. Memory rushed at me and I gasped with the horror of it. Anne and Patrick — my own sister — Anne was pregnant by Patrick!

I could not bear it. I would surely not survive pain like this. I moaned and twisted in Gerrard's arms in a futile attempt to escape the appalling truth.

"Shh, it's alright, Lass, hush now."

But it was not alright — it was unbearable. It sucked out my breath and burned like a searing, white blade in my chest, and as

Gerrard laid me on my bed, I curled into a tight ball and turned my face into my pillow.

Mother was there, asking why I had reacted so violently and Janet was replying with traitorous eagerness, details I'd never guessed she knew.

She told how Patrick and I had been lovers – for far longer than we in fact had been – she said we went riding together, described early-morning assignations in the park, his late night visits to my room, how he left his clothes on my floor, holding hands at Fountains Abbey, "Right under My Lord's nose," she ended with righteous indignation.

Mother listened without speaking. I knew the outraged look she'd have on her face for though she thrived on scandal she would not tolerate it beneath her own roof. Yet, she would know a certain satisfaction, for everything she'd planned for her daughters, was falling into her lap.

Lord Thorncliffe's defence of his son had fallen silent for the evidence was irrefutable.

The bed dipped and Mother spoke, surprisingly gently, by my shoulder. "Is this true, Alexandra? Were you and Patrick lovers?"

My throat constricted and I could not answer.

"You must know you can be honest with me. Patrick's reputation precedes him. That he has seduced both you and your sister … I cannot hold either of you responsible."

"We …" it sounded like a croak. I swallowed and tried again. "He said … we would be married …"

Mother scoffed. "I expected something more original than that from him!"

I could think of no reply. The weight in my chest was overwhelming. I'd had no concept that such pain existed – such intense, physical pain, a pain so bright, so debilitating, that it drained my strength rendering me unable to control such basic functions as breathing and speaking.

Mother grunted and rose from the bed. "Well, what say you in defence of your precious son now, Gerrard?"

I pictured her standing upright, confronting, with hands on hips and chin thrust out. "Nothing – as I thought. There's nothing you *can* say for the evidence is right there alongside every slattern with his bastard on her hip. And now look what he's done to my daughters. One is pregnant, while the other – you're not pregnant are you, Alexandra?" I shook my head. "While the other breaks her heart. I shall write to Lord Elginbury and confirm the marriage immediately."

"*No! Mother please …*" I cried thickly, "I can't."

"Alexandra," Mother's voice was deceptively kind, "There's no other way."

I clasped my pillow to my face, rocking and moaning with despair.

"You *will* recover, believe me, you will." She moved away. "Gerrard, write immediately to that philandering son of yours. Tell him he will marry Anne – better he meet a cannon-ball on the battlefield than cross me in this. Janet – fetch water and bathe your mistress' face. And get some laudanum from Eleanor to help her sleep."

"Yes, My Lady." Janet's voice was ingratiating. "Anything else, My Lady?"

I heard the door open and Mother hesitated on the threshold. "Yes – wipe that toadying look off your face – your keenness to betray your mistress this night was *despicable*. The only reason I don't dismiss you for disloyalty is that I'm grateful of the information."

The door closed and all was silent but for my ragged breathing. Finally, I heard the pouring of water, and then Janet was at my side.

"Miss Alex?" she said hesitantly. "I've some water to –"

"Go away," I snapped, throwing my pillow to the end of my bed. She stood beside me, her face white and her eyes wide.

"But Lady Thor –"

"*Go away!*" I screamed with the full force of my lungs.

Without another word she placed the bowl on the table beside my bed and hurried from the room.

And I was alone, but for Jemima, and my agony.

CHAPTER 22

The sky grew light. Exhausted from the force of my grief, I felt I'd lived longer hours than had actually passed by the clock. In the short time since I'd leaned from my window to catch a moonbeam, my life and hopes had crumbled.

But I do love you … I'm yours and I'll save myself for you only. My whoring days are over – gladly.

I had been hoodwinked, completely and thoroughly duped, for Patrick had gone directly from my arms to those of my sister, and how many others in between? Adrienne? Various wenches in Wolstone, Leeds and beyond? Sluts in taverns he frequented with Deon? At balls? Parties?

It was only that Anne had fallen pregnant that the events of this night came to pass, otherwise I'd never have known and … had he ever intended to marry me?

It was clear now that he had not.

I merely explained I was not the marrying kind but rather enjoyed a bevy of mistresses.

Were these the only true words he'd spoken during our time together? What could he possibly gain from spending two months pretending to be in love with me? He must have a wondrous talent for deception for surely no one could sustain such pretence for so long. All those afternoons together, the secret kisses, the irises … *the irises!* Why would someone only pretending to be in love, plant flower bulbs in the forest at sunrise like some pagan ritualist?

But I had given myself to him – he hadn't sought me out, even when he had opportunity, he had never …

Oh Alex, I'm in love like I've never known. Love me enough to be patient …

He hadn't wanted to bed me until we were wed, yet it seemed he wasted no time in bedding my sister. It didn't make sense. I could send myself insane with these thoughts. I needed to see Anne. Perhaps he'd enacted a similar sham with her.

Do you trust him?
Of course I do.

What a fool I've been!

The sun was above the horizon when I finally fell into a tormented sleep only to awaken much later with puffy, sore eyes and my cheek resting on a sodden pillow. My thoughts immediately flew to the night before and I moaned aloud, aggrieved to think that my heart had continued beating and I'd be forced to live with Patrick's betrayal.

I splashed water on my face, bringing small relief to my burning skin before attempting to dress myself.

When Anne knocked at my door, I was sitting on my bed, avoiding the day.

Italy had been good to my sister. The pretty girl had blossomed into a confident and stylish woman. She wore a lemon linen dress with sheer white sleeves and white lace trim. Her shiny chestnut hair curled to below her shoulders and was pinned at her temples with little pearl clips.

At 18, Anne had become the elegant and sophisticated young woman she'd promised to become in her childhood. She moved with an innate grace and her lovely hazel eyes looked about my room.

"Nothing's changed, it is all just as I remember," she said.

"Your lisp has gone."

"Yes." She smiled. I smiled in return for this was not her doing, and truth to tell, she was in more trouble than I, for Patrick, bounder we now knew him to be, would be most unlikely to marry her.

She approached and we hugged for a long time, then I indicated the chair by my window and pulled over my desk chair to sit opposite. We talked of her time in Italy, Catarina's excellent marriage, Maeve's continued residence in Europe, and as we did, the years dropped away, and I discovered – like a revelation, for I'd been so involved in Simon's world – the sister I'd never really known. But too much hung unspoken between us, and when finally our conversation stalled, I said, "So tell me, what happened?"

She knew what I was referring to and shrugged. "There's not much to tell, really. Mother had called me home. I arrived in London late April and was staying with Grace while I booked a coach to Leeds. We were taking tea at the Grand Marquis – her little boy was with us – and she told me Patrick had just arrived in London, and that she'd invited him to join us."

I knew her next words were going to be painful, but I needed to hear them. I said, "Go on …"

"Alex, he was so fascinating, and so … so different from Italian men who fawn all over you, full of false flattery and braggadocio. Patrick was so … I can't explain … understated … he has something … magnetic."

I nodded knowingly. Julia had said once that Patrick made her think of *doing things* with him. It was a good way of putting it.

"He asked me to go with him to Waterville. I'd heard so much about that house from Maeve, and he was so charming that I couldn't resist. I never thought, Alex, he's our brother – well sort of – *who* would have thought?"

"He seduced you," I said plainly.

She bowed her head and I knew she was quietly weeping. "He said it was alright because we'd been matched years ago." She added miserably, "Mother said he seduced you too."

"He said we would marry."

She dragged a handkerchief from her sleeve and blew her nose delicately. "Alex, he's not worthy of us. He has used us both. But at least you have Hamish. Marry Hamish, as intended. Patrick won't marry me – no-one will marry me now."

I sat quietly, knowing she was right; indeed what man would marry her now? I was not so badly off, there *was* Hamish, but I needed time to lick my wounds and gather my strength.

Watching my sister now, and battling my own pain, I realised that Patrick Washburn, heir to an impressive title and vast fortune, was nothing more than a heartless, self-gratifying libertine, taking maidenheads for trophies, and weaving webs of lies and deception, a trail of broken hearts behind him.

But then, my conviction failed me for surely there was some mistake. I could not marry Hamish. I loved Patrick – even though the truth sat opposite me now. He did not love me, he never had. Perhaps he was simply answering some primitive masculine call to scatter his seed.

And yet he'd been so passionate, so sincere, so tender in his lovemaking, how could it not be fuelled by honesty and genuine affection?

Was I being vain and naïve? No doubt he'd been as passionate and tender when making love to my sister and dozens of others.

Oh, I could go insane with it! I squeezed my temples between my palms to still the thoughts spiralling round and round like a whirlpool of love and betrayal.

"Alex?"

Anne was watching me, concern marring her pretty face. "Are you alright?"

My hands fell to my lap and I looked at her. "I believed him, Annie. I truly believed he loved me."

She nodded. "We both did but we'll survive this. At least you'll not carry the fruits of your foolishness around like a brand on your forehead."

She sighed and smoothed the skirt of her gown over the vague roundness that was there. "We were only in Devon two days before he put me in a carriage and deposited me back in London. He boarded a ship to Europe that same day. I knew within two weeks that I was with child – I was never late before. I wrote but heard no response. I wrote again and I waited in London until last week hoping to hear from him."

I reached across the space between us and took her hand. "I'm sorry you're in this mess, Annie."

She smiled wanly. "Do you think you will marry Hamish?"

"I'd prefer not to, but there is no other option, really. I've been living a beautiful fantasy. Do you know he even talked about making a financial offer to Hamish?" I laughed mirthlessly. The idea sounded so ludicrous in the harsh reality of his duplicity.

Anne looked at me sadly. "We've both been played for fools."

∽

Some days were better than others; vacillating between anger and denial, the only constant was my grief. On the one hand I raged with bitterness over his betrayal, and on the other, I was firm in my belief that there was some mistake. But the weeks slowly drifted by and Anne's belly distended with undeniable evidence.

August gave way to September and the leaves on the Great Oak turned bronze and fell. While I'd like to say my acquiescence to marriage with Hamish was under duress, the truth was that I could see no other future for myself. It was time to put aside foolish romantic notions and become a wife and a mother. So it was, that I offered no opposition other than a last feeble plea to Mother that I knew was futile.

And her arguments were persuasive; though in my heart I wished it differently, I knew in my head she was right. Regardless, it would always prove easier to bend to her will than to stand against her. Given time, perhaps I'd grow to feel something for Hamish – many successful marriages were founded on less.

Meanwhile, Gerrard had been unable to locate Patrick. I suspected he hadn't gone out of his way, though Mother was furious.

"He'd better be dead and mouldering on a battlefield somewhere!" she raged. "If he so much as shows his face again I'll cut off his cock and shove it down his throat – so help me I will!"

Into this storm, Simon arrived. It was early October and Anne's pregnancy was quite evident now, and the preparations for my December wedding were underway. We'd just completed dinner and Emily was clearing the plates when Mrs Grainger announced a carriage had driven up and gone immediately to the stables.

No mere visitor would arrive thus and I looked at Anne meaningfully. Mother had told her about Simon's injuries and she'd reacted quite badly, having always been fiercely proud of our brother's exceptional looks. Now, as we all gathered on the porch, flanked by the servants – for the master of the house was returned – we waited anxiously.

The crunch of gravel signalled their approach and two figures rounded the corner on foot. Under any other circumstances Anne and I would have scrutinised every inch of the woman who'd stolen our brother's heart, but we afforded her barely a glance – noticing nothing more than the glossiest black hair I'd ever seen.

Simon advanced slowly, and I don't recall what I saw first; the empty shirtsleeve tucked into his trousers or the angrily puckered scar running the length of his beautiful face and across one misshapen eye.

He halted boldly before us, allowing us to see him and become accustomed to his disfigurement. And in that moment, I admired and loved him so much, that by contrast, Patrick was shown for the shallow, selfish bastard he was.

I was the first, probably for that very reason, to come to my senses. With a cry, I flung myself at my beloved brother, and he caught me with his one arm and held me tightly against him as I sobbed my relief at his return and felt his own tell-tale tremble.

Then Anne was there, and we three wept and clung together, each of us with our own pain finding solace in solidarity, united emotionally for the first time in our joint histories.

Finally, we released each other and Simon introduced Maria. The girl was patiently standing to one side, allowing Simon time with his family, but now she came forwards. She was first presented to Lord Thorncliffe, then Mother, me and finally Anne, dropping formally into a correct curtsy before each of us. Despite her unfashionably straight hair and cheap travelling costume, she was extraordinarily pretty – even Mother was impressed. Maria carried herself with such dignity that, if she were dressed in finery and her hair styled appropriately, Mother's cronies would already be plotting her downfall behind their fans.

"Welcome to the family," Gerrard said kissing her cheeks.

"Thank you, My Lord. I am so very pleased to be here," she responded in English that had an accent warm and smooth as chocolate.

Though Mrs Grainger had ever held us in disdain, Simon's charm had wormed itself into a secret crevice in her stony heart. She stood now with her chin quivering. Beside her, Cook openly dabbed at her eyes with the corner of her pinny.

Mrs Grainger immediately issued orders to unload Sir Simon's and Miss Maria's luggage. "Hop to it, the master is home!" she commanded, masking her emotional lapse with severity.

Simon looked up, his head slightly cocked to the right and I realised he could not see properly from his injured left eye. "Cook! Mrs Grainger! You old boilers still kicking?"

That was when Cook lost her composure. She burst into tears and rushed to hug him like a long lost son.

"Clara, who's that?" a juvenile voice shouted from behind us. Meg and Clara were standing on the threshold and Simon, releasing Cook, moved towards them.

"Meggy? It's me, Simon."

But the little girl had never seen disfigurement before and, thoroughly terrified, gave a piercing shriek and burst into tears. Simon halted at the foot of the stairs, his face registering deep anguish as Meg clutched fiercely at her nurse's skirt and hid her face. "Meggy, lamb," Clara said placatingly, "it's your big brother, Simon. You remember Simon?"

"Noo!" the child wailed. Maria was beside Simon in an instant, her hand gently touching his arm in support.

"I'm sorry, Sir Simon," Clara said.

"It's alright Clara, she'll get used to me."

"Let me, *mi querido*," said Maria gently.

We watched curiously as the Spanish girl slowly but purposefully mounted the steps. Approaching Clara, she formally introduced herself. Then, as though surprised, she exclaimed, "*Madre di Dios*! You've a little girl growing from your behind!"

Meg peered cautiously around Clara to look at the pretty lady. "I'm not growing here."

"But how can I know when you are so hidden?"

Maria crouched and began a private conversation with the child whose face slowly relaxed. At length she nodded solemnly and eyed her brother less fearfully.

"I've had the master suite prepared for you," Mother said as we drifted into the house, "Maria may use Maeve's —"

"That's not necessary, Mother. Maria and I married in Spain."

Mother stiffened, "Married? But you are the master here. Your tenants and neighbours would have expected —"

"Indeed. I am the master here and returned from war. They will have expected nothing."

∾

That evening a wild storm blew over the Chevin making our gathering beneath the Great Oak impossible. Since the custom conjured memories of lazy, sultry nights in happier times, I was content to remain indoors.

Maria was lovely. She and Anne chatted in a strange Italian-Spanish dialect of their own making, inducing much laughter from the pair. Gerrard poured wine, and Simon toasted the future, thus beginning the exchange of nearly three years of news.

Simon and Maria described some of their experiences, telling of the poor medical facilities, crude instruments and conditions.

"It's amazing how inventive one can be when forced by necessity," Simon said. Every time I looked at him I was shocked by his appearance, but like everyone else I pretended all was as it should be and behaved accordingly.

"Tell them about little Jack," Maria urged, shoving Simon playfully in the arm. No-one witnessing their interaction could deny the sincerity of their love and, though my heart ached for my own loss, I was thrilled that my brother had found such happiness.

"What about little Jack?" prompted Anne.

Simon grinned with half his face, but it was the same disarming grin I remembered. "Jack was a small boy found wandering along the roadside outside of La Albuera. A wagon carrying wounded to our hospital picked him up."

"We called him Jack because he was confused and didn't know

his name. He helped in the hospital, carrying plates of food and so on, but because he was often getting underfoot, one of the Spanish surgeons gave him a guitar, not realising that he could actually play with a talent far beyond his years. So every evening this youngster entertained the hospital with his music.

"One day they brought in a Spanish soldier, so badly injured, he was not expected to last the night. He begged the nurses to leave him to die so he could be reunited with his deceased wife and son.

"That evening, when little Jack began playing, the soldier cried out that he was rising to paradise for he could hear the playing of his deceased son."

"The Spanish nurse – what was her name?"

"Angelina," Maria supplied.

"Angelina took Jack to the soldier's pallet and Jack cried out *Papa! You've returned for me!* It was indeed his father."

"The soldier was so excited," Maria interrupted, "that we feared this would be his end. They said there was nothing to be done for him and that all effort and medicines would be wasted. But Simon …" she pronounced his name See-*mon*, "would not let him die for he was all the little boy had in the world.

Simon added, "I sat with him overnight and in the end he survived for I told him I'd track him down in the afterlife and drag him straight to hell should he leave his son now."

"You didn't!" Anne gasped full of pretended outrage.

"I did, but more likely it was Jack sitting beside him playing his guitar, and the man could not bear to leave."

"A wonderful story, Son, you did well," Gerrard said.

"That was when I fell in love with him," Maria said brushing Simon's hair from his face.

He turned and kissed her hand. "I was already in love."

We all smiled, a little embarrassed in the presence of their intimacy and perhaps in that moment, even Mother decided that Maria truly loved her son.

"Wine anyone?" Gerrard asked brandishing a fresh bottle.

Mother and Anne declined, and as everyone else's cup was filled, Simon said, "So, what news here? I didn't expect to find Annie home. Where's Maeve? Is she here too?"

"Maeve's still in Italy. She met some fellow – an archaeologist," Anne explained. "Isabella was suspicious but he proved to be quite a fascinating chap. And entirely safe – seems he's one of *those* types – you know, prefers the company of men.

"Maeve was quite taken with the – whatever you'd call it, science, or whatever – living in a tent village with him and other diggy types."

"Good for Maeve – always was a bit eccentric. Is Missy with her?"

"Certainly, and holding court in Maeve's tent, earning her board by keeping the rat population from the food stores, apparently."

"What's the latest from the front, Son?" asked Gerrard.

"Well, you've probably heard that Wellington returned from the winter break with a vengeance."

Gerrard nodded. "We had read that. Seems he stormed his way through Burgos and Vitoria and got as far as the Pyrenees – that's all we know."

"So you wouldn't know that they finally broke through into France?"

Gerrard shook his head.

"Bit of luck really. Some local shrimp fishermen guided them in boats. It meant that they got there before the French. *Their* commander was leading them across the mountains by foot. While all this was going on, other allied forces were laying siege to Pamplona. Now that Wellington's in France – I think Patrick's with one of his troops – it will go … what?"

At the mention of Patrick's name Mother had visibly stiffened and Anne and I had exchanged looks.

No-one spoke and Simon said *what* again.

Mother jerked her chin towards her husband. "You may as well tell him. He'll know sooner or later."

"Tell me what?"

Anne spoke up and announced unflinchingly, "Simon, I'm with child. Patrick is the father." She bowed her head shamefully.

I felt the tears sting the backs of my eyes and quickly sipped my wine.

"I thought you appeared rather round in the middle," Simon said. Then he asked the forbidden question, the one I'd not been brave enough to ask. He said, "Are you certain it's Patrick's?"

Mother gasped and her hand flew to her mouth. Anne leapt to her feet, her face aflame, "Of course I'm certain. What do you think I am, Simon?"

"We both know the answer to that, don't we?" he replied, evenly.

My own mind returned to a time in the woods; Simon and I searching for and finding a half-naked Anne in the arms of a servant. A glance at Gerrard revealed that he also remembered.

To this day the incident had never been mentioned again, and Mother, unaware of her daughter's history, was disgusted that Simon would question Anne's integrity.

"Simon, you owe your sister an apology. She was a virgin until that … that debaucher got to her. Patrick is the father – I have no doubt about it."

"You were there at the conception, were you?" he asked directly. Even I gasped then and Anne buried her face in her hands and fled the room.

"*How dare you!*" Mother demanded. "If Anne says Patrick is the father, then *he is the father!* Lord knows, he tried his damnedest to impregnate Alexandra as well."

Simon's eyes swung to me and I flushed with humiliation.

Meanwhile Maria sat quietly with her hands in her lap, her eyes discreetly downcast, and I thanked her in my heart for I felt such excruciating abasement at that moment.

"Has Patrick confirmed this?" His look moved between Mother and Gerrard.

Gerrard spoke for the first time, "I've received no reply to my mail."

"Then my first question remains unanswered," Simon stated flatly.

Mother pursed her lips and regarded Simon with a cold stare. "I'm sorry the war and all you've endured has changed you so." She rose, gathering her book and pelisse from the table beside her. "But if there's any justice in this world, Patrick Washburn will meet an unpleasant end. Good evening, Maria. I hope you sleep well tonight. You've travelled quite a distance; feel free to sleep late tomorrow."

"*Gracias*, My Lady."

Mother nodded regally and left the room.

That night, I lay in my lonely bed, weeping softly, as I had many nights before, but tonight my tears included Simon and all he had suffered. I, who rarely considered God but to blaspheme, gave thanks for Simon's safe return, suppressing the urge to apportion blame for all that had come to pass.

Composing myself for sleep, I wiped my nose on the sodden handkerchief balled in my fist and snuggled beneath the counterpane. Jemima stirred in her basket and began to snore. I envied her untroubled slumber.

There was a soft knock on my door, and it opened a crack, "Zan, are you awake?"

"Come in, Sime."

He was carrying a single candle that threw a yellow arc of light around him. His disfigurement was brought into gruesome relief by its dancing glow, and I stared at him as he approached.

"It is quite horrible, isn't it," he said sitting on the edge of my bed. His words were a simple statement of fact.

"It's not as bad as I'd pictured."

"Well, at least Maria knew me before it happened so I don't have to brag about how handsome I *used* to be." His rueful grin touched only half his face. "She'd never have believed me."

"You're still you though," I murmured.

"I know, but it is amazing how people's attitudes and the way they treat you are influenced by your looks."

We fell silent and I thought how good it was to have him home again. I said, "What did you want to talk about?"

"Anne."

I sighed. "What about her?"

"Well, perhaps not Anne. Patrick."

He paused to consider his words. "Just say it," I prompted impatiently.

"Alright – here it is: that baby is not Patrick's."

I made a tutting sound. "It is. I've spoken with Anne privately and she's confided everything."

"I don't care. I just have this feeling."

"So you upset your homecoming and insult your sister because you have a *feeling*? I'm tired Sime, I want to go to sleep."

"Not only that, but I think her pregnancy is more advanced than she says."

"Your professional opinion?" I suggested, sarcastically.

"Perhaps. It doesn't matter, I know she's our sister and all, but I don't trust her."

"It's true, Sime. I don't know what Patrick was thinking or why he did it but the fact remains, Annie's pregnant and he's the father."

"You believe her then?"

"Why would I not? She's no reason to lie, and she says there's been no-one else. If you think she looks further along than she says perhaps it's a large baby."

He sounded unconvinced. "I'm sorry, Zan. I cannot simply accept that Anne has been with no-one else. You and I know she's always been a bit … you know, *forward*. And then there's Pat himself. He's ever been oversexed – that's undeniable – but he's always cautious. I just can't believe that he would let this happen. To be so careless is not like him."

I thought about how controlled Patrick had been with me, but in the end he'd relented and we'd risked pregnancy. "Well, it appears he is careless," I said. "And furthermore, I don't know why I'm so surprised – no female has ever been safe around him."

"Zan …"

"You, as well as anyone, know what he's like."

He ignored the bait. "Regardless, there's something else. Something Pat said once about you."

"*Me?*"

"He mentioned once that he thought Hamish was not right for you. I was being a bit flippant – I said I supposed he thought *he himself* was and he looked at me, very intensely, and said, *yes*. Now I know Pat – as you say, better than most – and I know when he's being serious. He liked you – he has never liked Anne."

Faint hope sparked within me but died just as quickly. "That doesn't mean anything."

"So that's it? You're accepting Anne's version without question?"

I shrugged. "What choice do I have? As much as I'd like to believe otherwise, it has happened, and there's an end to it."

He sighed unhappily. "I just don't understand it."

"Only Patrick knows his reasons. In any case, I'm marrying Hamish. I was signed over and paid for years ago."

"You're resigned to it then?"

"What else is there for a woman in this world? I can live on the charity of my brother and be known forever as the spinster sister – the appendage, the one who no-one ever wanted to marry." I thought of Miss Bradbury, the pink sister of Adrienne's mother, sharing her brother-in-law's home and delighting in romantic conspiracies. "I don't want to end like up that," I went on. "You and Maria have your own life, you'll have children. I shan't be the maiden aunt. I have a chance to marry, have my own children and run my own household. I'll not have anyone's charity."

"So you'll marry Hamish because you've nothing else," Simon said without malice, though his words stung. Only a short time back, I had hopes of enlisting Simon's support to avoid the Elginbury match. I could see he would indeed have supported me. But it was too late for that now.

I touched his hand where it rested on my counterpane. "I had a fantasy for a short time, but it turned out to be just that. I must live in the real world."

"So it's true then, Pat seduced you?"

"It wasn't like that, and I really believed he loved me."

"You wouldn't be the first."

I snorted bitterly. "Evidently I wasn't the last either."

"You've loved him for years, haven't you? And you're in love with him still," he stated plainly.

Quick betraying tears sprang into my eyes and I didn't have to answer. He touched me gently on the cheek. "Perhaps marrying Hamish will be best, I just want to be satisfied you're doing it for the right reasons. Marriage is for life – there's no going back once it's done. It seems Patrick has changed – he's not the person I thought I knew. This, new Patrick would not have married you, nor will he marry Annie."

October gave way to November and I watched like a spectator as Mother flitted about full of importance and excitement. Eager to impress her friends, associates and even those she didn't like; she embarked upon a frenetic campaign to spend a fortune on tradespeople and merchants and anyone else that could ensure my wedding was the society function of the year.

Yet I remained removed from the arrangements. She did not consult with me – a circumstance we both knew was satisfactory – and as the preparations advanced, I sensed a vague shift within me.

It wasn't happiness. It definitely wasn't excitement. Was it a faint glimmer of hope?

And as the leaves on the Great Oak piled at its base in crisp, bronze mounds, I stood on the porch, wrapped in a thick woollen cloak and turned my face towards the north. A cold November wind was blowing down and I closed my mind to its symbolism for soon Hamish will come riding in and we shall be wed.

Then, my life will begin.

EPILOGUE

The kitchen was almost dark; lit only by the banked coals in the fireplace. Jemima lay before the hearth, nose on paws and bathed in its warm golden glow.

The dog occasionally spent the night here – much as she enjoyed the comfort of her basket in her mistress's room, the kitchen was the most pleasing place in the house due to the tantalising smells that lingered.

The kindly woman who prepared the food had long since extinguished the lamps and gone to her own bed, leaving Jemima alone.

The dog sighed, licked her lips and allowed her eyes to close.

Somewhere in the house a clock chimed once ... twice ... and Jemima's ears twitched. The clock was a familiar sound, but the other, the slow drag of slippered feet, was less familiar and she raised her head.

Her first reaction was to growl; a low guttural warning to the intruder, but as the apparition appeared in the kitchen doorway, Jemima abruptly grew silent and she stared.

With the acceptance animals have for things that humans might dismiss as impossible, the dog recognised the old woman. She had bounded and frolicked in the garden earlier that day, with the woman's much younger self – the child, Meg.

Yet Jemima felt no fear – only interest – as the colourless shade shuffled into the kitchen, carrying what appeared to be a tin box, and muttering to herself, "It's for the lady, Meg, keep it safe for her ..."

Pausing, the old woman reached for something not visible to Jemima, then she turned towards the door that led outside. It seemed that Meg grasped the handle and pulled the door open, though Jemima could see it remained closed.

And as she watched, the vision of the old woman melted through the solid wood, as if it weren't there.

A MESSAGE FROM KAREN

Thank you for reading *Torn*.

Alex's story continues in *Inviolate*. Visit my website to find out more: www.karenturner.com.au

If you enjoyed reading *Torn*, I would be very grateful if you could post a quick review on Goodreads or Amazon so that others can discover and enjoy *Torn* for themselves.

Karen.

ACKNOWLEDGEMENTS

When it was suggested that I write an acknowledgements page I initially baulked at the idea; acknowledgments often rattle on and don't tend to mean a lot to people other than those mentioned.

However, when I started to think about it, I realised that there really are a number of people without whom this book would never have progressed from concept to where it is today.

So, here we go.

First and foremost is my long-suffering and unwaveringly supportive husband Stuart Turner. At various times throughout the writing of *Torn*, Stuart has been sounding-board, researcher, therapist, reader, editor and coffee-maker. Without you, dear, this book would not exist and I would not be the fortunate person I am today.

Next is a list of friends – too lengthy to document – who have encouraged me each step of the way. I thank all of you, particularly those who read *Torn* and answered my endless questions with honesty and patience. You know who you are, although one lady who deserves special mention is Liliana Vacis. Beautiful woman, your belief in me over the years has never failed. Gracias.

To my terrific editor Jane Woodhead, you made a gruelling

process virtually painless. It was great working with you — let's do it again some time!

This page would be incomplete without reference to Panda and Katie, my pussycats. These two kept me company for hours on end as I typed, cursed, talked to myself and read out loud. And if I occasionally lost myself while wandering the corridors of Broughton Hall and your dinner was served late — I apologise, but warn that it will probably happen again.

Finally, to Paul Higgs and the team at Palmer Higgs Publishing, thank you for holding my hand.

Other books by Karen Turner

ALL THAT & EVERYTHING

Ever wondered what life looks like from a cat's perspective?
What about the funny side of daily train commuting?
Are things really what they seem in the mirror?

From Regency London to the Australian bush, *All That & Everything*
is an enchanting collection of award winning short stories.
   Karen combines a selection of her late father's sketches with
these carefully chosen stories to offer something for everyone.

Other books by Karen Turner

COUNTERPOINT

1808

When Alexandra first meets Patrick, her handsome and enigmatic stepbrother, he tears apart the fabric of her quiet world...

So begins the epic love story that had fans of *Torn* gripping their seats. But there's another side to the story, a darker side: Patrick's side.

Welcome to a world of lust, decadence and violence.

Counterpoint is a retelling of *Torn*, told in Patrick's own words, and by those closest to him.

Just as *Torn* ushers readers into the very proper parlours of Regency England, where young ladies live within the bounds of the social restraints of the time, *Counterpoint* thrusts readers onto a rollicking ride through a clandestine world of wealth, privilege and dark passions.

In glittering ballrooms, sordid London backstreets and bloodied battlefields, Patrick Washburn comes of age in a time of licentiousness, when profligate young men, seasoned by war, live life for the moment, with no restraint and no regrets.

INVIOLATE

1813

Inviolate continues the story of Alex Broughton, the passionate and determined young woman readers first met in *Torn*.

This remarkable sequel continues from where *Torn* left you wanting more.

From *Inviolate*:

And in my quiet moments – those moments just before sleeping, or when I lay down my sewing to stretch my neck – the memories of Patrick came, unbidden, and always with the power to evoke intense emotions. In time I hoped they would fade to snatches of conversation or secret kisses, to be hidden away in a dusty, rarely explored corner of my mind. But when they appeared without warning, like glittering gem-stones, they were so exquisite that I forgot the hurts and betrayals and saw only the beauty so briefly enjoyed. And despite being deceived in the worst possible way, I remained haunted by a fleeting and impossible love affair.

Other books by Karen Turner

STORMBIRD

1941

Stormbird returns readers to the once beautiful rural home, Broughton Hall, the setting of Karen's previous books, *Torn* and *Inviolate*.

It's now 1941, England is at war and Broughton Hall has fallen into disrepair. New owner, war-widowed young mother, Jessica is struggling to raise her two children and run a small dairy.

When she encounters a wounded German fighter pilot hiding in her barn, she commits to helping him.

At first, the barriers of ignorance and prejudice separate them. Yet in a world where danger lurks behind every door, an unlikely friendship becomes a story of love, loyalty and understanding.